COUGAR POINT

BOOKS BY GREGG OLSEN

COUGAR POINT

GREGG OLSEN

bookouture

Published by Bookouture in 2024

An imprint of Storyfire Ltd.
Carmelite House
50 Victoria Embankment
London EC4Y 0DZ

www.bookouture.com

ISBN: 978-1-83790-491-4
eBook ISBN: 978-1-83790-490-7

PROLOGUE

Victoria awakens to complete darkness. Her head is fuzzy and she tries to say, "Where am I?" but the words are muffled by a rough cloth that cuts into the sides of her mouth, and she can barely breathe. A little air comes through the gag but her nose is swollen and her breath whistles.

She's lost track of time. All she knows is that she hurts all over and is reminded of it every time she awakens. She knows it has been quite a while because she's lain in her own filth, unable to move, and she's very thirsty.

Oh dear God! *she thinks.* What do they want from me? Why are they doing this? *She forces herself to calm, to think, try to remember what happened. She recalls being in her room at the resort. She and her daughter drank champagne and talked for a while. They were going to meet in the morning. Rebecca had left the room and there was a knock at the door. She remembers thinking that Rebecca had forgotten something, and she had opened the door.*

An object had come at her, and her nose exploded in pain; and some material was pulled over her head and face. The last thing she remembers is a pinch on the side of her neck. Nothing after that until they dragged her into this place and that part is hazy. They must have drugged her.

The next thing she remembers is waking up on the cold floor, maybe hours ago, maybe yesterday, with her arms bound behind her and her ankles bound too. Her clothes have been removed but she doesn't remember it. The bag was on her head the first time she came to but it must have been removed because now she is blindfolded and gagged.

Her thoughts turn to her daughters. Rebecca will be worried to death. And her youngest: What will happen when she finds out her mother is gone? Taken. There is so much she needs to tell her daughters. If she goes through with her plans, they will find out eventually, but she had wanted them to hear it from her. Not Jack, who would put a spin on it.

It's hard to breathe around the gag so she has to try harder to calm herself.

Why would someone do this to her? It doesn't make sense. She has nothing of her own. Some expensive jewelry maybe. An expensive car. Credit cards. A small bank account. But Jack holds the purse strings and doles out the money as he sees fit.

She closes her eyes tight and tries to jog her memory of the last moments before she woke up here. Was there anyone paying attention to them at the resort? Try as she might, she can't remember who she saw, who she knew, or even what she ate. Her mind was totally on what she was planning to do.

The divorce? Is that what this is about? It's not possible. Jack would never harm her. At least not physically. And he would never frighten his daughters.

Where is Rebecca?

Dear God, has she been taken too?

ONE

FRIDAY

Rebecca Marsh sits on the back deck of the Semiahmoo Resort, located in the furthest northwest corner of Washington State, looking across Drayton Harbor and from there to the Pacific Ocean. Seagulls screech and dive along the shoreline looking for whatever breakfast has washed up on the sand and rocks.

It's late on a Friday morning. She's soaking up the sun while waiting for her mom to come downstairs to join her. At dinner last night, Victoria promised to tell her this morning why she's been so distant and distracted lately. They'd shared a couple of glasses of champagne but not enough for her mom to be sleeping so late. She may be putting on makeup and trying on one of the outfits she's brought for their weekend getaway. Her mom packed enough clothes to stay a week.

Rebecca doesn't understand why Victoria has become so obsessed with her looks. She's a beautiful woman. Not that Dad ever notices, but plenty of other men do. He used to adore her, and had even bought the resort because her mom loved their stays here. He'd dedicated three of the suites for family use and one of those had family signage on the door. It was a Valentine's gift and Rebecca remembered her mom had squealed with delight. She wondered if she would ever be that deeply in love.

The whole family had come to the resort over the years, but then her dad had started sending the rest of them while he attended to business alone. And then Veronica had moved away to Port Hadlock. Of all the careers Veronica could have chosen, why she would pick a dangerous one was beyond belief. Her rebellious decisions had rubbed their parents wrong, especially their dad. He had hoped she would get a taste of the chaos society served up and come to her senses. But she had stayed true to her convictions, and Rebecca admired her sister for that.

Rebecca, two years older, finished law school and now works for Dad's law firm. Corporate law. As her father was wont to say, "That's where the money is." And he is right. Rebecca drives a new Lincoln Navigator. Veronica has a little mini car. Their parents offered to buy her something less likely to fold like a tin can in an accident, but she won't budge. Just like she hasn't budged on her career choice. Her little sister is determined to make her mark without anyone's help.

Their dad had shown his disappointment a little too much and too often, and as a result Veronica has kept her distance. Eventually Rebecca gave up inviting her to these getaways.

Semiahmoo Resort is beautiful and it promises to be a perfect weekend. She and her mom had arrived at the resort yesterday, mid-morning, had lunch on the deck, walked along the beach, and taken in the beauty that surrounded them. But something was bothering her mom. At first Rebecca thought it had something to do with Veronica preferring to live in Port Townsend instead of closer to home. Her best attempts to find out what was causing her mom's distress were met with responses such as, "Let's just enjoy being here," "I'm fine," and "It's nothing." Rebecca knew nothing was fine.

Now, as she reclines on the deck, a feeling of unease comes over her. She turns over possible reasons for her mom's unhappiness, from financial reasons to poor health, and it strikes her that her mom has been unhappy for a while. Sure, she puts on a brave face, but there is a conflicted and sad Victoria underneath. Rebecca will give her a little longer and then she'll go to her mom's room.

Rebecca is pulled from her thoughts by someone tapping her shoulder.

"Miss. There's a message at the front desk."

She peers from under her sunglasses at the messenger. "Is it from my mother?" she asks the young woman wearing a housekeeping uniform.

"Mr. Whiting said you were out here and to tell you to come."

Roger Whiting is the general manager. "Where is my mom? Did she come down?"

"I haven't seen her, ma'am."

"Tell Roger I'll be right there."

She looks out over the bay. Storm clouds are gathering, promising a cloudburst. She and her mom wouldn't be going for a walk along the shoreline today. She gathers the few things she's brought out to the deck and notices resort staff busily taking down umbrellas and folding Adirondack chairs.

Roger Whiting is a small man, late fifties, thin, balding, and barely five feet tall. He stands on a raised wooden platform behind the counter. He knows everything that has anything to do with the resort, and a lot that doesn't.

"Are you holding something for me, Roger?"

He hands Rebecca a piece of resort stationery with something printed in black ink. The handwriting resembles a child's scrawling.

you promised dinky

Roger says, "One of the staff found it outside the door to your mother's room."

"It can't be for me or my mom, Roger. Give me the key to her room." She hands the note back and holds her hand out for the key.

"Is everything okay, ma'am?" Roger says, handing her the key.

"Fine, Roger. I'll just go see what's taking her so long."

Roger calls after her. "I had a floorman knock on the door and she didn't answer."

"She might be in the restaurant."

"My floorman checked the restaurant and the other places she frequents when she's here. She's usually having a late breakfast in Packer's Lounge this time of day. I personally checked Packer's and the spa. No one has seen her. Maybe she's running an errand?"

Rebecca doesn't think her mother would leave the resort without telling her. "I take it no one has actually gone inside her room?"

"I didn't want to disturb her if she was, uh, indisposed."

Rebecca doesn't know what he means by that but feels her pulse tick in her temple and she rushes to the elevator.

TWO

SUNDAY

I'm just about to get out of my Explorer and go into Purdy Women's Prison when my phone rings.

"Detective Carpenter?" Nan asks as if she doesn't know who she just called. I bite my tongue.

"It's me, Nan. Megan Carpenter. What's up?"

I can almost see her snooty look. She doesn't like smart-ass remarks. But then she doesn't like anything except herself.

"Hold for Sheriff Gray, please." She's being very professional. I'm on edge knowing I'll be face-to-face with my bitch of a mother in a few minutes. I take back the snarky remarks I just made about Nan.

"Megan." Tony's voice comes over the phone. "I'm glad I caught you. Are you working on a case? Do you have a minute?"

Sheriff Tony Gray can have all of my minutes. I owe him. He found me just surviving, using street smarts, and got me into the police academy, hired me, and soon I was a detective. My entire world changed from day-to-day survival to having a family. A police family.

But I'm about to do something I'd promised myself I'd never do. I'm going to visit my mother at Purdy Prison. Tony has no idea about this part of my life. Well, maybe he has a tiny suspicion because of a recent case where the killer had pictures of me from high school when I used the name Rylee, and had left the pictures to be found at a murder scene. Tony had found them and secreted them away until he could give them to me. He didn't ask questions. He has trust in me and I would do anything for him. Except I don't want to let him know where I am. Not that I couldn't be going to a prison to interview someone about a case, but I'm not. So I tell a white lie.

"Yes, I am involved in something at the moment."

"Oh. Okay," Tony says, and I can hear his disappointment.

"But it can wait, Sheriff?"

"Great. This thing with Councilman Johns and his wife... Just a moment."

I hear Nan asking him if he wants coffee.

"That'd be nice, Nan."

"Cream and sugar, Sheriff?" Nan asks.

"Just cream, Nan. Oh, and a donut."

"Oh my goodness, Sheriff. They're all gone," Nan says.

I wish she'd get gone.

"I'll get some down the road from that new bakery that just opened."

"Just a moment, Megan." He puts his hand over the mouthpiece but I can still hear him. "Nan, I'm on a call so just get whatever you want. I'll pay you when you get back. And can you shut the door to my office, please?"

I hear the door shut, and Tony is back. "Sorry about that, Megan."

"Office emergency?" I ask, and he snorts.

"Just Nan sucking up. Now where were we? Oh yeah. Councilman Johns and his wife."

"She didn't stab him again, did she?" The councilman was having an affair, and his wife caught them together and stabbed him. Johns has quite the reputation for being a consummate liar and now a cheat. Deputy Davis was first to arrive and told me the wife caught the councilman with a naked woman on her knees bent over the bed and spanking her.

"Now, Megan, you know we would never be able to prove she stabbed him on purpose."

On purpose? The stab wound was on his lower groin, near Captain Happy. Another inch to the left, it wouldn't have been happy any longer. But Tony's right. We could never make a case since she claimed she was doing dishes and was drying a boning knife when he came up behind her and surprised her. We knew their stories were bullshit. They called an ambulance and the paramedic called us. The blood was on her clothes and the bed sheets. But he refused to press charges and backed up her story. We never located the spanking victim.

I ask, "Did anyone get injured?" *Or lose an appendage?*

"Councilman Johns wants to hire you to discreetly follow his wife. He suspects she's cheating on him."

I say, "First of all, Washington State has a 'no contest' divorce. They don't have kids. She gets half of everything. Secondly, I don't do that kind of stuff. Cheating isn't a crime."

"That's what I told him."

"Tony, I need the morning off. I'm not on a case. It's personal."

"You got it, Megan. If you need the day, just let me know. I've got some other things backed up here but nothing urgent."

"I won't be long and then I'll take whatever you've got." At least I hope this will be brief.

THREE

The visitor parking lot is surrounded by chain link and razor wire. Two guard towers rise above the front and back sides of the prison, catacorner to each other. It reminds me of a castle in a picture book I once read to Hayden.

Purdy Women's Prison is the largest women's prison in Washington State. If it weren't for the concertina wire surrounding the thirty-two-acre grounds, it would look like a sports complex with the spacious well-kept grounds, outdoor tennis courts, batting cages, and two Olympic size swimming pools.

Inside, a guard takes my weapon and I empty my pockets, including a roll of Tums. A female guard has me step through the metal detector. For good measure I'm subjected to a pat down. She touches places where only my boyfriend, Dan, has permission. I'm led through two more sets of iron-barred doors to an interview room.

The room next to mine has a glass front, a dozen desks and chairs, a chalkboard and projection screen. "What's that room for?" I ask my frisky friend.

"It's a classroom."

"Seriously?" *Do they teach them how to avoid being arrested?*

"Profs from Washington State University and some trade colleges teach classes, preparing our clients for a job on the outside."

"Rehabilitation?" I say this, and want to gag.

"Yeah. There are two other classrooms here and a library, a video room where they watch the latest movies, a computer room and a sauna."

Now I really do want to throw up. "You've got to be shitting me?"

"We don't have a sauna." She says this like she's really gotten one over on me so I play along, grin and punch her on the arm. I want to punch her in the face.

"Who pays for all of this?"

"You, me, everyone."

Except the prisoners. Prison is the ultimate Student Debt Relief Program. If you want a free college degree, go to prison.

The interview room isn't like the ones you see on television or on the big screen. It's worse. The concrete block walls are unpainted and stained from years of neglect, and although prisons across the U.S. went smoke free in the 90s, the smell of cigarette smoke lives on. No windows. No coffee bar. I sit in one of two chairs at a table that's bolted to the floor. My only contact with the guard will be to scream. I'm not afraid.

The door opens and a female guard who is built like Arnold Schwarzenegger with a blond wig comes in leading my mother. Courtney Cassidy, someone who betrayed and murdered my stepfather, the only man I've ever thought of as a father. She betrayed me and my little brother, Hayden, and lied to me my entire life. I'm not proud to call her my mother. She is in orange coveralls and black mules on her manicured feet, her hair is shiny blond, stylishly cut just above her ears, and she's wearing bright red lipstick. She's tan. Even more so than I am. She no longer looks played out, scared, lost, like the last time I saw her. Instead she's alert, self-assured, and I notice the bags are gone beneath her bright, almost-cobalt blue eyes. She's in better physical shape than I ever remember her being. Prison life agrees with her.

She sits across from me, her smile reaching her eyes; she's at ease. A feeling of hate and love and anger sweeps through my heart and mind. She doesn't deserve to smile, or feel safe.

I offer my hand to my mom and say, "Detective Megan Carpenter."

She doesn't take it. "I wasn't expecting a visit today."

My face betrays my disgust at the remark. Maybe I interrupted her makeover. She says, "Freyda, please close the door. We'll be fine."

"I'll be right outside, Mrs. Cassidy."

"Thank you, Freyda," Mom says. The guard gives me a sharp look and shuts the door.

Mom turns those beacon eyes on me and the smile disappears. The bitch is back.

"You're a detective now, Rylee. I'm glad you've done so well."

FOUR

Victoria has been left alone for so long she wonders if they've abandoned her, and the thought of being left to die frightens her more than being kidnapped. She hears a noise and a door opens. Footsteps approach. A foot nudges her in the side causing her to jerk in pain.

A woman says, "Wake up, bitch," and kicks her in the hip; the only place on her body that doesn't hurt. "I know you can hear me. Nod your head or you'll get it again."

Victoria lifts her head from the floor and sobs. Bloody snot runs down her gag and drips from her chin.

"You've had it easy all of your life. Now it's time to see what the other side is like."

Victoria braces for another blow but the woman just laughs.

"How much are you worth to him? Huh? A million? Two? Five? Don't worry. I'm not going to hurt you. Yet. But if your husband wants you back, he'd better come up with the money."

Victoria hears a derisive snort. "Five is pocket change for the King of Cougar Point. Am I right?"

Victoria hurriedly nods.

"Damn right. Maybe we'll ask for ten. If he balks, we'll send

him pieces of you to bring him in line. How's that, Miss High and Mighty?"

Victoria wonders if they've already contacted Jack. Do they intend to let her go? But she's afraid to mumble or do anything to set this animal off again. And so she doesn't reply and a shoe pushes her head down into the concrete hard enough to bring tears to her eyes.

"You don't have to answer. What happens to you is up to him. He'll either get you back or find your body. His choice."

Victoria hears the woman step away and a door open. Her heart is beating in her throat and tears stream down her face, puddling on the floor. She thinks of Jack and the way they left things. She doesn't know if he'll pay the ransom. She doesn't think it matters. After the beating she's just taken they would never let her live. They're going to kill her.

FIVE

18 MONTHS AGO—FEBRUARY 2023

Whatcom County

Dr. Stephanie Wright looked way too young to be a shrink. In fact, she looked way too young to be out of high school without a note from the principal. But then, looks can always be deceiving. After close to thirty years in the Whatcom County Sheriff's Department, Sergeant Michael Lucas knew that better than most.

The slim, blond-haired counselor made another lengthy note on the yellow pad in front of her, taking her time, seemingly impervious to Lucas's gaze. She seemed to finish, then her perfectly smooth brow creased a little and she made a correction before putting the pen down on the leather-topped desk. She let out a long sigh, adjusted the position of her red-framed glasses and looked out of the window of her small office at the rows of markers in the cemetery across the road.

"Nice view," Lucas had said when he had entered the office more than an hour ago, though right now it felt closer to a decade. "Must help put things in perspective."

Dr. Wright had acknowledged the crack with a polite and perfunctory smile. She hadn't repeated the smile since.

Lucas restrained himself now from making another comment, or even from prompting Dr. Wright to speak. If there was anything that he had learned in the past hour and change, it was that nothing he could say would hurry this process up. Quite the reverse. Any unguarded comment had seemed to prompt another line of questioning, another page of the notebook flipped over. So instead, he adjusted his position in the seat and looked expectantly at his interrogator, his face carefully devoid of expression.

After what felt like another decade, she sighed again and turned back from the window to look at him. She didn't say anything at first, simply examined him like he was a normally docile lab rat prone to the occasional urge to bite.

Lucas placed his palms down on top of his knees, trying to look as relaxed and unflappable as possible, and smiled back at her. Perhaps being a counselor wasn't so different from being a detective. Both professions taught you to deploy strategic moments of silence that your subject would want to fill; to tell you more about themselves than they might want to.

Good luck with that, Lucas thought. *I've been doing this since you were an embryo, Dr. Wright.*

Eventually, she spoke. "I'm not convinced."

"I don't know what you mean," Lucas said. "I'm not trying to convince you of anything."

"You don't think this is a little soon to be contemplating a return to work?"

Lucas took a deep breath through his nostrils and breathed out. He shook his head.

"No, I don't. If anything, it's been too long."

"My job is to make sure you're not making a mistake. If you come back before you've had a chance to process your trauma, it won't be good for anyone. Not for you, not for the department, and not for the public."

If Lucas had known her better, or even if he had gotten the impression there was a sense of humor buried somewhere behind those cold, sea-green eyes, he might have said something like, *I'm not going to go straight to the workplace shooting on my first day back, I promise. Maybe day three.* But he knew that would have been the quickest way to another five pages of note-taking, and almost certainly his request to return getting declined.

"I appreciate that, Doc, and I wouldn't want it any other way. If you don't think I'm ready, then I'm not ready."

Dr. Wright sat back and loosely folded her arms. "And what do you think?"

Lucas paused for a moment to give the impression he was giving this careful thought. "I think I've taken a few weeks and I've come to terms with what happened. Sitting on the couch watching home-makeover shows isn't doing anybody any good, and I think it would be of benefit for me *and* for the department if I could get back to work."

Dr. Wright looked down at her notes again.

"My recommendation would be a phased return. Not rushing back. And we would have to schedule a regular session. Twice a week, at first."

"I have no problem with that." He had a big problem with that. But if it was the price that had to be paid...

Dr. Wright bent her neck a little and peered at Lucas over the rims of her glasses, in the manner of someone not entirely sure if they're being conned.

"I hope I won't regret this, Sergeant Lucas."

* * *

Lucas took a breath of the cold, fresh air as he stepped outside and loosened his collar. Being in that overheated room, answering Dr. Wright's incessant questions, had been tougher than he had let on.

He walked across the parking lot to where his car was parked and got in, massaging his eyelids with his thumb and index finger. The moment he closed his eyes he saw flashes of the scene. *Blood pooling on the hardwood floor. Matted hair and splayed limbs and the smell of gunsmoke.*

His eyes snapped open and he stared himself out in the rearview mirror for a minute.

Get it together.

There was a sheen of sweat on his brow, cooling in the air. He wiped it off and turned the key in the ignition. He drove the four miles to the Sheriff's Office. The sun was still low in the sky, the trees lining the highway still shrouded in mist. It had been a drawn-out winter, and spring seemed a long way away.

He parked in his usual spot and walked into reception. Kelly on the desk looked up and blinked in surprise as Lucas entered, then said hello, tilting her head in a way that was probably supposed to convey sympathy.

"The boss in?" Lucas asked.

She nodded and gestured at the door marked *Sheriff Longbow.*

Charlie Longbow looked up from his desk as Lucas knocked and entered. Longbow was in his late fifties, with hair that was more gray than brown now, and a paunch that spoke of too many years behind the desk. A worn black Stetson sat on the desk beside a nicotine-stained desk phone that was probably an official antique. The office was smaller than the shrink's had been, and with cheaper furniture. The view was of the diner across the street, instead of a graveyard. Longbow glanced at the phone on his desk, then back at Lucas.

"Dr. Wright just called."

Lucas smiled. "Oh yeah? She give you the good news?" He pulled out one of the rickety wooden chairs on the visitor side of the desk out and took a seat.

Longbow steepled his fingers on the desk. "She's not convinced, Mike. Tell you the truth, I'm not either. It's barely been a month since—"

"How long does it need to be?" Lucas asked. "You think six weeks will make it all better? Eight?"

"No, but—"

He leaned forward. "Charlie. I'm ready. I need to come back. And you need me."

Longbow stiffened slightly. "We're doing fine."

"Sure you are."

Longbow almost smiled at that. He shook his head.

"Believe it or not, you are not indispensable." He sighed. "But it will be good to have you back. If you're ready."

"What did I miss?"

"Nothing much. You might have heard that Larry Stroud quit."

Lucas nodded. "I'll try and contain my disappointment."

"I know you two never saw eye to eye, but he really blew up after..." He stopped and reconsidered.

"It's all right," Lucas said. "And let's face it, he saved you the trouble of firing him for drinking on the job. And worse."

Longbow bristled a little, which was weird because Lucas knew there was no love lost between his sheriff and his former partner. "He was a decent cop."

"Maybe once."

Longbow gave Lucas a rundown of the current caseload. Nothing out of the ordinary. When Joyce had... when Lucas had had to stop work abruptly, he had been working a case involving a narcotics gang from a neighboring county making incursions beyond their turf. Pete Stimpson had taken over and resolved it in his absence. Stroud's departure had left a pile of work on the desk, which Lucas surmised was a big reason Longbow was willing to welcome him back a little sooner than expected.

"Why don't you come back in tomorrow?" Longbow said. "You can take a look at Larry's backlog, see if we can close anything off. We'll keep you riding a desk for a little while, let you take it easy."

Lucas was opening his mouth to say that easy was the very last thing he wanted, when the phone on Longbow's desk rang and took that decision out of their hands.

Longbow picked it up on the second ring and said his name. He listened, his eyes narrowing. Lucas couldn't make out the individual words, but whoever was on the other end of the call was talking quickly.

"Yeah... no, tell them to sit tight, we'll be there in ten. Yeah. Okay, thanks, Arnie."

He replaced the phone on the hook and picked up his Stetson from the desk and got up, digging in his pocket for the keys to his SUV.

"That was Arnold Cooney. They just found a body in a gully. A woman."

SIX

The upshot of visiting my mother in jail was that it was a big mistake, like I had always known it was going to be. But at least it's made my mind up about one thing: I've decided to tell Hayden the truth about his family. My mother can spin the facts until she throws up.

Back in the parking lot I'm still soaking up the A/C when my phone rings.

"Megan, are you at home?"

I avoid the question. "What's up, Ronnie?"

"Can you come by my place?"

I hadn't told anyone where I was going and Ronnie's place is at least forty-five minutes away. It's my day off, but being a detective means I'm subject to being called in at any time. This doesn't sound like a work thing, and I'd promised the Sheriff I'd look into his councilman issue.

I say cautiously, "I'm about an hour away and Tony needs me for a project."

"Oh. I just..."

"What is it, Ronnie? I'm heading home first." I'm not. I'm going to get a stiff drink.

She says, "I'd really appreciate your help with something."

"Can you tell me now?" I'm hoping to get tipsy and maybe call my therapist, Dr. Karen Albright. The meeting with my mother has left me unsettled. In truth I'm wrung dry from conflicting emotions and don't feel like dealing with anything else today. Or tomorrow. Or the next day.

"It can wait until I see you again, Megan."

I was so caught up in my mother issues I didn't recognize the need in Ronnie's voice. Now I feel guilty. "We can meet at Moe's if that works for you." That will cut about fifteen minutes off my travel time, and I'm relieved when she agrees.

The drive to Port Townsend and Moe's takes me up State Road 16, through thick forests that sometimes almost block out the sky. As I head north and the road curls around Sinclair Inlet, I catch a magnificent view of the Puget Sound Naval Yard, the late-morning sun glinting off the hulks of the ships in the yard. It almost makes me want to pull over and take a picture. But then I remind myself I'm not the "stop and take a picture" kind of person.

I skirt the inlet by hopping on State Road 3 at the little town of Gorst, located on the shores of the Puget Sound in an area of primarily antique stores, clothing stores, car dealerships and espresso stands. My mouth waters at the smell of espresso but I don't stop. Ronnie will be waiting for me at Moe's.

Recently, Ronnie met my baby brother, Hayden, and though I've tried to discourage her from going down that path, she's persisted in her interest. They're not dating yet, but he seems to show up wherever Ronnie and I are having drinks or when we're at my apartment discussing a case, and I see the looks they give each other.

They'd make a perfect couple but I have selfish reasons I don't want them to get together. Mostly because Ronnie already has a paramour. His name is Marley Yang, divorced, two kids, a very nice nerd, and he's the supervisor of the crime lab. Ronnie is beautiful and can get Marley to put us at the head of the line and sometimes to unofficially look at evidence. Her infatuation with Hayden will only hurt my chances of having priority at the lab.

I come out of auto drive when I reach downtown Port Townsend and spot Ronnie's tiny car parked outside Moe's. I'm emotionally drained from the confrontation with my mother so I hope Ronnie's issue is an easy fix. And then I remember it's Ronnie I'm talking about. Nothing about her is ever simple.

SEVEN

Moe's has outside seating and a magnificent view of Port Townsend Bay with its sailboats and cabin cruisers and the comedy of tourists needing directions. A lot of Moe's clientele are coming from or going to the marina and drawn to the smell of burning grease and hot fries. Moe's is popular with tourists and locals and a hangout for hungry cops who eat free. Today is no exception. I count no less than three police cars in the lot.

Ronnie is sitting at a booth by the window, and Moe is leaning on the counter chatting her up. Moses Adamos. He's in his early thirties, olive complexion, Mediterranean dark curly hair.

"Hi, Megan. Your regular?" Moe asks.

"I didn't know I had a regular, Moe."

"Coffee, cinnamon bun, two eggs over greasy, two pieces bacon semi-crispy, white toast buttered lightly."

"Sure. Sounds regular enough for me."

He brings coffee for me and refills Ronnie's mug before taking my order to the back. The cops exchange a look, get up, and leave. I might have yelled at one of them at a crime scene for being a dumbass. Of course he won't tell his buddies he was a dumbass. He'll say I'm hormonal. Screw them. They won't say it to my face.

One other couple, teens, horny teens, sit in the corner thinking they're hidden by the booth. They're all over each other like stink on sweat socks. I want to yell, "Stop that at once!" But it will take Moses to separate them like parting the Red Sea.

Grease is my friend now, but when my pants are too tight, I'll curse my weakness. "So what's the dilemma?" I ask Ronnie a little sharply, and then regret it.

"What's wrong, Megan? Can I help?"

I'm ashamed. She asks for my help and when I snap at her she offers to help me. That's Ronnie. "Bad morning," I say. "Got up on the wrong side of the Red Sea."

"What?"

"Never mind. You said you needed to meet." She's quiet. For Ronnie, silence is as unusual as Congress working. "Whatever it is we can fix it." I don't know what needs fixing. But that's what you're supposed to say when a friend is feeling down.

A tear falls into her coffee, and I say, "Tell me. You'll feel better."

"It's my mom."

You too? Sheesh!

"You know I'm not super close to my family." Ronnie stirs several teaspoons of raw sugar into black coffee, then adds enough creamer to half fill the mug.

Ronnie is dressed in one of her best outfits and has traded her work boots for moderate high heels. Her makeup is perfect, not that she needs any. She is a beauty and I've taken advantage of her appeal many times to get things from men.

"Are you going somewhere?" I ask.

Using a manicured fingernail to remove a coffee ground from her mug, she doesn't seem in a hurry to tell me why we're here. Instead she excuses herself to use the restroom. "Give me a minute, Megan."

Moe comes with a carafe and casts several looks at Ronnie's retreating figure and shakes his head. "That girl is troubled, Megan. You take good care of her."

I just nod, and Moe disappears into the back room.

Ronnie returns from the washroom and sits looking out of the window.

"Ronnie," I say and reach across the table taking her hand. She takes a breath before turning toward me. Her eyes are red from crying. Her cheeks are red and puffy.

"Ronnie, do you want to talk here or back at your place?"

She sniffs and dabs her eyes with a napkin. "We can talk here. I don't want to be alone right now."

She'll tell me when she's ready so I sip my coffee to brace for what might be coming. I'm just hoping she's not pregnant. Marley Yang. Or, God forbid, Hayden.

"It's my mom," Ronnie finally says.

Welcome to my world.

"She's missing and my sister thinks she was kidnapped."

EIGHT

"Is it possible your mom left for her own reasons?" It's a good question considering the rift between Ronnie and her family. From what I'd garnered about her father he sounds like a man who's used to having his way. Ruling the roost so to speak.

She says, "Rebecca doesn't think so. She wants to involve the police but is unsure if she should."

"Rebecca?"

"My sister."

Rebecca. Of course. "So why does Rebecca think this is a police matter?"

"Mom's been gone for two days with no word to anyone. Dad didn't want Rebecca to call me or the police. But she called me and I told her to call the police anyway. She agreed with me and called the local Sheriff Department."

"So the police are looking for her?"

Ronnie's face drops. "No. They told Rebecca they had to wait forty-eight hours to report her missing. But it's Sunday morning now, almost the full forty-eight, and they still haven't taken a report."

Her dad doesn't want the police involved. Ronnie knows, as

well as I do, that most domestic murders start this way. But I say, "I'm thinking maybe your dad knows where she is. They've had a fight. It happens."

"Rebecca doesn't think so. You'd have to know our dad to know how prideful he can be. He's going to try to handle this himself. He'll hire investigators that he can pay to keep quiet."

"Has there been a ransom demand?"

"Why? Do you think she's been kidnapped, Megan?"

"I'm just throwing out ideas. Do *you* think she's been kidnapped?"

"I'm worried. I don't know what to think."

"Let's start at the beginning. Tell me what you know."

"First, you need to know my parents are extremely wealthy. I've already told you some of that, and that Dad owns a law firm and Rebecca works for him. "

So kidnapping's not off the table.

"My dad bought a resort in Semiahmoo, and my mom and Rebecca were staying there the day before Mom went missing." She pauses and then clarifies, "They checked in on Thursday, had dinner and visited, and Friday morning Rebecca couldn't find Mom.

"Rebecca said Mom seemed anxious about something on Thursday night when they had dinner. They planned to meet for breakfast or a walk along the beach on Friday morning but Mom didn't show. She called Mom's cell phone several times but didn't get an answer. She said Mom had promised to tell her what was bugging her. Rebecca was told a note was left at Mom's room and the manager said the note was stuck under Mom's door."

"What did the note say?"

"It said something like 'You promised Dinky'."

"Dinky? Is that a name?"

"We don't have a clue. I've never heard a name like that."

"What does your father think?"

"He hasn't said much to Rebecca, and I haven't called him. Rebecca doesn't think he knows she called the police."

"Could your mom have left the note for your father? Is there another man?"

"Rebecca and I talked about that but of course it's ridiculous."

"Why?"

"Well. Because it just is. You'd have to know my mom. According to Rebecca, Mom took enough clothes and necessities to stay a week, but she always does that. And her best jewelry is still at home. She wouldn't have gone anywhere without her jewelry or without telling Rebecca."

"Okay. I take it you only found out today."

"Last night. I've barely slept."

"What has your dad or Rebecca done to find your mom?"

"Rebecca's getting Mom's phone records. She's checked with the bank and credit card companies and there's been no activity. She called the police again this morning and they don't seem interested. My dad is furious."

"With your mom?"

"Everyone. He didn't want Rebecca to call me. He doesn't want me to come. He doesn't want the police involved because it's an embarrassment to the family. He's mad at Mom for worrying everyone."

Boy. What I thought was a rift is more of a Grand Canyon. I had no idea. "Has Rebecca called your mom's friends? Relatives?"

"We only have grandparents on Dad's side but they wouldn't know anything. We seldom see them except on some holidays. Mom's parents are deceased and we've never talked about other family members. I seem to recall she has a brother. They must not have been close. Mom is on several committees. Charities, art museum, unwed mothers, Friends of the Library book club, and the library's restoration committee. As far as real friends, I don't know of any."

"Has your sister called the committees?"

"Dad finally gave in and he is going to call the committee co-chairs."

"Will he ask if they know where your mom is? Or is that too embarrassing for him?"

"My dad doesn't like airing family business. I don't really think he'll make the calls. He said she'll come home when she runs out of money. He has already put a hold on her accounts."

He's more worried about his money than his wife. Now I really don't like him. "Maybe she has accounts he doesn't know about."

"I highly doubt it. My dad keeps a tight rein on the money. His accountant probably keeps track of Mom's transactions."

Of course he would trust his accountant. Not the police, or his daughters.

"What can I do, Ronnie?"

NINE

Victoria lies still, slowing her breathing, listening. But she can only hear the wet sound of her breath coming through her broken nose. She doesn't know how long she's been here. One day? Two? She's beyond feeling humiliation at being naked and lying in her own excrement. She hasn't been offered any water or food and she's thirsty and hungry. She's slept randomly, jerking awake with a whimper and curling into a fetal position. The sides of her mouth and her tongue are raw from her muffled screams.

She thinks, I'm still here. I'm still alive. But she doesn't know how much more she can take. The sinus drainage of snot and blood runs down her throat and causes her to retch painfully.

She knows she has to do something, anything, if she's going to be saved. If she could talk to them, she could plead with them. Give them whatever they want. Promise not to tell anyone. She'll tell Jack that she was mugged and left unconscious. Regardless of how they want to do this, she'll make sure they get their money and that will be the end of it. She'll refuse to cooperate with the police. She just wants to live.

Her breath comes in hitches. She sucks in air around the gag and is about to cry out in despair when something stops her. She hears the sound of footsteps coming from somewhere.

Victoria lies perfectly still, feigning unconsciousness, praying they can't hear her heartbeat pounding. She's surrendering to her death and prays to God that her Rebecca is safe.

TEN

FEBRUARY 2023

Whatcom County

Longbow insisted on driving the two of them over to the scene in his SUV. Perhaps it was his way of telling himself he was still easing Lucas back in gently, despite bringing him into what was pretty clearly a murder investigation in his first ten minutes back on the job.

"You know, Mike, if you want to talk about anything..."

"Thank you," Lucas said quickly, cutting him off. "I appreciate that, Sheriff."

They drove north, beyond the outskirts of town and into the country. The trees were still bare, their skeletal fingers reaching up into a sky the color of gunmetal. Longbow slowed as they reached the turn that would take them to the bridge over the creek. He slowed even more as the bridge came into view. There was a black-and-white patrol car parked across the road, though there was no sign of Deputy Cooney.

Longbow parked up at the side of the road and they got out. The air seemed colder out here than it had back in town. Lucas could see his breath. He turned up the collar of his coat and started to walk toward the parked patrol car, pausing when he heard the sound of an engine back at the main road. He looked back down the road and saw the coroner's van make the turn.

As they reached the bridge, Lucas peered down the slope to the creek that flowed beneath. Deputy Cooney was standing just below the crest of the hill. Twenty feet farther down the slope, there was the body of a woman, lying in the shallows at the edge of the water.

She was naked, face down in the water. Her blonde hair was trailing with the westward current. The overcast sky and the surroundings made Lucas feel like he was looking at a monochrome image—the bleached hair, the skin so pale it was almost the color of the sky reflected in the water.

Lucas became conscious of Cooney's eyes on him. He looked over at him, and the younger deputy looked away. That was one of the problems of life in a relatively small department: everyone always knew everyone else's business.

Or thought they did.

Cooney cleared his throat. "Kids found it. One of the moms called it in."

Longbow looked around. Only the three of them were there. "You talk to her yet?"

"No, sir. I called you as soon as I got out here."

Longbow glanced down at the body again, and then over at Lucas. "Mike, are you sure...?"

Lucas sighed. "Take the kid gloves off, Sheriff. Let's go take a look."

Being careful to keep his footing, Lucas descended the steep slope, reaching the water line in a matter of seconds. He glanced behind him to see Longbow following in his footsteps with a little more difficulty. Deputy Cooney was standing by the body. Lucas realized he had removed his hat, and was holding it absently against his chest, like a mourner at a funeral.

"First body dump?"

Cooney blinked and nodded. "Yes sir. First one."

Lucas reached out, pulled the kid's hat out of his grasp, and put it back on his head. "You get used to it after two or three."

He knelt to get a closer look at the body, careful not to touch it. The woman was half-submerged, the face fully underwater. There were yellowed bruises on the arms and back. Lucas took a closer look at the right arm that was outstretched. It looked as though the woman was trying to swim, even though he knew that was just the position it had come to rest in after it had been dumped off the bridge. One of the fingers seemed to be curled. Then he realized it wasn't curled, it was missing.

"What is it?" Longbow asked, out of breath and looking relieved as he finally reached the water's edge.

"Somebody cut one of her fingers off," Lucas said. "And she's been beaten." He indicated the bruising on her back and arms. The bruises varied in color and in contrast. "Not just one incident, this happened over a longer period."

"You think she killed herself?"

Lucas turned at the sound of Cooney's voice. He had almost forgotten the kid was there.

"Say again?"

Cooney pointed up at the bridge.

"Maybe she was, you know... depressed."

"Arnie," Longbow said sharply, before Lucas could say anything. The kid snapped to attention. Longbow pointed up at the road. "Get up there and wait for the coroner."

When Deputy Cooney had retreated back up the hill, Longbow turned back to him.

"I'm sorry, Mike. He didn't mean anything by it."

This time, Lucas didn't even acknowledge the unasked-for sympathy.

"Thing about suicides," Lucas said, his voice even. "They don't ordinarily leave the house naked in February and walk five miles from the nearest town to kill themselves. Somebody beat her, tortured her and killed her. He was holding her for days."

"Holding her?" Longbow repeated.

Lucas gestured at the outstretched arm. Longbow had focused on the missing finger, the way Lucas had at first too.

"Ligature marks around the wrists. Looks like cable ties, not cuffs. This is a kidnap and kill."

The engine of the coroner's van sounded above them and they heard doors open and close.

"I'm out of the loop, do we have any live missing persons cases?"

Longbow shook his head. Nothing.

"Which suggests she's not local," Lucas said. "First thing we need to do is work out who she is and where she's from."

"Could be difficult," Longbow said. "No clothes, no ID. Probably a hooker. The perp could have picked her up in Tacoma, brought her out here for a good time, dumped her. Maybe there's nobody to miss her, easy prey."

Lucas shook his head. "I don't think so. Look at the hair and nails." He gestured at the body. "She took care of herself. Like I said, she's not local, but somebody's missing her."

The coroner investigator appeared at the top of the hill; a tall, wide-built man in his forties who looked like he'd be more at home doing manual labor than the thankless task of retrieving bodies from wherever they fell and working out how they met their maker.

Longbow beckoned him down. He descended the hill with more grace than Longbow had mustered, despite being encumbered with a large bag full of equipment.

Longbow introduced Lucas, and the coroner shook his hand and identified himself as Boyd Sutherland. He gave the body a look over and snapped a few preliminary photos.

"Anybody touch the body?" he said without looking up from his work.

"It's as it was when Deputy Cooney found it," Longbow replied.

"Good."

Sutherland yelled up to his partner to bring the litter down and then asked for Lucas's help carefully pulling the body out of the river, handing him a pair of latex gloves. Lucas grimaced, thinking about how he had just polished his shoes this morning, but stepped into the freezing flow to help move the body. Boyd Sutherland directed him to get the feet while he reached under the dead woman's arms to lift her from the water.

The body was surprisingly light. They moved it over to the bank, where Sutherland's partner had laid out the litter.

"It's your lucky day," Sutherland said, addressing Longbow. "We have an empty dance card today so we should be able to schedule your Jane Doe in this afternoon."

"I'd like to sit in," Longbow said, before casting a hesitant glance at Lucas.

"Yeah, we'll be there," Lucas said. "Soon as I pick up a new pair of shoes."

Sutherland glanced down at his own waterproof boots and grinned. "Be prepared, right?"

Lucas shook the water off his hands and peeled the gloves off as he watched Sutherland and his partner carefully scale the slope again with the body on the litter.

"Mike," Longbow said, "I don't mind covering the autopsy if you want to go home and change."

"Boss, with all due respect, you treating me like your frail grandma is going to get old real quick. I'll meet you at the chop shop. Now..." He gestured up at the slope. "You want me to go get a winch to get you back up there?"

Longbow couldn't help but laugh. "Fuck you."

ELEVEN

"You're going where?" Sheriff Tony Gray is sitting behind his brand-new desk, a gift from the same billionaire that bought our entire department new police vehicles, including my Explorer. The Sheriff is wearing a starched and pressed khaki uniform, and that tells me his wife laid his clothes out today. He's far past retirement age and twenty pounds overweight, as opposed to the thirty extra pounds he'd carried around four months ago. His wife, Ellen, put him on a forced diet and since she's the force, it's working. He'd met Ellen at the hospital several years ago after he had a heart attack and wrecked his truck. Ellen nursed him back to health and he has been fighting a losing battle of the bulge since. He has to control his sugar and grease addiction to keep healthy. It's a Herculean task.

To help Ellen out I've brought him two large cinnamon rolls from Moe's and an extra strong black coffee. The way to a man's heart is through diabetes and caffeine. I should be ashamed but I'm not. At least I didn't bring a bag of bacon cheeseburgers.

He greedily accepts my offering, and I steel myself for a battle. Ronnie lets me do the talking. I brought the rolls so I'm the one he owes.

"Sheriff, about this thing with the councilman..."

He's already shaking his head. "Forget about it," he says through a giant mouthful of cinnamon roll.

I sit back in my chair, surprised. That was easy. "Oh?"

He finished chewing and swallows. "I decided you were right. I've convinced him to hire a private investigator and not get our department mixed up in it."

I exchange a glance with Ronnie, who looks relieved. I had warned her I would have to get out of this before we made our request.

"Now," the Sheriff says, holding up what's left of the cinnamon roll. "I assume you want something from me."

That kind of perspicacity is why they pay him the big bucks. Or at least, bigger bucks than I get.

"We need to go to Whatcom County. We might be gone a couple of days."

"Am I allowed to ask why?"

No. "Yes. Ronnie's family has asked for our help with something personal." I know he won't ask. He knows more about me than almost anyone and he's never asked questions. He doesn't pry.

He thinks it over for a moment, then shrugs. "You both have vacation time coming, so I don't see why not. Can you give me an idea when you'll be back?"

I look at Ronnie and she doesn't have any idea, but to be safe I say, "A week or less." Maybe more.

"There's not much going on here, other than Councilman Johns's wandering wife, which we've already agreed is out of our purview. Do either of you have anything needing reassigned?"

We both shake our heads. Nothing much has happened lately outside of a couple of burglaries where only liquor was stolen and some teenagers going for a series of joyrides. Both

stopped when the teens wrapped a stolen car around a tele-
phone pole. Coincidence? I think not.

"Okay then. Approved but I might have to call one or both
of you back."

"Understood," I say.

"Thank you, Sheriff," Ronnie adds.

He stares at the second cinnamon roll and a look of guilty
indecision comes over his face.

I say, "I can take it with us if you want to—" I don't get to
finish before he snatches up the roll.

"Evidence," he says. "I'll keep custody."

We anticipated getting permission from Tony and both of
us packed a small bag. Ronnie said we would be put up at the
Marsh house. If it gets awkward, I'm going to a motel and she's
on her own.

TWELVE

It's after 4 p.m. by the time we reach our destination. The Marshes live on a peninsula north of the city of Birch Bay, bordered by Drayton Harbor and Semiahmoo Bay. Ronnie directs me down Birch Point Road and north along Semiahmoo Drive. We pass a sign reading: SEMIAHMOO GOLF AND COUNTRY CLUB and a mile later come to a private drive flanked by a stone arch with steel gates. A plaque is mounted above the arch. COUGAR POINT.

"Cougar Point?" I ask.

"The peninsula is shaped like the head of a cougar, and our property is the nose. My granddad thought so when he named it."

Ronnie takes out her keys, hits a button on a fob and the gates slowly open. A camera and a speaker are mounted in the stones on both sides of the arch. The aggregate drive is lined with miniature pine trees and the paved road rises slightly and turns from aggregate to yellow bricks.

"I don't think we're in Kansas anymore," I remark.

Ronnie smiles. "The yellow brick road is Dad's idea of a

joke. *The Wizard of Oz* was Rebecca and my favorite movie when we were kids."

The waterfront residence sets on a promontory overlooking Semiahmoo Bay; a mixture of Tudor and Cottage style with spectacular west-facing sunsets . I park and follow Ronnie along a meandering walkway lined with weeping cherry trees. A monkey tree sits to one side of the door; on the other side is a stone path that disappears and reappears at a sandy beach and a boathouse the size of Ronnie's apartment in Port Townsend. If I owned this gorgeous view, I'd never go inside. I might take up painting. But first I'd have to learn to draw.

A slightly older replica of Ronnie comes out of the front door and greets us with a serious look. She hugs Ronnie.

"Megan, this is my sister, Rebecca."

"Detective Megan Carpenter," Rebecca says, and takes both of my hands in hers. "I've heard a lot about you. When Ronnie calls she regales me with your adventures. You're just what she needs to keep her safe."

Ronnie looks uncomfortable and I immediately defend her. "Actually she's saved my life more than once. I'm proud to have her for a partner."

Rebecca blushes. "I'm sorry for that remark. That was our dad talking."

Nope. That was all you, Rebecca. I can see why Ronnie doesn't talk about the family.

Rebecca redeems herself. "Sorry, Ronnie. I worry about you but I know you can take care of yourself. I hope you don't think bad of me, Megan."

Too late. "Absolutely not. Ronnie is your biggest fan. " *She never talks about you. I didn't know your name until today.*

Rebecca's not buying it. "Does she? Well, please come in. Forgive the mess. Dad has dismissed all the help for a few days."

We enter into a high-ceilinged lobby furnished with floating

glass shelving filled with expensive-looking vases and trinkets
on one side, and on the other is a sitting area with high-back
chairs facing tall windows with a view of a rock garden and out
over the bay. Rebecca becomes our tour guide. She's obviously
proud of the house, and should be. It's beautiful and I've only
seen the entrance. If this is what she calls messy, she'd have a
stroke in my place.

A wrought-iron staircase leads down to a salt-water pool
with a jacuzzi, seating at least a dozen visitors, a stone fireplace
and kitchen. Steps carved into the rock lead to a private
boathouse and four-acre sandy beach. I can see why Ronnie
gave this up to live in a converted barn and become a deputy.

"Where's Dad?" Ronnie asks.

Rebecca ignores the question. "Let's go to the kitchen."

Ronnie holds me back a moment. "She's not a bad person.
She's just nervous."

"I can understand." She's not nervous. She's condescending.
And she has no reason to think she has a better life than Ronnie.
More money doesn't make a better person. But I do understand
about missing mothers. Although, some mothers are better off
not being found.

"Not just that. She's nervous about what Dad will say when
he finds out we're here."

"He doesn't know? Or he won't approve?" I ask.

"Both, I guess. He's very private. But he won't make a scene
in front of you."

I don't want to stay somewhere I'm not welcome. "If I'm
going to create trouble, I can go get a room somewhere else."

"No, Megan. I don't think I can do this without you. If
anyone can find Mom, it will be you."

"I was kidding. You couldn't get rid of me with a cattle prod.
But you're not giving yourself enough credit. You're the best
detective I've ever met." *Besides me.*

In the kitchen Rebecca is starting an espresso machine. I've got to get one of those. And then learn how to use it.

"Sis says you like yours extra strong."

"I like it to walk on water," I say, and Rebecca giggles. Honest to God. She giggles just like Ronnie. It must be genetic.

"Sis said you were funny."

"What else did she say? And remember, I'm armed." I put my hand on my gun.

She doesn't even smile. I don't suppose much laughing goes on here. Rebecca hasn't told her dad she called us so I wonder if he'll laugh or scream. He's a father, but he's an attorney. I don't generally like attorneys. After I taste the espresso I'll decide if I like Rebecca.

"She said you would listen and tell us what you think, Megan."

Down to business. "You talk and I'll listen."

"Find a seat. Cream or sugar, Megan?"

"Surprise me." I sit and wait until she gets her own espresso just right, which reminds me of people in Starbucks. I go in Starbucks to get a cup of regular coffee, and it never fails the person in front of me orders a string of ingredients that will take a supercomputer to figure out. There should be a line for "just coffee" customers and a "high-maintenance buffet" for the others.

Rebecca gathers her thoughts. Their dad is wanting to avoid embarrassment, which tells me their mom may not be missing-missing, as in kidnapped or tied to the train tracks, but rather, she's gone off on her own. But I never rule out foul play.

Ronnie and I have just worked a missing persons case, a mother and son, where the prime suspect was the estranged husband. He had a mistress who ran a close second, but she was eventually cleared of the kidnapping when her head was blown off by the real kidnapper. In that case there was money involved, and betrayal, and sex, and hatred, and love. All the ingredients for a messy investigation. But in reality, in nine out of ten missing person cases, the missing person comes home on their own. That means one out of ten never come home, or if they do, it's in a zipper bag. For Ronnie's sake I hope her mother is one of the nine.

THIRTEEN

Rebecca blows over the top of the steaming espresso and gazes across the bay. The view is astounding and I have to tear my eyes away to listen more closely. "Mom was being Mom. She needed a getaway at our resort and insisted I come with her. We had dinner and went to her room where a bottle of chilled champagne was waiting. She moped during dinner, and I had the feeling she wanted to tell me something. We sat on the veranda and drank the entire bottle." A look passes between the sisters. "I asked what was bothering her, and she said she just wanted to have a pleasant evening and we would talk about it in the morning. We agreed to meet for breakfast and go for a walk. I got up early but she hadn't come down, so I went out to watch the sunrise. I knew she would be along when she woke up. I fell asleep and it was noon before one of the resort staff woke me and said I had a note at the front desk."

Rebecca puts a scribbled note on the table. Three words.

you promised dinky

The writing was either from a five-year-old or deliberately

made-up. The sisters exchange another look, and Ronnie uses a napkin to pick it up for closer examination.

I ask, "Who's Dinky?" They shake their heads and once again I see the close resemblance. Not just in appearance but in the way they move and their facial expressions.

Rebecca says, "Roger showed it to me around noon on Saturday. Roger's the manager at Semiahmoo Resort. The note was found outside Mom's door. It wasn't there when I left her the night before but I couldn't swear it was or wasn't there when I went down to sunbathe. I went down the stairs at the far end of the hall and wouldn't have passed by Mom's room. We were supposed to be staying until Monday."

"Who found the note?"

"The night manager, I think. The general manager, Roger, was on the front desk when I came in to get the message."

"Did you talk to the night manager, sis?" Ronnie asks.

"The night manager was already gone but Roger said he hadn't seen Mom come down for breakfast, and when he didn't see her around lunchtime, he remembered the note and thought it might be important. I went to her room, checked the café and then out on the deck to see if we had just passed each other. She hadn't left a message for me so I went back to the room to see if she had left a note there. She hadn't. She couldn't have left on her own because we were in my car."

Your mom could have gotten a ride, or called a Lyft. I ask, "What did you do then?"

"I tried calling her phone and left voicemails. I finally called my dad to see if she was home. He thought she was with me."

"Did you call the police?"

"Dad said not to panic. He was sure she would show up and would be embarrassed if the police were looking for her."

Ronnie says, "But you called them anyway."

Rebecca nods. "They said they couldn't do anything for forty-eight hours. I stayed at the resort overnight Saturday, and when she still hadn't made contact, I called the police again and demanded an officer come to the resort and take a report. They said they could send an officer but he couldn't put her in the system until the forty-eight hours were up. I tried to reach the Sheriff here but it was a weekend and I got a deputy who gave me the same bullshit line. Police policy. She wasn't in jail or in the hospital. There was nothing. It's not like our mom to go away like this. She would have told me where she was going. She's never spent more than a few nights away, and those were with one of her committee groups. And that's why I called you."

Ronnie says, "You said Mom wanted to tell you something. Are you leaving Dad's firm? Was she upset about something? Remember when she faked an injury to get me to come home from the police academy?"

"What did you expect her to do? You wouldn't listen to reason. She thought it would make you see how important family is. Her heart's in the right place, sis. She only wants what's best for you. For us. But I see what you're hinting at. The answer is no, there's nothing going on. She's not faking this or I wouldn't have worried you."

"Mom always wants what's best for Mom. She wants to control our lives. Just like dear old Dad."

Rebecca gives Ronnie a stern look. "Don't be disrespectful. You're where you are today because of them."

"Point taken. But Dad hasn't changed, Rebecca. Did he come to the resort and help look for her? Or did he try to talk you out of doing something that might cause him embarrassment? That's how he is. That's why I left. I wanted my own life. Not his. Not Mom's. Not yours."

"And so you just take off. Leave me to deal with Dad and the fallout. I'm your older sister, not your caretaker, Ronnie."

"Rebecca the martyr. You could have left. You have a good job. You don't need to work here anymore. You could be happy like me. You can do something for yourself for once."

"How can you even say that? Someone had to stay and take care of them. To hold this family together. Our parents deserve one of us they can be proud..." She bites her words off and covers her mouth.

Ronnie's face gets hot. "They're not proud of me?"

I put a hand on Ronnie's arm and hold my other up like a referee, but I want to hit the mute button on Rebecca. "Time out, kids. Let's cool things down so you can tell me what I'm doing here." They turn away from each other. I say, "And don't forget I'm carrying a gun."

Rebecca says, "I'm sorry, Ronnie. I didn't mean it. I'm just upset."

"Me too. Let's just find her."

What have I gotten into? "Ronnie said there has been no activity on the bank or credit cards? Is that right, Rebecca?"

"Nothing. That's not like Mom. She loves to spend money."

"Boy does she," Ronnie adds.

I think for a minute about next steps. "I guess checking her room at the resort for clues again isn't possible?"

Rebecca brightens. "I've insisted Roger keep her room closed in case you needed to look at it. So far the police haven't shown any interest."

Ronnie says, "Way to go, sis. I'll make a detective of you yet."

"No, thanks. But we do need to talk when this is settled."

A loud gong startles me, and Rebecca gets up. "I'll get it." She leaves the room.

"What's going on?" I ask.

"Someone is at the gate," Ronnie says. "Dad has a state-of-the-art security system."

Ronnie turns on a small plasma screen fixed to the bottom of one kitchen cabinet. A clear picture of a black SUV with dark tinted windows is coming through the gate. "That's not Dad's car."

FOURTEEN

Voices come toward the kitchen and I recognize Rebecca's asking, "Would you like some espresso?"

A man's deep and loud voice answers, "Sounds perfect."

I imagine some hulking figure, but when the man walks into the kitchen, he looks more like a smarmy version of Mister Rogers. Instead of the robin's-egg blue button-up sweater and tennis shoes, this one is wearing a shiny shark-skin suit with fancy Italian-made shoes. Not someone you'd want to be your neighbor.

Rebecca directs him to a seat at the table next to me, and the stench of cigars assails my nose.

"I'll take mine with four shots, black," he says. "Do you have any cookies, Miss Marsh?"

"I'll look while you introduce yourself, Sergeant." She begins opening each cabinet and drawer. It's obvious she's never been in the kitchen without being served. I'm jealous.

"Detective Sergeant Lucas," he says, and runs his fingers through a hair-gel extravaganza of black hair. Too black. *Dyed.*

"Megan Carpenter," I say, and don't offer to shake the hand he doesn't offer.

Ronnie smiles at him. "Ronnie Marsh."

He says, "You look alike."

No shit, Sherlock. I feel like I have to say something. "They're sisters. I'm not related."

He gives me a dismissive look then turns to Rebecca. "Is it okay if I call you Rebecca?"

Rebecca comes back with his espresso and a pack of Lorna Doone cookies. "It would be a lot easier, Sergeant."

"You can call me Ronnie. That's Megan."

He doesn't acknowledge us. Rebecca sits, and the sergeant's focus is turned to her. Lucas says without enthusiasm or concern in his voice, "You called about a missing person. Your mom."

"Yes. And I've called a couple of times and was told a report couldn't be taken until she was missing for forty-eight hours. I tried again today and they said a detective would have to take the report."

He runs his thin fingers through the gel and wipes it on a napkin. "That's forty-eight hours for adults unless there are exceptional circumstances. Children are twenty-four hours." He pops a cookie in his mouth and slurps some espresso. "Why don't you tell me everything. I'll make sure someone takes the report. I want to get started on this as soon as possible."

Or until he runs out of coffee and cookies. I say, "If you brought a missing person form with you, I'll be happy to fill it out while you talk. Rebecca told us her mom has already been missing since Thursday night. It's Sunday afternoon now. That's way over forty-eight hours."

"But she wasn't suspected missing until Friday morning, so we're just over forty-eight, so I'm here. Happy, Ms. Carpenter?"

Again the dismissive look. I size him up. Sixties, close to collecting his pension. A "do what you have to and no more" kind of cop. He's here because he has to be.

"Detective Carpenter," I correct.

He nods, as though it had slipped his mind. "That's right. You two are detectives from... Jefferson County?" He says it with disdain, like his patch is so big-time.

Ronnie shows her credentials but I say nothing. I know what's coming. He does us the courtesy of asking for details on the case first, though.

Rebecca tells Sergeant Lucas what she told us. He doesn't take notes. He doesn't ask questions. I hope we're not keeping him awake. When she finishes he nods and gets up.

He addresses Ronnie. "You have no authority in Whatcom County. If you're here to emotionally support your sister, fine. If you're here to meddle in my business, you need to know I won't stand for it." He turns is gaze on me. "Am I making myself clear, ladies?"

Ronnie looks shocked. I'm not shocked. I say, "Yes, we're detectives. We know we don't have police authority here. But as private citizens you have no right to tell us what we can or can't do. We can, and will, ask questions. Am I making *myself* clear, Sergeant Lucas?"

He waves a dismissive hand at me as if I'm a gnat and turns his attention to Rebecca again. "You should not have called them. It was a mistake I hope you don't regret."

Rebecca bristles. "The mistake is you don't see how valuable their experience is, Sergeant. I called them because your department is doing absolutely nothing. And you don't appear to be interested either."

He ignores her anger. "If your mom contacts, you give me a call." He puts a business card on the table and reaches for another cookie, but I grab the pack. His eyes sparkle. He thinks he's funny.

Rebecca shows him out. I expect Ronnie to have a meltdown, but she says, "It's a good thing Rebecca called us. I'm glad you came with me, Megan. And that Rebecca didn't show Lucas the note."

"Lucas doesn't deserve to know what we know," I say. "He's going to continue to do nothing. Like Rebecca said, he's not interested. Call the resort and tell them we're coming?"

Rebecca comes back in the kitchen. "Roger knows we'll be coming. I'm coming with you if I may."

"Of course." I was going to insist. "I'll drive." I want to show off my new ride.

FIFTEEN

FEBRUARY 2023

Whatcom County

Boyd Sutherland tapped the button to activate the recording on the mic that dangled over the steel autopsy table and dispassionately recited his name, the date and time, and the fact that two other attendees were present: Sheriff Longbow and Sergeant Lucas. Finally, he assigned the corpse in front of him the customary holding name: Jane Doe.

Longbow cleared his throat and suddenly became very interested in the strip light on the ceiling as Sutherland made the preliminary incision. Lucas didn't blink, watching as the scalpel cut through the pale flesh of the woman's abdomen. Blood and fluids ran down the steel surface and collected in the gully as Sutherland cracked the chest and opened it up.

Lucas closed his eyes for a moment and immediately saw the scene in his living room several weeks before. Tangled limbs, blood spatter, broken glass. He opened them again and focused on the more orderly carnage in the here and now instead.

Lucas looked to his side and saw that Longbow was forcing

himself to watch. The older man had never enjoyed this. It didn't usually bother Lucas either way but he couldn't deny it felt a little different this time, after seeing the immediate aftermath of such violence so much closer to home.

They watched as Sutherland removed organs and took samples, narrating every motion in the same matter-of-fact voice, like he was a bored TV chef putting together a casserole. He barely glanced at the two cops watching his every move.

"Subject was dehydrated, probably a couple of days with no water..." He paused and looked up at Lucas and Longbow, his blue eyes focusing on them above his mask. "Sergeant Lucas, you speculated she'd been held captive for some time?"

"That's my guess," Lucas said.

"Mine too. Not much in the way of stomach contents either. What looks like dry crackers, most of the way digested."

"Excuse me a second," Longbow said, covering his mouth and making for the door.

Lucas watched him go and then looked back at Sutherland in time to see the grin distorting his mask.

"Sorry about that, I had to take a call." Longbow's skin looked a little less green than it had as he had hurried out of the autopsy room. Lucas just smiled and said nothing. He was betting his boss was regretting whatever he had eaten for breakfast.

They were in the back office at the coroner's, away from the chemical and human smells of the autopsy room, poring over the transcript of the recording while Sutherland washed up.

"Starved, dehydrated, beaten, finger cut off," Lucas said, totting up the damage. "Ligature marks on the wrists. Not just one kind—different cable ties and maybe a set of cuffs over several days. The bruising happened at different times too. She was held captive and tortured."

"Sick son of a bitch," Longbow said. "You think it's a serial? Like I said before, maybe he picked her up in Tacoma or Seattle and held her in the back of a van for a few days."

Lucas shook his head. "I don't think so. The finger being cut off doesn't go with that."

"How do you figure? These bastards like to torture their victims. Gives them a sense of power, or a sexual kick."

"Sure. And somebody sure seems to have taken pleasure beating her to a pulp, but the finger is different. Why stop at one finger?"

Longbow shot him a look that said he was starting to wonder if Lucas had indeed come back too early. "Say again?"

"Cause of death is blunt trauma, a blow to the head. If this is some psycho killing purely for the thrill of it, he doesn't stop at cutting off a finger. That's the only time a blade was used. So why take a finger?"

"Trophy or something? I don't know. I don't want to think like one of these diseased fucking animals."

"I think she was being ransomed," Lucas said. "Happens all the time. The drug cartels love to do it—they show the family they mean business by mailing them a piece of the victim. Ties in with her being well-groomed. This wasn't a junkie or a hooker."

"So in that case, I guess we just have to wait for somebody to call us to say they got a finger in the mail, huh?"

Lucas shrugged. "Maybe."

"What do you mean 'maybe'? This'll let us ID her as soon as we find a kidnap that fits."

Lucas thought about it for a minute, not entirely sure what he had meant himself. As his mind worked, he was distantly conscious of the fact he was enjoying himself. For the first time in weeks, he was able to focus on something other than what had happened in January.

"I think something went wrong. Maybe they didn't have the

chance to mail the finger before she was killed. Or maybe they got the money and killed her anyway."

His phone buzzed in his pocket. It was Deputy Cooney. Lucas had tasked him with going through missing persons reports while they attended the autopsy. He had told him to start local but then keep widening the search beyond the state lines if necessary.

"Sergeant Lucas?"

"I hope so," Lucas said, rolling his eyes at Longbow. "Otherwise somebody stole my phone. You got something?"

"I don't know exactly."

Lucas took a second to absorb that. "You don't know exactly," he repeated.

"There's a missing person's report filed in Ohio, matches the description. Caucasian, blonde, thirty-seven years old."

"Ohio?" Lucas repeated. "That's a little farther out of state than I expected. What's her name? How long's she been missing?"

"Well, that's the thing. She's not missing anymore."

Lucas rubbed his forehead. He felt the beginnings of a migraine. "Cooney, if she's not missing, then she's probably not the fucking body on the slab in there, is she?"

"The husband called the police when she didn't show up after booking into a luxury hotel for the weekend. Then he called again saying he thought she'd been kidnapped. Four hours later he called to say she showed up at the house. There had been some big misunderstanding."

"Still not following the connection. All we have is a blonde of about the same age that went missing a couple thousand miles from here and came home."

"There was a picture with the report. It's the woman we pulled out of the creek, I'd swear to it."

SIXTEEN

The Semiahmoo Resort is situated at the eastern end of the peninsula on its own 130-acre tract surrounded by water. White Rock, BC, Canada, is just across the water about two miles as the crow flies but probably an hour by road. With White Rock on the north, Blaine and Drayton Harbors on the south, the resort seemingly spreads across the horizon with the pristine blue waters of Semiahmoo Bay as a perfect backdrop for a Hollywood set.

I've never been here before but it's now on my vacation list. As soon as I can take a vacation. Which is never. The scenery is breathtaking. I wonder what Hayden would think of this place. Maybe I'll take some days off if I can bring him with me. A sibling vacation. It would be like when we were on the run, but a lot more fun without the murder and panic and having nowhere to hide.

The inside of the resort is as beautiful as the outside. Hardwood floors gleam. The lobby has floor-to-ceiling windows looking toward a spectacular view of snow-covered Mount Baker. Rebecca introduces Ronnie and me as detectives from Jefferson County to the manager, Roger Whiting. He isn't concerned she has brought us to search the vacated room, or that we want to question the staff. Rebecca is part owner.

The thing I notice first about Roger Whiting is that he's standing on a box when he steps down to retrieve a key for us.

"No one has been in the room, Miss Marsh."

I ask, "Have the police come by?"

"No. They never write. They never call..." he answers, very deadpan, and makes me smile. That phrase is as old as the hills but I could get to like this guy.

Ronnie says, "A detective named Lucas is going to be calling."

"I know Sergeant Lucas. He hasn't been here either." He reaches down and comes up with a silver tray filled with Biscoff cookies—the kind they serve on airplanes—and sets them on the counter. Roger sees me eying them.

"Would you like some, Detective?"

"Megan Carpenter," I say. "This is Detective Marsh."

"I know," Roger says. "It's been a while since I've seen you here. Your mom said you're a famous detective now."

They chitchat but I'm fixated on the cookies. I've never been on an airplane, but Sheriff Gray went to a Sheriff's Conference in Indianapolis once and brought some of those cookies back for the office. Picking up several packets I stuff them in my blazer pocket. Just to clarify our authority in case Lucas actually does come here, I say, "Mr. Whiting, we're not here in an official capacity. We're consulting for Rebecca if anyone with a badge asks."

Roger feigns ignorance. "You were never here?"

Now I really like him, and so, I take a couple more packets of cookies. I wonder if these cookies go with box wine? Roger must be a mind reader and offers the tray again. It would be rude to refuse. I hope there's none left for Lucas.

Ronnie says, "Roger, are there any staff here who worked the day my sister and mom checked in? And the next day?"

"One of our desk staff is off with a sick child so I checked your mom and sister in on Thursday afternoon. Let's see..." His eyes look toward the ceiling. He returns from memory retrieval mode and says, "Mrs. Marsh went to the pool. Then she and Miss Marsh"—he nods at Rebecca—"had lunch in the restaurant." He looks to Rebecca for verification then continues. "If you like, I can find out who your waiter was."

Rebecca says, "It was Alan. He always waits on us when we're here."

"Ah, yes, Alan. I can call him in."

"I'll pay for his coming in on Sunday to talk to us. And I'd like all the staff that were here on Friday and Saturday to come in too. I'll pay extra," Rebecca offers.

"Miss Marsh. Your money is no good here. Let me see." Again his eyes drift to the ceiling. "Let's see. Connie is here this morning. She cleaned and resupplied your rooms both nights. And then there's the night manager."

Ronnie says, "I'd like them to come in if that's doable. They might remember more in person."

"Of course. I'll arrange it. And I'll be here if you need me."

Take-charge Ronnie says, "I'll need the key to the room. And we'll need a place to do the interviews."

Roger hands Ronnie a brass key. "You can use Packer's Cafe for the interviews. I'll have someone come and make you coffee or whatever you need. I don't think there are any guests in there, but if they are, you can use the conference room on the second floor." He gives her a key card.

Rebecca puts her hand over Roger's. "Thank you, Roger. This means a lot to me."

"It's the least I can do. Mrs. Marsh will be fine. I'll say a prayer for her and for you. Is there anything else?"

"Not this minute," Rebecca says. "Send whoever you can find to Packer's one at a time, please. I won't forget your help."

Roger blushes and gets on the phone to call his employees.

Ronnie says, "I'll go to Mom's room. Rebecca, you and Megan can interview the staff. Let Megan do the talking. When I'm done, I'll find you at Packer's."

We agree. I'm not used to this side of Ronnie but I'm glad she's running the show. It will give her something to do besides worry. And it will assure Rebecca that Ronnie is the right one for the job.

Ronnie says, "If I miss something, Megan, please jump in."

"You've got this, Ronnie."

"But if...?"

"You're the boss."

Ronnie heads for the stairs, and Rebecca leads me to Packer's.

* * *

Packer's is an upscale café. One entire wall is floor-to-ceiling glass looking out toward Drayton Bay. In the distance is a ramshackle building that reminds me of an abandoned timber mill. Rebecca says it was a salmon packing operation. Hence the name Packer's, I guess. Roger was correct about the café being unused except for a lone man sitting by one of the windows banging away on a laptop like the keys are a whack-a-mole arcade game. He doesn't even notice we're there. He reminds me of one of those wannabe writers hanging around Starbucks, taking up a table and drinking free refills. I don't recognize him so he's probably no one. Then again, I don't read a lot.

Rebecca pulls the velvet-encased barrier chain across the entrance and latches it. We're stuck with the Pulitzer Prize guy but he's off in his own world. If he wakes up, he'll hopefully see the chain up and leave. Or I can yell, "FIRE!" Nah. He's actually kind of cute, in a nerdy way.

Rebecca and I take a table facing the entrance and wait. We don't have to wait long before a middle-aged woman in an honest-to-God maid's outfit, complete with white cap, sees us and ducks under the barrier.

"Connie?" I say, and she nods. Her expression is concerned, like she's been called to the principal's office or is being audited by the IRS. I stand and take her hand. "Let me assure you that you're not in any trouble. We just want to ask some questions." She doesn't relax. I try again and soften my expression with a smile. "I'm Detective Carpenter and this is Rebecca Marsh. Have a seat."

"I remember you, Connie," Rebecca says. "Thank you for coming so quick."

Connie sits and I can hardly shut her up. The only pertinent information she has is that she cleaned Victoria's room on Friday somewhere around two in the afternoon. She cleaned it extra special because they all knew who Victoria was. She kept sneaking shy glances at Rebecca as if she were in the presence of royalty. She said she was instructed not to clean the room later by the manager and hasn't been in the room since.

My gut tells me there's more and she's covering it with her incessant chatter. "Connie, it's very important for you to be straight with us. Did you see anyone come or go from that room?"

She looks down and I can barely hear her response.

"Can you say that again?"

Rebecca says, "It's okay to tell us, Connie. My mom is missing and anything you know might help."

She peeks at me and then looks down again. "I clean the rooms starting just before noon but Mrs. Marsh is always up early and having breakfast with you." She looks at Rebecca. "That morning I thought she wouldn't mind if I straightened up a bit so I went in and cleaned. Then a few hours later Roger said to leave the room alone."

"Did you know my mom was missing?" Rebecca asks, and then looks at me. "Sorry."

"Go ahead and answer, Connie," I say.

"Not then. I told you I cleaned the room around two o'clock, but it was before noon. Roger doesn't want us in the guest's rooms before noon. And when Roger told me not to go in the room, I thought maybe I'd done something wrong, so I didn't tell him I'd already been in there. When I found out from Roger that she was missing, I kept quiet. I was afraid I'd messed up something. I'd get fired if I did something that was evidence or whatever. I'm real real sorry. I hope you find your mom, Miss Marsh. She's such a sweetheart to all of us."

"Connie, what was the room like before you cleaned? I need all the detail you can remember," I say.

"The covers weren't down like Mrs. Marsh had slept there. I guess Mrs. Marsh could have slept on top of the covers but hardly anyone ever does because they're afraid we don't clean them." She hurriedly says, "But we do."

Myself, I never sleep on the duvet. I pull it off on the floor where it belongs.

"I'm sure you do a thorough job, Connie. Go on."

The dam breaks and the rest spills out. She has a good memory. She went in the room a couple of hours before Roger told her to stay out. Rebecca would have been on the back deck waiting for her mom at that time. There was an empty champagne bottle lying on the floor. She put the bottle in the trash, then cleaned the room. She took the trash away and threw it in the bin outside. If she can be believed, she hadn't touched anything else. She hadn't seen the note on the floor outside Victoria's room. I took Connie's contact information and let her go.

With Connie gone I ask, "What time did you have dinner with your mom Thursday night, Rebecca?"

"Maybe seven or eight. Then we went to her room and sat on the veranda and talked. There wasn't any champagne in the room. I'm sure of it. Mom is not much of a drinker. And when I looked for her, I went to her room and there was no bottle of champagne. Unless it was in the trash. I didn't think to look there. Connie said she threw the bottle away so I wouldn't have known."

"Maybe she ordered another bottle that night after you left the room?"

"I'm sure she wouldn't have."

I call the front desk. Roger answers.

"Mr. Whiting. This is Detective Carpenter. Is Connie still around?"

"She's right here. I'll put her on."

She answers in a hesitant voice. "This is Connie."

"Detective Carpenter, Connie. I just need to clarify something."

"Okay."

"You found a champagne bottle on the floor. Do you remember if there was anything left in the bottle?"

"Yes."

"There was some left?"

"Not much though. Is it important?"

"How many glasses for the champagne were in the room?" I'd forgot to ask that question.

"There were two. But now that I think of it, they hadn't been used."

I mull that over and then ask if there's anything else she can recall that might be helpful. You'd be amazed how often that "anything else" question bears fruit.

She hesitates for a second. "Well, there was one other thing. Sort of."

"Sort of?"

"I didn't think it was important enough to mention because you asked about unusual things. This isn't unusual."

"Tell me." *Before I strangle you.*

"It's probably nothing. People are always coming and going."

"Tell me."

"It's just, I didn't think it was worth mentioning. I was getting some ice and I ran into Missy. She always likes to make sure I'm doing everything right. Anyway, when she was talking to me, we saw a guy and a woman going out of the downstairs back door. I just saw them for a second. I thought the woman was a little drunk, the way she was draped around the guy."

"Were they guests?"

"I don't know. Maybe. They could have checked in before my shift. It's not a totally unusual sight so I didn't pay much attention." She stops and considers. "Do you think it could have been Mrs. Marsh I saw with the man?"

I fight back the excitement. "Can you describe them?"

"I only saw them for a second. He was taller than me. White. Dark sunglasses. Long hair with a ball cap. I'm sorry. That's all I know. I'm horrible with descriptions. Oh yeah. He had acne. I remember because my cousin suffered with it in high school."

I ask her a few more questions, but that's all she can recall. I let her go and make a note to ask her colleague Missy about it. Perhaps she'll have a better eye for detail.

"Miss Marsh," a young man says from the entrance. "You wanted to talk to me?"

"Come in, Alan," Rebecca says with a smile. "Have a seat."

"Let me get you some coffee first. Roger keeps a pot going for day shift. He said you might want something to eat. I'm not much of a cook but I make a mean grilled cheese." Without waiting for an answer, he goes behind the counter and through the batwing doors into the kitchen.

Alan is quite hot in his tight cut-off shorts and tie-dyed shirt. He couldn't be more than eighteen years old, beach-boy blond hair, dark tanned, perfect white teeth, in shape and knows it. I give Rebecca a look, and she turns red in the face. "You and him?"

"He's nice to me because of Mom."

I seriously doubt it. At twenty-six years old, Rebecca is an attractive older woman to this younger horny stud. I saw the way he looked at her. Lust was in the air. Hormones were on overdrive. Not that I noticed his perfect tight little... Hey, I've got a steady boyfriend, but I'm not dead. "None of my business."

"What are we going to ask him?"

"Same as Connie. Did he see your mom with anyone? Where did the champagne come from? How late was he at work? If he saw her, what was her mood like. That kind of stuff. I'm not hungry yet. You?"

She shakes her head and goes to the counter to tell him just coffee is fine. The writer dude looks over at her annoyed that we're making noise. If he does it again, I'll give him something exciting to write about.

SEVENTEEN

Victoria hears someone enter and a light switch click.

"I know you're awake, bitch," the man says, and the pointy toe of a shoe strikes her in the side and takes her breath. She begins hyperventilating and blackness clouds her consciousness. She is going to die. She is going dark like a light switch had turned off, but a hand is shaking her.

"Stay awake."

She hears a click and then something whirring. She recognizes the sound, He's taking pictures with an old Polaroid camera, the kind where a photo pops out of the bottom and develops itself. He slaps her several times on the face and her broken nose, and when she cries out he takes several pictures.

Her eyes are still watering from the sudden pain in her nose when she feels the gag being removed; now he's wiping her nose and mouth with it.

"I thought you were a goner there. That would be a damned shame after all the effort it took to get you here in one piece. Tell me your name and where you live."

Victoria's mind is fuzzy. "Wha...?" Her jaw aches and the

sides of her mouth feel raw from the rough cloth that cut into them.

"The gag came off so you could answer some questions. I can put it back on."

Victoria hacks up a wad of blood and spits it on the floor before another coughing fit overcomes her.

"I know you didn't just spit at me. But that's okay. I'm glad to see you have some spirit in you. We'll break that soon enough. Now. Are you going to answer my questions? Or do I have to wear your kidneys out?"

"Sorry," Victoria says in a weak voice. She hadn't spit at him. She was choking on it and he probably knew that. "My name is Marsh."

"And what's the rest of it. I need to make sure my girl didn't give you a concussion."

Victoria felt a sliver of hope. They wanted her lucid. At least for now. Maybe they'd release her. "Victoria Marsh. My name is Victoria Marsh. I live on Cougar Point."

EIGHTEEN

Alan came back with mugs, a coffee carafe, sweetener and cream, and loaded with pastries. He didn't come back with any usable information. I hated to see him go. So did Rebecca.

"That leaves us with the night manager and his assistant," I say as I see the last of Alan.

"Her," Rebecca corrects. "The night manager is a woman."

As if on cue, a striking young woman, twenties, slender, with dark skin and the largest brown eyes I have ever seen, comes in. The writer stares at her until I give him the glare of death. I tell the newcomer to have a seat, and I go to the writer.

"We're here on police business," I say. It's not a lie. We're just not the police here. "Do you mind working in the lobby?" *Or anywhere away from here will do.*

"And just when it's getting interesting," he says. He gets his crap together and leaves, looking back at our new arrival until he trips and almost face plants.

I sit and ask the woman, "You are?"

"Missy. I'm the night manager. Beverly is the real night manager but she's home with a sick daughter. I'm covering for her."

She seems bright and open and friendly and not the least bit curious as to why she's here. "Missy, do you know Victoria Marsh?"

"Yes. She's your mom," she says to Rebecca. "Roger—Mr. Whiting—checked you and your mom in but I had a bottle of champagne delivered to your mom's room late that evening. Rog... Mr. Whiting said she has been reported missing and I was to cooperate with you. Have you found her? Is she okay? I really like your mom, Miss Marsh."

"Call me Rebecca. This is Detective Megan Carpenter. My mom loves this place. Is Roger a good boss?"

The question takes her by surprise. "Well. Yes." Any time someone starts a response with "well," it means they have to think about it. In this case it was an easy answer. Yes or no. She's young enough to be Roger's daughter, or granddaughter, but when she called him by his first name and not by his title, there was a sense of familiarity. Maybe he has been making passes at her. Or the other way around.

"You're a detective?" she asks me.

"Yes, but I'm just consulting," I say to keep this above board.

"I wasn't aware it was serious enough for the police to be involved."

"I'm not the police, Missy. I'm a friend of the family."

She nods but doesn't look convinced.

"Did you talk to Connie?" I ask.

"Yes. I'm her supervisor. I wanted to know why you were talking to her."

She works nights so she's not Connie's direct supervisor, but I let it pass. "No problem. I just wondered who delivered the champagne to the room? You?"

"No. Hold on. Yes. I was going to have one of our night staff, but no one was around so I decided to do it myself."

I pause a long time and she doesn't take her eyes away from mine. "What time did you take the champagne to her room?"

"Ten thirty. Eleven. Maybe a little later. Why? You don't suspect a crime has been committed, do you?"

"Just covering all the bases." *Bitch.* "Did you hand it to her?"

"She was in the shower."

"How do you know that?"

"I assumed. I heard the shower running. I left the bottle on the table in the suite."

"Did Mrs. Marsh order the champagne?"

"She always... Excuse me, Miss Marsh, but I have to explain myself. Mrs. Marsh always has a bottle sent up when she visits. She generally likes it late in the evening."

I see the look Rebecca is giving Missy and put my hand on hers to be still. "Does she get one glass or two?"

"One. Sometimes two. I only took her one bottle on Thursday night. Was there something wrong with the champagne? Am I in trouble?"

"Was the champagne chilled?" I ask, and Missy's inscrutable façade slips just slightly.

I'm not disappointed when she says, "Should I have an attorney?"

"You're not a suspect, Missy, so no, you don't need an attorney." *Yet. Neither Connie nor Rebecca have said anything about a champagne bucket.* "We don't know if there was anything wrong with the champagne. Was there another bottle in the room? An empty bottle."

"Of champagne? Yes. I took it. I didn't want the day maid to think your mom was a... you know."

Rebecca can't stop herself from saying, "No. I don't know. If you know something about my mom, you'd better tell me."

The smug look on Missy's face tells me she's enjoying punching Rebecca's buttons. I don't have a clue why that would be. Rebecca gets up and goes to the windows and stands, arms across her chest.

"How long have you worked here?" I ask, knowing it may not be much longer.

"A year now. Roger said I had *potential* and promoted me. I've been a part-time night manager for six months."

Roger? I want to ask if she and Roger are a thing but I don't want her to tell him I asked.

"Were you the one that found the note under Mrs. Marsh's door?"

"I did rounds at midnight and found it. It wasn't there when I delivered the champagne earlier and I didn't see anyone in the elevator or in the hallway, so I can't tell you who left it. The note was right up against her door so I knew it was for her. I knocked but there was no answer. I pushed it partially under her door for when she was, uh, able to read it."

I throw Rebecca a cautioning look to let it go.

"I guess I shouldn't have touched it but I was afraid someone would find it and throw it away. In hindsight, I should have been the one to bring it to the front desk."

"How could you have known to do that? You couldn't. Right? So when did you give the note to Roger? Mr. Whiting. Your boss?"

"I didn't bring it to the desk."

"You didn't read it?"

"I told you I didn't."

"Back to Thursday night, Friday morning. Did anything unusual happen during your shift?"

"What do you mean by unusual?"

"Something not usual, Missy. Attention getting."

Her lips tighten and she cocks her head. "There was one thing."

"Okay."

"I went up to make sure Mrs. Marsh was okay. This was before I made rounds so it must have been after eleven o'clock."

"Why was that necessary?"

"Well—and you're going to be mad about this too, but I swear it's the truth." Rebecca has turned from the window and is staring daggers at Missy, and Missy seems to be fighting back a smile. "Mrs. Marsh sometimes leaves her room and sits on a bench at the end of the hall. I've found her asleep a few times and helped her to her room."

"What are you trying to say? That my mom is an alcoholic? That's bullshit and you know it."

Missy feigns being chastised. "I'm sorry. I told you it might be upsetting."

"Did you have to help her Thursday night?" I ask.

"No. I wasn't sure she was okay. Just a feeling. So I knocked and didn't get an answer. I knocked when I found the note during my rounds. I guess the note was left between those times. Anyway, when she didn't answer my knock I thought she might be asleep. I finished making rounds and went back to the office. I only wish now that I had let myself in. I'm sorry, Miss Marsh."

"Is that everything, Missy?" I ask.

"That's it."

I pause for a moment. "What about the couple you and Connie saw that night?"

Her brow wrinkles in confusion. "What couple?"

I tell her about the pair Connie told me about: the guy with acne and the drunk woman who might have been Victoria Marsh.

"Oh, that," Missy says airily, like she forgot to put the milk back in the fridge. "Yeah, that was just a couple of drunks. I don't think that's anything to do with this. I didn't really get that good a look at them."

"Connie said the man had a lot of acne, do you remember that?"

She shrugs. "Didn't get a good look at his face."

"Can you remember anything at all? Clothing? Shoes? Anything else?"

She frowns, to show me she's thinking Really Hard. "He had some kind of jacket with a hood. I can't tell you anything more than that."

"What about the woman?"

She shakes her head. "Just drunk. Light-colored hair. I had the impression she was white. I can't tell you how old or anything. I just caught a glimpse."

"Could the woman have been Mrs. Marsh?" I ask.

She answers quickly. "I didn't get a good look, like I said. I just kind of glanced at them because he was almost carrying her out." She gives Rebecca an odd look and once again I wonder what Rebecca has done to earn her dislike. "Sorry I couldn't be more help."

She doesn't look sorry. "Thanks, Missy," I give her a card and get her contact information. "Can you tell Mr. Whiting to send someone else back?"

"There's no one else, but I'll tell Roger." Missy leaves, and Rebecca sits again but she's still fuming.

"I've never liked her and now I remember why."

"Why is that?" I ask.

"She's one of those people who hates people she thinks are rich. I don't for one minute believe what she said about my mom. And why wouldn't she tell us about the man and woman going out of the back door in the first place?" Good question. "Part of her job is to keep the guests safe and report anything or anyone that might be a problem. This is a nice resort. I don't care what she says that kind of behavior doesn't happen here."

"Connie saw them too," I point out. "Did you see anyone matching their description while you were here?"

She thinks for a moment. "No. Not from the resort. But I may have seen someone like that man somewhere else. Let me think a moment." She sits quietly and runs a finger around the mouth of her coffee mug and then looks up. "It was in Blaine. No, Birch Bay. Yes, it was at a little tourist shop. Mom and I stopped there before we came here. She never buys anything but she likes to look. I bought a water and this man came up behind me at the register. Mom was by the entrance. He winked at me and smiled at Mom and then left. I'd caught him looking at us several times while we were in there. He was creepy."

"What makes you think it's the same guy?"

"I mostly remember the acne. Except his were scars. When Ronnie and I were in high school, one of the boys had bad acne and the kids called him pizza face."

"Okay. Let's find Ronnie."

NINETEEN

Ronnie is at the registration desk talking to Roger.

He says, "I'm sorry. I left strict instructions to leave that room alone." He addresses Rebecca. "No one has been in there to my knowledge since you were here, Miss Marsh. No one has a key and I changed the code."

Ronnie turns to me. "Someone has cleaned the room. The bed is made. New towels. It smells strongly of disinfectant. Mom's toiletries are in the bathroom. Her bags are still there and her clothes are in the closet."

Rebecca asks, "Was there a champagne bottle on the dresser?" and Ronnie shakes her head. "Was there a champagne bucket?"

"No. Did you see one when you were looking for her, sis?"

Roger says, "I gave strict orders. No one was to go in the room. I guess one of the cleaning staff didn't get the word."

And there goes the champagne bottle and any other evidence of who was in the room.

I say, "Your night manager said she took a bottle of champagne to the room before midnight. If the café and restaurant were closed, where would the champagne have come from?"

"We keep a few amenities in a locked cabinet in the office."

"Would there be record of what was taken?"

"No."

"What time does Missy come on duty?"

"Eleven but she's always here by ten or ten thirty. Was she helpful?"

I dodge the question. "Missy told us she was working Thursday night and covering for another employee. Who was the employee?"

"We have another night manager who is out with a sick child. Like I told you. But she's been gone for a month and wouldn't know anything. Missy has been kind enough to work her nights. She's worked under me for a year now."

I'm sure she has. I give him the description Missy gave us of the drunk couple.

"It doesn't ring a bell. Sorry."

He would remember the acne if nothing else, so it probably wasn't a guest.

"Missy indicated it wasn't unusual to see drunks carried out the back door."

He hesitates before answering. "If she says she saw them, I believe her. I guess they may have come in for the restaurant. That's not our typical guest."

"The restaurant closes at eight. Right?"

"That's right. But Packer's is open until nine in the evening."

It was after that but this isn't going anywhere. "Would you still have the trash taken from the room?" I ask on a hunch.

"We might. I doubt it though. They pick up the trash bin on Saturday morning. The bin is out back if you want to look. There's no way of telling what came from each room unless it's something the guest has their name on."

Dumpster diving should be an Olympic event. I've done it numerous times. "Can we use the café a little longer?"

"Of course."

We go to the café and out a door leading to another deck. To my right I see a wooden enclosure for the trash bin. "I want to have a look." I go to the waste bin and pull myself up to look inside. Empty. Unless we want to go to the dump and rake through all the trash, that's it. Inside we get the same table. The writer dude is back. He looks up, sees me, gets his stuff together, and leaves in a huff. He's smarter than I give him credit for.

"So let's backtrack a little. Thursday night you have dinner with your mom, go to her room, sit on the veranda and talk. You go back to your room around..."

"Ten or ten thirty," Rebecca says.

"You saw no one suspicious. No one watching you during this time?"

Rebecca shakes her head.

"Your mom seemed to have something on her mind during that time but told you she would discuss it with you in the morning. She doesn't show. When you get the note from Roger, you go to your mom's room and she isn't there, but her clothes and other items are still there. You didn't see a champagne bottle. Have I got that right?" She nods. I tell Ronnie what Missy had to say about the note and Connie's story about finding a champagne bottle on the floor.

Ronnie addresses the question. "The room looked like Rebecca said. I didn't smell any liquor, just disinfectant."

"Connie was in your mom's room Friday before noon and then Roger declared it off limits. When were you in the room, Rebecca?" I ask.

"Maybe noon Friday. It would have been after Connie cleaned and found the note. I didn't see a bottle but it could have been in the waste-basket. I didn't look there. The room wasn't messed up like there had been a... you know."

"Like there had been a fight, you mean?" I ask, and she nods. It's too bad Victoria didn't tell Rebecca what was bothering her. But for now we have to find out who wrote the note. And hopefully find the guy who Missy saw helping a woman out of the back entrance. "Rebecca, you said your mom didn't drink much. Could she have gotten drunk?"

Ronnie answers, "I think Rebecca was comparing Mom's to Dad's drinking. He can put it away. But, no, she wouldn't have finished a bottle."

That's interesting. Maybe the champagne was a ploy to get Victoria to open her door to a stranger. There was no sign of a fight or a struggle so whoever took Victoria convinced her to come peacefully, or they knocked her out. There was no sign of blood on anything, but Ronnie said she smelled disinfectant. Maybe it was from Connie's cleaning. Whatever happened, it happened quickly. That leaves the question of the two bottles of champagne. Did her abductor bring a bottle? And then there's the drunk couple near the exit door. In my mind I can imagine Victoria opening the door to someone pretending to be a waiter. She's knocked silly and helped along to go to the stairs. A second person may have staged the room to look like Victoria had gotten drunk. Maybe I'm wrong on each count. I'm frustrated. This is going around in circles.

"We need to look at the surveillance camera footage. There must be cameras in a place this big."

Rebecca says, "I checked on Friday before I went home. The system was down Thursday night until 3:17 Friday morning. The last thing on Thursday night is before we went to Mom's room."

"I'm going to call Tony," I say. "Ronnie, ask Roger to get the times the camera was turned off and back on. And tell him not to erase anything."

Ronnie and Rebecca leave, and I go out onto the deck for privacy. When Tony answers it sounds like he's speaking with his cheeks stuffed like a chipmunk. "Wait one." I hear a paper bag being crumpled and imagine the office smells like Moe's famous cheeseburgers. The sound of someone sucking the bottom out of a paper cup ends. "Okay. Go."

"Hi, Sheriff. Can you check records for Missy or Melissa Milligan, Melissa with one 'L'?" I don't feel bad about interrupting his munchies. His wife will thank me. His heart will thank me too. I hear keys clacking and Tony comes back on the line.

"Melissa Sue Milligan. Lives in Bellingham. I'm sending you her personal information. Looks like she's single. Next of kin is her mother, also in Bellingham. She has a DUI and a couple of other misdemeanors in another state, plus one arrest last year for aiding and abetting a fugitive."

"Can you send me the information for that arrest?"

"Do you need it now?"

"No hurry. Anytime in the next ten minutes will work."

I hear him chuckle. "What's up with her?"

"I just wanted to know why she said she's the mother of your child." I can hear him almost choke and sputter. "I'm just kidding, Sheriff." I hang up before it gets nasty.

TWENTY

FEBRUARY 2023

Whatcom County

Lucas's phone buzzed with an email notification as he got into the passenger seat of Longbow's car. As promised, Cooney had sent through the missing person's report for the Ohio woman. Lucas stretched the screen to zoom in on the photo at the top and whistled. The picture looked as though it had been taken in a restaurant. It showed a woman smiling, sitting at a table in front of a candle. Her shining green eyes and blonde hair reflected the candlelight. She was a dead ringer for the woman in the creek.

"Looking good?" Longbow asked as he steered the car out of the lot.

Lucas waited for him to check both directions and pull out onto the road before he showed him—he didn't fancy being T-boned by a truck because his boss was distracted.

"Looking real good," he said, holding the phone up so Longbow could look at the image.

A glance was all Longbow needed. He took it in and looked back at the road.

"That's her, isn't it?"

Lucas nodded. The blonde hair, the blue eyes, the cheek-bones, even the hair style, was all a match for the woman they had pulled out of the creek this morning and watched the coroner cut up this afternoon.

"Name's Olivia Greenwood," Lucas said. "She's an interior design consultant from Cincinnati."

Longbow raised an eyebrow. "*Interior design consultant.* What's her husband do?"

Lucas smiled. He had had the same thought. Hobby job for the trophy wife. "Investment banker. He was the one who reported her missing... and then unreported her missing."

"Huh?"

"Let's get back to the station and we'll take a proper look at it. I hate squinting at a phone screen."

* * *

It didn't make a whole lot more sense back at the station, with the missing person's report and associated documents up on the big screen in the briefing room.

Olivia Greenwood was either their victim or her identical twin, and according to the record, she was an only child. She was a thirty-seven-year-old housewife who lived in a tiny suburb of Cincinnati; almost two and a half thousand miles east of Whatcom County. She had checked into a luxury hotel just over a week ago but didn't show up when her husband showed up to pick her up at the appointed time. She wasn't answering her phone, and the hotel staff hadn't seen her since the previous evening.

The husband, a sixty-two-year-old investment banker whose DMV photo made him look like the Republican senatorial candidate for Stepford, had called their mutual friends first. Then he had called other local hotels of a standard acceptable to Mrs. Greenwood. Then, with slowly mounting panic, he had called the local emergency rooms. Finally, he had called the Cincinnati Police Department to say he thought his wife was missing.

The officer in charge had initially tried to fob Edward Greenwood off with the usual policy that a person had to be out of touch for forty-eight hours before they could be reported as missing, in the absence of any suspicious circumstances. Edward Greenwood, unsurprisingly, had picked up his phone to a buddy in the mayor's office. Okay, *the* mayor. Five seconds after that, the CPD had started looking for Mrs. Greenwood.

The report, unsurprisingly, given the pressure that had been brought to bear, was unusually detailed. Officers had questioned staff at the hotel, contacted Olivia Greenwood's known associates, and put an APB out on a pickup truck seen by security video leaving the hotel in the dead of night after someone was seen bundling a woman who might have been Olivia Greenwood into the elevator down to the parking lot.

That's when it got interesting.

Less than twelve hours after Edward Greenwood had made his first call to report his wife missing, he got back in touch to say that it was all a misunderstanding. There had been a miscommunication and his wife had taken a room at another hotel. She had left her phone in a taxi. Greenwood was very apologetic and embarrassed, and Lucas detected a slightly smug tone in the report conclusion. The officer who had been raked over the coals by city hall had taken great satisfaction in being proved right: ninety-nine times out of a hundred, a supposedly missing person will show up again all by themself, given time.

But there was something the police hadn't done. Or if they had, it was nowhere in the report.

They hadn't conducted a follow-up interview with Olivia Greenwood.

So it seemed as though Olivia Greenwood had disappeared

a week ago only to reappear almost immediately safe and well. If they were right about the identity of the body in the morgue, why had she turned up dead, having been held in captivity for a period of time that seemed to match the period since she had been reported missing?

Lucas sat down at his desk and picked up the phone. He punched in the number for the CPD Homicide Department and asked to speak to an available detective.

A gruff-sounding male voice came on the line after a minute, introducing himself as Detective Frank MacDonald. "To what do we owe this honor?"

"Well, Detective MacDonald... can I call you Frank?"

"You can but it would make you the only one. Everybody else calls me Mac."

"Mac, great. If I say the name Olivia Greenwood to you, what comes to mind?"

There was a chuckle. "A great, big, fiery pain in the ass. And that's just her husband." He paused and Lucas waited for the penny to drop. "Wait a minute, how do you know that name? Whatcom County is a long way from the Buckeye State. What's happened?"

"I've got your report in front of me," Lucas said. "All about Edward Greenwood reporting his wife missing and then unreporting her missing after you fellas had wasted a day looking for her."

"Yeah. Like I said, a pain in the ass. Probably cost us a collar on a real case we were working. Are you going to tell me what this is about, friend? If I want to play guessing games, I have a pimp down in the box who's acting less cagey about the murder he just committed than you are about this."

"I'm sorry, Detective. We just found the body of a woman dumped in a creek out here. And we think it might be Olivia Greenwood."

There was a long silence on the other end of the line. Lucas was about to prompt the other man when he heard the sound of a long sigh. It was the sigh of a man who had realized he suddenly had a lot more to worry about.

"I knew there was something off about that. I fuckin' knew it."

Mac asked for the details, and Lucas gave them. Viewing the body dump site, his initial impressions, speculation about who and why.

Then he went over the autopsy report. The details of how the victim had died, and how she had been treated before she died. The dehydration, the bruising from multiple beatings, the finger that had been cut off.

"So what I want to know is, do you have any idea how she came to be all the way out here?"

"You got me, son," Mac said. "And now we get all the fun of working it out."

Mac gave him the brief background of what he knew of the report by Olivia Greenwood's husband, though he said he would need to talk to one of the other detectives to get some of the details. It matched up with what Lucas had already gathered, plus a few extra details. The husband had seemed panicked, like he knew something bad had happened to her. But then he had dropped the whole thing after pulling strings to get damn near the whole department involved in the hunt for his wife.

"And nobody spoke to Mrs. Greenwood after he called off the hunt," Lucas said, careful not to allow any hint of judgment into his voice.

"Not my call, man, but you know what it's like. We got enough work to do—especially after chasing our tails for hours—without going looking for more work. The husband was happy, the mayor was happy. That means we were happy to close the book and get back to work."

"I get it," Lucas said. "But we have to open that book again now."

Mac let out another sigh. "Send me everything you got. I guess we need to go and tell Mr. Greenwood the bad news. I'll be interested to hear his explanation for why his wife is dead in Washington State after he said she wasn't missing anymore. And I guess you and me'll be having the next conversation in person."

TWENTY-ONE

Ronnie and I briefly interview half a dozen other staff over the phone. Maintenance, one security officer who I'm guessing spent the time sleeping in one of the rooms, two other cleaning staff, two kitchen workers. Nothing interesting there and we didn't get a feeling any of them were lying.

It's after seven o'clock by the time we get out of there and I realize I haven't eaten since breakfast. Driving away from the resort I notice two large totem poles guarding the entrance. One is of an eagle with wings spread wide, the other is identical to the bear carving setting in my apartment. The totems remind me of my boyfriend, Dan, whose wood carvings are just as colorful. Dan told me the totems have spiritual meaning with attributes of some animal spirit. I'm curious but I need to change the mood. "Do either of you know what the totems represent?"

Rebecca says, "The bear is industrious, instinctive, powerful, guardian of the world, a watcher with courage and great strength. The eagle is a divine spirit. It represents sacrifice, a connection to creator, intelligence, renewal, courage, and freedom, and a risk-taker."

Ronnie smiles at her. "Dad was always going on about these. He commissioned them and had them installed when he bought the resort. He said the eagle reminded him of Mom. The bear was like him."

The bear sounds like me, but he bought it so he can think whatever he wants. Any direction I look, the causeway that separates Semiahmoo Bay from Drayton Harbor reminds me how the Pacific Northwest is beautiful and breathtaking country. It's home. Even though there is evil present, I wouldn't want to live anywhere else.

But I have to get my mind back in the game. Roger hadn't noticed the issue with the security cameras and apparently neither did Missy. There would be no video of the drunk couple leaving the resort, or any of the hallway outside Victoria's and Rebecca's rooms.

Rebecca asks, "What did your sheriff tell you about Missy?"

I tell them what Tony had on Melissa Milligan and that he is sending the complete records.

Ronnie says, "I had the feeling when I talked to Roger that he was covering for someone. If he's close to Missy, maybe she did something he doesn't want us to know about."

"Like what?" I ask.

"I don't know. She has a record for harboring a fugitive and lied to police for him."

The mean things Missy said about their mom runs through my mind. There is some kind of old grudge there on Missy's part. Maybe Rebecca's right and Missy's problem is with anyone who has more money than her. Roger didn't seem very upset the room had been cleaned against his orders. I wonder if he has a grudge against the family as well. Roger is a likeable enough guy. A nice guy. But even nice guys lie.

We reach the Marsh house and Rebecca opens the gates. I park under the portico in the front. The house is so magnificent I expect a bellboy to collect our luggage.

The weather turned nasty as we left the resort and the rain challenged the wipers to keep up. Now the rain has let up, the evening sun is out, and the puddles left behind by the storm reflect the sun and sparkle like diamonds.

Rebecca says, "Why don't you get your things and bring them upstairs. I have your rooms ready."

I'd need to tell Tony we might be here a while. I brought a small bag with some personal items: toothpaste, brush, mascara, etc. But I always keep a "go bag" packed away in the trunk of my vehicle with a change of clothes, spare ammunition, running shoes and some necessities like Cheetos and Payday candy bars. You never know when you might need those things.

Rebecca shows us up a wide staircase to a long hallway with doors on either side. *Other bedrooms.* She takes me into a room facing out over Semiahmoo Bay with a view across the Strait of Georgia. There's a walkout balcony/deck and I can see Point Roberts. It's a small community that's a part of Washington State but can only be accessed by traveling through part of Canada.

Rebecca says, "I hope you'll be comfortable. This is our best room. Ronnie's room is just down the hall." She opens the door to my ensuite bath. No expense has been spared but there is no tub, only a glassed-in shower with a number of rain heads mounted on one wall. "You'll love the shower. Dad just had it put in."

I lay my go bag on the California King bed and say, "Perfect." *Compared to this room I live like a homeless person.*

She smiles. "I'll just check on sis and we'll go to the kitchen where we can have coffee and talk."

"Don't wait for me," I say. "I'll just follow my nose."

"Then I'll get the coffee ready and wait in the kitchen."

My extra blazer isn't too wrinkled from being folded and crammed into the little overnight bag for the day. I put it under the mattress to press the worst of the wrinkles from it. It takes only a minute to unpack but it takes more time to pull my gaze from across the strait. Ronnie gave all this up for the life she has now. I'm glad she did but I don't know if I could have done it.

"I'm in the room next door," Ronnie says, coming up from behind me. She's getting to be very stealthy. "Is your room okay?"

I'll tell you after your father throws us out. "It's perfect."

"Mom kept my old room just the way it was when I left so I stay there when I come home. The only thing different is a bookcase full of law books my dad must have added. He never gives up."

"When was the last time you were home?"

"Six months and I didn't stay the night. Every time I get the urge to come home, I remember the arguments and the pressure and the guilt. My dad is the king of guilt trips. He doesn't come right out and say, 'Look at all the things I've given you. All the opportunities that others would die for. You're wasting your life.' But his actions say he's very disappointed in me."

I wish I had a father who would have berated me and not tried to kill me. But I don't whine. I've got what I need. "He cares about you. How long did you say your family has lived here?"

"This land has always been in the family. My dad will tell anyone who will listen that we can trace our lineage back to his namesake Jack Marsh who settled in Virginia in 1635. The first male child has always been named Jack. My dad had a genealogist trace our history. But I've talked to the genealogist and the original Jack Marsh was a blacksmith."

I've gone by so many names. I'm not really sure who I am or who I came from except for my mother who calls herself Courtney now. If she were only a blacksmith and not a lying criminal bitch I would be in heaven. It would be virtually impossible to trace my family history. For me it all started after I killed my bio-father. Future generations—if there are any future

generations—will look back on me and Hayden and deny knowing us.

"You should be honored," Ronnie says. "This is Rebecca's
room and she wouldn't give it up for anyone. But don't make a
fuss about it."

This is more than I expected and I don't know what to say,
but I'm saved from embarrassment when a gong sounds and
Ronnie makes a scary face and says, "Daddy's home." Of course
she's referring to a different Jack and not Jack Nicholson from
the horror movie *The Shining*, where Daddy gets possessed by
homicidal ghosts.

Debating for a moment whether to wear my shoulder
holster, I decide it won't be prudent to shoot our host, so I go
down unarmed to greet Jack. He's waiting for us in the kitchen,
directing Rebecca on the correct way to make coffee. Espresso
actually. The man is not what I expected. There are numerous
pictures of him and the family on the stairway walls, and in all
of them he looks like a cowboy. He's square jawed, shorter than
Ronnie or Rebecca, fit, and a ruddy complexion with a thick
mustache that would make Sam Elliot jealous. My boyfriend,
Dan, has been trying to grow a handlebar mustache and I don't
have the heart to tell him to give it up. He has a beard but the
mustache has got to go.

In person, Jack's smile doesn't reach his faded sky-blue eyes.
He takes my hand. "You must be Megan Carpenter." He's very
attractive. His eyes are more striking than the rug on his upper
lip. They are an intensity that demands respect. He says,
"Ronnie talks nonstop about you."

Ronnie does sometimes talk nonstop. But I doubt she's
talked to him more than a handful of times since I've known
her. Then I remember he's an attorney and he's got his "smoke
and mirror" machine running, laying down cover and
concealment.

"She talks about you too, Mr. Marsh." *Never.*

"Please. Call me Jack. You have quite the reputation, young lady. I somehow pictured you as older."

And I pictured you as taller. "Thanks, I think." I'm older than Ronnie, a year younger than Rebecca. I guess he expected me to be gray-haired and senile. I smile letting him know I'm not offended, which I am. "This is some place."

"It's home. We raised our daughters here. Of course my girls are busy with their own lives now." He gives Ronnie a look that silently rebukes her. She was right about him giving the "Jack" glare. It is impressive. I'll have to practice it on the little punks who live around my neighborhood.

"It was nice of you to put us up, Mr. Marsh."

"Jack. Please. Any friend of my Ronnie is welcome here. I hope Rebecca has you settled. Is the room satisfactory, Detective Carpenter?"

"I'm not on duty so call me Megan. And yes. It's perfect. And that view! If I didn't have to go back to work, I'd ask you to adopt me."

His expression grows serious. "I hope you see the sights while you're here. I assume you'll need to get back to work soon."

"I've asked them to stay and help find Mom," Rebecca says.

His expression darkens like the sky outside. "Rebecca has told you Victoria's missing?"

Rebecca blushes, but Ronnie isn't going to be intimidated. Good for her. "We're here until Mom comes home."

"So. I assume your partner will be here as well?"

I'm right here. "I wouldn't be a very good partner if I didn't offer my help, would I? I don't have to stay in your home."

"I appreciate your willingness to help, Megan, but this is a family matter and should be handled as such."

That does it. I'm not going anywhere. "Ronnie is worried about her mom and her sister and you. I'm worried about

Ronnie. We're all worried about each other. So why don't we quit worrying and get down to business."

After a moment's silence he says, "You're welcome to stay if my daughters want it."

The sisters say nothing. I guess he's outvoted. I'm not leaving in any case. "Mr. Marsh"—I don't call him Jack this time because my professional reputation needs to be voiced—"I've worked many missing person cases and had excellent results. I can be the soul of discretion."

"Has Sergeant Lucas talked to you?" he asks.

"He made it very clear to stay out of his way. We will." *Not.* "But he has no authority over us as civilian contractors working for Rebecca." Veins stand out on Jack's neck and one throbs at his temple. "You won't find better help than us. We're experienced and motivated." I don't say Sergeant Lucas doesn't appear to be motivated beyond mooching coffee and cookies. "I understand this is a family matter, but the more you help us the sooner we'll find her. Have you hired a private investigator?" By his reaction I can see he has. "Have they started working?"

"No."

"If you use the investigator, we may run across them, so it would help us to know who they are?" *Better yet, fire them.*

He ignores my question.

"Can you trust whoever it is?"

"Megan, I've been a corporate lawyer for more years than you've been alive. I don't trust anyone. But I know people. Molly Quinn is very good at finding people. Expensive, but the best to my way of thinking because you get what you pay for."

"I'll charge you double what you're paying her if it makes you feel any better. You should fire her so Sergeant Lucas doesn't feel overwhelmed." *And get all defensive again.*

His stern look cracks and he suppresses a smile. "Your reputation is you're incorruptible... and incorrigible."

I cock my head to the side and smile. "Ronnie's incorruptible. I'm incorrigible. Glad to meet you."

He looks at Rebecca. "Okay. You win. They can help. I'll tell Molly she's fired."

Leave it to an attorney to look at everything in life as a win or loss. Either way he might not like what we find.

"Now," he says, consulting his watch. "It's getting late. Have you two eaten?"

Now he's talking. Jack suggests ordering in, and I willingly agree. We should get an early night. I suspect it's going to be a long day tomorrow.

TWENTY-TWO
MONDAY

I sleep like a log for a change, probably all that sea air. I wake just after dawn, dress, and go downstairs, following the smell of coffee.

Kitchens are the most used room in a house. The Marsh kitchen is the exception. It's completely decked out with all the newest appliances but Ronnie tells me they barely know how to use the espresso machine. Rebecca said Jack gave the house staff the next couple of days off. I don't know if he's just being a nice guy or if he doesn't want us talking to them. The walls have ears type of thinking. Jack is sitting at the head of the table with Rebecca and Ronnie on one side, me on the other.

"Have you shown your dad the note?" I ask.

Jack answers, "I've seen the note. Roger made a copy and texted it to me. It could be from anyone. It could mean anything or nothing at all."

Rebecca says, "Yesterday we talked to Missy, the night manager that found the note."

He gives Rebecca a stern look. "You started talking to people without my permission."

"That's right," I say. "The police haven't been there and they haven't formally taken a missing person report. You can't find a missing person if you don't look."

With a self-important look Jack says, "I know Sheriff Longbow personally. He assured me his best detective has been assigned. Sergeant Lucas has already started an informal investigation."

I assume by "best" and "informal" he means it will be low key and eyes only, which means slow and casual and most of all "quietly".

"Some detectives I've known are satisfied to wait and see if the missing person shows up. They feel justified because over ninety percent of missing person cases are family drama related —the spouse decides to leave, the child runs away and is staying down the street with a friend. In ninety percent of the cases, the missing person either comes home or makes some kind of contact within a few days or weeks."

"And the other ten percent?" he asks.

"I won't lie to you. Some are never found. Some are found too late."

"You mean dead."

"Mr. Marsh, your wife has been missing for almost three days and she hasn't made contact. An informal investigation is not what you need. More is at stake than your reputation or hurt feelings. Let us work on this. The worst that can happen is that we find her and she doesn't want to come home. We apologize but at least we know what happened."

"Let's not get ahead of ourselves," he says.

"Look, Ronnie is better at finding missing persons than I am." I don't mind telling a lie in this case. "You are in a unique position to help us know your wife's mindset. Her relationship with your daughters. Her best friends. Extended family members. All marriages have ups and downs. We need to hear all of it. Don't hold anything back. The one tiny thing you don't tell us, no matter how personal or embarrassing it may be, might make a difference in finding her quickly."

He's a lawyer so his expression is unreadable. If he won't talk to me, maybe he'll talk to his daughters. However, if this starts looking more like an abduction than a wife leaving her husband, I'll have to advise Ronnie and Rebecca to push Sergeant Lucas to take off the kid gloves.

Ronnie puts a hand over his. "Dad, if one of us were missing, you would do anything to find us. I know you would. You love us. We love you. I know you and Mom don't always get along and sometimes she gets on your last nerve. But you've been together through hard times. I remember you telling us stories about your own childhood and your own dad and how you all struggled. It wasn't easy then, and it's not going to be easy now. Please don't wait until it's too late. Megan's right about me being good at this. I know you don't approve of my life choices but I love my job. If something happens to Mom, you'll never forgive yourself."

And Ronnie will never forgive you. The stiffness of his posture tells me she's gotten through.

He surprises everyone and says, "I would prefer to talk to Megan alone."

Ronnie and Rebecca exchange a look, get up, and both put a hand on his shoulder as they leave the room. This family is not as broken as I first thought. They're just pigheaded. I've never been that way myself.

Jack makes us coffee and puts the cup in front of me, waiting for me to speak first.

I oblige him and start with, "Did your wife leave you?"

Jack sputters a mouthful of coffee back into his cup. "You don't pull your punches, do you, Megan?" He dabs at his mouth with a table napkin. "I respect that. I'll admit things haven't been good for a while now. We sort of—grew apart. We married right out of college. She became involved with charities. First a little. Later it was all-consuming. I didn't think it was appropriate and it was sometimes dangerous being around those types of people. But it's what she had always wanted to do and I finally had no say in that matter."

Boy, this is sounding so familiar. I wonder if he sees the parallels to what he's been doing to Ronnie?

"That's the long answer to your question. Has she left me? The answer is no. Through it all, we still have an active sex life."

Eww! TMI. My fault. People my age don't like to hear about people his age *doing it*, but I told him not to hold anything back.

"Are either of you having... seeing other people?"

"I'm not and I'm sure Vicki's not."

"Does anyone hold a grudge against you or your wife?"

"I'm a lawyer. So yes, take your pick. But Vicki. No. She's kind to everyone."

"Anyone in particular have something against you?"

"I've thought about it. I've made enemies. But no one comes to mind that would do anything to her or my family just to get at me. I don't deal with those types." He looks uncomfortable. "But I think I know who the note is from."

And you didn't think that was important enough to tell me?

"I should have told you up front. But the person who wrote it isn't likely to harm her. She's had nothing to do with him for years."

"Maybe you should tell me and let me determine if he's a problem."

Jack never loses eye contact. The man is a professional. "Her brother, Vinnie. Vinnie Lombardi. The note is signed Dinky, and Vinnie used to call her Dinky when they were kids. He's an alcoholic, drug addict and has a gambling addiction."

I guess this is what he meant by Victoria having baggage. "Why would Vinnie leave the note? What did she promise?"

"He's most likely in over his head gambling, or he owes his dope dealer. Any of a dozen other things. Take your pick. In the past I bailed him out but I decided to be done with him. If he was going to ruin his life it wasn't going to be at the expense of this family's reputation. He knows I won't agree to any more handouts. Vicki knows I won't agree. Even if that's what the note is about, I can't see him doing anything like this. He's an idiot but this would be a new low, even for him. I'm guessing I'll hear from her soon asking for money for Vinnie."

"That's why you don't think she could have been taken?"

He doesn't hesitate. "No. Absolutely not. There hasn't been a ransom demand. I have money. It's been two days. Why wouldn't they contact me if she'd been... taken?"

I could tell him about our last case where the abduction wasn't for money. There are a lot of motives for taking someone against their will. Love, rejection, shame, vengeance, sometimes murder. The cases Ronnie and I worked shared all of these. The obvious suspect is not always the right one. Even now I have to look at what Jack is telling me with a jaundiced eye. Jack could be my guy. He's admitted they were having problems. In most missing person cases that end in murder, the spouse or significant other is always the first suspect.

"Could your wife have her own money to give her brother?"

"I give her an allowance and house money. I've set up an account for her charity work. I give her everything she needs. She has no large amount of money to give anyone."

"Has she given her brother money in the past and hid it from you?"

"She did a few years ago. Like I said, I put a stop to it."

"I need a list of her family members. Names, addresses, phone numbers, where they work, children, anything you know about them. Ronnie and I will find Vinnie. It may be nothing but at least we can talk to him."

"It will be a short list," Jack says.

"Okay. So it should be easy putting it together."

Ronnie sticks her head in the door. "Megan, we need to talk. In private."

TWENTY-THREE

Ronnie motions for me to follow her toward the back of the residence. She says in a quiet voice, "We're being warned off. Rebecca just got a call. The voice sounded disguised and they told her to stop what she's doing or something will happen to Mom. They know she called us and that we're detectives. Let's go outside."

Ronnie leads me through the back and onto a stone deck where stairs hewn out of solid rock lead down to a larger landing. "I hoped Dad was right and she wasn't in any danger. But now we know. And the threat to harm her means there will be a ransom demand."

"They called on her cell?" I ask, to clarify.

Ronnie nods. "We can talk to the phone company, see if they can tell us where the call came from, but..."

She doesn't need to finish the sentence. The odds of the caller being dumb enough to leave a trail to their door are pretty long.

"Was the caller a man or a woman?" I ask.

"Rebecca thought it sounded more like a woman's voice but it was muffled."

"How do they know we're detectives?" *Someone has been talking.* "The only place we asked any questions was the resort."

Ronnie says, "I've known Roger a long time. He would never discuss this with anyone."

I say, "Missy knew your mom was missing. Tell me something, Ronnie. It might be none of my business."

"Ask."

"When we were talking to Missy at Packer's, I had the feeling that Missy had a bone to pick with Rebecca. Or your mom. She seemed to be pushing Rebecca's buttons and getting off on it."

"I don't know her. I haven't stayed at the resort for a long time. I can't imagine what my mom or sister could have done to her. We always treat the staff nice. Dad gives Christmas bonuses. Maybe she was just having a bad day."

Or maybe she's just a bitch? Maybe I should have pressed Missy harder. One rule of investigation is to not worry about what you can't change. Sheriff Gray taught me that early on. But I can feel time pressing on us. If Victoria has been taken, her kidnappers won't wait forever to finish this. I'm surprised it's taken them this long to play their hand. They're amateurs. That gives me hope they'll make a mistake and we'll catch them. On the other hand they may cut their losses and that would be bad.

"Tell me what you know of your mom's side of the family."

"Is it important?" Ronnie asks.

"I won't know until you tell me."

"I'm ashamed to admit it but I don't know much about them. I've never met them. I believe her mother and father are deceased. She never talks about any of them and I've never seen pictures." She tilts her head and asks, "How can that be?"

"Where is your mom from?"

Ronnie blushes. "I'm not really sure. I know it's horrible but they never talk about it. I mean, we may have asked when we were younger. I don't know. Maybe Rebecca knows."

One entire side of Ronnie's family doesn't exist except in very general terms from a long time ago and the one Jack told me about is a drug addict. Jack's side of the family had money, but his family ancestry is made-up. But I'm not one to judge.

I never talk about my mother, or father, or stepfather. Not even about my brother until very recently. Ronnie knows a little about my past. She shot the woman who was trying to kill me because of my past. You never know what your past will drag up from the depths of Hell. Is this some of Victoria's past coming back? Or maybe Jack's? Ronnie may be estranged from her parents but she's fiercely loyal. I respect that. I'm that way with Hayden.

Ronnie says, "On the Marsh side my dad's an only child. My grandparents are great. I visit them as often as I can, and we talk on the phone a couple of times a year. But I don't think this has anything to do with our family unless it's just about money."

"Your dad knows who wrote the note," I say. "Have you heard the name Vincent Lombardi?"

"Mom's maiden name is Lombardi. Now I remember. Vinnie is her younger brother. Does Dad think he is involved?"

"Your dad said Vinnie called your mom Dinky when they were kids."

Ronnie's eyes widen. "So the note was from Vinnie."

Or someone that knows Vinnie, but chances of it not being him are slim to none. "The note mentions a promise. Your dad says your uncle is an alcoholic and a gambling addict. Maybe some drugs are involved. He's gotten into trouble with gamblers in the past, and your dad bailed him out. He said your mom had helped Vinnie out in the past but your dad says he put a stop to it. Could your mom have been giving Vinnie money without your dad knowing?"

Ronnie says, "Dad has a tight grip on the money. I don't

think Mom could get much but apparently I don't know a lot of things."

"We need to find Vinnie. Get Rebecca and meet me in the kitchen."

I don't want to bring it up with the sisters but maybe Victoria has left Jack or is faking her own kidnapping to get money for Vinnie's gambling debt. It's not a long stretch. Ronnie said her mom faked an injury to get Ronnie to come home from the police academy. But this doesn't sound like it's a fake. If Vinnie really is an alcoholic and drug addict, he might not be thinking straight. Maybe he's holding her against her will to try and get money from Jack. But who knows what a drug addict will do if they're in a bind? Maybe it's the people Vinnie owes that are behind this. I have a lot to consider.

TWENTY-FOUR

The man is asking personal questions, and that makes Victoria feel some small hope she will be released soon. She feels like the man and the woman are playing good kidnapper, bad kidnapper with her. The woman is always brutal but the man sometimes softens. He is the least violent of the two in any case. His method of taking the "proof of life" pictures left something to be desired. His hand felt like a club, and she'd probably have black eyes from his slaps. Her eyes are still watering, and she is having trouble breathing through her broken nose.

The man asks, "How big is Cougar Point?"

"I honestly don't know."

"Wrong answer," he says, and grabs a fistful of hair, yanking hard until she thinks her hair is being pulled out. She cries out, and the woman giggles. "Now you know the rules. I ask a question and you answer. Another 'I don't know' out of you and I'll scalp you." He grabs a handful of her long hair, and she can feel him cutting it off near the top of her skull. "Maybe I'll send this to your husband. Jack, right?"

She nods, and he grabs another handful of hair.

"Yes, his name is Jack," she says, her voice an octave higher

than she intended. She's frightened. He isn't sane. "I'll answer your questions."

"Good. You learn fast. Now. How big is Cougar Point?"

"It's huge. Maybe one hundred acres of mostly wooded land. It covers the tip of the peninsula and overlooks the bay."

"Is it surrounded with a wall?"

"Yes. Well, at least the area around the house. The wall goes all the way to the bay."

"Tell me about the entry."

"There's a tall metal gate. It's electric."

"Cameras?"

"Yes."

The questioning continues and intermittent photos are taken until he is satisfied. Now she has time to think and feels a little anger at her cowardice. He already knew about the wall and the gate and the camera. Those questions were a test and a lesson to put fear in her. It didn't take much to scare her and she hates herself for the weakness.

If he knew about her home's security, he didn't need to grill her. If he didn't know about the security, she'd told him everything he needed to enter the property and even the house. He'd forced her to give him the alarm codes.

She'd asked again if he'd contacted Jack, and she could feel his anger building and had to say she was sorry and would be quiet. He warned her that if she asked again, he'd put the gag back on, but he didn't and he'd left.

Now she is worried about Jack and Rebecca. What if he hurt them? It would be her fault.

TWENTY-FIVE
FEBRUARY 2023

Whatcom County

"Mac" MacDonald and his partner were on the first direct flight from Cincinnati to Seattle the morning after Lucas's call. Lucas picked them up at the airport. Standing at arrivals, he spotted them immediately; cops always stuck out in a crowd, even two cops as visually distinct from one another as these two.

Detective MacDonald looked pretty much as Lucas would have guessed from hearing his voice. A big, barrel-chested guy in his early fifties with a shaved scalp and a suit that was a little too small for him. His partner was a petite woman with reddish brown hair, glasses, and a dark blue pant suit that somehow looked as though it had been freshly pressed, despite the fact she had stepped off a five-hour flight.

Lucas wasn't carrying a sign, but MacDonald immediately homed in on him when he saw him. They shook hands and MacDonald turned to his partner.

"This is…"

"…Detective Anderson," the petite woman said, extending her hand. "Kyra Anderson. Good to meet you."

Lucas took her hand and was struck by the smoothness of her skin as well as the firmness of the shake. Her gaze told him that she wasn't one for wasting time on pleasantries.

"Have you two eaten? We can grab something here before I take you to see the body."

"We're good," Anderson said.

"I could eat," Mac said, drawing a sharp look from his partner. "And we both need a coffee. But we'd like to see the dump scene first."

"Not a problem," Lucas said. "It's on the way."

They bought coffees to go at a place in the terminal, and Mac added a breakfast burrito to his order, paying for both of them with a crumpled twenty he dug out of his pocket. He was still eating it when they reached Lucas's car in the short-stay parking structure. Lucas had tried to slow the walk from the terminal down a little to avoid just this, but Detective Anderson had set the pace, striding forward, steadily clutching her go-cup like she was competing in an egg and spoon race.

Lucas wound his window down as soon as they got in and hoped Mac wouldn't drop any of the filling from his burrito in the passenger footwell. As it was, the car would be smelling of egg and grease for a week.

He pulled onto the on ramp for I-5 and merged into the northbound traffic. The sun was still low in the sky.

"First time in the Northwest?"

"First time for me," Mac said, then craned his neck around to address Anderson. "How about you?"

"Closest I've been is San Francisco," she said, staring out of her window.

Lucas let Mac fill him in on their activities since they had spoken the previous afternoon.

"We brought the husband in for questioning."

"How did he take it?" Lucas asked.

Mac shrugged. Neither of them had gone into this side of

things in detail on the call yesterday, but that was because a lot of it went unsaid. Even in a homicide case with slightly more everyday parameters, the first person you look at is the victim's spouse. The fact he had apparently covered up his wife's disappearance made him look even guiltier, though Lucas was keeping an open mind until he spoke to the man personally.

"If he was acting upset, he's a good actor. We didn't have to say anything. He went to pieces when he saw us at the door. Didn't ask for a lawyer, either. Not at first."

"What's his story?"

"Same as it was a week ago, minus the part where his wife showed up safely."

Mac consumed the last inch and a half of the burrito in one mouthful, then crumpled the foil and the wrapper together and stuffed it into the pocket of his pants. He reached for his coffee in the cup holder and took a sip, wiping his mouth with the back of his hand.

"She checked into the hotel and then vanished. The husband called everywhere he could think of and then contacted us. A couple of hours later somebody contacted him and told him to call us off, say his wife was back home." He turned to fix Lucas with a hard stare. "A couple of days after that they checked in again to make sure he wasn't going to spill. They made a compelling argument."

"His wife's little finger arrived in the mail?" Lucas asked.

"FedEx," Anderson said from the back. "The box arrived with the finger and a note with a phone number on it. Greenwood called it and they told him they had his wife and if he didn't want more digits arriving, he would call us off."

"When it absolutely, positively has to be there overnight," Lucas said.

"What?" Anderson said.

"Before your time, kid," Mac said, before winking at Lucas. "The younger generation, huh?"

"Is he going to ID the body?" Lucas asked. He was interested in the answer.

"He assumed it was being transported back to Cincinnati. When I told him it was staying here for the foreseeable, he demanded to come with us. Thankfully I got to pass on that. He's on his way out here."

They ran out of shop-talk after a while, and Mac started talking about his hobby of breeding pit bulls. Lucas tuned him out and made the occasional comment to make it seem like he was paying attention. Detective Anderson didn't even try to pretend she was interested, tapping out emails on her phone from the back seat the whole time.

Eventually they reached the outskirts of Bellingham and the dump site. The creek ran across the county, passing under a bridge on a back road. As Lucas slowed, he could see that the area around the bridge was taped off, even though the forensic work had been completed and there was no longer anything to see here.

He parked in the wide spot at the side of the road, and the three of them got out.

Lucas led them to the start of the slope down to the creek and indicated the spot where the body had been found, and told them the timeline. The initial discovery by the kids, the 911 call, Deputy Cooney attending, and then Lucas and Longbow arriving at the scene.

The two Ohio detectives did just as Lucas had done the morning before. They took a moment to take in the immediate surroundings, judged why the site had been chosen for a body dump, then climbed down to the spot where Olivia Greenwood's body had been found. Anderson asked a couple of questions relating to timings: if they knew roughly how long the body had lain there before discovery, whether there was any clue on the vehicle that had been used to transport her here;

and Lucas told her what he had been able to discern, which wasn't a lot.

It was a good dump site: miles from anywhere, no cameras or tolls, no mud on the road to show up tracks, and the creek could have carried away trace evidence remaining on the body. The coroner's best guess was that time of death was at least twenty-four hours before the body had been found. The body could have been left in the creek at any time in that window, though logically overnight would have been the safest time for the perpetrator to do that.

"All right," Mac said, clearly bored already but satisfied that he had checked one item off his itinerary, "let's go say hello to the deceased."

They got back in the car and Lucas drove them into Bellingham.

* * *

Ten minutes later, they pulled up outside the coroner's office. Longbow's SUV was parked outside. As Lucas pulled into the next bay, the driver's door opened and the sheriff stepped out.

The three of them got out of Lucas's car, and Lucas made brief introductions. He knew Longbow was no great fan of other cops on his patch, even those with good reason, but he disguised it well.

"Good to welcome you both to Whatcom County," he said. "I hope your trip is worthwhile."

The coroner showed them into the chiller room and pulled out the drawer that was Olivia Greenwood's temporary resting place. He pulled back the sheet that was covering her enough to expose her head and shoulders and stood back. Lucas suppressed a shiver and hunched his own shoulders, longing for the relative warmth of the office.

The two Ohio cops took their time looking at the body, then exchanged a glance.

"Husband'll do the official ID later today, but that's her," Mac said.

"Okay, that's out of the way," Lucas said. "So perhaps you can help us out with why your kidnap victim ended up in a creek all the way out here."

"That's what we're going to work out," Mac said.

Lucas exchanged a glance with Longbow across the body. The sheriff got the message and cleared his throat.

"And is that going to be 'we we', or 'you we', Detective?"

"This is CPD's case," Anderson said. She had been crouched to examine some dirt under the corpse's fingernails but straightened up to look Longbow in the eye. "Victim is from Cincinnati, she was abducted in Cincinnati, maybe even killed in Cincinnati for all we know."

Lucas doubted the latter piece of speculation, but he ignored that in favor of his strongest hand. "...and the body was dumped right here, in Whatcom County Sheriff's Department jurisdiction."

Mac held a hand up to stop his partner from answering. "I don't think we need to get into a pissing contest here. From what I've seen, this is either going to be straightforward or it's a mess. Either way, we all have to pitch in on this. We have work to do here and back home. We can waste a bunch of time fighting over who gets the credit—if there is any—or we can cut to the chase and get working."

There was a silence. The four of them standing on opposite sides of a cold body. Finally, Longbow broke the silence.

"Sounds fair to me. Sergeant Lucas and I will help you out however we can here, but we want to be kept in the loop." He held up a finger. "Don't go Big City Cop and jerk us around on this, Detective MacDonald."

"Likewise," Mac said. "If we can skip the part where the locals bitch about their turf, I'll be a lot happier."

Anderson said nothing, but Lucas noticed she had the air of a long-suffering spouse waiting for her husband to finish dickering over a hotel bill.

There was a knock on the door. The receptionist appeared, head tilted, lowering her voice like she was interrupting a small group of mourners in the waiting room of a crematorium.

"Mr. Greenwood is here to identify the body."

TWENTY-SIX

Ronnie made espressos when Rebecca and Jack joined us in the kitchen, and now we all sit around the table. I need something stronger but I need a clear head more. Rebecca tells Jack about the call.

I ask, "Who else knows we're trying to find your wife, Jack?"

"You went to the resort and spoke to several people. I've only talked about this with Sergeant Lucas and now you. I didn't even tell the private investigator about Vicki. But maybe *she* could have kept it quiet."

I ignore the dig. "What did the caller say, Rebecca? Exactly."

"They said, 'Stop your detective friends from meddling or what happens to your mom will be your doing.' I demanded to talk to Mom and they said they would send us proof. What does that mean? Are they going to hurt Mom?" Rebecca's face is a mask of terror. "Did I do something wrong?"

She's challenged them and there's no telling how they will respond. I say to keep things calm, "It just means they're serious. They didn't mention a ransom or the note found at the resort?"

I say, "They just want us to stop what we're doing." I notice Jack looks away. "Your dad says the note is from your mom's brother."

Ronnie says, "I told Rebecca about Uncle Vinnie. She remembers the name."

Rebecca says, "Mom hasn't had any contact with our uncle that I know of. But she's never talked much about her family."

"I can promise you Vicki hasn't had contact with Vinnie," Jack says.

I ask, "Rebecca, you say the caller might have been a woman?"

"It was distorted, but that's the impression I had. Maybe the note and the call are from the same person?"

Jack says, "Not necessarily. It could be a coincidence. Vinnie is asking for money. The caller is wanting you to stop what you're doing."

I find it interesting that Jack doesn't include himself in this effort and says *what you're doing* and not *we're* doing. He still doesn't get it. "The resort's video system was shut off Thursday night and not turned on until your wife was gone. We have the note and now a call. This is too much for mere coincidence, Jack. Has anyone contacted you?"

He indicates no one has contacted him. He's got an attorney's face and gives little away. He's very convincing.

Rebecca asks a question that's bothering me too, "Why haven't we been contacted about a ransom?"

Victoria's been gone since Friday morning, maybe as early as late Thursday evening, and it's now Monday. A ransom demand has to be on the way. The sisters seem convinced their mom would have let them know she was leaving. Rebecca saying she felt her mom was trying to tell her something at the resort makes me lean toward the idea that she was going to tell Rebecca she's divorcing Jack. But there are two complications to that theory. The call from an unknown woman, and the note from a possible brother that has a drug and gambling problem. Taking these two incidents in turn it looks like the brother left the note for Victoria and when Victoria didn't do what she "promised" the woman, or brother, or both, kidnapped her.

The implied threat in the call strikes a personal nerve. I seem to draw violence to me like a black cloud brings rain. Those around me are targeted for my sins. Now this person calling Rebecca knows we're here. Knows I'm here. Knows I'm looking for them. Are they willing to hurt Ronnie's mom to stop me? Or am I giving myself too much importance? My heart beats faster and I feel a fist squeezing the breath out of me.

A dear friend, Monique Delmont, was murdered in a savage manner because of her association with me. She had helped me change my name, get through college, which resulted in my going to the police academy and ending up where I am. Recently, Dan was drugged and almost killed by the same psycho that killed Monique to send me a message. Both were collateral damage for a war they hadn't started. I can't be responsible for anyone else being killed because of me. For a moment I consider packing up and going home. But only for a moment. I know Ronnie will never stop. And I owe her.

Jack sips his espresso and says matter-of-factly, "This is best handled by the authorities now. Your clumsy involvement has jeopardized a peaceful resolution."

He looks at me when he spews this crap. The *authorities* he's talking about seem to have done nothing so far and it's two days since Victoria's disappearance. The police aren't even keeping Rebecca abreast of what they are doing. "Does Sergeant Lucas know about the note found at the resort?" I ask.

"We've discussed it."

It's strange Lucas wouldn't have brought this up when he was reading us the riot act. "Does anyone else know about the note?"

Jack calmly says, "I told you no. Do you think I'm lying?"

Yes. "That's not what I meant. I want to know how much of her disappearance is known so we can limit the suspects." That sounds good, and actually is true.

Jack looks incredulous. "So you're not going to stop what you're doing?"

Ronnie doesn't show any lessening of her resolve to keep going. I take my phone out and go outside. Ronnie follows.

"Who are you calling?"

The phone is answered and I put mine on speaker. "Sheriff, we need some help."

Tony's new chair squeaks worse than his old one did when he leans back. He's already ruined it. He really needs to lose some weight. "What can I do for you, Megan? I assume this has to do with Ronnie's family."

I mouth the words to Ronnie asking if it's okay to tell the Sheriff what's going on. She nods. "She's on the line with us, Sheriff. Do you know the sheriff of Whatcom County?"

"Yeah. Charlie Longbow. Full-blooded Lummi Indian."

"So you're friends?"

"I wouldn't go that far. He's a straight shooter. Good guy. Why?"

I fill Tony in on the situation with Ronnie's mom without telling him everything. I tell him about the lack of enthusiasm shown by Sergeant Lucas and his threats to send us packing—or worse, to arrest us for interfering in an investigation.

"You need me to put in a word to Sheriff Longbow?"

"Yes." *Get Lucas off our backs.*

"Are you looking to be deputized so you can legally work on this?" Tony asks. His tone of voice says it's never going to happen.

"That would be great." I would ask Sheriff Longbow myself but I think he would have laughed in my face.

"I'll call him. Can I do anything else?"

"I'll let you know. Thanks."

I put the phone in my pocket, and Ronnie asks, "And what if Sheriff Longbow won't deputize us, Megan?"

"We'll wing it."

"Like we always do. Right?"

Rebecca comes outside. "It's almost noon. Dad said I should take you to lunch. We have no staff, and I don't cook. And no one can make espresso except Ronnie."

Say what you like about Jack Marsh, he takes care of his guests' appetites. I hadn't realized how quickly the morning had passed, though the rumble in my tummy should have given me a hint. Some detective I am.

I can relate to Rebecca's lack of culinary skills, though I do make a mean pack of Ramen noodles. "I could eat pizza. Do they deliver here? Or does the driver need a background check to get in?"

Rebecca gives a nervous chuckle and I can see she's barely holding herself together. Going to eat is a great distraction.

"I'm taking you out for a sit-down meal. Dad wants to stay here in case we get another call or Mom comes home."

"Good idea." I didn't want to eat with him anyway. I hate to be a downer, but I don't hold out hope Victoria will walk in the door.

Rebecca asks, "Do you like oysters, Megan?"

"Who doesn't?" I've never had oysters. I've never deliberately swallowed snot either. Hayden tells me I need to try different things. Explore. Experience. He told me about some of the things he ate in Afghanistan. Described them in great detail until I told him "shoot me now." Hayden thought I was kidding.

TWENTY-SEVEN

We load into my SUV and exit the Marsh empire. Drayton Harbor Oysters is on the outskirts of Blaine and faces the harbor. As we approach I get a phone call. I put it on speaker.

"This is Sheriff Longbow's secretary. He would like to see you in his office."

Ronnie and I exchange a look. Either we're in trouble or Sheriff Gray has convinced Longbow to deputize us. We can wait on food. Rebecca takes us to Bellingham.

Sheriff Longbow is standing in front of a WWII Army surplus desk. He could be a twin to Sheriff Tony Gray except he's Native American. He's wearing a black Stetson with a silver-and-turquoise sweatband around the crown. His black Western boots have a high shine. His heavy leather duty belt is held together with an overlarge silver-and-turquoise cowboy buckle that peeks from under his paunch. His face is devoid of any expression.

"You're Tony's people," he says. "Charlie Longbow." He holds out his hand, his lack of expression remains as we introduce ourselves.

"Your dad says Victoria is missing," he says when we're done.

"My mom has been gone since Friday morning, but no one has taken a missing person report."

"Your dad reported it to me and I assigned Sergeant Lucas."

There's plenty of seating in the office but he hasn't offered us a seat. I take the lead and pull up a chair for myself. I ask, "Sheriff Longbow. You talked to our sheriff this morning. He told you why we're here and what we need."

"He did." He sits behind his desk and sighs deeply. "Take a seat."

When we're seated, Longbow says, "First of all let me say how sorry I am. Victoria has a lot of respect around here. Her charity work is needed and appreciated. We'll do everything we can to find her safe and get her home."

"Your sheriff and I go way back. We went to the Academy together. He said you're his best detectives. Sergeant Lucas is mine. He'll work alongside you."

Sheriff hadn't told me he knew Longbow from way back. Maybe he didn't remember. Or think it important.

"I haven't seen Tony since the last Sheriff's Conference. He kept us all laughing." He looks at me. "I owe him and he never lets me forget."

I want to ask what the debt is. And I want to know about the comic sheriff that I've never seen. But I don't get off the subject. "We're not here to interfere with Sergeant Lucas or the investigation."

"You're here to support your partner, Megan, and I commend you for that."

I use one of his remarks. "And I owe her."

"Tony says you don't always do things by the book and can be very creative."

"We do what we have to... within the law," I lie.

"Glad to hear it. I like self-starters. But I won't brook cutting corners to make an arrest. Same as lying in my book and I can't stand liars."

"I agree completely," I say.

He gives me a hard look like he knows I'm lying. He's very perceptive, but I'm a very good liar.

"We play by the rules," I say. The same rules the criminals play by.

His eyes linger on mine until he's satisfied then leans back and his chair squeals. I wonder if that's a sheriff thing. Or if it's because of their girth.

"Ronnie Marsh," he says. "I've heard good things about you from the Academy. I still have contacts there. I teach an interrogation class from time to time. A good interviewer is worth their weight in gold. We teach firearms four times longer than we school on interrogation and I wonder sometimes if it shouldn't be reversed. I understand you're proficient at firearms and interviewing. Good skills to have. We could use more of that here. Now. Let's get back to your mom. Sergeant Lucas is the best detective I've got. If I ever have need of assistance in your county, I expect you to give us what help we need."

"Goes without saying." I'll give Lucas something all right.

"Well, if you're going to be working in my jurisdiction, I need to do something."

TWENTY-EIGHT

"Well, that went fairly smooth," Ronnie says, We're heading back to Drayton Harbor to eat.

"Until Lucas has a meltdown." But I don't care what he does as long as he doesn't get in our way.

As we approach Drayton Harbor Oysters, I notice several people down by the bay wearing muddy boots and using pronged hand rakes to dig in the dirt and then pitch something into a laundry basket. Fresh from the mud to your mouth.

We settle at a table inside with a nice view across the harbor to Semiahmoo Resort. At least from here I can't see anyone digging my food out of the mud. And there's a bar. Ronnie can drive home. Perfect.

Ronnie and Rebecca order oysters on the half shell and Sprite. The cook is kind enough to grill a hamburger for me. I'd been thinking about the call to Rebecca and wondering if it might have something to do with her job. It just doesn't ring with me, but then I've never been sued or worked a case involving a lawsuit. And there's Victoria's involvement with charity work. A disgruntled soup kitchen visitor? In any case we have to find Vinnie Lombardi.

Ronnie says, "I'm ashamed to admit it, but I know very little about Mom's life outside of the house. She likes to shop. She doesn't have a favorite restaurant. If she has a best friend, I don't know who it is. She never talks about anything but us. She's always concerned with our lives and listens more than she talks." Her eyes mist over. "I'm a horrible daughter."

Rebecca to the rescue. "If you are, I am too, Ronnie. We both could have paid her more attention. She got on my nerves wanting me to become someone successful like Father, date the right guys, make the right friends. I never once thought she was looking out for my happiness. I never once thought of her happiness or what she'd given up to be a stay-at-home mom."

The sisters are silent, lost in regrets that cause me to rethink my relationship with my own mother. She's a bitch and all I can come up with is my mother was horrible to me and my brother. She never was concerned with our welfare. Only her own. Never wanted us to succeed, only to hide, lie, and steal. Thanks, Mom. I hope you rot. No, I don't. Hayden loves her and I hope she loves him enough to try and change. To become someone worthy of his love and loyalty. No matter what she does she will never have mine. She threw that chance away long ago.

"Should we call Tony and thank him?" Ronnie asks as they bring our orders.

"He'll get the big head. Let's talk about Vinnie first," I say, and turn to Rebecca. "Does your mom keep an address book?"

"She keeps it with her. I didn't see it in her room at the resort." She looks startled. "Oh my God. I didn't even check for her purse."

Ronnie says, "I didn't find it."

"I got in her computer at home and found the addresses and email for her committee members. All the emails involved her charity work. There was nothing personal, or any threatening items. Our mom threw herself into her charities. I can't imagine any of them wishing her harm."

"Does your mom have an office? One at home?"

"She has a little office where she reads and keeps correspondence. Her computer is in there."

"Did you look for an actual address book? Letters?"

"I've really just expected her to come home. I didn't want to rummage through her private things. It felt disloyal even getting into her email."

"It's been three days, Rebecca. I think you'll be forgiven for violating her privacy."

"I'll have to ask my dad."

Sweet Jesus. Rebecca is a grown woman. Taller than her sister, taller than me, much taller than her father. She's an experienced corporate attorney, evidently has smarts to go with her blue eyes, blonde hair, and high cheekbones, hence her fashion model appearance. Ronnie is a knockout but with red hair, and I always notice that when she's with me the guys think I'm her ugly wingman. Rebecca is a little older than I am. Probably late twenties, and still has to ask Daddy. I'll ask Ronnie to check her mom's office when we get back. "Would your dad know how to contact her family?"

"I have no idea."

I look at Ronnie and she shakes her head. I say, "It's too bad Sergeant Lucas isn't more helpful. Ronnie, can you get into the utility company data and see if Vinnie Lombardi lives near here? I know it's a long shot but we have to start somewhere." Ronnie is my Internet geek. There's very little data that is safe from her prying fingers. I'm lucky to have her as a partner.

Ronnie starts to take her iPad out but I stop her. "Let's eat first."

She ignores me and starts punching and swiping. When she stops she says, "There are dozens of Lombardis. The local criminal record system can only be accessed from a terminal at the police department unless you want me to bypass them."

I mull it over, "We should talk to Longbow first."

Ronnie directs her gaze over my shoulder. I turn and see an angry Sergeant Lucas headed our way. From the look on his face, I guess his boss told him the good news.

The restaurant isn't full by any means, but he says loudly enough for all to hear, "I want you to know I don't appreciate you going over my head. You may be hot shit in Jefferson County but you're nothing here. I was putting criminals away when you were just getting out of grade school. I close every case. Can you say that?" He doesn't wait for an answer and turns on Rebecca. "I hope you know your friends' interference is going to cause major problems."

"Sheriff Longbow told you he's deputized us as Whatcom County Sheriff detectives. And he's told you to include us, right?" Lucas's red jowls are the answer. "We need access to your computers. We need to see everything you have."

"Sure. Why not. Sheriff Longbow said to bring you to the station. I'll give you whatever he orders me to. But listen closely, *detectives*." He looms over our table and spits the word "detective" out like its distasteful. "This is my case. If you step one foot over the line, I'll haul you in the same as I would any other criminal."

I calmly say just to piss him off, "We're not in competition, Lucas. We want the same thing. And I promise, if there's any credit it will go to you."

"This isn't your jurisdiction. You can't give me credit." He backs up a step. "You can follow me to the station now."

Ronnie says, "We're still waiting on our food. I'm sure we can find your office when we're through. I don't think Sheriff Longbow would appreciate you pulling us away from this wonderful food."

Several diners are still looking our direction and our waiter is watching wide-eyed, no doubt hoping for a fracas. Lucas doesn't seem to notice, or care, and leaves in a huff. *Good one, Ronnie.*

To insult him further I say, "Or you can eat with us." I'm sure the chef has a hand rake and a bucket. Lucas clamps his mouth shut and stomps out.

The sisters have oysters and a salad and wine. My hamburger is perfect but I skip the wine. I want to go into this meeting with a clear head and clean breath. And I don't want to give Lucas a reason to discredit me.

I get up to use the restroom and splash some water on my face. As I'm coming out, a man wearing a blue baseball cap brushes past me on the way to the exit, head down, grunting an apology. A moment later, I hear a word that turns my blood to ice. The word is my name. Or at least, it used to be.

Rylee.

For what seems like eternity, I'm frozen. Then I make myself turn around. There's nobody there. I imagined it. Or did I? The man with the baseball cap is nowhere to be seen, and the door is still swinging shut.

Without even thinking about it, I move toward the door, pushing it open and spilling out into the afternoon sunshine. The lot is empty. There's no one there.

I return to the table, feeling shaky, like I just avoided a car wreck. My imagination, that has to be it. I'm so wound up about this case, I'm hearing things. *And seeing things too?* the little voice at the back of my head adds helpfully, thinking about the disappearing man in the hat.

My dining companions haven't noticed anything was amiss. They're laughing at some joke I missed.

Ronnie says, "I was just saying, Lucas hasn't changed a bit. When we went to grade school, we all called him Officer Unfriendly because he was such a hard-ass."

Hard-ass, or just an ass, I ponder. Whatever, I need him on my side. I have enough enemies. I motion the waiter over and a dessert to go. The sisters pick at their food. Not me. I'm starved. I even eat a couple of oysters. I don't know what I tasted. Maybe it's for the best. I take a breath mint from the little container on the table, pop it in my mouth, and chew it. Rebecca and Ronnie give me their mints and we head into the lion's den.

After that little scare on the way back from the restroom, I'm just grateful to be anywhere but here.

TWENTY-NINE

The Whatcom County Sheriff Office is located in Bellingham, which is the county seat. I park on Prospect Street, and Sergeant Lucas meets us at the entrance with a scowl on his face.

"Was your meal satisfactory?" he asks.

I open the box we brought from the restaurant. "I brought you and the sheriff a peace offering."

Lucas looks inside. "Cherry cheesecake."

I say, "I thought donuts would be a little personal and we barely know each other."

Lucas says, "Sheriff doesn't like donuts."

I say, "I thought Donut 101 was a mandatory class at the Academy."

The three of us step through the metal detector setting off the alarm. Ronnie and I are both armed. Lucas nods at a deputy sitting behind thick glass in an office ahead of us and the alarm is silenced. The deputy buzzes us through and calls out to Lucas, "How goes it, Sergeant?"

Lucas smiles but I can tell he just wants to fob the conversation off. "We're getting there."

"Like the Greenwood case all over again, huh, Sarge?"

Lucas frowns at the deputy as if he's just given away a state secret but says nothing.

We follow Lucas inside another locked area and down a hallway to a door marked SHERIFF. Like our sheriff, Longbow has no need of ornate placards to declare his authority. Lucas knocks and a froggy voice tells us to enter. Once inside he explains the deal to Lucas and once again informs us we will do everything by the book.

Lucas hurriedly says, "I've put out bulletins to local law enforcement. I have the missing person report ready for Miss Marsh's signature when we go to my office."

Longbow dismisses us, and we follow Lucas. Lucas's office is crammed with stacks of file folders on the floor, on top of the filing cabinets, on top of his desk and the two visitor chairs. If he was a civilian, I would call him a hoarder but the stacks were divided into bundles tied with twine. I hope he has a system to remember what's what.

"We only have one missing person detective working this week and she's covered up with other cases, but she said she'd help out if we need her."

I say, "Judging by all the case files on your desk, it looks like you're a little busy, Sergeant." Or you don't do anything.

"Not all of these are active cases, Detective Carpenter. I know it looks like a mess but I've found many a career criminal by going through old unsolved cases. There's always some mistake made the investigator didn't catch. Sometimes that investigator was me."

This catches me off guard. It's good to be self-critical. Maybe Lucas is okay at his job after all.

"You said you've put bulletins out?"

"All surrounding counties and Canadian authorities. If you have a recent photo of your mother, Miss Marsh, I'll make up a poster and circulate it to my guys. Our missing person unit has a format for a poster and an email list that's quite extensive. The businesses put them on their counters and windows."

Rebecca says, "The bulletins are fine if they go to the police. However, my dad wouldn't like her face plastered all over the business community. At least not yet. He still thinks she'll come home when she's ready. Can we hold off on that?" Lucas looks at her a long while then nods. "Call me Rebecca so we know which sister you're addressing, Sergeant Lucas."

"Okay. Rebecca. Don't take this wrong but you've got some big bucks. Someone may target your family for that reason alone. The note that was found at the resort may or may not be relevant. Your dad said it was from a brother who is always begging for money. And the cryptic call you received telling you to stop looking for your mother. There's always the chance this is personal. You've had more time to think about it, so do you have any idea who might harbor ill feelings toward your mother?"

I ask him, "How is the call to Rebecca 'cryptic'? It was a direct threat. So why haven't we gotten a ransom demand, Sergeant Lucas?"

"Since we're working together, just call me Lucas." He ignores my question. "Now, tell me what you have."

Ronnie says, "Dad told us very little about our mom's side of the family. I know we have an uncle on Mom's side, Vinnie Lombardi. Dad said Vinnie called Mom Dinky when they were kids. He doesn't believe Uncle Vinnie would do something like this but Uncle Vinnie was into drugs, alcohol and gambling, and so you may have a record on him. Megan and I think we should find him."

Rebecca says, "Maybe Vinnie is the reason we haven't had a ransom demand."

Lucas's expression slips a little. I think he knows more than he's letting on. Jerk. He hits some keys on his laptop, and I hear a printer in another office whirring. "I'll be right back."

He comes back with several pages and lays them out on his desktop. On top is a full-color photo of a hard-looking man in his forties. Jack told us Vinnie was Victoria's younger brother. It's hard to tell his age exactly because he looks like he's been beaten recently. Black bruises around gray eyes say he was still stoned when the photo was taken. Dirty, greasy-looking blond hair hangs to his shoulders. His face is thin and you can almost see the cheekbones through the flesh. Vinnie Lombardi. Jack said he was a drug addict but this is a death wish and it won't be long before his wish is granted. Now the note makes sense. He's desperate. Whether it's for another fix, or to pay off an arm-breaker.

Ronnie says, "My dad said he's paid gambling debts off for my uncle in the past, but he and Mom decided to stop doing so. Maybe Vinnie thinks my mom will take pity on him but I can't imagine a reason my uncle would kidnap her."

Lucas looks through the other papers. "He's had several arrests over... well, apparently since he became an adult. Drugs, illegal gambling, theft, robbery, assault, vehicle theft." He looks up from the pages and hands them to me.

I skim through them and ask, "Lucas, can you see if Vinnie showed a next of kin or emergency contact in the records."

He hands me the arrest records. "If he does, it will be in these records. There may be something in the jail, but I don't have access to their database."

There is no mention of an emergency contact in the papers. But there are dozens of arrests. Most are felony with a few misdemeanor battery charges. A few of the battery charges are on deputies. The arrests go back to when Vinnie had just turned eighteen. Not surprising to me because there wouldn't be a record of any juvenile arrests, but that doesn't mean there weren't any.

I say to the sisters, "According to the computer Vinnie's last arrest was in Blaine two years ago. Assault and attempted rape.

He's used different addresses for each arrest and seems to use some more than others."

Lucas says, "Most probably those addresses are made-up or just places he's crashed for a night or a few days. He doesn't seem to stay put."

Ronnie and Rebecca give each other a look. I know they're thinking they had an uncle they'd never met and that he was a felon. No wonder their parents didn't talk about him.

This has been a bad day for the Marsh family. It's no wonder Jack didn't want anyone else involved. He was trying to protect his daughters from the truth. From experience I know that's still lying, but I protected Hayden from the truth about our mother and real father for the same reasons. I didn't want my brother to feel our biological father's evil blood that coursed through our veins. But now, just like Rebecca and Ronnie need to know the family secrets, I believe Hayden needs to know and come to grips with who we are and try to make peace with it. He deserves the truth from me and not the spin my mother will put on it. She has a master's degree in telling lies.

Lucas hits some keys. I hear the printer start up again. "I'm getting you all the detailed arrest reports for the brother. The last address we have for Vinnie is two years old. It's from when he was last arrested here in Bellingham. I'll call the jail to see if he listed a next of kin or emergency contact person. Current records don't show him in custody."

"What was Vinnie charged with in court?" I ask. Sometimes the police charge is changed by a prosecutor. In this case I'm hoping the attempted rape charge was erroneous.

Lucas consults the computer screen. "Sexual battery. Criminal confinement."

This just gets better and better. Poor Ronnie and Rebecca.

"Can you ask the jail if he had visitors?"

Lucas gives me a funny look and says, "But what are you hoping to get?"

"I'm not sure."

He looks at the clock. It's almost 4 p.m. "This might take a little while. Visiting hours are just starting at the jail. If you want to get coffee, there's a little café nearby. We have a break-room with a coffeepot but Sheriff takes his so weak you can see through it. Go out the way we came in and turn left outside. You can't miss it. Come back here after. I'll tell the deputies downstairs to let you in."

We find the café and order four coffees to go. Sure enough, when we come back we are waived through the metal detector without a word. The deputies give Ronnie and Rebecca the once over again but ignore me. Ronnie makes heads turn wher-ever we go, and now I feel like I'm the comedy relief. What am I? Chopped liver? I dress for the job. No high heels or designer clothes. Just black lace-up boots, dark slacks, dark button-up shirt, and kind of a sport jacket.

We re-enter Lucas's office and he's just getting off the phone. We hand over his coffee and take our seats.

"Vinnie didn't list an emergency contact. The jail commander said he'd be happy to talk to you after visiting hours are over. You have an hour-and-a-half wait. Come back and get me and I'll go with you."

"Not necessary," I say. "I'll let you know if we get anything useful."

"Have you been in a maximum-security facility before?" he asks.

He would no doubt have something funny to say if I told him I just visited my mother in women's prison. So I don't.

Instead, I say, "I've been in a few." Not a lie. "I'll take you home before we do this, Rebecca."

Rebecca starts to say something but I shut her down with a look and pick up the computer printouts.

Lucas says, "I'm sorry if I came off as a jerk earlier. It's just I usually work alone these days. I had a partner a couple years back and it went south. And I didn't know you. Can I trust you?" He narrows his eyes and for a moment it almost seems like he's flirting. Would that be so bad? All in all, Lucas is a very attractive man, A little old for my taste, but he has a certain charm. I want to smash his face.

"Of course, Lucas." Until you can't anymore. He doesn't say anything more and we leave.

Back in my SUV I think about Lucas's about-face from his earlier rudeness. It seems contrived. But then, I might act the same way if the tables were turned. I still need him. He has the home-court advantage. He can get records. Knows the towns. Has connections. I'll take what I can get from him and keep him in the dark.

THIRTY

FEBRUARY 2023

Whatcom County

It took a while for the formalities to be complete, but by five o'clock, it was official. The woman who had been recovered from the creek was Olivia Greenwood, positively identified by her husband.

Lucas took a break to eat before driving over to the Sheriff's Office, where they had scheduled the interview with the husband. He arrived a little late, and Kelly showed him straight through to the interview room. Longbow was already there, along with Mac and Anderson. The three of them sat around the medium-size table opposite a man in a gray suit with salt-and-pepper hair with his back to the door. As the other man turned, Lucas recognized him from his picture as Edward Greenwood.

Mac stood up and gestured at the two new arrivals.

"Mr. Greenwood, this is Sergeant Lucas of Whatcom County Sheriff's Department. He's assisting us with the investigation out here."

Greenwood turned and rose to his feet. He was in his early

sixties, and well-preserved in the way only money can do. His skin was clear and unwrinkled, and the shadows around his eyes was the only hint that anything was amiss.

"Sergeant Lucas," he repeated, shaking Lucas's hand. "I understand you were the one who found Olivia."

Lucas decided not to be pedantic and tell him that he was probably the fifth person to view the body, and instead offered his condolences. First impression: if this guy had had anything to do with his wife's death, he wasn't making it obvious.

Lucas sat down next to Greenwood.

"I believe in not beating around the bush," Greenwood said, fixing Lucas with a steady stare. "I know how this works. You need to assume I had something to do with my wife's murder, because statistically, I'm the most likely to have killed her."

Lucas nodded and couldn't help being a little impressed with Greenwood's candor and self-possession.

"That's true, Mr. Greenwood. But I'm sure the detectives here have already reassured you that we don't make the mistake of homing in on one suspect without good reason. Having said that, the fact you lied about your wife's return raises other questions."

"Which I think I have addressed."

"If you don't mind, Mr. Greenwood," Mac began, "it would be helpful to go through it fresh with Sergeant Lucas."

Greenwood looked at MacDonald and then nodded. Lucas wondered if MacDonald was this polite with all his suspects, and decided there was almost certainly a net-worth threshold.

"I had a meeting in New York the sixteenth of last month, so Olivia decided she would check herself into the Park Plaza for the night. She did that sometimes. You know, me-time. Spa treatments. Pampering. I was pretty caught up with work so I didn't call her that last night. We had arranged for me to get the early flight the next day, pick her up, and we were going to have lunch."

"And this would be the seventeenth," Anderson said. Not a question, just clarifying for Lucas's benefit.

"That's right. So I got to the hotel around noon, parked underneath the building and called Olivia from the car to see if she was ready. No answer. That wasn't unusual, sometimes she's too busy to pick up the phone. But I had had no messages from her in a while either. I decided to go up to reception. I told her I was meeting my wife and asked if she had checked out yet. They asked me for her details and looked her up on the system and found she hadn't checked out. I asked for her room number, and of course they gave me the usual runaround, so I asked for the manager by name."

Out of the corner of his eye, Lucas saw the hint of a smirk at the corner of Detective Anderson's face. *Of course this guy asked for the manager by name.*

"You know the manager?" Lucas asked, trying to look mildly impressed.

"Sure, we stay there all the time. Phil's a good man. Anyway, Phil wasn't there, but the deputy manager took me up to Olivia's room. It still had the DO NOT DISTURB tag on the door. This was when I started to get a bad feeling, you know?"

"You were worried that something had happened."

"Yeah. I mean, it's not like she was depressed or anything and she wasn't some kind of drug fiend, but... accidents happen, you know?"

"Sure. I can understand why you were concerned. No contact by phone, late checking out and so on."

"So the deputy manager knocks on her door. Then he knocks louder. I can tell he really doesn't want to go in there, but I made him. He opens up the door and the room is empty. Olivia's clothes were still there, including her makeup on the dresser, and her phone. That's when I knew something really was up, because she doesn't go anywhere without her phone or her makeup."

"And that was when you called the police?" Lucas prompted.

Greenwood shook his head. "No, not then. I asked the deputy manager if she could be anywhere else in the hotel. He was pretty on the ball; called down to the gym and the spa, but nobody had seen her since the previous day. Her car was still in the garage downstairs. I asked if we could take a look at the security cameras. He called his security team and asked them to check out the cameras in the corridor on her floor."

"They let you see them?"

"Of course," Greenwood said. "They found a man escorting a woman along the corridor around 2 a.m. It was Olivia. It all made me concerned enough to contact the police."

Lucas listened as Greenwood went through the rest of the story: contacting the police, spending the next few hours frantically searching for his wife, and then the terrible moment when he had been contacted by the kidnappers and forced to make the decision about whether to follow their orders. Only once did his voice break a little: when he described opening the package containing his wife's finger.

"Up until that point I thought... I thought this could be resolved," Greenwood said, clearly holding back tears.

Lucas asked a few more questions, with Mac occasionally pitching in too, while Anderson kept her own counsel. The only time she spoke was at the end of the interview.

"Is there anything else you need to tell us, Mr. Greenwood?"

Lucas was watching his face, and for a split second, he saw something in the other man's eyes that suggested a brief internal conflict. But then he just shook his head.

"No, Detective Anderson. That's it."

THIRTY-ONE

We drive out to the jail, arriving around five thirty. It's a depressing hunk of concrete garlanded with barbed wire that is smaller but otherwise pretty much indistinguishable from the one I visited my mother in the other day. The guards don't smile or acknowledge us. We're just three more bodies to be counted in.

We go through all the usual security and then sit in the little café; killing time until visiting hours are over. Ronnie and Rebecca spend the time chatting, distractedly catching up with each other's lives, but neither one's mind is on anything but the revelations plaguing them.

A crowd of women come in, chatting about incarcerated family members and how they were innocent, or guilty, or the same old assholes that they don't feel sorry for. Visiting hours are over and we approach the deputies at the metal detectors. We have to surrender our weapons this time in order to enter the jail. One deputy operates the metal detector while two others watch us. Of course the machine blats and the two deputies' hands rest on their sidearms. Ronnie and I show our badges, and Rebecca shows her Washington State Bar card.

The deputies relax, and the one running the machine smiles and says, "Sergeant Lucas said you'd be coming. You need to put any weapons, change, bags, knives, anything metal in the locker over there and take the key. Who are you here to see?"

Sergeant Lucas can kiss my ass. He's probably watching us and laughing at our discomfort.

Before I can answer a tall man in uniform comes off an elevator and says, "It's okay. They're with me."

The deputy gives the man a semi-salute and motions us forward.

"I'm Captain Roberts, the jail commander. You need to lock everything up and then we can go to my office upstairs."

Roberts is a head taller than us. His wrinkled face and head of white hair gives his age away but he appears to be in good physical shape evidenced by the corded muscles in his forearms. "Captain Roberts, I'm Megan Carpenter. Ronnie and Rebecca Marsh," I say by way of introduction and to save time.

After putting a death grip on our hands, he says, "I'm aware. Charlie Longbow is a good friend of mine. I know a lady working in your sheriff office. Nan something. I never knew her last name but, boy, can she put away the margaritas."

"Yeah, that's our Nan," I say. "We call her Margarita."

He chuckles. "I know you're telling a fib but it's funny. When you get home tell her Roberts says hello and she should call me if she gets back up this way."

I think I'm going to be sick. He's talking about S-E-X and that word doesn't mix with my image of Nan. 1970s hairdo, thick lipstick that comes off on her teeth, beady eyes. Not really, but she's a pain in my ass and nosy to the point of needing a search warrant or being arrested if she goes through my desk again. I'm almost to the point of using crime scene tape to warn her off.

We step on the elevator with the captain and he says,

"Lucas had good things to say about you. To what do we have the pleasure of this visit?"

And here I thought Lucas put out "Shoot on sight" bulletins on us to all law enforcement.

"We're looking into a missing person case," I say.

Roberts turns to Rebecca. "You're Jack Marsh's daughter. The attorney."

"That's me. Ronnie is my sister. Our mom is missing and we hope you can help us find her."

"Lucas said you might want to talk to some of the jail staff."

"And maybe some of the inmates, if possible," I say.

"If you follow me to my office, I'll see what we can do. I don't have much time but I'll have one of my lieutenants take care of you."

We get off the elevator at the second floor. His office is accessed by a steel door operated by a deputy after verifying our identities via camera. The heavy steel door slowly slides back, and we follow him down a long hallway to an office at the end. The door rolls shut behind us and slams with a thunderous finality. I wonder how many times my mother has heard that sound. I wonder if it even bothers her.

The captain's office is even more minimal than Sheriff Longbow's. On the wall behind the desk are framed pictures of Roberts shaking hands with two ex-presidents, another showing him getting an award from President Bush senior. On an opposite wall facing the desk are pictures of Roberts and Longbow displaying a swordfish longer than Roberts is tall. In his fishing shorts I notice Longbow is slightly bowlegged with a thick jagged scar running the length of his shin from ankle to knee. Next to that is one of Lucas and Longbow on either side of a smaller swordfish. Longbow and Roberts are wearing orgasmic smiles. Lucas still wears the trademark frown.

I say, "Fishing buddies?"

"Longbow and I are stepbrothers. We were raised together

on the Lummi Nation Reservation. His dad married my mom."
He tells us to have a seat and he gets on his phone. He relays
what he needs into the phone and a harried-looking jail matron
brings in several heavy logbooks. "That'll be all for now, Trish."
She leaves and pulls the door shut.

Casting a bemused glance at the twelve pounds of paper
that's just been dropped on the desk, I venture: "You don't have
this on a database?"

"Of course we do," Roberts says. "But I insist it's all printed
out and bound as well, and Trish does a damn fine job on it."

As Roberts opens one of the books and begins flipping
pages, I exchange a meaningful glance with Ronnie, and hope
that Trish has a good health plan to cover all of that heavy
lifting.

Roberts stops and turns the book facing our direction.

"Vincent Anthony Lombardi is a frequent flyer. Battery,
robbery, dealing, possession, assault on a police officer, theft,
drunk and disorderly, and several other small-time things. He
was a trusty; that's a prisoner who is allowed to leave the jail for
short periods to run errands for the jail."

Ronnie and I know what a trusty is, but we let him
continue.

"When he stayed here at the iron bar motel, he made coffee,
cleaned, ran errands, ran the library, that sort of thing. But he
didn't last long. He was an untrustworthy trusty, if you get my
meaning. I should have never let him be one in the first place.
He didn't show any next of kin. For all we knew he didn't have
any. I wouldn't have figured him for one of your relatives."

WTF? It just gets better and better.

I say, "You say Vinnie ran errands. Did he always come
back?"

"He did. But he couldn't go far. He knew if he fled, he'd be
charged with escape and do hard prison time. He wasn't a bad
sort. If you ask me, he just liked to gamble and drink and dabble

in drugs. When he ran out of money, he'd do something stupid to get put in here. Three hots and a cot, we call it. Three hot meals and a roof over his head. We have a few of those men. And women too. That's progress for you."

I knew what he was talking about. I'd arrested an older gentleman for setting off an alarm at a business last year. It was winter. Two feet of snow. All he wanted was to get out of the cold to sleep. In most cases the homeless don't resist arrest and so we have to get creative with the charges—trespass, public intoxication, disorderly—just to get them off the street and let the jail nurse look at them. Vinnie has an addictive personality and his addiction is more powerful than his common sense.

"Lucas told us he wasn't in jail now."

"Released two weeks ago. Bonded out."

Rebecca mutters, "Dad was right."

Roberts says, "I know your father and I told him about Vinnie a day or so ago. How is he by the way? He sounded stressed over the phone. Is it because Victoria is missing?"

I don't want to get into it so I say nothing.

Roberts reads the log. "Victoria Marsh paid his bond." He looks at the sisters. "Is that your mother?"

The look on their faces is one of disbelief. Ronnie says, "That's our mom."

Roberts looks uncomfortable. "Sorry for asking. I've never met her but Jack always speaks of her fondly."

So he's close to Jack too. Jack, Robertson, and Longbow. I want to ask how he knows Jack but it really doesn't matter. Jack's very rich.

I ask, "And you never show a family member, emergency contact, anything on his record?"

Roberts shakes his head. "That's one reason I took him off trusty."

"I understand. Thank you, Captain. We were hoping to talk

to some of the other jail staff. People that know Vinnie. And we'd like to see the visitor log for the dates Vinnie was here."

Roberts picks up the phone and asks someone to come in. "Lieutenant Sitzman will help you. He has more hands-on day-to-day contact."

Lieutenant Sitzman comes into the office. Roberts introduces us and says, "James, I want you to give these detectives any help they need. Detective Carpenter will tell you where to start. I've got to go to a budget meeting and may not be back for several hours."

Lieutenant Sitzman gives the captain a strange look. "Uh, okay."

"You can use my office. There's Cokes in the mini-fridge." He says over his shoulder, "I'm leaving you in good hands."

THIRTY-TWO

The man had come back and pulled her across the floor and leaned her in a corner sitting up. Victoria has scooted on her butt to a wall. It's so dark she's disoriented but at least she can breathe. Loud footsteps reach her ears and the door opens, the light comes on, and she hears the rattle of metal on concrete. Something has been set on the floor near her.

Strong hands grip her shoulders and pull her forward as far as her bindings will allow. The shoulder she'd been forced to lie on for days now erupts in pain, but she bites back the moan.

"Good girl. I'm going to cut your hands free. Don't touch me or the blindfold. If you do, I'll hurt you. Understand?"

Victoria nods and says, "I understand. Please don't hurt me again."

The plastic ties are cut and fall away, and a groan escapes her when she moves her arms in front of her.

"Raise your arms over your head. That'll get some circulation going."

She forgets modesty and does as he says. Her injured shoulder pops and she immediately feels relief. Not good, but better. Her arms automatically come down and cover her breasts, *and the man chuckles. The embarrassment makes her face flush and she swallows a sob at her helplessness.*

"Next to you is a bucket filled with water. You can drink some but use the rest to clean yourself up. You really stink."

She hears the bucket scraping across the concrete and feels it touch her leg.

"Listen to me. Your life depends on you doing as I say. I'm keeping your ankles bound so you don't think you can escape. Not possible. Keep the blindfold on and keep quiet. Don't make a problem." He chuckles softly. "It's all I can do right now to keep my girl from tearing you apart."

The boots walk toward the door and stop. "I don't want her to kill you, though. You're not bad looking for your age. If your husband doesn't pay up, I might have a go at you." He laughs and the door shuts and latches.

She grabs the metal bucket and gorges on the water until she retches. It tastes like heaven. She bends her knees and sets the bucket between her legs so she can stretch her arms over her head and pushes her legs out to work her ankles and toes to get the circulation back. She pulls her knees up and feels the bindings on her ankles. Thick zip ties like he'd used on her wrists. The kind she's seen on police shows. No way is she going to break these. But she has some hope in her heart. If this man wants her alive, it must be for a reason. Maybe Jack has seen the pictures and is arranging to pay a ransom.

THIRTY-THREE

Before we left the jail we had talked to half a dozen of the jail staff and a couple of trusties and left contact numbers with several, including Lieutenant Sitzman. None of it was very helpful. Most said Vinnie was a good guy when he wasn't high or drunk, which was his usual state when he came to the jail. One jailer said the last time he was arrested, he had bruises all over his body and two black eyes. Vinnie hadn't told the jailer what happened and the jailer didn't ask.

I was interested in Vinnie's bruises. The note said, "You promised." Maybe Vinnie needed money and was running from a debt collector. The kind that talks with a baseball bat. Lieutenant Sitzman said he could have the medical officer call me when he came to work. With all the right of privacy issues though, he wasn't sure the medical officer would be able to tell us much.

The visitors log was no help except to verify that Victoria Marsh had visited during Vinnie's incarceration. She had left a modest amount of money for his commissary account so he could buy snacks or other items. I had the lieutenant look up the amount of money Vinnie carried on the books. It wasn't much, maybe fifty dollars each time Victoria left money, and it was gone as soon as it was available.

I wondered if Vinnie gambled his money away in jail? I'd learned from our own jail that prisoners would gamble on almost everything by using commissary money. If the loser didn't have the money to bet with, he'd been found by the jailers after he'd gotten a good beating.

Rebecca says, "The one trusty, Duke I think his name was, wanted money to talk to us. Can you believe it?"

I can. "I gave him my number. Maybe he'll call."

My phone chirps. I look at the screen and it shows the jail number, so I answer.

"Detective Carpenter?" the caller says.

"Duke?"

"Yes, ma'am."

He's whispering and there is laughing in the background. "I can't talk. Too many guys around. I'm going on an errand for the jail right now. If you can meet me somewhere, I got something you might want."

I can't believe this guy. "I'm not paying you, Duke."

"I don't want money, ma'am. I liked Vinnie. He was a stand-up guy. A little off, but he was a good guy."

He gives me an address, and I turn the car around and head back downtown. The location he gave was maybe ten blocks from the jail. When I get there Duke is standing on the street corner waiting for us. We're in a part of town where you lock your doors and carry a gun. Rebecca is uneasy, but Ronnie has been in worse places. I pull past a car with two flat tires and park. One side of the street is WWII shotgun-style houses; the other side is mostly boarded-up flat-roofed and wood-sided little shops. On the corner where Duke is waiting is a Mom & Pop store that seems to be the only place still in business. Urban renewal has forgotten this street.

Ronnie and I meet Duke at the back of the car. Rebecca stays put.

"Detective Marsh. Detective Carpenter," he says, and his smile looks like he's never been introduced to a toothbrush. Duke is early twenties, white, skinny, with greasy brown hair pulled under a red bandana the same color as his rampant case of acne. His arms, face, and neck are covered with tattoos. In other words, the dictionary definition of a scum bag. While we were at the jail, I'd wondered if all these guys were related. Since Duke's a trusty he's in street clothes and not the orange jumpsuit that has JAIL printed on back and front. In this case, faded and tattered jeans, black Hard Rock Café T-shirt, and bone-white Reeboks. Despite his looks he speaks intelligently and politely.

"It was wrong of me to ask for money. I want you to know I'm not like that. I only said that so no one would think I was snitching. And I couldn't tell you anything on the phone. Too many ears. If they knew I talked to you, I'd get hurt. I can take care of myself, but it's never one-on-one."

"I understand, Duke." I don't care. "You have something to tell me?"

"I'm probably the only friend Vinnie has."

I look at the car and Rebecca is giving us an expectant look. She wants to go but we're not done here.

"I'm sure you have to get back. What have you got for us?" He seems a little put-out by my tone of voice but if he doesn't stop wasting my time I'm going to be put out.

"I know where Vinnie is staying."

"We have the address, Duke."

He shakes his head. "The address he gives the police is always wrong. They never check. They just ask where you're staying and you can tell them anything."

"Does he live in Custer?" We'd been given an address in

Custer, a little spot in the road halfway between Blaine and Bellingham.

"No, ma'am."

"Where does he live?" I'm about through with this guy but Duke points across the street to the Mom & Pop store. "He lives there?"

"Yes, ma'am. Upstairs."

The building is two-story. The top floor has windows covered with newspapers. Condemned is too kind of a description.

"Are you sure?"

"Yes, ma'am. He has a card game going there from time to time. I played once and didn't go back. Too rich for my blood. Vinnie is lucky. Good enough to take most of the players around these parts. Some guys approached him and offered to front him if he paid them back and gave them half his winnings."

"He didn't pay them anything."

Duke smirks. "No, ma'am. Vinnie is plenty slick. But you don't take money from those guys. Not if you want to walk around on two legs. He's always strapped for money. He wouldn't have been able to eat if his sister didn't give him money."

"His sister?"

"Yeah, I seen her a time or two when she'd visit." He describes Victoria and I can tell Ronnie is convinced.

"Is there an apartment number?"

Duke laughs. "No, ma'am. The front is storage upstairs. His place is in the back. Or at least that's where he crashes. Sometimes at least. He moves around a lot."

"But you think Vinnie is up there right now?"

Duke shrugs. "I just got here. I didn't go up. I don't think he'd like it if I checked on him and then cops show up."

Of course he's right and he's protecting his reputation that he's not a snitch. "Anyone live with him?"

He shakes his head.

"Weapons?"

Duke laughs again. "Vinnie? Not that I ever knew about."

I ask, "Have you talked to Vinnie since he got out, Duke?"

"Maybe a week ago. He was supposed to meet me, but he wasn't around and I had to get back to the jail. He doesn't have a phone. I feel sorry for him, ma'am."

"Why's that, Duke?"

"He's twice my age and he's never grown up. He just keeps digging the hole deeper. I learned my lesson this time. I'm going to Narcotics Anonymous when I get out. I won't be back."

I've heard that before. I take a tenner out of my pocket. "We're here to help Vinnie so I seriously doubt he'd be mad at you. I'll tell him I threatened you with a gun." *Which I'm about to do.* "So, if I give you ten dollars, will you go and see if he's there? If he is, don't say anything about us. You only get the money if he's home."

"I don't want your money. But I'll take a kiss from one of you girls." He's eyeing Rebecca, who quickly turns her head and stares ahead through the windshield.

I hand him the ten. He chuckles and crosses the street.

I say to Ronnie, "I just saved you and Rebecca from a lifetime of nightmares."

"Thank you, Megan," she says, and nods toward Duke's backside as he walks around the building.

I say, "Let's go over there in case Duke warns him, or if he runs with our money."

We cross the street, and a girl comes along pushing a shopping cart filled with aluminum cans. She's maybe nine years old, dirty-blond hair, dirty clothes, brand-new Nikes. She gives us a defensive look and crosses the street in case we might mug her for the cans. Or the shoes.

Ronnie says, "You've made quite a haul, young lady. What are you going to do with all those?"

She answers, "It's for a science project."

"What kind?" I ask.

She gives me a sarcastic look, says, "I'm going to turn aluminum into money." She then gives us the bird and continues on her way. She's a poster child for celibacy. *We should arrest the little brat for stealing a shopping cart.*

We locate a side door and stand on each side of it, listening. Wait five minutes and then ten. How long does it take to see if Vinnie's there?

I say, "Duke should be back by now."

"I'm right here." Duke has come up behind us holding three Styrofoam food containers. He pulls his shirt down but not before I see part of a plastic baggy sticking out of his waistband. I smell marijuana. Smoking dope must make him hungry.

"Well?" I ask.

Duke says, "Someone's up there. I didn't see who but I don't think it's Vinnie. Do you want your money back?"

It probably paid for the dope. "Keep it. If anything else comes to mind, call me."

He leaves, but he's not headed in the direction of the jail. Not my problem.

I take out my phone and dial a number. Ronnie's phone rings and she answers with a quizzical expression. I say, "Keep this line open in case I need you. I'm going up."

"I'll go with you. He's my uncle."

"Exactly. You might hesitate if he's armed. You'll be able to hear everything and come if I need you."

"Don't hurt him."

"You'll know when I locate him. I won't hurt him." *I will if he makes me.*

I go to the back of the building and find a door standing open. The screen door is trashed and lying on the ground. This must be how Duke snuck up on us. I enter. Inside on the left is a door that leads to the market. Straight ahead is a set of rickety wooden stairs with smelly indoor/outdoor carpet nailed to it. I smell marijuana and something else. Like dirty sweat socks mixed with Lysol and bleach. I hope I'm not walking into a meth lab. As I reach the top of the stairs, I draw my gun. The smell starts to burn my eyes and I almost turn around to go down. Drugs are not my thing. But I hear someone moving around and I whisper into my phone, "Someone's up here."

There's a hallway that runs left and right, with three doors along its length. I pick the door straight ahead and think, *What do we have for our guest behind door number one, Johnny?* If whoever is in there is armed, I have some lead bullets for them.

I put the phone in my pocket so my hand is free and push the door open. I brace my feet, push my gun in front of me and prepare to force the door open. My breath catches as a man steps out of the room right in front of me, holding a gun of his own. I ease up on the trigger recognizing the black suit and slicked back hair.

"What are you doing here?" Sergeant Lucas asks, and looks at my gun. We both lower and holster our weapons, and I notice Lucas is wearing latex gloves. "Well?" he asks.

"Same as you. We came to find Vinnie."

Ronnie comes up the stairs holding a Kleenex over her nose.

Lucas looks around. "As you can see he's not here. It doesn't look like anyone has been here for some time. Did you check the address in Custer that you were given?"

First of all, how does he know we were given the Custer address? Secondly, how did he get this address? It wasn't on any of the records we were shown. As I suspected, Lucas was holding back. "Not yet. My guess is the Custer address is older than this place."

"Is that how you do things in Jefferson County?"

He thinks I'm sloppy. That's a good thing. "We were on our way there when one of the trusties at the jail called and gave us this address."

"Duke?" He laughs. "Did you pay him?" When I don't answer he laughs again. "He called me too. Just think what the boy could do if he put his mind to work on getting a job."

Rebecca comes onto the landing. "Sergeant Lucas?"

"Miss Marsh, Rebecca. I thought they were taking you home?"

"I couldn't stay in the car. I thought I might be useful."

He goes across the room and opens a window. "Will one of you prop the door down there open. We need to let this air out a moment and then I think there is something you should see."

Rebecca stumps down the stairs, and the breeze created is lifegiving. At least for my eyes and nose. I look around and there is another room looking out over the store front and it looks empty except for some boxes. Lucas leads us into that room where a toilet sits against one wall and flies buzz around it. A plastic table with a broken leg leans against another wall. A cracked plastic chair sits in the middle of the room. A couple of sofa pads lie on the floor with varying lengths of rope on them. No sheets. No blankets. No sofa. Empty containers of Chinese food, paper wrappers from Sonic and half-full Styrofoam cups growing mold litter the floor. The only thing alive besides us are the flies.

Lucas moves the pads away from the wall and reveals several items of used drug paraphernalia. A burnt spoon, hypodermic needles, matches, a tiny mirror complete with razor blade. All in all, the place was cleaner than a homeless camp—but not by much.

There is such a litter of trash it would take hours to go through it all.

"Any mail, paperwork, anything showing Vinnie was here?" I ask.

"Knock yourself out."

He peels off the gloves, and I have to ask, "Where is the ammonia smell coming from?"

He looks down at his expensive Italian shoes and a liquid has splashed on the toes. "I kicked over a bucket. Vinnie must have been cleaning things up. He's smarter than I gave him credit for."

I don't see anything to make me believe Victoria might have been here. Except the rope. I can't imagine her being here of her own free will. Of course, I couldn't imagine her visiting her brother in jail. Or supporting him financially and hiding it from her husband. Ronnie and Rebecca don't really know their mom. It reminds me of my own mother. Two-faced. Four-faced. She can be whatever she needs to be at any moment in time. The only thing constant about her is she's always a lying bitch.

Lucas says to Ronnie, "If your mother was here, she's gone now. The rope makes me wonder but with this mess who can tell what was going on. Maybe some kind of kinky sex. I'll go check the address in Custer, and I suggest you take Miss Marsh home. She needs to be near the phone."

Does he know about the threatening call? Maybe he's just suggesting her mom might call, or the kidnappers. He is right. But I don't trust him to go to Custer alone. "How about I ride with you and Ronnie can take Rebecca home."

He raises a thick eyebrow.

"I think we need to talk."

THIRTY-FOUR

I ride with Lucas. Ronnie will drop Rebecca off and check on her dad and then come to meet me. She doesn't like Lucas. She doesn't trust him. She has good instincts. I do too. I don't want him finding Vinnie without me.

Lucas is driving a Chevy Suburban, black, shiny with whitewall tires. Definitely not a police unit. It smells strongly of pine scent. "So you're helping Missing Persons out *and* driving your personal vehicle. Will it get you a promotion?" I ask Lucas, and he thinks that's funny even though it isn't what I intended.

"First of all, it's not my personal vehicle. I borrowed it from our Narcotics Unit. To come to the part of town where we were, it's best not to attract too much attention. A county vehicle would attract the roaches. This looks like a drug dealer's vehicle. Yours might as well have a bull's-eye painted on it."

No one likes a smart-ass. Unless it's me. "Captain Roberts says you're fishing buddies."

"You saw the picture."

"Yes. Quite a catch."

He laughs again. "He photoshopped the picture. Not that the one we caught wasn't a prize too. You said you want to talk.

I don't think you're into fishing. Unless that's what you're doing right now. Fishing."

"My grandfather has his own trawler in Maine. I went out with him a few times."

He looks sideways at me trying to judge the truth. Of course I'm lying. I don't know who my grandfather is. I've never been fishing in my life except battered and fried at the Tides restaurant.

"Was your father a fisherman?"

"No. He was a serial killer and a cop. But he's dead so who cares." That makes Lucas take his eyes off the road and he turns his head. "Just kidding. My dad was in the Army. Killed in Desert Storm. I barely remember him." At least it's what my mom told me. She lied.

"So you broke the family mold and became a cop."

Not completely. I've killed, but not for kicks like my bio-father. "How about you?" I ask.

"My dad died in prison. He was a murderer. He's the reason I went into law enforcement. He was everything I never wanted to be."

I relax a little. We do have something in common.

He asks, "Now that we've bared our souls to each other, what did you want to talk about?"

"I think we should be honest with each other. I don't want any credit, but I do want to finish this. I don't think Victoria has run off. Do you?" I ask.

"It's a possibility, but... no, I don't think so."

"So what do you think? Why is she missing?"

He thinks for a few miles. I don't interrupt.

"Mr. Marsh is a hard man." He glances over at me to judge my reaction before he continues. "Mrs. Marsh has been giving money to her less-than-law-abiding brother. I'm guessing Jack doesn't know and if he did, he wouldn't approve. He's proud to the point of arrogance. In any case, I don't think he would want to continue supporting his wife's brother. Apparently his daughters know little to nothing about their uncle or that side of their family. I did some research on Victoria Lombardi Marsh. She comes from a lower middle-class family. Stay-at-home mom, father had a lawn-care business until he became disabled.

"Victoria paid her own way through college. She met and married Jack Marsh. He was an up-and-coming lawyer who went on to have his own firm and continues to make a name for himself. Two children. Rebecca followed him into corporate law and is with his firm. Ronnie is a detective with Jefferson County. Both daughters are talented and have distinguished themselves, which is not surprising given the family they come from.

"On the Lombardi side of the equation however, the Lombardis had Victoria and Vinnie. Vinnie is a criminal and a little off. No other children or grandchildren except for Rebecca and Ronnie. Mrs. Lombardi is in a long-care nursing home paid for by Victoria. Dementia. Mr. Lombardi is on Social Security Disability, living in subsidized housing and drinking himself to death. Shall I go on?"

I don't let on that I'm surprised Victoria's parents are still alive. I had assumed they were deceased. This guy has really done his homework. He knows more about the family than the family knows. How the sisters will react to this news is beyond me, so I'll tuck that away for now.

"Okay, here's what I know so far," I say. "Before we came to see you this afternoon, Rebecca received a phone call. The caller disguised their voice and said she should stop. They indicated they knew we were detectives. They said if she didn't stop us what happens next will be her doing."

"Do you need me to trace the call?" Lucas asks.

"Ronnie is very good at that kind of stuff. She looked into it and said the call was untraceable."

"So all we have is Vinnie Lombardi writing a cryptic note

and leaving it outside Victoria's room at the Semiahmoo Resort. We assume he was asking for money she promised to him," Lucas says. "That's pretty thin but Vinnie is what we've got."

I add, "According to Duke, Vinnie owes some big-time money for gambling debts."

Lucas passes a car that was already exceeding the speed limit. "Do you think the people are after Vinnie and have something to do with the disappearance?"

"Maybe Vinnie can tell us. If you know anything else, you'll share it with us. Right?"

Lucas says, "Agreed. Maybe we should meet each day to discuss strategy?"

I don't expect this to last long, but he's at least making an offer to work with us. "Sounds good. You can buy us dinner. I always think better with a full stomach."

He laughs. I'm getting to him. He's getting to me too. I feel a little queasy.

"Let's see how this goes."

"And while we're being open," I say, "what's the story about the Greenwood case?"

Lucas narrows his eyes. "What?"

"The deputy earlier, he said this was like the Greenwood case all over again."

Lucas looks pained, like he had been hoping I hadn't picked up on that. "It's not your concern."

"Okay. You can ask me a question and I'll be honest with you."

"Are you always this annoying, Detective Carpenter?" Lucas is getting pissed.

"Yes. Okay, I was honest with you, so tell me about the Greenwood case. Was it another kidnapping?"

"It's not related to what we're doing."

"Then what is it related to?"

"Christ! Do you ever give up?"

"Is that your second question? You still haven't answered mine."

Lucas rubs his eyelids and inhales through his nostrils, like he's counting to ten. When he opens his eyes, to his disappointment, I'm still here, still waiting.

"Okay. Last year, we found a body in a creek. A woman. It took a while to identify her because of what was done to her. Do you want the graphic details?"

"Not yet. Continue."

"We managed to ID her as an Olivia Greenwood. She was reported missing from an upscale hotel in downtown Cincinnati, Ohio. Her body turned up here a week after her disappearance. She'd been tortured and sexually abused. The husband was a person of interest. He'd been contacted by the kidnappers but refused to pay the ransom. By the time the police were informed of the ransom call, it was too late to do anything for her."

I start to say something, and he holds a finger up. "I wasn't through."

I sit and listen as he continues. "There was no suspect information, no suspects except for the husband, but there was one interesting tidbit."

He's quiet, wanting me to drag it out of him. I want to choke it out of him but I wait him out.

"The husband had a girlfriend on the side. He and the victim have three children. The girlfriend is built like a model, younger and prettier than the wife. The girlfriend is a co-worker of the wife. The victim. The co-worker/girlfriend was recently divorced and has two children. According to the Ohio investigators, the husband was planning on getting a divorce and leaving his kids with his wife. She upset the plan when she found out about the girlfriend and promised a nasty divorce battle. He didn't care about his kids, but she wanted to keep his dogs and vintage cars. According to the detective I talked to, she probably would have gotten what she wanted and he would pay through the nose."

"Did they arrest him?" I ask.

Lucas pauses before answering. "No. Turns out they couldn't make the case."

"So, no named suspects, and no arrests," I say.

"I just told you no."

"The body was transported from Cincinnati to Whatcom County. Why? What's the connection?"

"None that anyone could find. The victim's body has been sent back to the parents in Cincinnati. They couldn't prove the husband did it. The girlfriend has an alibi. End of story."

"Lucas, you can't tell me it's not eating you up to not know how she was kidnapped and how she was transported here?"

"It's not eating me up. The case is closed. Ohio is done and so are we. Why? You want to reopen that case too?"

He has no idea how badly I want to do just that. Only on my own time. I'll keep it in mind.

"Don't you think it's odd? The Ohio woman is taken from a hotel. Victoria is taken from a posh resort. Are we going to wait until her body turns up in a ditch outside of Cincinnati?"

He turns toward me. His eyes are burning like hot coals. I've hit a nerve.

"Don't you ever accuse me of not doing my job," he says trying to control his anger. "I was a detective when you were still shitting yellow. Don't get on my wrong side."

Sheesh! "I'm sorry. I didn't intend it that way." I really did. But I don't want to walk back to Bellingham.

He watches the road for a couple of miles and we sit in uncomfortable silence. Eventually, he speaks again.

"The Greenwood murder is not connected to this case. You get distracted by shit like this and we could lose our chance to find Victoria Marsh."

"But how do you know it's not connected?" With an effort, I keep the exasperation out of my voice. Mostly.

He looks across at me, long enough that I get worried he's not paying enough attention to the road.

"I don't trust you enough to tell you how I know yet, Detective Carpenter. Maybe I'll tell you another day."

I hold his gaze until he looks back at the road. I know that's all I'm getting from him right now. And I'm not holding my breath for him telling me in the future.

THIRTY-FIVE

FEBRUARY 2023

Cincinnati

Delta 447 from SeaTac to Cincinnati/Northern Kentucky airport touched tarmac a little ahead of schedule at five thirty in the afternoon, local time.

Lucas was carrying hand baggage only, so he made it to arrivals within ten minutes. Detective Anderson was waiting for him in the terminal. Today, she was wearing a dark-gray pant suit, and her hair was tied back. She didn't return Lucas's smile, just gave him a brief nod of recognition as he emerged from the throng of commuters spilling out into the terminal.

Longbow had quibbled about the budget, of course, which was expected, but had agreed to let Lucas travel out to Cincinnati to shadow MacDonald and Anderson as they worked the Greenwood kidnapping.

"Cheap hotel," he had ordered. "And no fancy restaurants."

Anderson's car was a dark blue Ford Taurus with a couple of thousand miles on the clock. It still had the new car smell. Lucas wondered if Mac was authorized to eat breakfast burritos in this vehicle and doubted it.

"How was the flight?" Anderson asked as she pulled out of the lot. It was only the second thing she had said to him since they had met at the terminal. Lucas couldn't work out if she disliked him because of the usual tensions of a case spanning multiple jurisdictions, or if it was just a personal thing. Maybe it didn't have to be either-or.

"Uneventful. The way I like it," Lucas said. "Where's your partner?"

"He had a status meeting with the deputy commissioner," Anderson said. "We're meeting him at headquarters."

"The deputy commissioner. For the Greenwood case, I take it?"

Anderson nodded.

"Some victims are more equal than others, right?"

Anderson said nothing.

They took the 71 north into the city. Signs for Crescent Springs and Fort Mitchell flashed by. Lucas looked out of the window as miles of flat, unremarkable landscape passed by: low-rise buildings and acres of parking lots and big box stores.

Traffic was slow this time of day, and it took them almost an hour to reach the center of Cincinnati, where the police HQ building was. Anderson parked in the basement lot beneath the building, and they took the stairs up to the foyer, where she signed a couple of forms and issued Lucas with a pass.

"Good to be official," Lucas said.

"Don't arrest anyone while you're here."

They took the elevator up to the floor where the homicide department was based. It was a big, open-plan space with windows looking out over the city. As Lucas followed Anderson through the office, he took in the hustle and bustle of the busy department. Dozens of cops were working at the desks, talking on the phone, typing reports furiously. No one glanced up at the pair of them as they passed through the hive of activity. Lucas had always wondered if he would have

preferred the noise and pace of working in a big city department, and part of him felt the pull now, but he knew there were
compensations to working in a smaller patch. Lucas liked
control, and there were too many cooks stirring the broth here.
Even the commissioner in a big department like this only had
the *illusion* of control. It was impossible to know everything in
a city this size; not the way a smaller community could be
completely knowable.

Anderson led him to one of the doors lining the north side
of the office and opened it onto a good-size room with a floor-to-
ceiling window with a venetian blind. Detective MacDonald
was waiting for them. He was on his feet, looked like he had
been pacing.

"You tell him?" Mac asked Anderson.

"Tell me what?" Lucas asked. He looked around the room
to confirm it was just the three of them. "I thought Greenwood
was going to be here."

"We're trying to get ahold of him," Mac said. "There was a
development while you were en route."

"Don't keep me in suspense, Mac," Lucas said, throwing
Anderson a side-eye that bounced off her like a BB pellet off
Kevlar.

"Turns out Mr. Greenwood still wasn't entirely forth-
coming with us."

"He has a girlfriend," Anderson added.

Lucas looked from one to the other. "Oh?"

"We've been talking to his friends and family, people at
work," Mac continued. "We talked to everyone at his office but
his PA, who called in sick. Her name is Elizabeth Shaw. We
went to her home to interview her earlier this afternoon."

"And she told you they were having an affair?"

"She didn't volunteer that information," Mac said.

"Not verbally," Anderson clarified. "But it was written all
over her face. We threw her a few softball questions before we

asked her straight out. She stared at the floor for a long time and then asked us if she was in trouble."

Mac nodded. "She admitted she had been banging him for the last two years. The wife found out about it because Greenwood's PA had left a diary entry with the girlfriend's name in it public and it flashed up on Greenwood's iPad. She wanted a divorce. Seems that was the reason she went to stay at the hotel. You get where I'm going with this. Maybe they did the math, worked out that a life insurance payout coming in would be better than a divorce settlement going out."

Lucas was facing Mac, but he saw Anderson shake her head a little out of the corner of his eye. He turned to her. "You don't think so?"

Anderson folded her arms, looking irritated that Lucas had read her reaction. "I don't know. I don't like to jump to conclusions."

"Sometimes, you just have to accept the conclusion staring you in the—"

Mac broke off as his phone buzzed in his pocket. He took it out, glanced at the screen and answered with his name.

"Tony? You at Greenwood's place? Tell him I—"

He stopped again, and his eyes widened. Lucas and Anderson exchanged a glance.

"Jesus. Okay. Okay. I'll be there in a half hour."

He hung up and ran his hand over his bald head.

"What happened?" Anderson asked. "Is he still coming?"

"He ain't coming anywhere. They just found Greenwood's body in his study. He shot himself."

THIRTY-SIX

What Lucas told me of the kidnap/murder disturbs me. I won't tell Ronnie's family. There's no need to frighten them. Yet.

But I can't help but see parallels between that poor woman from Ohio and Victoria's disappearance. Jack denied he and Victoria were having bad marital issues, but it was the first thing that came to mind for both Ronnie and Rebecca. And Jack didn't want to involve the police. He was pissed Rebecca had called Ronnie. And then I show up. Surprise! He's making all kinds of excuses for her absence, but they all fall short of being remotely believable. I make a mental note to have Ronnie check Jack's personal finances. See if he's moving large sums of money around to hide it from a divorce attorney.

A road sign announces we've arrived in Custer. It's a wide spot in the road kind of place. The kind of place you leave if you walk outside. I look behind at the sign and say, "The other side of the sign says, 'LEAVING CUSTER.'"

Lucas slows and watches for our destination. "Custer's only claim to fame is Loretta Lynn. The country singer, may she rest in peace."

I'm young but I know who Loretta Lynn is.

He feels the need to continue. "Loretta lived here when she started her career."

"Wow!" I can see why she left.

The houses we pass coming into town are newer ranch-style brick and stucco with swimming pools, but as we get closer to the center of town all the houses are trailers or wood cabins. It is a shanty town. More shanty than town. One or two homes have rusted and tireless cars or trucks on cinder blocks in front of the house. The wealthy ones have both a car and a truck on blocks. Another has lawnmower parts strewn across the lawn and front porch. A sign on one mower advertises "Mowr and Small Ingne Repare." I want to tell Lucas to stop and let me correct the spelling. But I'm being unkind. These people are probably happier than those that measure happiness by possessions. Take Jack for example.

The address Lucas is looking for turns out to be a tavern on a corner that boasts the only stop sign we've come across. There's no signage on the place but I'm sure it's a tavern because of all the pickup trucks parked outside and the neon beer mug sign in the window. I imagine this place to be too small to have a police presence, but I'm wrong.

We park outside the tavern among the work trucks and go inside. It's only 8 p.m. but every person inside looks as though they've been there for a while. Five men inside and a middle-aged woman bartender, who is bigger than any of the men, turn and look at the newcomers. I'm expecting someone to say, *Ya' ain't from around here, are ya'?* I only hope they don't say, *You sure got a pretty mouth.* But the bartender says to the men, "Make room for the paying customers. I've got a business to run and don't have time for all this chatter." The men grumble but it's friendly and they make way for us newcomers.

"What would you like?" she asks. "Wait. Let me guess. The lady wants Scotch, no ice. The gentleman wants Jack Daniels with ice on the side."

She doesn't wait for our answer to pour our drinks, drops some ice cubes into a glass and puts our drinks in front of us. One of the men down the bar says, "Tammy's a mind reader. She tells fortunes too. She told me not to marry my wife and, boy, I should 'a listened."

After the guffaw dies down, another man says, "I thought you was widowed, Hank?"

"I am." He holds up four fingers. "Three times now."

Someone can't count or he's already stupid drunk. All of them are grinning so I sip my Scotch and watch the show.

"What happened to 'em, Hank?"

"First two died from mushroom poisoning."

They all fake a shocked expression. "No! What happened to the last one?"

Hank looks around with a wicked grin splitting his face and says, "She wouldn't eat the mushrooms so I took her and her cat out in the country and left them. She never came back." Even Tammy is laughing so hard I think she'll spit her false teeth on the bar.

I smile. Lucas downs his drink. Tammy goes to fill it again, and he puts a hand over it. "We're hoping one of you can help us find someone."

The jovial atmosphere is sucked out of the room like losing pressure in outer space. Tammy puts the liquor back on the shelf and turns with her arms crossed below her ample breasts.

I say, "We're looking for Vincent Lombardi." They look at each other like they genuinely don't know the name. I say, "Vinnie." This animates them.

Tammy smiles and takes the Jack from the shelf again and sets it in front of Lucas. "You should 'a led with that." The rest of the men laugh like I've told a joke.

"Does he live here in Custer?" I ask.

Hank says, "You mean Vacuum Vinnie."

"Vacuum Vinnie?" I ask.

Hank looks around at his audience. "We call him that cause he sucks liquor down like a vacuum. He gets the half-empty drinks and pours 'em into a beer bottle and takes it back to the camper when he's out 'a money."

The man next to him says, "And he's always out of money." They all agree.

"The camper?" I ask.

"What's he done now?" Tammy asks.

Lucas says, "We're not at liberty to say."

Hank says, "It's an ongoing investigation, then?"

Lucas nods, and a man at the end of the bar comes over to us, reaches in his back pocket and pulls out a leather wallet with a gold badge inside. "Thomas Tittle. I'm the town constable."

The men all snicker, and Hank stands, puts his thumbs in his belt and mimics the constable. "Town Constable Tommy Tittle. You got a problem, it better be little." Tammy hides a smile behind her hand. Hank says, "Go get 'em, deputy dawg."

Tammy holds a hand up. "Be nice, Hank. Tom did get us a stop sign."

Tittle says, "We had speeders coming through town and I got the county government to pay for a stop sign to slow 'em down."

Hank says, "You mean Tammy convinced her friend on the town board to get it. She hoped it would divert some traffic to her tavern. How'd that work out, Tammy?"

Tammy gives him the bird and everyone chuckles again and pats Hank on the back.

Comedy night in Custer!

I finish my Scotch to be polite while Tammy tells us about the camper Vinnie crashes in when he's on the run. The camper is gone and so is Vinnie.

"Your friend should be here by now," Lucas says.

"Do you mean Detective Marsh?" I correct him. "Let's go see."

We step outside, and Ronnie is waiting for me with the windows up and the engine running to keep the air conditioning going.

"I've got some things to do," Lucas says, waves to Ronnie, gets in his pimp car, and leaves.

* * *

"Find anything," Ronnie asks as I get into my Explorer. I let her drive so she quits fidgeting.

"He's not here, Ronnie. That's something eliminated."

"Yeah. I guess. What was Lucas like?"

"Lucas is an encyclopedia on the Marsh and Lombardi families."

Ronnie raises an eyebrow. "I barely knew who Lucas was."

"Well, he knows you. At least all he wants to know about you. I don't guess I merited more than a cursory look."

"So, what's Lucas doing now?"

"I told him about Rebecca's call. We promised to share information now." *Not.* "He'd done some digging and the address Vinnie gave on his arrests was an empty lot in Custer, but it turned out to be a camper parked behind the tavern. He doesn't live there. The owner let him stay in an old VW Bus camper. He did some work around the place but drank more than he was paid and took off. He came back the day after he was bailed out by your mom and paid cash for the VW. It's gone now and he hasn't been heard from. No one here knows where he might have gone."

"Can we trace the VW?" she asks.

"Tammy said it's a '68 or '69 and gave me a description. Primer red paint with a cartoon wizard painted on both sides, and a florescent green grill. She unsurprisingly didn't have paperwork on it and it didn't have license plates. I asked her who she bought it from and she said she didn't have a name.

She'd let some guy park it behind her tavern to sleep in. He was gone the next day and left it behind, so she owns it. Finders keepers."

"Sounds like it's stolen," Ronnie says.

Sounds like a circus vehicle. "I'm more interested in where Vinnie got the cash to buy it. She said she sold it to Vinnie for two thousand cash."

The road is straight and the scenery passing by is making my eyes heavy. Too much Scotch.

"So my uncle is in the wind," Ronnie says.

"Yep. Anything new at the house?"

"I left Rebecca with Dad. He said there was nothing new."

It's starting to get dark. I'm tired and the Scotch has taken its toll. "I know you want to keep at this, Ronnie, but we need to eat and get some rest. Let's start early in the morning if you don't mind?"

"You're right. I guess we need to get a fresh start."

I can tell she's thinking about her mom being out there somewhere. Victoria's scared out of her mind. Maybe hurt. Ronnie and Rebecca are frightened out of their wits. I can relate to that feeling. I was out of my mind with worry when I was looking for my own mother. Every minute spent sleeping or eating felt like I was betraying her. But I'm relieved I don't have to try to talk to anyone else tonight. My stomach is talking trash to me. I'm worn out from my session with my mother yesterday morning and worrying about what poison she's put and is putting in my brother's head. I feel guilty about not pursuing my first thoughts about telling Hayden everything when he first got home from Afghanistan. Well, almost everything.

And I get a chill thinking about the story Lucas told about the Ohio kidnap victim. Maybe I'm making similarities up. I'm tired and a tired mind does what it wants.

I debate whether to tell Ronnie about the Ohio woman that was murdered, body dumped here, and what was done to her. It would only cause Ronnie and her family more distress than they are already going through. I'll tell Ronnie in the morning and let her decide what to tell Rebecca and Jack. There's no reason we both lose sleep.

We're in our own heads until we get to Cougar Point. We say goodnight and go to our rooms. I strip and put my blazer and khaki pants under the mattress. Rebecca has laid out a toothbrush, toothpaste, water glass, thick luxurious towels and hair dryer. It was very thoughtful of her. The fancy high dollar shower is a treat. The water is hot unlike my sometimes-working water heater. The multiple shower heads can be set as a rain shower or can strip the skin right off your body. I like it hot and blasting. I get out, dry off, comb the tangles out of my hair, and brush my teeth before getting in bed.

The bed is just right. The pillows are soft and fluffy and numerous. The lights across the bay twinkle artfully.

My mind drifts back to the Ohio case. I haven't had time to process what Lucas told me yet. I take out my phone and Google "Cincinnati," "Greenwood," and "Whatcom". There's only one news story on the case, in the Cincinnati *Enquirer*. I'm guessing there aren't follow-up articles because there was no trial. The *Enquirer* piece relates some of the details Lucas relayed to me earlier: that a woman identified as Olivia Greenwood was found dead in a creek thousands of miles from her home. There's a line at the end requesting that anyone with information contacts Detective MacDonald at Cincinnati PD. I make a mental note to call tomorrow, if I have time. Maybe MacDonald will be able to tell me why they couldn't charge the husband.

In the meantime, I'm hungry and too wired to sleep so I rummage in my bag for the candy bars and chips. It's been a long couple of days, and I've accomplished very little. Some hotshot investigator I am.

I put the wrappers back in my bag. This place is too nice for my tastes. My father was a killer. Ronnie's dad is an asshole. We have some things in common. However she has a sister that loves her. I have a brother that hated me, but he's warming. In another twenty years maybe he'll forgive me. Ronnie just discovered her mom has quite a few secrets. I discovered my mother had been lying to me all my life.

THIRTY-SEVEN

I was twenty and a college student, when I first met Dr. Karen Albright, a psychiatrist who also became my friend when I most needed her. During my sessions with her, I poured out my soul and she helped me process my hideous history and the ideas that I was doing good while doing bad things. She taped these sessions and when I was finished therapy, she gave me a box of cassette tapes of the sessions and a tape player. I remember crying during that conversation and that was the first time I'd allowed my emotions to show. Crying was a weakness that my mother never allowed. I had to be strong and emotionless like her. Sure she could turn the tears on and off like a faucet, but only when she was manipulating someone.

I remember that conversation with Karen like it was yesterday. Karen said, "You'll want these someday." To which I'd responded, "I can't see that happening." She'd smiled at me and said, "Trust me. You will. The day will come when listening to the tapes will make you stronger." I didn't feel strong. She had put her arms around me, and that was the first time I'd allowed someone to touch me in that way and I welcomed the comfort. I knew it wasn't goodbye forever. But it was my last therapy session; therapy that had spanned a year and a half. At that time I was graduating from the university with a degree in criminology and had enrolled in the police academy in suburban Seattle. But more importantly I was graduating from therapy. Karen thought I was ready. I wasn't so sure, but Karen was the only person I could trust completely in life.

She was right about me needing the tapes. I've listened to each tape many times, and each time I've found answers I didn't know I was looking for, some tidbits to help me solve a case, or just get through the day. Over the next several years I visited her sporadically when I felt like I was sliding back into the whirlpool of blackness.

The original tapes are still in a box in the bottom drawer of my desk at home, but I never felt comfortable with them being accessible to anyone else. For one thing, Hayden has a skill I didn't teach him. He picks locks. I've come home and found him in my kitchen making himself at home. If he found the tapes, they would tell him everything about our past, about our mother, about our real father, about what I'd done. I don't want Hayden to find out that way.

It took me several weeks, sitting at my desk, my iPhone recording what my cassette tape player was playing. But I don't need to listen to the recording to remember the conversation with Dr. Albright.

Karen: Take your time, Rylee. I'm here for you. Let's go through this together. You found your stepfather murdered? And your mother was gone. It was just you and your little brother. Why did you think your mother had been kidnapped?

*Me: Hayden was on the floor kneeling in a pool of blood beside Rolland's body. On the wall behind Rolland a word was written in blood. **Run**.*

Karen: Tell me what the word 'run' meant to you back then.

Me: It was my mother's code word. It meant we'd been found.

Karen: Found by who?

Me: The man we'd been running from my entire life. The one that had taken her.

The message from my mother makes me think of another message left at a crime scene.

The note Rebecca was given at the resort was scrawled in barely legible letters. *You promised Dinky.* Promised what? To Vinnie or to someone else? Was it code? Did Victoria go back on a promise? A promise that would cost her freedom and maybe her life. Was she running from someone? I know so little about Victoria's past, only that she has a brother that doesn't have the approval of her husband and that entire side of the family has been erased from memory.

I press STOP. Victoria has been missing for two days. Victoria's daughters love her. Her husband is still questionable. The note must be related. I don't believe in coincidence. The Ohio case is another thing. Coincidence? I'll have to tell Ronnie and see if she can get the police file on that murder from Ohio and here. Lucas will be pissed off that we're messing in another of his cases. Screw him.

A clap of thunder rolls across the bay, coming from miles away, and rushes past my window like a freight train. The patter of raindrops turns into a full-blown storm. It will help me sleep. But what of Victoria?

"I'll find her," I say the words in a whisper. "We're coming for you, Victoria, and God help whoever took you."

THIRTY-EIGHT

When the man leaves the room and she hears the door latch, hesitantly she lifts the bottom of her blindfold. The room is dark except for a sliver of light at the bottom of a door. She can make shapes out. She quickly looks around the room expecting to see instruments of torture. No furniture of any kind. On the wall furthest from the door is a small rectangle window. She remembers her father calling it a hopper window. It's a foot tall and maybe three feet wide. She can't escape through it; there are bars welded to the frame.

Something hard presses into the bottom of her calf. She finds the zip tie that had been used to bind her wrists. The scuffing sound of boots is coming down the hall. She scoots over until the zip tie is under her buttock and pulls the blindfold back in place.

The door unlatches and she feels a waft of air on her face as the door opens. She hasn't felt this before. The air is fresh and damp and reminds her of how wet asphalt smells after a hard rain. She thinks maybe a door leading to the outside has been left open. Maybe there's a chance she can run? But where if she doesn't know where she is? She inhales the air but blood and snot run back in her throat and gag her.

Something metal clumps to the floor beside her and she can hear liquid sloshing.

"I'm going to cut your ankles free. Don't get any ideas. My girl is just outside the door and believe me, she will enjoy killing you."

"Please try something," the woman's voice comes from the doorway.

Victoria shivers. It's cold. The ground is cold. But it's her fear that has frozen her.

Something about the woman disturbs her even more than the man, who is more physically imposing. The woman really seems to despise her. But how can that be, when she doesn't even know her?

Victoria knows she has to get out of here. She'll crawl if she has to. The woman is going to kill her in any case. Better to die gaining her freedom than trussed up waiting to be butchered. She puts both palms on the floor and leans forward but a hand goes on her head and pushes her back.

"Victoria, you don't want to try that. For one thing, even if you got lucky, you'd never find your way out of here."

He puts the metal bucket beside her and takes the old one. "Here," he says, and the woman answers, "I'm not her damn maid."

"Take it," the man says forcefully, and the woman mutters but apparently has taken the bucket from him.

Victoria finds her voice. "Have you contacted my husband yet? Is he going to pay you?"

"Well, now, that's what we need to talk about. You and me. Let me cut you loose and you and me will talk."

From inside the room, closer now, the woman scoffs. "Talk. Yeah. We'll all talk and talk and talk."

"Shut up and do what I told you," the man says.

Victoria straightens her back and waits with her arms to her sides. Before she can say anything more, his strong hands grip her right hand. She can't pull it back and almost yanks the blindfold off, but she knows they will kill her if she sees them. She relaxes the hand. What else can she do? The grip grows tighter and her hand is pinned against the man's chest.

"Straighten your fingers," he says, and she can smell cigarette smoke on his breath. His face is a mere foot away from hers. She does what he says, and he forces her fingers out and bends them back until the pain is excruciating. Is he trying to break her finger?

And then something cold and hard presses around her little finger, and she realizes it's worse than that. Her heartrate quickens and she mumbles, "No," trying to pull her hand away.

The man holds firm and before the pain comes, she hears a snip, like a branch breaking. The pain is sudden and excruciating. She screams out and writhes against the arms clutching her. She can feel blood running down her crushed wrist.

She goes lightheaded. As she starts to slip into merciful unconsciousness, she dimly registers the man tightly wrapping a piece of cloth around the severed finger stump.

"Keep that tight and you won't die," are the last words she hears before she blacks out.

THIRTY-NINE

Sleep comes in fits. It's like being paralyzed and running possibilities through your mind like a black-and-white film. The storm gave up hours ago and moved south. I lie on the bed with my mind churning like a vortex. It dissipates as the door opens and Ronnie rushes in.

"Meg, you need to come downstairs." She takes off without waiting for me. I haul myself out of bed and tap my phone on, the screen glare dazzling my eyes before they adjust to see that it's 2:12am.

Rebecca and Ronnie are pacing in the kitchen, and there's no sign of Jack. "What's up?" I ask.

Rebecca touches an icon on her phone and a voice comes through. A man's voice. Deep and undisguised.

"Hi, Rebecca. I guess you know who this is. Don't talk. Just listen." There's a short pause. "If you go to your mailbox where I left the pictures, you'll find a present. I've warned you and your police friends to stop. You've caused this. Only you can stop it.

"After you open your gift, you'll believe. I will kill your mother if I don't get the money. But since you seem to ignore me, I'll send another gift, and another, until you comply. The price

*has gone up. I told your father two million. Now it's ten million
and I don't want any more excuses or delays. Let's just say, her
life depends on it.*

"I'll be in touch unless cops are still involved."

The call ends. I ask, "Where's Jack?" He's got some
explaining to do. There *was* a ransom demand and he's received
pictures. He's lied the whole time.

The front door opens and closes, and we all stand, staring as
Jack comes in the kitchen. He's unsteady on his feet, holding a
legal envelope that is stained red. Rebecca is closest and steers
him to a chair. His legs give out and he plops down on the seat.

"You're scaring us, Dad. What is it?" Ronnie says.

Jack pours the contents of the envelope onto the kitchen
table, and Rebecca puts a hand over her mouth and backs away
from the table like she's just seen a snake. Ronnie just stares. It's
the gift the kidnapper promised. A pinky finger with chipped
red nail polish, red raw tissue, white bone. Blood has soaked
into the envelope.

FORTY

FEBRUARY 2023

Cincinnati

Several hours after the discovery of Edward Greenwood's body at his home, Lucas checked into a Days Inn on the southern edge of the airport and wondered what he could do with the rest of the evening, seeing as how his schedule had been thrown off and he seemed to be surplus to requirements in the CPD investigation of Greenwood's death. Mac promised they would call him with an update later on, but he wasn't holding his breath.

Did Greenwood's suicide mean he was guilty of his wife's murder? Mac certainly thought so. But Lucas knew there was a lot more to the story.

He took out his laptop and opened it up on the small, scuffed desk in the corner of the room.

The day before, Detective Anderson had showed him the security footage of what was almost certainly Olivia Greenwood's abduction from the Park Plaza hotel. He had asked her to send the link by email and had watched it several times now. The footage was of acceptable quality, but he could see how it would have been inconclusive enough for the investigation not to have been a priority.

The footage was time-stamped for the early hours of February 17th. The clip opened at 02:07:36 on an empty corridor that could have been from a million hotels across the world. Doors on both sides, a beige carpet, low lighting from wall lamps.

At 02:07:52, a moving, indistinct shadow appeared in the bottom of the frame. It was followed by two figures shuffling into view. A man and a woman. The man wore a long coat and a baseball cap. His hair was dark and looked like it was short. Using the doors in the corridor as a guide, he looked about five-ten. It was impossible to tell anything else about him. He could have been black or white, skinny or well-built, twenty years old or seventy.

The woman was a little easier to place. She had blonde hair that looked unkempt. She had a coat, but she wasn't wearing it; it was draped over her shoulders. Bare legs showed below it, and Lucas couldn't be sure, but it looked as though she was wearing slippers.

At 02:07:56, she glanced back down the corridor, as though she had forgotten something, and showed her face to the camera. On a freeze frame, despite the quality, it was clear it was Olivia Greenwood.

Then the man, without turning back, steered her back around and kept her walking down the corridor. Her gait was unsteady, like she was drunk or drugged, but the man walked steadily, guiding her with an arm across her shoulders.

They reached the elevators at the end of the corridor, and the man pushed the button. Lucas noticed that he kept his face away from the camera at all times, and positioned his body in front of Olivia's while they waited. Ten seconds later, the car appeared, the doors opening and casting a brighter wedge of light out onto the dimly lit corridor. The man guided the woman inside. The doors slid shut, cutting off the light, and that was it. The video clip ended at 02:08:49, and that, as far as anyone could tell, was the last sighting of Olivia Greenwood.

Edward Greenwood had said that wasn't his wife on the tape at the time, that he had been mistaken, and so the line of inquiry had been discarded. Piecing it together weeks later, the investigating cops had searched in vain for more footage of the couple on the 19th floor of the Park Plaza in the wee hours of February 17th.

The foyer had several cameras, but the elevator allowed access to the basement parking lot, which had only one operational camera that did not cover the elevator. The couple could have taken one of the cars parked there, or even climbed the ramp to the street on foot and gone from there. The only vehicle seen leaving the lot within an hour of the video was a black Nissan Frontier pickup truck. The Ohio license plate was visible. It hadn't been run at the time, since by the time the footage had been recovered, Edward Greenwood had called off the search. Now, a week later, it turned out the plate was stolen.

"We'll take a look at black Nissan Frontier, see if we can find anything," Mac had said, adding, "I'm betting there's a lot of them out there."

Lucas was thinking about that when his phone buzzed. To his surprise, he saw Anderson's number on the screen.

* * *

She was waiting for him in the foyer.

"Mac wanted to see you again before you go."

Lucas smiled. "And you didn't?"

She didn't return the smile, bounced her car keys in her palm. "He's downtown, you coming?"

Lucas asked if they could make one stop on the way: the Park Plaza. It was a twenty-story building that looked like it had gone up in the middle of the last century. The hotel manager, Philip Morgenstern, was expecting them and greeted them with the air of a funeral director welcoming the family.

Morgenstern was mid-fifties. Thin and on the short side, with a neatly trimmed goatee and a widow's peak that made him look like a vampire, especially when paired with the black suit and the bow tie. He ushered them into a large office behind reception.

"Detectives," Morgenstern said as he closed the door, so quietly it was almost a whisper. "It's good to see you again, and I'm so sorry it isn't under happier circumstances."

Anderson only rolled her eyes a little, then turned to introduce Lucas. "Sergeant Lucas has joined us from Whatcom County, where Mrs. Greenwood's body was recovered. He's liaising with us to get to the bottom of what happened."

Morgenstern's face took on a pained expression. "Such a tragedy. Mr. and Mrs. Greenwood were such dearly loved guests. Part of the Park Plaza family."

"Any idea who the guy who crashed this family party might have been?" Lucas asked.

Morgenstern shook his head. "We had every member of the staff on duty that night watch the video, none of them could identify him as a guest or anyone else who had business in the hotel. Though, of course, it's difficult to be certain with the coat and the hat."

Lucas glanced at Anderson, raising his eyebrows. An unspoken request for permission to ask a question. Anderson nodded.

"Forgive me, I know you've probably been through this already with the detectives, but did you speak to Mrs. Greenwood at any time during her stay?"

"I regret I did not see her this time. I'm told she spent most of the time in her room before she..."

"Before she disappeared."

"Yes."

"You ever have anything like this in the hotel before?"

Morgenstern's brow furrowed. "Anything like this? Detective, I'm sure I don't have to tell you that as a large hotel we occasionally have to deal with... delicate situations, but no, we've never had a kidnapping. It's unfortunate, the circumstances of this case. If we had known earlier... if Mr. Greenwood had not called off the search..."

Anderson sat back in her chair and blew a lock of hair out of the way of her eye, sharing his frustration. "I hear you."

They were all picking up the pieces more than a week after the event, and far too late to do any good.

* * *

They met Mac at a late-opening coffee shop four blocks from the hotel. It was one of those self-consciously hip places with lots of exposed brick and spiral-filament light bulbs. Mac was sitting at the back with a glass of iced tea.

"It's been too long," Mac said as the other two pulled up their chairs and joined him. "This case is so cold you could put up a couple of goals and play hockey on it."

"How does the Greenwood thing look?" Lucas asked. "Mr. Greenwood, that is."

"Definitely a suicide, crime scene guys say nobody else involved," Mac said.

"He leave a note?" Lucas asked.

Mac shook his head. "I guess he didn't need to."

"Can I ask you a question?" Anderson said, addressing Lucas.

"Fire away."

She held eye contact with him for a moment before asking. "You think he did it?"

There was a long silence. Lucas held Anderson's gaze, and

he could feel Mac's expectant gaze on him from across the table. He realized why they had made the time to catch up with him. It wasn't just professional courtesy; they needed to hear from someone with a little distance from the department.

Eventually, Mac replied with his own question: "What do you think?"

The two Cincinnati cops exchanged glances. Lucas could tell they were reluctant to show their hand first. But after a minute, Anderson shrugged and jutted her thumb at her partner, "He does. I'm not so sure."

Mac gulped the last of his tea and slammed the glass down on the coaster like a judge banging his gavel. "Innocent men don't do the things Greenwood did." He held up his index finger. "One, he reports his wife missing, then says she showed up fine. Which we now know was a lie."

Middle finger next. Lucas was gratified he hadn't led with that one.

"Two: he says later the kidnappers told him to say that. How do we know? There's no note, no email, no goddamn carrier pigeon, nothing to tell us anyone else was involved but him. Just the finger, which he could have done himself."

Mac raised his ring finger. "And three: right after we find the body and work out he had a sidepiece, he kills himself. It's like an admission of guilt. He knew he was caught; he knew what he did."

"We didn't have anything concrete," Anderson said, examining her own drink in the glass.

"Sometimes you don't need anything concrete," Mac said. "You know what you know. And I have probability on my side too. Nine times out of ten, when a woman dies violently, the husband or the boyfriend did it."

Lucas held his gaze and, without even consciously thinking about it, said, "My wife died violently."

It was as though someone had hit the mute button on their

conversation. Anderson's eyes widened. Mac's jaw hung open like he had just taken an unexpected punch to the gut. Perhaps it was just Lucas's imagination but he thought the chatter from other tables around them ceased immediately. Even the song playing on the speakers seemed to be quieter. Lucas felt the pulse thudding in his head. *Why the hell had he said that out loud?* But he held Mac's gaze, unblinking.

"Oh my god, seriously?" Mac said after a minute. "Jesus, I'm so sorry. What happened?"

Lucas cleared his throat, a little worried that his voice would catch, but the words came out sounding normal, matter of fact.

"She killed herself. Put my Glock to her temple and pulled the trigger. Right after she killed our daughter."

Anderson blinked. He saw her fingers tighten on her glass.

"Jesus," Mac said again. "When did it happen?"

Lucas made a decision. He had said what he had said, and there was no taking it back. But if he wanted to make any sort of progress with this investigation and with these two cops, he would have to start rowing back toward normality. So he lied.

"It's okay, it was a long time ago," he said. "It stays with you but eventually you learn to live with it."

Anderson nodded. She hadn't said a word since Lucas had dropped his bombshell, but he was grimly amused that her ever-present look of mild contempt had vanished for the first time. Perhaps his unplanned opening up might even pay dividends.

Lucas shrugged, leaning into the part of the trauma survivor who's made it through the worst. "And what helped me was the job. Helping other people. Finding the people who took the lives of others. I think it's made me a better cop."

"Right," Mac said.

"Enough about the past," Lucas said. "Talk me through the present. Why is Greenwood guilty?"

Mac looked grateful to be steered back to the conversation they were having before. He continued, though his voice still had a hint of the quiet, shellshocked tone with which he had pressed Lucas on his wife's death.

"Okay, so he lied to us and he killed himself, like I said. But there's more. We looked into his background. Turns out he was in a little bit of financial trouble. His wife had a two-million-dollar life insurance policy."

"Not out of the ordinary, for a couple that rich," Anderson said, speaking for the first time since the revelation. "Greenwood himself was insured for the same."

"Still," Mac said. "Being in deep financial shit is a motive. And that's not the only one. There's the girlfriend. Maybe the both of them cooked it up. Wouldn't be the first time."

"Doesn't sit right with me," Anderson said.

Lucas was interested. He thought Mac's explanation was a little too neat himself. "Why not?"

"We interviewed both of them. They were both in shock about what happened to his wife. But neither of them acted guilty; not in that way anyway. I could believe one of them could put on a good enough act to fool me, but both of them?"

"So maybe the girlfriend didn't know about it," Mac said. "Doesn't mean Greenwood didn't kill his wife."

"You're both talking hunches," Lucas said, realizing he was enjoying the unusual opportunity to critique someone else doing his job. He looked at Mac. "What do you have that's solid? Can you actually put Greenwood in the frame for the murder?" He turned to Anderson. "And can you rule him out?"

Anderson shook her head. "We have a decent, if incomplete, timeline of his movements from the night of the sixteenth until he killed himself. Some of that from our interview with him, the rest from his work calendar, social events, and so on. But we don't have a minute-to-minute account of his whereabouts over the last couple weeks, if that's what you want."

"Why was she dumped twenty-five hundred miles away?" Lucas asked. "Almost certainly she was held there; at least immediately before she was killed. You don't transport a body across seven or eight state lines for no reason. You find the nearest dump spot to you, and I'm guessing you know all the hot spots out here."

"This is the problem. We have Olivia going missing on the seventeenth, we have you finding her body three days ago, and we have Greenwood offing himself today. In between the first two events, it's a black hole, thanks to Greenwood."

"Or thanks to the kidnappers," Anderson said.

"If there really were kidnappers," Mac said. "There's no evidence of that either. No notes, no pictures, nothing."

"What about the call Greenwood took?" Lucas asked.

"There's a call from a burner to his phone around three o'clock the afternoon after Olivia was abducted," Anderson said. "That matches with Greenwood's story. Supposedly that's when they called him, told him they had his wife and that he had to tell the police she was safe at home."

"Any other calls from that burner?"

Anderson shook his head. "If he was telling the truth, they communicated by another burner after that."

Mac still looked skeptical. Lucas could see both points, but he wasn't sure who he agreed with. There was one thing that didn't add up though.

"If Greenwood killed his wife, or hired someone to do it, why did they take her so far away?"

"We were kind of hoping you could tell us that," Anderson said, after exchanging a glance with her partner.

Lucas thought about it.

"Do you have access to Greenwood's bank accounts, his business affairs?"

"We know the gist," Mac said. "There are forensic accountants going through the fine detail right now, but we know that he was a lot less solvent than he appeared to be. That's the motive."

"But no big transactions in the last couple of weeks?"

"He moved some money around, seemed like he was trying to free up some capital," Anderson said. "Nothing had come to fruition, certainly no large sums being withdrawn or transferred."

"Which would be consistent with a man trying to pay a ransom," Lucas said.

"Right," Anderson said.

"Or consistent with a guy making it *look* like he was trying to do that," Mac interjected. "Remember, if this went to plan, he would have to show his working after the fact."

"So unless there's something you haven't found yet, no ransom was paid."

"Because there never was a ransom," Mac said. "He made it look like a kidnapping and was going to cash in on the life insurance."

Lucas said nothing for a while, deep in thought. It didn't make sense. If Greenwood had killed his wife, or had her killed, why overcomplicate it like this? Why take her so far away, risking discovery? But if he was telling the truth, and Olivia Greenwood really had been kidnapped and ransomed, why had she been killed before he had a chance to pay? And where were the kidnappers now?

FORTY-ONE

An hour after we open the grisly package, Sergeant Lucas is sitting at the kitchen table with coffee and a pack of cookies. Whatcom County Sheriff crime scene techs have come and gone with the evidence. I sanitized the table from the blood-stains. Jack is still staring into the void. I might have to slap him out of his trance. I want to but I resist. He's their dad. I won't hurt him in front of them.

"Are you sure the finger is Mom's?" Rebecca asks, but Jack doesn't answer.

"It's Mom's," Ronnie says. "Whose else could it be?" Ronnie says this a little too sharply, and Rebecca starts crying.

"Sorry, sis. Maybe you're right. It doesn't—"

Rebecca interrupts her. "No. You're right. I'm just…" Her words trail off and she dabs at her eyes with a napkin.

I know Ronnie has seen worse things in our career but this is her mom. She surprises me. Her police mind has kicked in and I can see the wheels turning.

Lucas, being the uncompassionate jerk he is, says, "Why didn't you tell us about the ransom demand, Jack? This changes everything."

Jack's cheeks redden but that pulls him out of his fugue. He faces Lucas and says, "They called and told me they would kill her if I told anyone. They already wanted Rebecca to stop. They were angry she'd called the police, and then Ronnie and her friend show up. I was getting the money together, but I don't have two million dollars in my back pocket. I told them I would pay and needed more time to get the money. They just hung up on me. It was stupid. I know that. They hurt her and that's all my fault. I can't live without her. She means everything to me. You have to believe me. I thought I could get her back and then I would tell all of you. I..."

Lucas interrupts Jack. "And you didn't have the gate camera recorder on?" It's more of an accusation than a question. But I get it. I'd wondered the same thing.

"I told you, Detective. I didn't know the cameras weren't recording. We mostly use them to identify who is at the gate so we can let them in. We don't record everyone. We've never needed to."

"Well, you know better now," Lucas says.

I want Jack to stand up to him. Lucas is bullying Jack. I don't like Jack but I like Lucas even less. Jack is paralyzed with guilt and fear that he's gotten his wife killed. Lucas is unfeeling. Even more than me.

In Jack's defense, I say, "What good would video have been? We don't know when it was left. It could have been left by a kid on a bicycle for all we know."

Jack looks at me and I can tell he's grateful even though he'd never say it. But in fact, the recording would have helped. For one thing it would have given us a time the envelope was left. Also some small description of who left it. I'm not done with Lucas yet.

"The kidnappers could at least have left you a return address, Lucas. That's how police work is done."

Now Lucas focuses his attention on me. That's good. I don't care what he thinks. "Sarcasm won't help, Carpenter."

"Detective Carpenter. Or Megan, if you like. Let's not make this ugly."

"Right," Lucas says, and finishes his coffee. "Well, that's that."

He gets up and straightens his tie. It has cookie crumbs on it. He's a slob.

"What do you mean, *that's that*? What are you going to do now?" Rebecca asks.

Ronnie and I know what he's going to do. Nothing. He'll wait for the kidnappers to turn themselves in. Now more than ever I wish we could have brought our own crime scene team with us.

"Mr. Marsh had pictures of his wife delivered to the same mailbox by the kidnappers yesterday and didn't inform any of us. A recording of the delivery would have helped, don't you think? You don't have to answer that. But I'm going to tell you all again. If you have any other information, you need to tell me now. And"—he holds a finger up like he's scolding children— "anything in the future will be run past me before you do anything. This is my case. If it goes badly, I'll blame myself and I'll blame all of you. Shame on you for being so stubborn. This isn't a competition."

Ronnie speaks up. "The same goes for you, Sergeant Lucas. It's your reputation but she's our mom. This isn't a competition, like you said, but you saw the pictures for yourself. And now they've hurt her. Cut her finger off. Believe me, we'll keep in touch but you have to recognize our value and accept our help."

Lucas answers, "Yeah. I get it. Well, there's nothing you can do tonight but get some sleep. We'll go over this again in the morning. I wish you'd let my crime scene techs take the pictures. They may be able to do something to identify where she's being held. Actually, I insist you turn them over."

I hate to admit it, but Lucas has a point. He knows the people and the area. We're playing catch-up.

Jack had let us examine the photos but he has handled them several times. His fingerprints will be all over them. They were taken with an old-fashioned Polaroid camera. I didn't think those existed anymore. Jack has the Polaroid photos in his top pocket and he's kept touching the pocket like he's afraid the photos will disappear. I put my hand out and he reluctantly gives me the photos and I turn them over to Lucas.

Lucas goes to the kitchen doorway and turns to Jack. "You should turn the recorder on. Better late than never."

Jack just nods. He's glued to his chair and touches his empty shirt pocket. He's still in la-la land. Rebecca gets up and turns the recorders on. I'm ashamed I didn't ask about the recording and that makes me dislike Lucas even more.

The silence in the kitchen is awkward but there's not much to say. Jack looks at his empty hands maybe thinking they can do something to fix this. He disturbs the silence. "I don't trust him."

Rebecca stands and puts her arms around Jack. "Why didn't you tell us about the photos or the ransom?"

Jack looks around the table. "I couldn't. I didn't want any of you to get hurt. I was afraid you'd interfere and get yourself killed. This is my responsibility. I'm your father."

Ronnie blinks and I suddenly have a bad feeling. I imagine it's how a vulcanologist feels right before he witnesses an eruption.

"Your responsibility?" she yells. "That wasn't your call to make! This is what I do for a living, Dad. It didn't occur to you that I might be able to help? That I needed *all* the information?"

"I'm sorry, okay?" Jack says, and looks like he's on the verge of tears. His voice cracked a little on the last word. Ronnie stares at him and when she speaks again, her voice has returned to its normal calmness.

"No more secrets," Ronnie says, and he quietly nods.

I hate to interrupt a tender moment but I have a question. "You said you don't trust Lucas. Why is that?"

Jack's mouth tightens into a straight line. He knows something else he hasn't told us. I can't wait to hear it.

"Spit it out, Jack. No more secrets," I say.

"Lucas knew about the ransom demand. I called him about the call and the pics. He's the one that told me my daughters would be in danger. He said Megan was messing things up and that he could get Vic back."

Ronnie is on her feet, both hands on the table. "That lying son of a..."

"Language," Rebecca says.

She doesn't have to worry about language. Ronnie wouldn't say "shit" if she was standing in a pile.

Jack says, "I trust you now. All of you. Whatever you decide I'll support you. I'll deal with Lucas later. Sheriff Longbow is a longtime friend."

FORTY-TWO

We grab a couple more hours of unsatisfactory sleep, and by 7 a.m., Ronnie and I are up again and sitting on the back deck drinking coffee that's so weak I can see through it. I need to teach her how to make real coffee. Rebecca comes out to talk to us.

Rebecca says, "I haven't been completely honest with you. I'm sorry for not trusting you with everything. Mom hasn't been herself for the last couple of months. She's more withdrawn. She's gone during the day and comes back late at night. Mom always said she was at board meetings, or shopping, or at one of her charities."

I say, "But you didn't believe her?"

Rebecca shakes her head.

"What did Jack think? Did he say anything?" I ask.

"At first Dad asked her where she was going but then he just stopped."

Ronnie adds, "Our parents were never very outwardly affectionate."

Rebecca says, "It's been months since they really spoke to each other. My dad has a home office, Mom has a reading room, and they spend most of their time at home in those rooms. They rarely have meals together. I eat with Mom but Dad always has some client he's taking to dinner. He normally doesn't drink, but lately he's come home intoxicated and goes straight to his office. We were never allowed in his office growing up but I think he hides a bottle behind in his desk."

Ronnie has found out more about her family—most of it bad —in the last day than she probably knew her whole life. I feel for her. At least I knew how screwed up my family was and there's never been a moment when I was blind to it.

I say, "Every marriage goes through ups and downs." I'd heard that from several people but they usually were talking about it ending in divorce.

Rebecca gets that ugly face people make just before they break down in tears. It hurts my heart to see her so distressed. She dabs at the corner of her eyes with her fingers and fights the emotion that God didn't intend us to ignore. Hurt should be let out. I'm not one to talk but lately I'm becoming a real girl, feelings and all. The hard edge to me is still there but another person is just below the hard scrabble.

Rebecca gets up and goes inside.

"I'm really sorry for what you're going through, Ronnie. Your sister will be okay."

Now Ronnie is crying. I put an arm around her shoulders and pull her into me, but she pulls away. "You're going to make me cry, Megan."

"Okay," I say. "I'll be mean to you. What's really bugging you? Spill." I feel better already.

She makes a fist and pounds the bench beside her. "Are they living a lie? Is it all a front? They've had quiet spells before but this is different. Rebecca told me she found a notepad that Dad must have left in the kitchen. There was a note on it to call his personal attorney. The one who drew up their wills. She asked Dad what it was about, and he told her it was nothing for her to worry about."

She takes a breath before continuing.

"After Mom went missing, Rebecca looked in Mom's reading room and it looked like she'd been sleeping in there."

Being the pessimist I am, I'm thinking wills, divorce, murder. I'm sure Ronnie knows this as well as I do. Domestic violence doesn't always take time to come to a boil. Sometimes the volcano blows and the one unprepared for the violence gets dead fast.

What Lucas said about the Ohio woman threatening divorce and that she was going to "clean him out" crosses my mind. From what I've seen of Jack he is very full of himself and protects his reputation at all costs. He's very much the alpha male. If he thought his wife was cheating on him, or going to leave him, he would have called his attorney to see what he could do to fight Victoria's claim to his wealth and holdings. I don't want to ask Ronnie but I have to.

"Have you ever had any indication your parents might split up? Any separations? Accusations of cheating?"

She shakes her head. "I don't know what to think. So we have to add possible divorce to the picture."

Tuesday morning, now. Five days was a long time for kidnappers to keep quiet. That made me worry that she was dead. Maybe by accident and the kidnappers didn't know what to do next. It's still possible they've killed her and cut the finger from her dead body, though forensics will tell us quickly if that's the case. And there's the opposite side. If she's leaving Jack anyway is it a possibility she would cut the finger from her own hand to move things along? I can't see that happening. She has two perfect daughters. Why do that to them?

The time has come for me to come clean with Ronnie like I should have last night. I say, "Lucas told me something yesterday on the way to Custer."

I tell her about the Ohio woman and give her all the details I have. As she listens, her expression grows more and more concerned. When I'm done, she can't keep the accusatory look out of her eyes.

"You should have told me yesterday."

"I know. I thought about telling you last night but we couldn't have done anything. Today we can get all the case file records from Ohio. I couldn't ask Lucas. The case is closed and he's not moving from that position."

"You should have told me, Megan. No secrets, remember."

"You're right. I should have told you."

Ronnie says, "I forgive you but don't do that again."

"I promise." *Maybe.* "One other thing is bothering me. How did Vinnie get two grand to buy a junk van? He'd just been bonded out by your mom so he wouldn't have had money. If she gave him the two grand, why would he leave a note saying she promised? Promised what? Do you think your mom promised him more?"

"Possibly. It sure seems that way, doesn't it? But Rebecca would have found it when she looked into the financials. Dad gives Mom a generous allowance, and he puts money in her charities accounts. Maybe she used that money."

Rebecca comes outside again and sits beside Ronnie. She's taken her makeup off and has bags under her eyes. "What have you been talking about?"

I deflect the question and ask, "Can you check on the bank accounts for your mom's charities?"

"I've done that. No big withdrawals or expenses."

"Can you check if the accounts are legitimate.? Who owns them? Where the money is going?"

"Are you suggesting my mom would set up a bogus account?"

"Of course not." *Hell yeah.* "But I want to know where the money is going?"

"I can do that but I don't see how it fits with her being gone."

In my job I've seen women hide money preparing for a divorce. Men too. Victoria might use the money. "We need to find out how your uncle got the money for the VW and how it's related to the note."

She quietly sips her coffee while she processes this.

Ronnie says, "And there's something else. Brace yourself."

FORTY-THREE

Ronnie assures her sister we're going to look into the Ohio case and see if we can rule out a link. We don't want to ask Lucas for the file. I know he'll tell us it has nothing to do with us and then we'll have to go over his head and start a war. I make another pot of coffee, this time it's strong enough to stand on its own, and go back outside to think in private. My coffee sloshes over the side of the mug when Ronnie comes running outside saying, "Come quick."

Rebecca meets us in the downstairs hallway, holding her phone out. "Listen," she says, and touches the screen.

Caller: "I guess you didn't believe me."

Rebecca: "I believe you. Please don't hurt my mom again. We're getting the money together and just need to know how to deliver it."

A long pause.

Caller: "Expect another gift. You kept Lucas involved after I warned you. Are those other detectives still with you?"

Rebecca: "No."

Caller: "Liar."

The call ends.

Ronnie asks, "Does Dad know about this one?"

"I came and got you as soon as the call ended."

Ronnie says, "No secrets. We have to tell him."

"But not Lucas," I say. "Not yet, at least."

Rebecca is gripping the phone hard enough to break the screen. "He said there's another gift. Oh, God! What do we do?"

Victoria might have been forced to give the kidnappers information about security at the house, but she couldn't tell them who was doing what. Either the kidnappers are watching the house, or they have someone that is keeping tabs on us and Lucas.

"Rebecca, you and Ronnie check the mail and search the front of the property."

Ronnie asks, "What are you going to do?"

"Give me your phone, Rebecca." She does. "I'm going to talk to Jack. He needs to get the money. They'll call again. They're greedy. Do you know where he is?"

"He's in his office. He hasn't come out this morning."

The call Rebecca just received reminds me of a warning I've been receiving. Someone calling themselves "Wallace" has been sending emails to my work and my personal accounts. The emails are becoming increasingly threatening. I've made some enemies since becoming a detective, but these threats are to expose my past. A past that if ever exposed, would be the end of my career. The end of my relationships. The end of me. I'd have to start over again. New name, new appearance, new apartment, new job. No friends. The thought makes me feel ill. Whoever Wallace is, he doesn't want me to let the past go. He wants to punish me with it. He doesn't seem to realize that my past should be a warning to him. Much like the warning given in the phone call to Rebecca. I still wonder if these threats are not payback of some sort for whatever Jack has done.

I remember my stalker's last email: *I doubt you know what*

it's like to be hurt so deeply you've lost part of yourself. I know what it feels like. Soon, Rylee, you will too.

Jack knows what it's like to be hurt so deeply he's lost. But he knows more than he's telling. He'd already talked to Lucas and tried to shut Rebecca down. He was too calm when Rebecca told him about the first call threatening his wife if we didn't stop looking into her disappearance. He only came clean about the photos and the ransom demand *after* his wife's finger arrived. Why? What does he know?

The calls may be made to Rebecca but directed at him. To make him afraid. To make him suffer. Maybe Jack did some bad things in his past and is being punished for it now. The kidnappers, a man and a woman as far as we know, may want more than money. They may want revenge. But for what? Because the Marshes are wealthy? If so, why Victoria? Why not Rebecca? I'm sure Jack is the target. He's the one with the power. And the money. I'm still not convinced one hundred percent Jack's not behind this.

I knock on Jack's office door. He doesn't answer but I'm sure he's in there. I knock more insistently, and Jack says, "It's unlocked."

Jack's office is spacious with every wall covered with shelves of books and pictures and paintings. One wall is full of legal tomes, some look ancient, some new. He's also an art collector. Leaning against the shelves are a dozen or more water paintings. Most are of the bay with sailboats and suns. I notice they are laid out in the order where you see the sun at its zenith and sequentially sinking toward the horizon. The last painting is of a beautiful sunset with reds and golds and blues saturating the striated clouds.

"You have quite a collection."

"Those are Victoria's. She has a small studio downstairs."

"They're beautiful. Does she show them?"

"She's given some away. But not these. She did these for me

when we first moved into the house. I plan to hang these some-day. She's quite talented."

He's sitting behind a mahogany desk, a bay window behind him, a credenza below the window. "You should hang them in order on the wall leading to the window. You can watch the sunset from here and it will be like going back in time."

A sad look crosses his face. "If only." He's quiet for a moment and I take a seat beside his desk. "I take it you've found something."

"Yes. Rebecca just got another call."

I wonder if he's heard me but then his eyes widen. "Oh my god! Is she dead?"

"We don't think so, but there's bad news. First I want you to tell me why your wife has been sleeping in her reading room."

"I don't have to explain myself to you. I suggest you leave that avenue for the real authorities."

Asshole. "Ronnie and I have been deputized by your friend. Sheriff Longbow. We *are* the real authorities. Your daughters are doing everything they can to find your wife while you sit here looking out the window. Don't you care?"

His expression is one of anger but his eyes are wet. "Don't you dare talk to me like that. You're only here at the invitation of my daughter. You're staying under my roof. If you persist in insulting me, I'll call your sheriff and you'll be home before you can say you're sorry. Do you understand me?"

I lean forward on the desk. "I'll speak to you any way that will bring you back to doing what you should be doing. What the police should be doing. What you have the resources to scour the state to do. I understand where you're coming from Mr. Marsh, but now you understand me. I'm going to find your wife. I won't stop until I do. And if you've harmed her in any way, you'll find your ass sitting in prison and not among your wealth. Got it? If you're holding something back that causes her death, I'll make you... sorry." *Get it under control. He's not the enemy.*

He says nothing. He's not accustomed to being put in his place or made to face facts. He's not accustomed to being helpless, and I can have some sympathy for how he feels. I've felt it a few times. But I don't give up and that's what he's doing.

I soften my voice and try to look compassionate although it's easier to be angry. "I want to help Ronnie. She's like a sister." That's true. Now for a lie. "If you aren't responsible for your wife's disappearance—and I'm sure that's what Lucas is thinking—then I think you know, or at least suspect, why she's missing. Talk to me. It's just you and me now."

One little tear starts to fall but he catches it with a fingertip and takes a deep breath. "This is hard for me, Detective Carpenter. I don't think you appreciate how hard. I don't know what you might have been told about our marriage. I know Vic has been in touch with Vinnie. She's kept in touch and doesn't think I know. The trouble between us started a couple of months back. I'd found out she was bailing Vinnie out and sending money to her parents."

I'm surprised and he can see it on my face. "You don't know about Vic's parents. My girls don't even know. I was unaware that she was still in touch with them, but I found out she'd been selling off stock. I thought it was unusual so I had my investigator look into it. Her parents aren't fit to be around my girls. Vic's dad is a drunk who is in constant rehab paid for by free medical in Canada. The wife has dementia and wouldn't know Vic if she saw her. But Vic kept bleeding money paying for an apartment for the old man, and put her mom in an assisted living home. An expensive one. Those two never did anything for their kids. Vic paid her own way through college and was dead broke when I met her. Don't get me wrong. I admire her spirit. I love her more than my own life. She's a fighter. I know the girls don't see it, but believe me, Vic doesn't give up if she thinks she's right."

I ask, "Does she keep in touch with Vinnie?"

"I was being truthful when I told you Vic kept bailing Vinnie out of trouble and I put a stop to it. It was like throwing money on a fire. I understand she felt an obligation but she was only enabling him. The only way for a man to rid himself of the devil is with his own will and maybe some sacrifice. Vinnie wasn't even trying to straighten himself out."

"You're telling me Ronnie and Rebecca don't know their grandparents? Their mom's parents."

"They might have heard Vic and I talking about them when they were younger, but they've never met them and it's going to stay that way if I can help it."

What a dick! If Victoria left him, I don't blame her. "You're still keeping secrets, Jack. I don't like secrets. Secrets get people hurt. You've witnessed that."

"Why do you keep after me? Do you think I'm behind this? You do. That's what cops do. They badger people until someone confesses. But I want Vic back more than anyone. If you don't believe me, I don't really care."

"Okay, Jack. Let's say I don't believe you. You know your wife better than anyone. Where would she be? Why did the kidnappers know your address and phone numbers and who is staying in your house? Why do they know Lucas is still working on this? Why haven't you made arrangements to pay the ransom?" I look around his office and say, "Look at all this. You can't tell me you were unable to come up with the money. And why was Lucas telling you not to pay? I want to know what's going on."

"No. I don't know where my wife is. You're wasting your time and frightening my girls."

I put a hand up to slow him down. "One of your *girls* is a

cop. And she knows exactly how important what we're doing is."

He's practically yelling now. "What you're doing is making people mad and endangering my wife. Just leave us in peace. This isn't your battle. You're not family."

He's right. I'm not family. And he's right about our digging alerting the kidnapper. I pray it doesn't make things worse for Victoria. But if I believe everyone else I've talked to, and I do, he's fooling himself. Lucas should have contacted the FBI. A case this big is what they eat for breakfast. I don't like to call them because it takes them a week to make a decision. But neither Lucas, nor the FBI for that matter, will do what Ronnie and I will do to get her back safe and sound.

He seems to be a little embarrassed by losing his temper. He grimaces and sits down, shooting me a look that almost looks like one of apology. I soften my voice.

"Could it be someone from your past? Someone that you've hurt getting revenge."

He waves the statement away but his calm is put on. "It's the nature of the business we're in. My office gets threats toward me all the time. Why didn't Rebecca tell me about the call herself?"

"It doesn't matter, Jack. We have to focus. Your wife is in danger." Or already dead. "We don't think Vinnie took her. I know there's been issues with your marriage. Did she ask for a divorce? Is that why you called your personal attorney right before this happened?"

"Who told you I called..." He catches his mistake. "I called about a business matter. It's none of your business. Besides, Vicki would never divorce me. The idea is ridiculous."

"Has she ever left for days without telling you or Rebecca?"

"No. When we were first married, she had the crazy idea of moving her parents in with us. I put an end to it right then and there. She got angry and stayed with them one night but came home the next day. She worked and put herself through school. Something none of her family had the desire to do. Moochers. That was what she had to put up with before I married her."

"Where are her parents living?"

"White Rock. Just across the border in Canada."

"It doesn't bother you that your daughters never had a chance to meet their uncle or grandparents?"

"Of course it bothers me. But the decision was made a long time ago to not introduce them to that side of the family. We never told them about Vicki's brother because I wanted my daughters to believe in themselves and not know they had relations that were criminals.

"Why are we going over this again? The note is proof her bother is involved somehow. I know for a fact she bonded Vinnie out of jail recently. Where she got the money, I don't have a clue. She's sold all her holdings. There's not much in her savings."

"Jack, if you don't take this seriously and your wife is injured, your daughters will never forgive you. If you love her, if you love them, you'll stop denying what's obvious."

He cups his head in his hands, and I can barely hear him say, "I can't. I just can't." His voice rises to a whine. "This kind of thing doesn't happen to a family like ours."

He's wrong. Victoria was leaving him. She was divorcing him and he knew it. Or at least he suspected it.

"Are you making any headway on the ransom?" It's gone from two million to ten because he probably asked for proof of life. Look how well that worked out.

"I'll get it. Now, leave me alone."

I leave him in his denial. He's from a different world and I can't show him the way back to mine. He has to find it for himself. I just hope when he comes to his senses it won't be too late.

The last threatening phone call has me worried that it's already too late.

FORTY-FOUR

Ronnie and Rebecca are in the kitchen when I walk in with Jack. He seems to come to a decision and turns to face me.

"I'd like to talk to my daughters alone."

"No way," Ronnie says. "Sit. Talk. Now."

Rebecca takes him by the arm and leads him to the table where he sits and puts his head in his hands. "I guess you'll want the truth."

"Damn straight. Everything. Now!" Ronnie says. I've created a monster. I'm so proud of her.

Jack takes a deep breath and begins. "Your mom is filing for divorce. She's been unhappy for some time now and she gave me an ultimatum. Change, or she would leave me. I didn't know what to do so I called her bluff. That's why she wanted to take you to the resort. She was going to tell you."

The sisters stare at him in disbelief. Or they believe but are hurt and disappointed and fighting back accusations. I'm not one of the family so I ask, "What did she mean by 'change'? Change what?"

For a long moment I don't think he's going to answer. It's

none of my business, but I know Ronnie would have asked if she wasn't so shocked by his revelation.

"The usual stuff," Jack says, like that's an answer.

Rebecca shakes her head. "What was the ultimatum, Dad?"

Ronnie says, "We're waiting, Dad."

"It's not about money," he says. "Well, not entirely. We've reached a point in our marriage where we've become comfortable with each other. Or at least that's what I thought was going on when we stopped talking. We stopped spending time together. Stopped almost everything. She wants me to be someone I haven't been in a very long time. We don't even sleep in the same room anymore."

I cringe. I hope he doesn't bring up their sex life again. He doesn't.

"She wants me to retire. Sell the business. Stay home. Spend more time as a family. Go on vacations. I told her we go on vacations, but she said what we do isn't a family vacation. She's right. We go and I spend my time on the phone running the business. It has grown too much for me to handle alone. I was making a place for my daughters to take over the company."

"He's making excuses, Rebecca," Ronnie says.

Rebecca nods. "I know it will be hard for Dad to slow down, but it sounds reasonable that Mom wants you to be home. You deserve a retirement. You and Mom."

"Well, you know I could never do that. Retire. I'd go crazy. Can you imagine me without my job. What would I do? I don't have any hobbies or talents like your mom does. I don't believe in charity work. I've fought for everything I have. No one handed me anything. You girls are where you are because of our hard work and sacrifices. Your mom and I have given you everything you wanted."

The sisters are quiet but they never take their eyes away from Jack's. I say, "So you told her you would never retire."

He nods and looks away from his daughters. "She would never divorce me. Or that's what I thought. When I found out she'd talked to an attorney, I woke up and realized I love her too much to let that happen. I wanted to make things right. I tried to talk to her but she put me off. Said she had to have time to herself. That's when she took you to the resort. I guess she was going to discuss it with you. Get your opinion. I was scared she would leave me. And then I got angry. I received a phone call the morning she went missing. I didn't recognize the voice but it wasn't disguised like the one Rebecca received. The man's voice said they had taken my wife. He said 'they.' He warned me not to tell the police or call anyone, but I thought it was a prank until Rebecca called me and asked if her mom was here. Then you came home—alone—and told me what had happened. By then it was too late. I'd called the sheriff. After you showed me the note you found at the resort I knew who wrote it. I called the sheriff again and he sent Sergeant Lucas to talk to me. I told Lucas what happened. I gave him Vinnie's name. He was familiar with Vinnie. He said he would find him."

His face stiffens and he's having trouble with his words. "I made a terrible... mistake. Decision. When you called your sister, I panicked. I had already been talking with Sergeant Lucas. And then you two show up."

He means me and Ronnie. I think he should have been more worried when he talked to Lucas. At least we are doing something.

He says, "I called Lucas and asked him what I should do. He said to try to discourage you from getting involved. But of course I knew you'd keep at it. How could a daughter of mine not?"

Ronnie asks, "What did the caller say exactly?"

With a distant look in his eyes he says, "The first call was a man who asked if I knew where Victoria was. I don't have time for foolish pranks and so I told him not to call here again and was about to hang up. Then he said she wasn't at the resort. She was with them. Don't call the police. That kind of stuff. He said he'd stay in touch."

"Nothing else?" I ask.

"Not then. I just hung up on him. I thought it was a prank like I said."

"So there was more than one call?" I ask.

"Yes. After I hung up on him, a woman called. She said Rebecca would be telling me about Victoria soon and they'd get back to me." He looks at Rebecca. "She called you by your name, Rebecca. I thought it was someone who knew you and your mom were at the resort. That made me think it was someone from the resort calling. I got a call from you an hour later. When you told me Victoria wasn't at the resort, I was still thinking it was some kind of sick joke. I was even more convinced it was someone from the resort. And Victoria and I had our problem and I thought maybe she'd gone somewhere to think. I could tell from your call she hadn't told you about the pending divorce. You already sounded worried and I didn't want to frighten you, so I told you we'd talk when you came home."

"Right after your call my phone rang and it was the woman again. I told her if she valued her job, she'd better stop this nonsense. She laughed. She said if I talked to anyone or called the police, they'd kill her. She said they wanted a million dollars to get Vicki back. They told me I'd get another call and not to tell the police. She said they would know."

He looks from one daughter to the other. "Somehow this woman knew you'd called the police and she called back. She didn't speak but I could hear screaming. They were hurting Vicki. I begged them to stop. I told them I'd do as they said. I told them I'd make you stop, Rebecca. I'd get the million. She laughed and said that was too easy. Maybe they wanted more. Then she hung up.

"After I got my head straight, I thought it wasn't possible. I hadn't heard Vicki's voice. Only screaming. Maybe it was a setup. It seemed like a bad episode of *Law and Order*. It made me angry someone would threaten my family, and the more I thought about it the angrier I got. That's why I called Sheriff Longbow. He agreed it was a prank but to be safe he said Sergeant Lucas would contact me. At that point I hadn't talked to you or Detective Carpenter yet. I didn't want to call the resort and talk to Roger and embarrass Rebecca or Vicki. But I did and he told me about the note. He faxed me a copy that I gave to Lucas."

"Jack, you're a smart man," I say. "You had to know something wasn't right. Did you seriously think your wife was playing games with you? I know why you told us about Vinnie. You wanted to put us on that trail to keep us out of the way. And when that didn't work you sicced Lucas on us."

"I'm not going to apologize for what I've done. She's my wife. She's not your responsibility and if you keep messing in this, you'll get her killed."

"There's more, isn't there, Jack?" I ask. He's not good at hiding his lies and that's surprising as he's an attorney.

He remains quiet, then gets up and walks to the window keeping his back to us. "After I'd talked to Lucas, the male called. He asked if I wanted my wife back. I told him I wanted to speak to Victoria for proof. You know? He told me not to be stupid. He wanted the million in untraceable bearer bonds. If I didn't agree, they would send me proof of life. One piece of her at a time." The sisters exchange a terrified look.

We've been wasting valuable time. Vinnie might be off feeding his addictions and has nothing to do with this. Lucas knew better, so why did he steer us that direction? "So when are you supposed to make the exchange?"

"That's just it. They never said. The woman called me right after the three of you went to the jail. She knew you were there asking questions. She asked if I preferred a left or a right hand. I told her I'd made a huge mistake. I said I would meet wherever they want and bring the money. She laughed and said the price was now two million and I had my daughters to thank. She said they would be in touch."

We'd talked to a couple of trusties at the jail but didn't tell them why we were looking for Vinnie. Only a small handful of people knew about Victoria's disappearance. Surely Lucas or the sheriff wouldn't have said anything.

"Can you get the money?" I ask.

"I'm working on it but it won't be easy. I don't have millions in bearer bonds. I need to get those from a bank and I can't do that until tomorrow. I'll have to sell some things but I will find the money. I just hope they give me a little time to raise it."

I wonder if he has any idea what his wife is going through while he's raising the money. She probably thinks he won't pay. She's divorcing him after all.

"And what is Sergeant Lucas doing?" Ronnie asks.

Jack points at the security monitor beneath a cabinet. "You can ask him yourself."

Sergeant Lucas has just pulled up to the gates.

"I'll get him," I say.

Lucas comes to the door and says, "I've got some news."

"Okay." I don't step back to allow him entry.

"I think this is best told to Jack and his daughters as well."

I let him in and he beelines for the kitchen. I can smell coffee brewing. When I get in the kitchen Ronnie has put a plate of cookies out, and Lucas is already munching. He sits at the table dipping cookies in his black coffee then nibbling off the wet ends. After he's eaten a handful of cookies, he pushes the pack away. "Sorry. I have a medical condition and I didn't have breakfast."

I don't care. Shut up and tell us. "What's the news?" I ask.

"I've got a good lead on Vinnie Lombardi. I put out a bulletin on him and the VW camper van. Officer Nelson is in

Lynden. Nelson said the camper is parked at a homeless shelter in Lynden called Word of the Lamb. He hasn't approached it. He thought we might want to meet him. I told him we didn't have a warrant but the van is probably stolen or has stolen plates. He said there are no plates. He's keeping an eye on it."

We haven't told Lucas that Jack finally spilled the beans. I want to see where this goes first. It's possible Vinnie is tied up in this somehow, so I want to be thorough. Finding him isn't as important as it was, but it still needs to be done. If he left a note on the door to Victoria's room, he probably didn't see her. But knowing when he left the note will help determine when she was taken.

FORTY-FIVE
FEBRUARY 2023

Whatcom County

The morning after he got back from Cincinnati, Lucas woke early and drove down to Blake's Diner on Main Street before he clocked in. He ordered black coffee and steak and eggs. He had a mandatory check-in with Dr. Wright at two, and before that he wanted to get a head start on some of his lines of inquiry. Since arriving back from his flying visit to Ohio, he had been chasing up new leads. "Mac" MacDonald might think he had worked it all out but Lucas wanted to tie up the loose ends closer to home. Something had gotten under his skin about this case. It didn't take Dr. Wright to work out that it might have something to do with his own recent history.

As he was getting into his car, his phone buzzed. It was the sheriff. He was at a conference down in California, and had set off before Lucas had returned from Ohio.

"Morning, boss, how's the Golden State?"

"Pleasantly warm," Longbow said. "You get back okay?"

"Yeah, last night."

"Worth the trip?"

Lucas considered. "I don't know yet. I think MacDonald wants to put this on the husband, close it down. His partner isn't so sure."

"And what do you think?"

"It would probably make life easier if he was right, but I don't know. I think if Greenwood did it, he had no reason to bring his wife all the way out here."

Longbow said nothing, mulling it over.

Lucas leaned his arms on the roof of his car and watched the traffic blow past the lot.

"There's no goddamn reason for her being dumped out here," Lucas said. "Mrs. Greenwood didn't have any connection with the area, and her husband didn't either. That tells me a third party's involved. I think Greenwood was telling the truth; it was a kidnap."

"Then why did he off himself?"

Lucas thought about it. "It looked bad. No evidence anyone else was involved, some circumstantial evidence he was involved, like lying to the police and concealing his girlfriend. Or perhaps he was just that broken up about his wife."

"If somebody else did snatch her, you think she was from around here?"

"I don't know. Maybe. But it's all I've got to go on."

There was a pause, and Lucas was about to wind up the call when the sheriff made an unwelcome change of subject.

"You got a session with Dr. Wright this afternoon, right?"

Lucas was caught by surprise. He hadn't added the appointment to his shared diary, so Longbow clearly had other ways of keeping an eye on his counseling schedule.

"Yeah. Two o'clock. I'll be there."

"Good. Don't even think about telling me you were too busy with the case. This comes first, got it?"

With an effort, Lucas kept the irritation out of his voice.

"You don't need to tell me that, I'll be there at two." See? He had even managed not to say it from between his teeth.

Longbow's voice softened. "Good. How you doing, anyway?"

Lucas rubbed the back of his head and wondered how much longer this was going to take. "I'm doing all right, thank you for asking. The work is helping."

"Okay. But remember what I said, don't push yourself."

"Got it. Listen, if I'm gonna keep to my schedule, I need to make a move."

"All right, talk soon."

Lucas hung up and got behind the wheel, gripping it tightly. He closed his eyes and found himself back in the living room as usual. It was something he was almost getting used to: the images whenever he closed his eyes.

He opened them, turned the key in the ignition and pulled out onto the road, headed west.

His first port of call was the creek. This was his third visit in the last week, but the first on his own. He didn't expect to find anything new, but sometimes it helped to visit the key scenes.

He parked at the side of the road again and walked up to the edge of the slope. He looked down to the spot. This time, when he closed his eyes, he saw Olivia Greenwood's body, not the living room.

Instead of descending the hill, he walked up to the bridge this time. It was pretty obvious how the dump was carried out. The perpetrator could have rolled up after dark and parked on the bridge. From this vantage point there was visibility for miles along the road in both directions. Any other vehicle would be visible a couple of minutes before it got close.

February. The road wasn't dusty enough for the forensics guys to pull usable tracks from the road surface. The body could have been transported in a van... or maybe a pickup with a tarp over the flatbed. The driver would have parked, killed the lights, then hauled the body out and dumped it over the edge. It could be done by a single man. Under two minutes. And then he was gone, into the night. A pickup truck with a dropping tailgate, like the one on the Park Plaza security video, would be ideal for the job.

This was a well-chosen dump site. The perp was familiar with the area. Lucas was surer of that than ever.

Lots of black Nissan Frontiers around, like Mac had said. But how many in Whatcom County?

* * *

This afternoon, Dr. Stephanie Wright was wearing a black pant suit and a lilac shirt. Her hair was tied back. It might have been Lucas's imagination, but he thought she had warmed a little since the early sessions.

"It sounds like you're adjusting to being back at work well," Dr. Wright said. "I have to admit I was concerned when I heard about the homicide case you're working on."

"How so?"

Wright sat back in her chair and looked back at him, waiting for him to fill the silence as usual. He suspected that was just muscle memory now. They both knew he wasn't going to oblige.

"A woman dying violently. A wife and mother. Many would say that's exactly the wrong case for you to be working given what happened to your wife and your daughter."

Lucas shrugged, playing up the philosophical attitude he had made sure to foreground a little more in each session. "You know what? I would rather it wasn't a case like this too. I would rather I had come back to deal with some nice petty fraud case in a lumber yard back office, but this is the job. You don't get to pick what comes in next. I guess it's the same in your line of work."

There was the faintest hint of a smile at that.

"I believe you went out to Ohio to speak to the detectives out there. How did that go?"

Lucas took his time answering, considered his response. "It was worth the trip. I think I got some valuable information and it feels like I'm on the right track."

"And how was Cincinnati?"

"It was nice enough. Not much time for sight-seeing. I was glad to get back home."

Wright nodded and scratched a note on her pad, and Lucas realized he had made a misstep.

"Speaking of home, you're still living at the house?"

Lucas nodded. He had carried out the cleanup himself after the crime scene guys had signed off on the scene. He had ripped the carpet up and stripped the wallpaper where it had been spattered with blood. The blood had seeped through the carpet and stained the floorboards beneath. The stains were still there, underneath the new flooring. He thought about that sometimes, those permanent stains beneath the nice new carpet. It was precisely the kind of thought he made sure not to share with Dr. Stephanie Wright.

"I won't lie, sometimes it's a little difficult. The memories and so on. But it's getting easier. Maybe some time you can come over for a coffee, I can show you the place."

"Mmm," Wright said, noncommittally.

The sound of a car pulling into the lot outside drew Wright's attention, and then she looked up at the clock, seeing that their session was almost out of time. One minute to go. Lucas always greeted the looming end of the session with relief. Like he was the point guard on a basketball team with a decent but not-insurmountable lead running out the clock.

"Well, I'm pleased to see you settling in again," Wright said. "I want you to call me if you think it's getting on top of you, if you start to find you're not coping as well as you thought you were."

"I'll be sure to do that," Lucas said. "I don't know if you noticed, but I may have been a little resistant to this whole... counseling thing when we started."

"I may have noticed," Wright said, deadpan.

"Anyway, I was wrong. It's really helped to talk things through, just as much as it's helped to get back to work. It's been a big comfort to know you're here, to know I can tell you anything."

If Wright was skeptical about that, she barely showed it.

FORTY-SIX

Rebecca stays with Jack in case the kidnappers make contact again. Ronnie and I follow Lucas in my car. I've been to Lynden once. My boyfriend had a booth set up for a downtown craft festival and was selling his wood carvings. Lynden is a pleasant city with quaint restaurants, antique stores, bookstores, micro-breweries, boutique hotels, art galleries, everything you'd find in a bigger city, but on a smaller scale. Lucas circled around some back streets and soon we passed in front of Word of the Lamb, which, in another life, was Abe's Auto Repair Garage according to the faded paint on one of the garage doors. A Lynden city police car pulls up behind us and a uniformed officer steps out and approaches. We get out to meet the officer but Lucas gets in front and extends a hand.

"Officer Nelson?" Lucas asks, and the officer nods. "I'm the detective you spoke to." He doesn't bother to introduce us.

Officer Nelson is closer to Ronnie's age than mine. Maybe twenty-three or twenty-four. It's hard to tell with his baby face. He's wearing the typical small-town cop getup: tight-fitting uniform, sharp creases down pant legs, bulges in shirt sleeves and chest, Smokey hat, mirrored sunglasses and a tan that looks like it was sprayed on. He's absolutely beautiful with a perfect set of pearly white teeth that he shows off with a smile. He's in love with himself.

"I'm Detective Carpenter and this is Detective Marsh," I say, and he gives us the full body exam with his eyes. I'm going to kick him in the balls if he makes one wrong remark.

Nelson says, "I think I found your VW unless there's a circus in town."

Well, Duh. How many '68 or '69 VW camper vans can there be with a wizard painted on both sides, orange paint, and a green grille?

His eyes are still examining Ronnie so I shake him until his head bobbles. Not really, but I want to. "Can you show us the camper, Officer Nelson?" I say it loud enough to break Ronnie's hold on him.

"Call me Trey," he says, and turns his teeth up to high beam for Ronnie.

"Okay, Trey," I say, "show us."

Lucas sees my discomfort and grins. Asshole.

"Follow me," Trey says, and leads us around the back of the repair garage/shelter to a rickety shed with no front doors. A VW camper, rust spots spray-painted bright orange with a wizard painted on the side I can see. The front has a green grille and bumper. The shed looks like a strong breeze will flatten it. The license plates are missing.

A woman with tightly permed gray hair, a deeply lined face, and glasses with lenses thick enough to burn ants approaches us. "Can I help you?"

Officer Nelson says, "It's okay, Annie. They're with me."

Annie smiles and the wrinkles on her face shift like tectonic plates. "If you want Vinnie, he left early this morning."

Nelson asks, "Do you expect him back soon?"

"I never expect anyone back. These poor children of God have no roots. They are lost like little lambs. I feed them and give them a bed for the night. I never ask where they come from, how long they're staying or where they're going."

Nelson says, "Annie's our own Mother Teresa. Our officers help out from time to time collecting food and clothing but she is full service."

"Vinnie was helping with the others," Annie says. "He's a good man. Always a kind word. Always there for anyone that needs him. I hope he finds what he's looking for."

I ask, "How long was Vinnie here?"

"Two or three days this time. He's been here before. Never stays more than a few days. This time he brought that." She indicates the VW. "He loaded us up with groceries and water and offered to buy a big-screen television. He donated some money, which we can definitely use, but I didn't know what we'd do with a television. These poor souls need something to occupy their hands, not rot their minds."

"You got that right, Annie," Nelson says.

Lucas hasn't said a word up until now but the mention of money catches his attention. "You say he made a donation?"

Annie gives Lucas a suspicious look out of the corner of her eye. "He would never steal from anyone." And that was all she had to say about that. "I did hear him say something about going to Bellingham. He has a sister he was going to visit. I didn't see him leave so I can't say for sure. You're welcome to talk to anyone here but most of them won't talk to you."

Lucas asks, "Can I search the van?"

"Don't you need a warrant?" She gives him a scathing look.

"Do I?" Lucas says, but it's not really a question. More of a threat.

"Go ahead. You won't find anything," she says, and shrugs.

Officer Nelson stays with Annie while Lucas goes to search the van. I agree with Annie that there will be nothing of note in the van. If there's anything of value, Vinnie would have taken it, given it away, or already sold it. Ronnie and I go into the shelter.

The shelter is divided into single bed bays by sheets draped over ropes. Several picnic tables take us to the aisle between the bays. Four men and two women of varying ages and ethnicity are sitting at two of the picnic tables. All of them are holding on to a backpack or wearing one, no doubt containing their worldly possessions. The rule for homeless that I've run across is to never let your guard down. Never trust anyone. All are silent except one of the women.

"I'm Hattie. You looking for Vinnie?" she asks.

She must have been eavesdropping at the door to see if she had to vacate the premises. Or if one of them was going to be busted. I can see the caution emanating from her like a heat-wave on blacktop.

"Hi, Hattie," Ronnie says, and introduces us as Megan and Ronnie. She already knows we're cops. "We are looking for him. He's not in any kind of trouble. I know you probably don't believe that since we're cops, but it's the truth. We have something important he needs to hear."

She eyeballs me to see if she can trust me. Of course she doesn't but makes up her mind to talk. Maybe tell us something useful, or just to defend a fellow traveler.

"He's not here. Been gone a long time."

She's going to protect him. It's okay with me. Loyalty is hard to come by and I admire anyone that shows it. I wait her out and Ronnie is silent also, although I can feel her impatience.

"You promise you ain't gonna arrest him?" she asks.

Ronnie says, "He's my uncle."

Suddenly Hattie smiles. Her teeth are missing but it's still a pretty smile. "Uncle Vinnie, huh? Ain't that a hoot. I didn't know he had a niece. You must be Vicki's kid."

"Two nieces," Ronnie says.

"Two? He never told me." Hattie examines Ronnie and seems satisfied that Ronnie's niece material I suppose. "I can tell you he's a looker. Must run in the family. I would have given him my number if I had a phone."

Ronnie chuckles but I know Hattie's serious.

I ask, "Does he talk about his sister, Vicki?"

She shakes her head. But she knew the name so she's still in protection mode.

Ronnie says, "Hattie, did he go to see Vicki when he left? It's important. We really need to find him."

"I told you he doesn't talk about her, but I know she's good to him."

Ronnie says, "Do you know where my uncle is or where he was going, Hattie?"

She shakes her head again. "I'm not under arrest, am I?"

"We're not arresting anyone," Ronnie assures her.

"Then I don't have to tell you nothing, do I?"

"That's right, Hattie," I say. "But Vinnie is her uncle and she's worried about him. She has some family information he needs to hear from her and she doesn't want him to hear it on the news. Family is important."

Her eyes fix on Ronnie and she says, "If family is important, how come he's living on the street? How come I never heard him mention you? How come you don't know where he is or even if he's got a phone?"

Ronnie's breath catches. The words hurt her. I'm getting pissed. "Hattie, you don't have to talk to us but you have no right saying those things to Ronnie." Hattie cringes like a dog that's being abused, and I regret my tone. "I'm sorry. Ronnie is my friend. Like Vinnie is your friend. I'm helping her find her uncle because we're friends. So if you won't help us, we need to look somewhere else. But if Vinnie is hurt, it's on you."

Hattie nods. "I just have to check, don't I? I don't have many friends. Well, he's not a friend really. But I don't have many that treat me kind. And he's that kind of man. Good to the core that one is. In another life I'd have..." Her words fade.

"Will you help us?" Ronnie asks.

"Okay. But you better not hurt him. He's had a rough time of it. Worse than me, I think."

I can't imagine anyone being in a worse condition than this poor woman and my heart goes out to her. In another life, she said. I can relate. My life sucked until Karen Albright fixed me and Sheriff Gray found me. It was fate or luck or both that I was able to change. Hattie's life will most likely never change for the better. She's one of the forgotten, the easy to forget, the fell-through-the-cracks, abandoned by our government and society because she's a reminder of what our own life could be. I wish I was a better person and could help her. I guess I'm being hypocritical. I'm not ready to take on anyone else's burden.

"Do you know anything about his sister?" I ask.

"Yeah. A little. Vin likes her." She looks Ronnie over. "We don't talk personal-like here usually, but he told me some things about his sister. She's married to a man that keeps her under his thumb and so Vinnie don't get to see her much. But past is past. Now is now. He's living with it. He don't complain but you need to spend some time with him. You'd like your uncle a lot. He's a great guy."

Ronnie says, "I'd love to do that. I wasn't aware I had an uncle until a few days ago."

Hattie says something that reminds me again that there are still kind people in the world and I feel my eyes moistening.

"You poor girl. If you were mine, I'd take better care of you. You need to know Vinnie. You look a little like him, come to think of it. Same eyes. And I can tell you're kind, like him."

"My mom is missing. I'm afraid for her and I need his help finding her."

"Vinnie loves his sister. Told me she's always been there for him. I asked him if that's who gave him the money and he hushed up quick-like."

"What money, Hattie?" Ronnie asks.

"He told me he didn't steal it." She pauses, ready to lie for him, or pounce on the first person who makes an accusation.

"I understand," I say. Understand it's stolen or from a drug deal.

"Well, it was a bunch of money. Hundred-dollar bills mostly. He said he hit the lottery. He was giving us all money. Bought us these clothes. Wouldn't say how much money but I seen a roll that would choke a mule."

"What about the van?" I ask. "Where did it come from? Did he buy that too." I ask to see if he's told her the same thing Tammy at the no-name-tavern told us.

"I guess he bought it. He ain't no thief. He said he didn't need it no more. His thumb would do him fine. He give it to Annie. That's the kind of guy he is. He brought us bags of food from McDonald's. He bought me a vanilla shake 'cause I'd told him I really missed them. I ain't had a vanilla shake from McDonald's for a while. I wanted to go with him when he left but he snuck away. I don't blame him none. I'm not nothing to look at and I'd just be wanting money."

Hattie smiles and her breath is putrid. She has gum disease, or something worse is going on with her health.

Ronnie asks, "Do you think he was really going to see his sister?"

Hattie scratches under her armpits and thinks. "He said she was the only one who done him right. He might be going to see her. Then again, he might not. He said he needed to get some more money. He owes some people and he always pays his debts."

"Who did he owe money to?" I ask. He was giving hundreds away and could have sold the van but he apparently gave it away. Maybe Duke was right about Vinnie being in Dutch to some gangsters and is on the run.

Her lips tremble and her eyes mist. "Don't know. He said he was taking me with him. He promised. I don't blame him but I sure would 'a liked to go with him. Your uncle is one good-looking sucker." The conversation is over.

Outside we thank Officer Nelson and give Annie our contact info. Lucas has searched the van and shakes his head at my questioning look. Annie promises to keep an eye out for Vinnie, but of course, she would say that.

"Give me your phone number," Ronnie says to Nelson. He does and a moment later his phone dings. "That's a picture of Vinnie. If you hear anything you can call me and Lucas."

He asks, "What about the van?"

I defer to Lucas. He makes the right call. "I should have it towed and let my crime scene people go through it. It doesn't have license plates and isn't registered to Annie."

Annie says, "I can't drive anyway. Lost my license moons ago. And I wouldn't let any of my people drive it without proper registration, license, and insurance." She says this to Nelson, and he laughs and says, "Annie, if you weren't already taken, I'd marry you."

Annie's face turns red and she whispers to Ronnie, "Watch out for that one. He's a womanizer."

"I wasn't finished," Lucas says. "I *should* have the van towed, but I'll leave it up to Officer Nelson."

Lucas, you old softy. You don't want to mess with the paper-work, do you?

Lucas says to me, "We're done here. I'm going to find Duke. I'll catch up with you later."

"*We're* going to find Duke," I correct him. "But *we* need to talk first."

*   *   *

We follow him back to Bellingham and to the store where Duke told us Vinnie had his upstairs apartment. We go inside what is a café of sorts with only two tables and several chairs. Lucas gets coffee and something to feed his cookie habit. Ronnie gets water and buys me a tall black coffee.

Lucas starts. "Before you say anything, I called Mr. Marsh on the way here. He told me you know about the ransom demand."

"When were you going to tell us about it?" Ronnie asks. She doesn't look pissed but I know that tone of voice.

"I had hoped I wouldn't need to." He sips his coffee. "Mr. Marsh said the demand is up to ten million now. He knew the note was from Vinnie and I've been after Vinnie since this thing started. I was getting close to finding him too when you two arrived and made a mess of things."

"Is that why you wanted us to go away?" I ask.

"I still want you to go away."

I say, "If you and Jack had been up front with us, we could have worked together." Probably not but I feel obligated to say that.

Ronnie says, "My dad is going to pay the ransom? Even though Mom might be filing for divorce?"

Lucas inhales a cookie and says, "He doesn't want the divorce. He said her intentions gave him a wake-up call. And now this. He's scared, Ronnie."

Lucas knew about the pending divorce. Something else he hadn't shared.

Ronnie asks, "Is my dad a suspect?"

"Of course," Lucas says. "Everyone is. You know that. But he's not a good one."

I think he's a good suspect. Jack stands to lose his ass and it might put a stain on his reputation if she divorces him. Half of a fortune is still a fortune. Besides the short call to Rebecca, Jack is the only person we're sure has talked to the kidnappers. Jack's willingness to pay the money is a nice touch. If Jack is behind this and something goes wrong and she dies, Jack keeps it all and everyone will feel sorry for him.

Vinnie's recent windfall complicates things. If Vinnie is the kidnapper, that would make him one vicious and immoral bastard.

Ronnie asks Lucas, "What about the call my sister got?"

"I agree with your dad. For all we know it's a prank made in bad taste. Someone he or she works with, or someone at the resort. Several people know she's missing. Not everyone likes your family, Ronnie. Could be jealousy. All it takes is an unintended slight for some crazy to want to frighten you or put you in your place." He stops and considers. "But if it's for real, it's for one reason: because you two screwed up."

"What have we screwed up?" I ask. I'm tired of being lied to, kept in the dark, and fed bullshit by this arrogant bastard.

"When you went to the jail and talked to the trusties, did you think that wouldn't get back to the kidnappers? A successful kidnapping is very hard to pull off unless you have some experience. Some of those experienced people have spent time in jail. I'm betting that's where this idea originated. Someone in the jail somehow knew where Mrs. Marsh would be most vulnerable. These criminals have criminal friends on the outside. It's the perfect cover."

FORTY-SEVEN

Victoria cried herself to sleep and when she awoke in the darkness, she was no longer afraid but angry. Neither the man nor the woman had come into the room to taunt her since they'd come and cut her finger off. After what they'd done to her, there was no chance they would ever allow her to be ransomed. She was free to move around her jail cell but it was hard with the blindfold still on.

She pulled the blindfold down and could barely make out her own hand, though it was mere inches from her eyes. She stretched her uninjured arm out in front of her and felt her way around the four walls. The walls were concrete block, the floor a rough concrete, one door, one small casement window. The bucket was useless as a tool and the room was empty of any item she could use to pry the door open. The door was metal, with an industrial-type handle and no keyhole. The hinges were on the inside and she'd torn two fingernails trying to pry the pin out of the hinge.

The woman especially took pleasure in inflicting pain and humiliation. The next time they came in, she would fight for all she was worth. She wouldn't die here. Not by these people. She'd fight them with her last breath. There were two of them but she had daughters, a husband, a brother. Someone would come for her.

She's standing in front of the door when it suddenly opens, knocking her to the floor. She scoots away from the door and suddenly the lights come on. Blinding her before she reflexively puts her hand in front of her face, blocking the light. Squinting through slits of her fingers she sees the white tennis shoes at the bottom of skinny blue-jean-clad legs.

"I wondered when you'd take this off."

He squats and pulls her hands down and yanks the blindfold up over her head, scraping it across her broken nose and causing her to cry out.

"Stop crying or she'll come back in here."

Victoria knows who he means by "she" and covers her mouth.

"That's better. I just want you to know this wasn't my idea."

"Who..." Victoria mutters before she stops herself.

"Who? Well, that's a good question. Why is a better one."

Her vision is clearing and the light doesn't hurt. She sees the man's face for the first time. He's late twenties, maybe thirty years old. A black bandana is tied around his forehead holding long greasy dark hair back from his face. His arms are covered with tattoos in what the kids call a sleeve. On his right wrist is a tattoo of a woven bracelet that hasn't yet healed. It takes all her will to not grab the tin pail and smash it into his head.

He wrinkles his nose and looks at the floor that she's been forced to use as a toilet. "Now look at the mess you made. Whoa! Number two? How disgusting. I hope you don't expect me to clean that up." A chuckle comes from somewhere outside of the room. "Well, it looks like you're in no condition to do it. But you'll have to. This is all the water you get today so ration."

The woman moves to the side of the door, and Victoria sees she's holding a camera. It looks like one Victoria had years ago for recording family outings. "Get it done," the woman says.

The man steps beside Victoria, close enough she can smell his sweat and horrible halitosis breath. "Oh, I almost forgot. Hold your hands out."

When she hesitates he raises a fist and she relents. He was going to hurt her after all. She holds her hands out and when he touches the injured one, she feels faint.

"Now the other."

She does as she is told this time and he grips her wrist so tight she can feel the bones grinding.

"That's a fancy wedding ring. What's these other ones?"

She is wearing a ring Jack gave her after Ronnie's birth. It had birthstones in it for both of her daughters. She doesn't answer fearing he'll steal them. It's a silly thought but she has nothing left. Not even her dignity.

"Will he know these are yours?" the man asks.

"What..."

"The rings. Will hubby know they're yours?"

"Why would you...?"

"Wrong answer again." His fist slams into the side of her face and she's falling.

FORTY-EIGHT

While we are talking Lucas gets a phone call from Lieutenant Sitzman at the jail. He puts the call on speaker so we can listen and asks, "Where was Duke supposed to be going?"

Sitzman says, "He went to get some stamps and envelopes. He should have been back by now. I just called because you and your partners talked to him yesterday."

Partners? I think that's stretching things a bit.

"Did you call to see if he's been to the post office?" Lucas asks.

I can hear Sitzman letting out a deep breath. Either he's offended, or he thinks Lucas is an idiot. I vote for the second one.

Sitzman says, "I did. He never got there. You know, these guys never wander too far. If he comes in liquored up, he'll get stuck in an isolation cell and that means no more trusty status."

"When you find him, call me." Lucas disconnects.

"Why would he go AWOL?" Ronnie asks.

"You heard what the jail said so you know what I know. The post office is five minutes from the station. Lieutenant

Sitzman isn't worried and I'm not either. Happens all the time. If I hear anything, I'll let you know."

Will we? It's possible they're right. Maybe Duke is scoring some more drugs to sell in lockup. I remember seeing what I thought was a baggy of pot in Duke's pocket. He's more than likely off somewhere, his head in a cloud, literally. But I don't think this is coincidence given our last discussion that the kidnapper may have someone in the jail pulling strings. Duke knew about Victoria and her cornucopia of money. He has a taste of freedom. He's jumped to the head of the class as a suspect.

Ronnie says, "I've got Duke's records from the jail but I'm sure you know more than is in those records. Is there something we don't have, Sergeant Lucas?"

"Nothing to speak of. Just feelings. Same as you."

I say, "Duke told us he was Vinnie's only friend." Lucas raises an eyebrow. "And Duke knew Victoria was leaving money for Vinnie."

Lucas shakes his head. "But Victoria wasn't leaving thousands of dollars on her brother's books at the jail. Jail policy precludes any large amounts. I'm guessing Vinnie spent a couple thousand; for the van, the food and another couple hundred he gave away. Maybe his sister gave him the money after he got out, but I can't see someone with a drug and gambling habit giving everything he has away. Can you? Unless he knows there's more where that came from."

Or if Vinnie won the money? Not likely. But Lucas is right. Duke told us Vinnie spent money the minute he got it. I say, "Hattie said Vinnie was on foot. She didn't think he would be capable of committing a crime." As soon as I say it, I realize how stupid that sounds. Vinnie is a criminal. He's committed numerous crimes and is always in need of money. Between him and Duke as suspects, it's a tie.

But then, not all criminals have a record. They just haven't been caught yet. My thoughts turn to some of the people we interviewed at Semiahmoo, and I ask Lucas if he's done any digging on that side.

Lucas says, "If you've got a notebook with you, I'll tell you what I know on."

We don't need notebooks, but Ronnie always has one that she produces like magic. She opens it on the table and says, "Shoot."

"Roger Whiting is a recovering alcoholic," he begins, and I must have a surprised look on my face because he adds, "All of us have secrets."

I'm no exception. My secrets are a lot worse than Roger's. I wonder what Lucas's secrets are.

"Roger was involved in a little scandal concerning the Lummi Indian casino several years back."

"What kind of scandal?" Ronnie asks.

"Money laundering. The feds didn't charge him because he never handled any of the money. A gambling outfit was running money through the resort, and Whiting was in a position to deposit the money into an account in Canada. The feds could never prove he benefited from it."

"Why would he do that?" I ask. "He's just the resort manager. Jack is the owner. Jack's accountant would have discovered the illegal transactions eventually."

"The accountant is the one that blew the whistle on the operation. My friends at the FBI said the mob had some dirt on Whiting. Your dad was going to fire him but they convinced him to keep Whiting in place until they could clean up the others. They eventually arrested most of them and Whiting was never charged. Mr. Marsh decided to keep him on."

I tell Lucas about Missy's arrest for Assisting a Criminal. Lucas already knew because she had her probation transferred to Whatcom County.

"Anyone else we should know about?" Ronnie asks.

Lucas sips his coffee, grimaces, and puts it down. "Len Thundercloud. He worked at the casino as a blackjack dealer before he got the job as a floor guy at the resort. He was tied to the casino thing but was a very minor player. The FBI thinks he was the one who gave the mob Whiting's name so they could blackmail Whiting. The FBI couldn't prove Thundercloud benefited from any of it either so they left him alone."

Ronnie asks, "What was Roger being blackmailed about?"

Lucas says, "Sex with a minor. It was over thirty years ago. He was eighteen; she was sixteen. The FBI said the girl had two children, a one-year-old and a four-year-old. She reported Whiting because her boyfriend was angry she'd cheated on him. Whiting was charged but it was eventually dismissed when she failed to testify."

"How would Thundercloud know about a thirty-year-old arrest?"

"He was the four-year-old son. Roger's son. Small world, isn't it?"

Or not.

"Is there a connection between Thundercloud and Victoria?" Ronnie asks.

"Nothing I could find."

Ronnie asks something I never would have thought of. "What does he look like? Thundercloud, I mean."

Lucas takes out his cell phone and flips through some pictures, stopping at one. He holds the screen toward her. Her eyes narrow.

"Can you send us the files and pictures. We were going to ask for them," I say. "But that was back when you were pissed at us for being involved."

"What makes you think I'm not still pissed?" He smiles and just like that we're all friends. Fellow officers. Band of brothers, or sisters. Whatever. Not quite coworkers because we will still lie to each other but we're beginning to win him over to our side.

"So how are these people connected to each other?" I ask.

Lucas says, "I was getting to that. Vinnie was arrested with Duke once. Theft of a vehicle. Duke took the car. Vinnie claimed he thought the car belonged to Duke. He was still arrested and went to court. He was found guilty and they both did a year in jail. Thundercloud was in jail during the same time. It's a big jail. I don't know if they knew each other but they were trusties at the same time."

Sheriff Gray had sent the file on Missy's arrest for harboring a criminal but I hadn't a chance to read it yet. I hold a finger up to wait and pull the file up. I find what I need near the front of the information, pull up a photo, and show it to Lucas. "Recognize this guy?"

The only change in Lucas's expression is in his eyes. "He looks familiar. Who is he?"

I hold a napkin over the top of the head of the man in the photo blocking out the bleached hair.

"Thundercloud," Lucas says.

"According to Jefferson County's arrest record, his name is Donald Sutherland. Probably made up. Different color and length of hair, no facial hair, but it's him. I guess he thought it was funny to take a celebrity's name. He's the guy Missy was hiding from the police."

Lucas takes my phone for a closer look. "Well, I'll be damned. That's why I couldn't find any other criminal record on the guy."

Never trust computers. Given what we now know I wonder if the resort's video surveillance was accidentally turned off, if Roger and/or Missy might be behind it, or know who was. Someone, primarily Whiting, had two days to erase the video so it might not have been turned off.

I ask Lucas, "Can you get a copy of the resort's video from Thursday night until Saturday evening?"

"I can. Why? You said it was turned off during those times."

I explain my idea.

"I'll have forensics see if they can recover any missing video. They know how to collect it as evidence. If you're right, we might have our kidnapper on video."

We leave Lucas to go about his business. He has been doing more than we thought but given time we could have come up with what he finally told us. The investigation has taken a different direction, and we head back to the house. Ronnie is busy tapping keys on her phone.

I say, "I saw the look on your face when you saw the picture of Thundercloud. What was that about?"

"He and Duke look very similar."

"You're thinking maybe he's the guy who was hanging around Rebecca and your mom in Birch Bay?"

"Rebecca isn't positive about Duke even. If we had shown her this photo before she saw Duke, she might have said Thundercloud looked like the man. She didn't really get a good look."

My phone dings and I hand it to Ronnie. She says, "It's from Lucas."

She opens the file and shows me a newer photo of Thundercloud from his personnel file at the casino. In this one his hair is a little shorter than Duke's. His acne is more prominent. "I'm going to send this to Rebecca. The hair's more of what Rebecca described." Ronnie sends the photo to her sister, and my phone rings almost immediately.

Ronnie says, "Hold on, sis," and puts it on the handsfree link.

Rebecca's voice comes from the car speakers. "That's him. I'm almost sure. He has the same sneer on his face, and I remember the rotted teeth. Who is it?"

"His name is Len Thundercloud, sis. He used to work at the resort. He's connected to Missy and to Duke."

Rebecca says, "I want to be there when you talk to Duke."

Ronnie says, "Duke's missing and can't be found."

"He escaped?"

I say, "The jail isn't considering his absence as an escape yet. They're trying to find him. They said it's not unusual for a trusty to be late coming back from an outside errand."

Rebecca's voice drips with sarcasm. "My tax dollars at work. So what do we do now?"

"We're coming home, Rebecca," Ronnie says. "We'll pick up dinner on the way."

"Dad had dinner delivered. Pizza. I'll heat it up when you get here."

Ronnie ends the call and hands my phone back. "Rebecca can operate the oven, Megan."

"I didn't say anything, Ronnie."

I'm starving. I'll eat anything. Cold or hot. I plan to get some sleep if nothing happens. Ronnie will most likely be on her iPad until late. The plan is to get up early and start looking for Duke. If he's not around, I'll settle for Missy or even Roger Whiting. Someone is going to talk. Someone always does.

It's already dark by the time we get to Cougar Point. We eat warmed pizza and wine, and I tell Ronnie I'm going to turn in. I want to leave the sisters alone to discuss sister stuff.

In my room I take another shower, shampoo my hair with this great product Rebecca must use, brush my hair and teeth, and slip on a new nightshirt and shorts Rebecca has laid out on the bed. I need her at my apartment.

FORTY-NINE
WEDNESDAY

I'm up before the sun. Ronnie and Rebecca have beat me to the kitchen and I can smell coffee brewing. I'm not fit to be around anyone until I have a caffeine fix. Or two. I pour a mug and wear an expression I hope warns them not to talk to me. There's no need. Rebecca's holding a mug in her hands and staring down between her feet with a blank expression. I sip the very hot and strong brew and wait for her to realize I'm in the room with her.

"Sis, tell Megan what you dreamed about."

Rebecca's blank stare doesn't change and I wonder if she's heard Ronnie, but her lips begin to tremble.

"Go on. We need to discuss this," Ronnie says.

Rebecca says, "There's nothing to discuss. It was a dream. I shouldn't have told you."

Ronnie is not to be deterred. "She dreamed Mom and Dad were fighting. She was accusing him of having an affair. He slapped her and told her to get out." She stops and looks at Rebecca before she continues. "Mom told him she was leaving. She'd found someone else and was going to take everything from him. He told her he'd kill her before he let her break up the family."

Rebecca adds, "It seemed so real." Her eyes brim with tears, and Ronnie looks at me, beseeching me to tell Rebecca it was just a dream. But dreams have a way of letting our minds explore things our waking self won't consider. Not that dreams are always true. But the feelings behind them are, just the same.

"Dreams can do that," I say. "But you can't make decisions based on a dream, Rebecca." *Like hell we can't.*

Ronnie says, "I called the jail and Duke is still missing. A judge is issuing a warrant for his arrest. I looked into Thundercloud this morning. He's living in Bellingham. Guess where?"

Here we go. "Ronnie, I've only had half a cup of coffee."

"Sorry. I checked with the post office and the address he's using is the same as Missy's. They are living in her mother's house. If we can't find Duke or Uncle Vinnie, we can go to Bellingham and see what those two have to say."

I suck down the rest of the mug and pour another. I hold up a finger to shush Ronnie. Rebecca grins and says, "Ronnie said you were a bear in the morning. You remind me of Dad. He's unapproachable until he's loaded with caffeine. Then he's just hard to approach."

Ronnie nods. "He gets in his own world for sure. He's usually up before us. I'll see if he wants to join us."

Jack comes into the kitchen and says, "Not necessary. I smelled the coffee."

Rebecca pours another mug and hands it to him.

"And don't believe everything these two tell you. I'm not unapproachable. They are."

Rebecca asks, "Do you want me to make some breakfast?"

I'm hungry but Jack says, "Let's not take the chance."

"I can make eggs and toast," Rebecca says defensively.

"You can't even find them," Ronnie teases.

Rebecca makes a face at her. What they're going through

has a way of dividing a family or bringing them closer together. It's good to see them at least reacting to each other in a positive way. Even if it's making fun.

Jack asks, "What is this Thundercloud I heard you talking about?"

"Not what," Rebecca says. "Who. He worked at the resort."

"I seem to recall a guy named Thundercloud from a long time back," Jack says. "Now I remember. He helped blackmail someone who works at the resort. That was a mess. What's he done? Is he involved with this?"

I tell him what we know about Roger and the connection between Missy and Duke and Thundercloud.

"It wasn't Lucas's place to tell you about Roger," Jack says.

Too late.

"So Vinnie is involved with these people?" Jack asks.

I say, "We can't prove anything."

"Have you discussed this with Sergeant Lucas?" Jack asks.

"Lucas is the one that told us," I say. "Duke, the trusty from the jail, is missing. Lucas is trying to track him down."

Jack looks frustrated. "I can't believe they would let a felon just walk around outside. He should stay behind bars."

My take exactly, but I say, "They said it's not unusual for a trusty to be missing for a while but they have a warrant out for his arrest. I'm sure Lucas will find him." I'm not sure at all.

Jack surprises me by saying, "You and Ronnie should find Duke. If Lucas finds him, he may not tell you. I'm glad Rebecca called you."

Ronnie beams a short-lived smile when Jack adds, "Don't let it go to your head, honey."

Just when I was starting to like this asshole.

I say, "I want to run an idea by you, Jack." Actually I'm going to do it whether he agrees or not. "If we find Vinnie, I want to bring him here."

Jack's coffee mug stops halfway to his lips and he puts the

cup down so fast it spills. "Absolutely not! He will not be in my house. I don't want him around my girls. That's a ridiculous idea."

I say, "He doesn't need to stay here. We could get a couple of rooms at a nearby hotel or motel. Ronnie and I can share a room next to him. We need to talk to him. Get him to trust us. I'm not sure Vinnie is behind any of this."

Jack seems to calm down. At least I don't see the vein throbbing on his neck now. "What good will that do?"

"Think about it. If Vinnie left the note on your wife's door, it probably means he didn't get to talk to her. Or..."

"Or what?" Jack asks.

I haven't even discussed this theory with Ronnie or Rebecca yet, but it just feels right so I have to consider it. "The kidnappers might be setting Vinnie up."

"Preposterous!" Jack says, and I see the shocked look on the sisters' faces.

"Just hear me out. Vinnie spent time in Whatcom County Jail. He was a trusty so he made contacts and is known to the jail staff and inmates. Like Duke. And Thundercloud. The kidnappers have known our every move. Rebecca said Thundercloud was the guy that was following her and her mom around a store in Birch Bay and smiling at them. Thundercloud worked at the resort for a while. His girlfriend is Missy who works at the resort. Thundercloud has connections to Roger, the resort manager who seemed stymied as to how the surveillance video was missing during the time we think your wife was kidnapped."

"That's fairly convincing," Jack says, "but what about Duke, and how does this make you believe Vinnie is being framed for the kidnapping?"

Ronnie picks up the thread. "Thundercloud knew Vinnie. Duke knows Vinnie. Mom had left money for Vinnie at the jail. She bonded Vinnie out of the jail. And it seems there's not much that goes on that doesn't get around in the jail. The note was scribbled like a child's handwriting. We only think it's from Vinnie because you remember him calling Mom Dinky. What if Vinnie used that nickname to talk about her in the jail?"

Jack is thinking. He connects the dots and says, "So you want to find Vinnie and question him about the note and if he talked to Duke or Thundercloud or anyone else at the jail and told them about the nickname. In that case you should put him somewhere safe. If the kidnappers are setting him up, they will find out he's with you and try to silence him."

I say, "I know I'm not part of this family, but I would never do anything to harm any of you. We need to find Vinnie. We need to find Duke to spread the word. Even if we don't find Vinnie, I want to spread the word Vinnie is with us and looking for his sister."

Rebecca asks, "But if you don't find Vinnie or Duke, what's the plan?"

"I'll make sure word gets around the resort." I even plan to let this leak to the jail. "We know how to find Missy and Thundercloud, Duke may show up, or the kidnappers will come and we'll be waiting."

"So, you're using Vinnie and my daughter for bait," Jack says.

"I wouldn't call it that." *It's exactly that.* "I'll be there too. Ronnie is tougher than you give her credit for." And I'm twice as tough.

"I don't think you're asking my permission at all. What part do I have in all of this?"

"I want you to get us a couple of rooms at a dive motel near the jail," I say. I would do it but I want Jack to feel that he has a part in finding his wife. If he's helping us, he may not stab us in the back.

Rebecca says, "Dad, we should let Uncle Vinnie stay here

with us. We have surveillance cameras and alarms. I don't like the idea of Ronnie and Megan making themselves targets."

"I don't want him to stay here in our home." His eyes soften and he looks at Ronnie. "As a last resort. Okay? But I trust you not to do something reckless. If they're armed, I want you to get out of there or call the police."

Because I'm a better liar, I say, "I promise we'll do that, Jack. We'll be cautious."

Part of my idea is that Vinnie might get word that he's at the motel and know what's going on. He seems pretty shrewd and I think he wants to find his sister. The idea he's behind this is less realistic in my mind. I could be wrong; in which case I might have to hurt him. Either way we'll find out.

"What about me?" Rebecca asks.

"You can find us a motel and Jack can rent the rooms."

"Why not stay at the resort?" she asks, but the answer is obvious.

I say, "Preferably downtown Bellingham where there's high foot traffic. Maybe close to the jail, or the Mom & Pop store. You'll stay here with your dad in case you're contacted. Rent one room in the name of Vincent Lombardi. Then rent the entire motel under an assumed name."

Rebecca asks, "Do you think a motel will let me do that?"

"Money will buy you anything, sis," Ronnie says.

"Will it be dangerous?" Rebecca asks.

"For us? Nah. Not any more than driving a car, or getting out of the shower without slipping." I try to make light of this but Jack's right. This kind of money breeds unconscionable greed. "Ronnie and I have trained for this type of situation."

Jack says, "I should have the ransom money together this evening. If you catch the kidnappers tell them, I'll pay them. Money's not important. My wife's best chance is for them to give her up. Right?"

Says the guy with plenty of money. "That's a good idea,

Jack." But they won't do that. "We'd better get going. Call and tell us what motel. And, Jack?" He looks at me. "If you hear from the kidnappers, what are you going to do?"

"If I hear from them, I'll call you. Not Lucas," Jack says.

"You can tell them we have the money. They may already have a place picked for the exchange. If so, tell us and we'll go. If you go, they might just kill you both. No witnesses that way."

"I didn't think of that. But I want to see Vic."

"Got it," I say.

I hope I'm not misplacing my trust in Jack. If this goes south, I'll be damned for life. Ronnie is more than a partner. I didn't think I'd ever feel this way but I'd take a bullet for her. And I know she would do the same for me. The only person I've ever felt more for is Hayden. If I've learned anything by being here, where secrets are abundant, it's that secrets are deadly. Secrets can kill. I just hope Jack's secrets don't get his wife killed. He should have come clean. Too late now.

Whatcom County

Lucas had never had cause to visit the Semiahmoo Resort before for a couple of good reasons. The first was that it was within ten miles of his home, so he had never had the need for an overnight stay, even if he could afford it. The second was that the Semiahmoo Resort wasn't the kind of place where the police were regularly in attendance.

Detectives MacDonald and Anderson had talked about the Park Plaza in Ohio like it was high-end, but the Semiahmoo Resort made it look like a Motel 6 by comparison.

Lucas parked in the lot outside and went into reception.

There was a brunette behind reception wearing a black blouse and gold stud earrings. She looked up from her computer as Lucas approached, the customer-service smile breaking out on her face unconsciously. The badge over her left breast read CHRISTI.

"Good afternoon, how may I help you?"

Lucas flashed his badge and told her who he was.

People react in all sorts of different ways to seeing the

badge. Some are immediately on their guard. Some sigh and resign themselves to a little more hassle than they had scheduled for the day. Some give away guilty consciences.

Christi was none of the above. Instead, she widened her eyes and her smile got wider. "Oh wow, exciting! What are you here for?"

"I was hoping I could ask a few questions in relation to an ongoing investigation."

"Are you working on that dead body they found up at the creek?"

Lucas stalled by patting his pockets, looking for his notebook, reflecting on the fact that it might be possible for someone to be *too* cooperative.

"I'm working on a few things right now." He took his notebook out and flipped through a couple of pages, pretending to look for something. "Let me see. Right. I'm looking into a report somebody made about a black Nissan Frontier being parked in your lot last Tuesday. Somebody complained about it, said it wasn't registered with a guest."

Christi told him she hadn't seen such a car, with her tone suggesting that she would have remembered a car like that in this place. She offered to check the security cameras, if Lucas had an idea of when on Tuesday the car had been sighted. He asked for the whole day, and Christi said she would get the manager to send it over.

Lucas was pleasantly surprised with how cooperative Christi was. No persuasion or cajoling had been required. Nobody had mentioned a warrant. He asked if she had worked for the resort long.

"I'm here for a good time, not a long time," she said. "I'm going to college in the fall. Criminology. Although I have been thinking I might like to be a police officer. Do you have any advice?"

Behind them, the elevator pinged softly. Lucas glanced back

and saw a well-dressed man and a woman step out. He looked back at Christi.

"Sure," Lucas said. "Stick to the lab. Better pay, less grief."

"Good afternoon, Christi."

Lucas turned at the pointed greeting to see a man in his fifties who had just exited the elevator. He was a little shorter than average, dressed in a slim-fitting charcoal suit with a white shirt and a gray tie. Lucas could almost see the reflection in his shoes. He had a suede overcoat draped over one arm.

His female partner, presumably his wife or girlfriend, was a step or two behind him, looking into one of the large mirrors that lined the wall and adjusting one of her earrings. She was younger than the man. Blond-haired and with striking cheek-bones. She reminded Lucas a little of Olivia Greenwood. She wore a long coat that hung down to just above ankle level.

The man's gaze moved from Christi to Lucas and back to Christi again, a questioning expression on his face.

"This is Sergeant Lucas, from the Sheriff's Department," Christi said brightly. Perhaps it was Lucas's imagination, but it looked like she had physically snapped to attention. By the looks of the man in the suit, this wasn't a mere manager, it was the owner.

"Jack Marsh," the man in the suit said, extending a hand abruptly. "To what do we owe the pleasure?"

Lucas took his hand, expecting a bone-crushing shake. He was not disappointed.

"Just making some inquiries on a vehicle that may have been sighted in your lot, Mr. Marsh. Christi has been very cooperative."

"Jack, we're running late," the woman Lucas assumed to be his wife said in a bored tone of voice, still adjusting the earring.

Marsh didn't acknowledge the interjection.

"What vehicle? What's this in relation to?"

"Nothing you have to worry about. It's of potential relevance to a case I'm working."

His wife finally seemed satisfied with the position of the earring and turned back to see that her husband was still occupied. "Jack..."

"Just a second, Vic," he said without looking around. "Do I need to be concerned?"

"I don't know," Lucas said, knowing he was being needlessly antagonistic. He couldn't help it, though. He had met this prick twenty seconds ago and already hated him. "What's your interest in this company?"

"I own the resort, Officer Lucas."

"Sergeant," Lucas corrected, not rising to the bait by sounding aggrieved. "Okay, then you can let me see the security footage for Tuesday."

"I'd be delighted to," Marsh said. "As soon as you produce your warrant."

Lucas sighed. "Can we talk privately?"

Marsh smiled imperiously. "Sure, as soon as you have that warrant."

Lucas glanced at the receptionist, who was making herself busy with some paperwork and trying not to look like she was listening. Mrs. Marsh wasn't paying any attention, but she wasn't pretending. He leaned in and lowered his voice.

"I don't want to be difficult, Mr. Marsh. But I'm investigating a murder here, and I'm trying to trace a vehicle that might be related and was sighted on your property. I can absolutely get a warrant, but it will take time, and I can assure you it will be more hassle for you."

Marsh stared back at him, and Lucas was suddenly sure he was going to tell him to go ahead. But then he rolled his eyes and looked over at the receptionist.

"Christi, let him have the footage for Tuesday." He looked

back at Lucas. "But anything else, you're going to have to come back with something official."

"Much obliged," Lucas said.

FIFTY-ONE

We left Rebecca and Jack at Cougar Point to make arrangements for the motel and traveled to Semiahmoo Resort. Roger Whiting is behind the registration desk.

"Detectives," Roger says with an apprehensive look.

"Hi, Roger. Have you remembered something?" Ronnie asks.

He says, "The police came and looked at your mom's room and did a thorough search of the resort and grounds."

I ask, "Roger, have you talked to Sergeant Lucas recently?"

He shakes his head but his eyes tell me he's lying, and so I push.

"Roger, Lucas said he talked to you."

"Oh. Oh yeah. I've been busy and I completely forgot. He was here yesterday for a few minutes and talked to Missy. His people took everything Mrs. Marsh left in the room."

"Ronnie wants to access your video footage and make a copy. Can you set her up?" I ask. Lucas was supposed to have already done this.

He hesitates only a second. "Well, I guess it will be okay. But what about the privacy of the other guests?"

"It will be okay," Ronnie says. "Give me a copy of your registration log from Wednesday until today. It's legal. In case Lucas forgot to tell you, Megan and I have been deputized by Sheriff Longbow."

"Well..." Roger looks around to see who is listening. "Lucas already made a copy and asked for the registration log. Can't you get this from him?"

Ronnie's mouth straightens into a tight line, and Roger relents. "Of course you can have those. Come into the office and I'll get you set up. The registration files are there as well."

"Is Missy here?" I ask.

"Uh, Missy. She called in sick. She won't be in tonight either."

I press him, "Can you give me her phone number?"

"I spoke to her mother and was told she's not to be disturbed."

"Give me the number and her address."

Ronnie goes behind the counter and tells Roger she can find the files herself.

I say, "Roger, I want you to take me around the resort and show me where Mrs. Marsh might have spent some time. I want to talk to you."

He doesn't ask about what. His shoulders drop and he comes around the counter. When he steps off the raised platform his head comes just above the counter. He's much shorter than I'd thought. Under five feet. Maybe four. I walk slow so he can keep up. We make our way back to the café where the interviews had taken place.

"So, Victoria came to the café?"

"Yes. She helped redesign the café and the restaurant. She loved coming in here and the staff were always happy to see her."

"What about Missy? Was she always happy to see her?"

"I have no idea."

"Come on, Roger. Tell me the truth."

He looks around again and it's like something on a sitcom. He lowers his voice and his eyes travel to the wannabe writer who is sitting near the window again. The man isn't typing and his head is cocked in our direction.

"Don't look at him, Roger. Talk to me."

"I don't really think I should talk about my staff."

"They talk about you," I say, and his eyes widen. "Didn't Lucas tell you what he heard from them? I won't say who told him but I know you've been in trouble several times in the past. An underage girl, laundering, FBI..."

Roger makes shushing motions with his hand. "Can we go somewhere more private, please?"

"I'm happy right here, Roger. Tell me why Missy doesn't like Victoria or her daughters."

What he tells me fits with what I had already surmised. Missy came from dirt poor, didn't finish school, had no place of her own, and was in some trouble with the police. He claimed he didn't know what that was about but thought it was about a guy. He guessed that was the reason she didn't like police.

Ronnie shows up while Roger is winding down. He sees her and asks, "Did you find everything, Detective?" I've pissed him off. Or he's regretting he left Ronnie in his office unsupervised.

I say to Ronnie, "Show him the pictures we have."

She pulls up pics of Vinnie, Duke, and Thundercloud and flips through them pausing at each one. Roger's eyes shift when he sees the pictures of Duke and Thundercloud.

Ronnie says, "You've seen these guys before."

Roger turns his face away. "I don't know them."

Ronnie persists. "But you've seen them."

He just nods.

I say, "Come on, Roger. Lying to the police is not a good way to stay out of trouble. Talk to us. We won't tell them we even talked to you."

His head is on a swivel. He says, "Miss Marsh, I'm sorry for not speaking. I've seen the last two guys. The very last one is Len Thundercloud, an ex-employee. I think he's Missy's boyfriend."

Ronnie asks, "How long ago did you see either of those men?"

Roger looks at me, and I give him my best bad-girl look.

"I know Thundercloud was here visiting Missy about a week ago. They were in my office and she knows no one is allowed there but the management. I would have fired her but she's good at her job. She has a chip on her shoulder about some of our wealthier guests but she keeps it from them."

"Do you know if he's been here when Victoria was here? And I mean ever."

He shakes his head. "I just caught them the one time. But I've seen him in town with that other guy. Bellingham, I mean. Thundercloud scares me."

I wonder if Lucas asked the same questions and how much of a lead he has on us in finding any of the three. He could be at Missy's place right now.

"We're almost done, Roger. I need a favor from you."

"Anything, Detective."

"If Lucas asks you, we were never here today. We never talked. He's seriously looking at you as a suspect in Victoria's disappearance. Ronnie and I know that's a load of crap but he's very set on you being involved."

Roger's hand goes to his mouth. "Oh my god! I didn't do anything wrong. You have to believe me."

Ronnie says, "We believe you but you know Lucas."

He says, "You were never here. I'm sorry about the surveillance stuff. Lucas told me to keep it to myself. He was angry that I told you parts of it were missing. I didn't know..."

Ronnie puts a hand on his. "It's okay. We understand. We're going to help you."

Into prison if you are involved in any minuscule way. I say to Ronnie, "Ronnie, I was about to tell Roger that we might have a lead on your mom's whereabouts."

"You do?" Roger says.

I say, "The first picture we showed you is Victoria's brother. His name is Vinnie. We've located him and he's beating the bushes for her. When we leave here we're going back to the motel to meet up with him. We might not need the video footage, but it's always better to be thorough. Don't you think?"

"Was it this Vinnie who Missy saw that night?"

"I guess we'll know shortly. Ronnie is a pure genius when it comes to recovering deleted video files. And I might as well tell you since you've been a big help to us, we think Vinnie is involved in the disappearance. Something about gambling debts. It has nothing to do with the Indian casino if that's what you're thinking. The FBI are in charge of that part."

"I don't know what to say." Roger looks pale. He's been through the ringer once over his activities and might still be in Dutch with the FBI.

"Nothing to say, Roger. I may need to come back. I want you to think hard about anything you might know. And I want you to call me or Ronnie if you see anyone we're looking for."

He just nods his head. His lips are dry and his eyes are focused on the tabletop.

Ronnie says, "You don't want to be involved in this, Roger. You've skated a few times already and you only get so many chances. You find out what you can and call me. Maybe I won't find that you doctored the video and arrest you for tampering with evidence. Maybe worse."

Roger's face goes pale and we leave him sitting there with his mouth hanging open.

FIFTY-TWO

Back at the car Ronnie calls Missy's home and puts the call on speaker. The phone is answered by a drunk woman, bellowing, "What. Well, crap. Hang on." Clatter, clatter. "Dropped my damn cigarette." I hear a grunt and then, "Where ya' at?" I wonder if she's talking to someone else or the cigarette. Then, "Okay. What ya' want?"

"Mrs. Milligan," Ronnie says.

"I ain't a Milligan," the woman says. "I never married that bastard. All he ever gave me is a kid and an ungrateful one at that. What's she done now?"

"I'm Detective Marsh. My partner talked to Missy at the resort. We need to pass on some new information. She's not in trouble."

"Well, she's, uh, asleep."

Ronnie says, "Can you wake her? I think she'll want to hear what I have to tell her."

"Nope. I don't go in her room. Ever. I just pay the bills and feed her and my boy when he comes here," she says. "You got any kids, Detective." Before Ronnie can answer, she says,

"Didn't think so. Well, take my advice. Keep your legs together. Too late for me."

"Good advice, ma'am."

The woman laughs and it turns into a coughing fit. When she recovers she says, "You don't mean that but thank you for agreeing with me. No one else does. It's been nice talking to you but I got things to do before her highness gets her ass out of bed."

"One other thing," Ronnie says. "Do you know a guy named Thundercloud?"

"Oh, Good Lord!"

"So you know him?"

"I should. He's my son, but I don't really claim him. He's no good, that one. And before you ask, I don't know where he is and don't want to know or talk about him, so goodbye."

Ronnie hurriedly says, "Just one more thing, ma'am. Can you leave Missy a note?"

She sighs, and says, "This is it but keep it short. I got to look for something to write with." The phone clatters and I hear, "Well, shit fire." When she comes back she's yelling into the phone, and Ronnie holds it at arm's length. "Okay. Damn pen. Hang on." The phone clatters again and then she comes back. "Okay. This one's working. What do you want to tell her? Not like she'll pay attention. She don't like cops. Not me, you understand. I don't have a thing against cops."

"Just say we're meeting Vinnie in Bellingham."

"Hold on a dang minute." The phone is muffled, and I can hear her speaking to someone else but the words are unclear. "Who's Vinnie?"

"He's someone she's helping us look for."

"Spell the name for me."

Ronnie does; it's like teaching calculus to a two-year-old. She has to repeat the phone number several times.

"Okay. I don't know if she can read my writing but I'll put it on her door."

"Thank you, ma'am. Have you seen Missy's boyfriend?"

She laughs. "Which one? Boyfriend. That's a good one. She's having it on with my no-good boy. How's that for a mental issue?"

"Tell her to call us. Thank you, ma'am."

"Ronnie, ask her if Roger called?" I say, but the call goes dead.

Ronnie and I look at each other in disbelief and a little disgust. Thundercloud is Missy's brother. How sick is that? Next stop, Whatcom County lockup.

We're shown into the sheriff's office right away as if he's expecting us.

"Glad to see you, ladies," Longbow says and indicates two chairs. We sit. "I hope you don't think I run a half-assed outfit. I've got everyone available looking for Duke. It's not the first time something like this has happened. Duke's been a good trusty in the past. I don't know what made him run, but I hope it doesn't have anything to do with him talking to you and Lucas."

Captain Roberts, the jail commander, knocks on the door frame. "You wanted me, Sheriff?"

"Anything on Duke?" Longbow asks.

"Nothing new, Sheriff."

A trusty is in the hallway with a floor cleaner running. Roberts tells the man. "Turn that off for a minute, Ludwig." The machine goes silent but the trusty doesn't leave. Good. I want him to hear this and pass it on.

Roberts says, "I've talked to all the trusties and staff. No one had any idea he was going to skedaddle."

Skedaddle. I haven't heard that word for a while. Sheriff Gray used to say it. He'd say, "Why don't you skedaddle off home." I'm sure Ronnie will look the word up when we leave here.

Longbow says to us, "What can you tell me? It might help us figure out what's got up Duke's ass. Excuse my language, ladies."

The trusty is still there. Ronnie says, "We've been looking for my mom and her brother, Vinnie, called last night and said he needed to talk to her. He mentioned Duke. He also mentioned someone named Thundercloud."

Sheriff Longbow and Captain Roberts exchange a look but say nothing.

I ask, "Is that name familiar to either of you?"

Longbow has a disgusted look on his face when he says, "Yeah. We know Thundercloud."

Roberts says, "He's a frequent flyer here. Bad dude. Dangerous. He was a cell boss. Do you know what that means?"

I do but I shake my head.

"We always had him locked up with the worst ones. He was feared even among that lot. His reputation is he bit a prisoner's ear off. The whole cell, that's twenty inmates, were scared of him and did whatever he said. He'd take their commissary. Stuff like that. If someone disrespected him, he'd have a few inmates pound the guy into hamburger meat. Sorry for the image but there's no other way to describe it. He was a trusty a very short time but spent most of his time here mostly in isolation."

"Was he ever a trusty when my uncle was one?" Ronnie asks.

"Could have been," Roberts says. "They're both gamblers."

Ronnie says, "They gamble in here?"

"They do a lot of things in here. We keep the worst of it out, but we don't have enough jailers to do much good." Roberts asks, "Any idea what Vinnie was going to tell you? Did he tell anyone?"

"No."

Longbow asks, "Do you know how to contact your uncle? Maybe he knows where our runaway is hiding."

"He's coming to Bellingham to meet us," I say. "I was hoping someone here knew where Duke was. Duke is Vinnie's only friend. Now Duke is gone and we were hoping he could get the truth out of Vinnie about his sister."

Sheriff Longbow looks at Roberts. Roberts says, "I've talked to everyone. Inmates. Staff. Kitchen help. No one has a clue."

Ronnie sighs. "Well, it was worth a shot." She hands Roberts a card. "Call me if you hear anything. Anything at all. I'm..." Her words trail off, and I put an arm across her shoulder.

"It'll be okay, Ronnie. We'll find her," I say, and look up at Longbow and Roberts with what I hope are sad and pleading eyes. Ronnie wipes a real tear from the corner of her eye with a knuckle. I didn't teach her that.

We get up and I say, "Well, thank you, gentlemen, for everything you've done. I'll get her home." Ronnie is making that ugly "I'm gonna cry" face and more tears roll. She even convinces me. Maybe it's not an act.

We get outside and I put my hand on Ronnie's arm. "Are you okay?"

She giggles. "How was that? Do you think I got their sympathy?"

Too good. "It was okay."

"Just okay? I should get an Oscar."

"Okay. I'll admit you did an excellent crybaby act. Even the ugly face was convincing." I smile on the inside. "Let's go."

FIFTY-THREE

To spread word that Vinnie's in Bellingham, we plan to go to Custer to the No Name Bar and then back to Lynden to the Word of the Lamb shelter. We arrive at the crossroads in Custer and get out at the No Name Bar. It's well after noon and we haven't heard from Jack or Rebecca.

"We can eat lunch here if you've had your hepatitis shots," I say.

Ronnie found a picture of Missy on Facebook and saved it along with the pictures of Thundercloud and Duke and Vinnie. "Do you want to show these people the photos of everyone?"

I was counting on it. I don't think the kidnapper will do anything to Victoria and risk getting nothing. I don't tell Ronnie this. I'm risking her mom's well-being on my gut feeling. "It's going on six days, Ronnie. We need to push the kidnappers and find your uncle. Jack *will* pay the kidnappers, won't he?"

"He will. I'm sure of it."

I'm not sure of anything. But this is Ronnie's family.

It looks like the same pickup trucks are parked outside. We enter and the regulars are debating the consequence of not paying their taxes. The conversation stops and all eyes are on Ronnie. The bartender, Tammy, doesn't look up and says, "Put your teeth back in your mouth, Hank." No one laughs. Hank swallows loudly.

Hank wants to say something so badly that if I had a needle, I could burst him like a balloon. I preempt him and introduce Ronnie.

"Hi, Hank. This is my partner, Detective Ronnie Marsh. She's armed. So am I. Play nice or I'll shoot you in the leg. Maybe the middle one."

This causes a chorus of laughs, and those near Hank thump him on the back.

Tammy grins and says, "She got you good, you old bastard."

"Who you calling old?" Hank says, and one of the boozers sputters beer in a fine mist and wipes his mouth with his sleeve.

I say, "A round of drinks on me." If you want cooperation, mention anything free, especially liquor.

One of the drunks asks, "What're we celebratin', princess?"

"You all helped me solve my case. I thought I'd buy you a drink." To Tammy I say, "We need to get some lunch. What do you have?"

"Cheese pizza or cheese pizza. Your pick."

"We'll split the cheese pizza. Burn it."

"Brown?"

"Cremated." I hate burned pizza but I have to play the tough girl. I should order a Scotch in a dirty glass but I'm not that crazy.

Tammy unwraps a frozen pizza and sticks it in an air-cooker then starts replenishing drinks for our audience. "What do you want to drink, ladies?"

"Diet Coke for me. Water with lemon for Ronnie. We're still on duty."

Hank says, "Good call. You wouldn't want Tommy Tittle to

get you for drunk drivin'.'" They guffaw and raise their drinks to me in a toast. "Here's to the best women detectives I know."

Another drunk says, "They're the only women detectives you know, Hank."

"The best damn lookin' ones I've seen anyway."

I cock an eye at him. "Remember we're armed, Hank."

"Yes'm." He puts on a solemn face.

"Say thank you," I say to all of them.

They all say thanks.

Tammy brings our drinks. My Diet Coke is in an ice-cold can. The water is in a bottle. She leans across and whispers, "We're out of lemon and I don't expect you'll stay long enough to eat the pizza. Why are you really here?"

"Tammy, I need your help again." She hadn't helped last time but a girl can hope. "We're looking for some other people now."

Tammy holds a hand out, and Ronnie puts enough money on the bar for another round of drinks and the pizza for us. Tammy scoops it up and stuffs it down the front of her tank top. She's not wearing a bra. Or deodorant either. "And you don't want these yahoos knowing nothing, am I right?"

"I want you to listen to us tell them something and call me if anyone makes a call or says anything after we leave. Will you do that?"

She nods.

I say loud enough to overcome the slurping and burping at the bar, "Take a look at these pictures, Tammy. We're trying to find them. Anything you can tell us will be appreciated." I show her the pictures of Thundercloud, Missy, and Duke—and Vinnie last. She recognizes Vinnie and Thundercloud. I can tell by her eyes. She takes my phone and slides it down the bar in front of the men. They gather around Hank, and he flips through the photos of the two men.

Hank says, "That's Vacuum Vinnie," and points to the picture of Vinnie. "I don't know the other." They all look then shake their collective heads and go back to their drinks. We do the same with the pictures of Missy and Duke with the only response being whistles at the picture of Missy. I guess free booze only buys so much. Tammy hands the phone back, then slides the pizza out of the air-fryer onto a couple paper plates and covers this with a wad of paper towels creating a makeshift to-go box. Our cue to leave. We leave.

Back in the parking lot Ronnie holds the pizza in her lap and hands me a piece on one of the paper towels. "Tough crowd," she says.

I take a bite and almost break a tooth on the hard crust. "Tough pizza too." I ignore the littering law and pitch the pizza out of the window. Ronnie does the same and settles for her water.

"This seems like a wasted trip," she says.

"We're going to Lynden. Nothing is wasted." Except the pizza. And Ronnie's money. "Call Rebecca and see where we're at with the motel."

"Maybe we should go to Missy's mother's place. We might find Thundercloud. Someone else was there when we were talking."

"We're not ready to talk to him yet. I just want to know where he is. Maybe a drive-by won't hurt. Can you check and see if he has any vehicles registered to him?"

Tammy knocks on the window. Megan powers it down, and Tammy is holding a bulging black trash bag. "You see what my customers are like. I can't say nothing in there or I wouldn't have any customers at all. Show me the pictures again. The ones of the guys with scarred faces."

Ronnie pulls the photos up on her iPad to make them larger. Tammy stops her at Thundercloud's photo. "I've seen him." She takes the iPad to get a closer look. "Yep. He was in here right after you and the rude cop were here."

She means Lucas. I ask, "What did he want?" I don't ask if Hank or his comedy crew had seen him. It doesn't matter.

"He was asking about Vinnie. Said he was a friend and had some news for him. I might 'a messed up."

I ask, "What do you mean, Tammy?"

"I might 'a told him some cops were looking for Vinnie too. Hank might 'a told him about the VW camper that Vinnie bought. I should 'a known he was lying. Vinnie doesn't have any friends as far as I know. But this guy was one scary looking man. Is he in trouble?"

I say, "We're going to arrest him for P.U. Public Ugliness."

Tammy chuckles. "In that case you'd better take everyone in my bar."

We thank her, and Tammy heads off to the trash bin.

"Thundercloud is looking for my uncle," Ronnie says. "He just made the top of my list of suspects."

"Along with Duke and Missy," I say.

Ronnie gets on her iPad. "I'm sending the pictures to Officer Nelson's phone. He can check with the shelter and save us some time."

"Good idea. There's still one person here we need to show."

There's no traffic so I run the stop sign hoping Tommy Tittle, the town constable I'd met earlier in No Name Bar, is hiding behind a billboard. Maybe he'll stop me and help us spread the word or at least listen in at the bar. But Tittle's not taking the bait. I don't wait for Ronnie to finish to see if we're going to Lynden or to Bellingham and pull out of Tammy's place running the stop sign. I then make a U-turn and run the stop sign again going toward Bellingham.

Ronnie gets off the phone. "You just ran that stop sign, Megan."

"Sorry. I was thinking." I was thinking there's never a cop around when you need one.

"I texted Nelson and he'll do that for us. I texted Rebecca too. She rented all the rooms at the Ocean View Motel."

Before I can ask where the Ocean View Motel is, a black car with wig-wag lights in the grille speeds up behind us almost tapping my bumper. The siren is blasting the peaceful stillness I'd been enjoying. I pull over, and a policeman in a khaki uniform, straw Western hat, large gold badge, cowboy boots and big mirrored aviator glasses saunters to my window.

"Ma'am," he says, and tips the silly hat.

"Officer Tittle," I respond.

"I'm afraid I'm going to have to cite you for running that traffic sign back there."

"I'm afraid too, Officer Tittle." I fake a shudder, and he chuckles.

He pulls a ticket book from his back pocket and writes something on it; not enough to be a citation. "I'm not really going to write you a ticket, Detective Carpenter. Who's your friend?" He lowers his sunglasses almost comically and assesses Ronnie.

"She's a murder suspect and she's holding me hostage. Help."

His jaw comes unhinged, and I have to quickly say, "Detective Ronnie Marsh. My partner. This is Officer Thomas Tittle. He's the law here."

He says, "I knew you was kiddin'."

He really didn't.

He says, "You got some quick come-backs, Detective Carpenter. That's good. Us lawmen—and women—he tips his hat, need to have a quick mind. Like for example I know'd you was trying to get my attention when you blew through the stop sign. Smart. And a' course I had to come after you to make it look real."

Ronnie looks at the ticket and there are smiley faces drawn across the form. She smiles, leans across me, and offers her hand. He holds it longer than necessary. She says, "Megan has told me about you. She said we can count on you, Constable."

His smile widens with each word.

"You can call me Tommy."

"Ronnie," she says, and has to ask for her hand back. "That's some grip, Tommy."

"I work out at the gym in Bellingham. Us lawmen have to keep in shape."

"Keep up the good work," I say, and want to gag. "We have some pictures to show you. Of course you can't tell anyone."

He puts two fingers to his lips and turns an imaginary key, which to me means he'll spill his guts to anyone and everyone.

"Ronnie will show you while you check her identification to make this look real."

He goes to Ronnie's window and checks out everything but her credentials. She shows him the photos of our quarry and in between lecherous looks he glances at each one. I hate using her like this. Actually, I don't.

Ronnie tells him the names. "These are persons of interest in a kidnapping."

Constable Tittle examines the photos and quickly points to the ones of Duke and Thundercloud. "I've seen these two guys together in Bellingham. I was taking a prisoner to the jail there since it's the closest and they were on the street across from the gym I go to. That was three weeks ago. I can get the date for you if you want."

"That's not necessary, Tommy," I say.

"The other guy is Vinnie, right?"

"Good eye," I tell him.

Ronnie says, "We showed these photos back at Tammy's bar so I would very much appreciate it if you would listen to the talk. Find out anything you can and call me."

She gives him a business card.

"I'll owe you. That's Megan and I'm Ronnie from now on."

His hand shakes visibly when he takes the card.

As we drive away, slowly, Ronnie buttons the top two buttons of her blouse.

I laugh. "You should be ashamed."

FIFTY-FOUR

Victoria comes to lying on her stomach in her own waste. Her hand hurts and she tries to move it, but it seems frozen and throbbing with excruciating pain. Her captors have left the light on. She rolls onto her back and attempts to sit up but the hand hurts too much to use. She examines it and where her hand should be is a stump wrapped with a filthy red bandana. First they took her finger and now her whole hand. She uses her good arm to sit up and cradles the injured stump in her lap. She can't stop looking at it. She can feel her hand, her fingers. How is that possible? She's heard about ghost pain from an amputated limb.

"My hand!" she cries out. "You bastards!"

Her breath is coming in hitches and screaming has made her nose bleed again.

"Dear God. Please save me. Please. I'll do anything you ask but please make this all go away. I want to go home," she says, and her throat feels like it's closing shut.

"Calm," she says. "Calm."

She coughs and blood spatters the top of her thighs.

She assesses her situation for her mind to have something to focus on besides her injuries. It doesn't help much but she is calming down. She tells herself not to scream. Not to draw attention because they'll come back.

FIFTY-FIVE
MARCH 2023

Whatcom County

The footage showed a beat-up black Nissan Frontier leaving the parking lot of the Semiahmoo Resort at 2:27 on Tuesday afternoon. It could be nothing, of course, but he couldn't pass up the coincidence of the kind of vehicle he was looking for being sighted in the area.

The quality of the video wasn't great, and the way the light reflected on the windshield meant there was no chance of getting a look at the driver anyway, but the license plate was visible as the car reversed out of the spot. This one wasn't an Ohio plate, and Lucas hoped it wouldn't lead to a dead end like the other one had.

Lucas jotted the number down and called Kelly at the station to run the plate. A minute later, she came back with a name and an address. A Duke Scanlon of 216 Burnham Street in Bellingham. The address was only five miles from the resort, and when Lucas looked up the quickest route, he saw that it would take him across the bridge over the creek where Olivia Greenwood's body had been found.

On the drive out, Sheriff Longbow called to say they were looking at recruiting a replacement for Larry, but it was liable to take a while, what with the budget cuts. That didn't bother Lucas. He had always worked better solo anyway, and having a partner like Larry Stroud had been worse than having no partner at all. He told Longbow he would like to be in on the process to make sure they got someone better this time.

"Don't worry, I'll want your take on whoever we pick," Longbow said. "How did your session with Dr. Wright go?"

"It went," Lucas said. "Why, did she call you again?"

"As a matter of fact, she did." Lucas could hear a smile in Longbow's voice. "She says she's impressed with your progress. Obviously she didn't go into detail, but it sounds like you said something right."

Lucas was pleasantly surprised. "Good to hear."

"I guess you worked out how to play her, then."

Lucas couldn't help but grin, tried not to let it show in his voice. "I have no idea what you're talking about, Sheriff."

Longbow laughed. "Anyway, keep up the good work. And let me know how you get on with the black Nissan."

As the sheriff hung up, Lucas reached the creek. He slowed as he crossed it, taking another moment to examine the scene in new light and conditions, and then sped up again when he reached the opposite side.

He reached the address of the registered owner of the Nissan Frontier five minutes later. It was an unassuming single-story house with white siding in a street of houses that looked similar. There was no black pickup truck in the driveway. Lucas parked at the curb and got out. The street was deserted, but then it wasn't the time of year for yard sales and kids running around outside. Was it ever the time of year for kids to be out of the house, these days?

He approached the door, keeping his eyes on the front of the house, alert for a twitch of blinds. There was a faded sticker underneath the doorbell with a big red NO at the top and then a list that included hawkers, salesmen, charities, religious groups, but not police detectives. Lucas pushed the bell and waited for a minute. He pushed it again and waited another minute, straining to hear any sounds from inside.

He stepped back from the door and glanced around the street. Still nobody around. He walked around to the back and found a small, paved backyard with a stack of tires in one corner and a garbage can in the other. The back door was locked. The window on the left of the door had a gap in the closed blinds inside. Lucas peered through the gap and saw a threadbare couch and a TV and an empty pizza box splayed open on the floor next to a crumpled can of Bud Light.

He took a pair of gloves from his pocket and walked over to the garbage can, slipping them on. He opened the can and wrinkled his nose at the smell. The remains of some Chinese food, an empty milk carton and some crumpled junk mail. He prodded around a little and saw that one of the items of mail wasn't junk. It was an envelope that had been opened and the letter stuffed back in before being tossed. Carefully, trying not to get sweet and sour sauce on his gloves, he extracted the envelope and removed the letter within.

It was a lease agreement on some property.

As Lucas was looking for a name, he heard the sound of tires on the road outside and springs creaking as a vehicle made a practiced turn onto a driveway. It sounded like it was this driveway. Lucas quickly folded the lease in half and slipped it into his pocket. He started walking back toward the front, removing the gloves as he walked.

The car that had pulled onto the driveway wasn't a Nissan Frontier, it was a blue Chevy Tahoe, and the guy getting out of the driver's side did not look happy to see a visitor on his property.

The guy looked like he might be in his forties, though that

could have been the acne scarring on his face making him look older. He wore white sneakers, blue jeans, and a leather jacket. A black tattoo showed on the skin of his left wrist. Lucas could feel the death stare from behind his sunglasses.

"Who the hell are you?"

Lucas took his badge out. "Sergeant Michael Lucas, Whatcom Sheriff's Department."

The guy took a step forward to take a closer look at his badge, then nodded at the back. "What were you doing around back?"

Interesting that he had asked that first, rather than the more standard, *Is there a problem, Sergeant?* Or even the blunter *Why are you here?*

"I knocked on the door and didn't get an answer, so I tried around the back." Lucas kept his voice casual, not a hint of defensiveness. "Are you Duke Scanlon?"

The guy opened his mouth to say something, then changed his mind, then glanced back at Lucas's car, probably checking if he had a partner.

"What's this about?"

"Are you Duke Scanlon?" Lucas asked again.

"No. Duke crashed here for a while after he got out of the joint. I let him use the address."

"I see. You got some ID?"

After a moment of hesitation, he reached into his back pocket, took out a wallet and handed over a driver's license.

"'Len Thundercloud'," Lucas read, then glanced over at the Chevy. "This your car?"

Thundercloud nodded.

"Do you also own a Nissan Frontier pickup?"

"What's it to you?"

Lucas put his badge back in his pocket, taking his time. He put his hands on his hips and looked past the guy at the Tahoe. There was a woman in the passenger seat, looking away from the two men on the driveway. He looked up at the sky, which seemed to be preparing for rain. He let about a minute elapse between the guy's question and his answer, taking all the time in the world.

"Look, if you want to make it official, we can do this down at the station. But if you can give me five minutes of your time, we can clear this up and I'll be on my way."

Thundercloud's eyes narrowed. "I think Duke does, I haven't seen him in a while."

"You know where I can find him?"

"Why would I?"

"You said he was a buddy."

"Drinking acquaintance. I don't know everything about him."

Lucas stared back at him, waiting for him to fill the silence. Eventually, Thundercloud relented.

"Ask over at the No Name in Chester."

"I will. When was the last time you saw him?"

"Why's that relevant?" he said, narrowing his eyes.

"Well, if I had to know what was relevant before I asked it, I wouldn't get very far. Humor me."

Thundercloud sighed. "I don't know. Last month?"

Lucas noted with approval that Thundercloud's initial hostility had abated since he had seen the badge. He just wanted to get this over with. But Lucas wasn't quite done.

He walked around to the passenger side of the Tahoe. The woman in the passenger seat was also wearing sunglasses. She had been watching the conversation intently but averted her gaze as Lucas approached. He tapped on the window with one knuckle. Reluctantly, the woman lowered the window. There was a purse in her lap. Lucas gestured at it.

"You got some ID in there?"

Without speaking, she took out her own license and handed it over without protestation. It identified her as Melissa Milligan, twenty-eight years old. Lucas took a mental note of the details.

"Do you live here, ma'am?"

She shook her head. "Just visiting."

"Do you know Duke Scanlon?"

She shook her head again.

Lucas didn't get the feeling he was going to get much out of her, but that was okay, he knew where to find her now.

"Are we done yet?" Thundercloud said from behind him.

Lucas took his time again before answering.

"Thanks for your cooperation."

He got back into the car and pulled away from the curb. Thundercloud stood in the driveway, still in that gunslinger pose—legs apart, arms suspended a little out from his sides—and watched him the whole way. His female companion still hadn't gotten out of the car.

Lucas took a right at the next corner, drove two blocks, and pulled into the forecourt of a gas station, leaving the engine running. He took the folded invoice from his pocket and flattened it out.

It was a lease agreement for a storage unit not far from the Semiahmoo Resort. Why would Thundercloud need a storage unit?

Lucas pulled up the map on his phone. The storage unit was part of a cluster of business premises. A part-worn tire place, a couple of garages. It was a little way out of the nearest town, probably deserted this late in the day.

He pulled out onto the road again and drove south.

FIFTY-SIX

We leave a mesmerized Tommy Tittle behind. "I should get a forensic sketch artist to do a composite drawing of your chest."

Ronnie blushes. "He forgot to give us the fictitious traffic ticket."

"Do you want to go back and talk to him?"

I'm not really jealous she gets all the attention. I've tried to keep a low profile my entire life. Attracting men has been the last thing I needed. Not that I can't charm some guy. I can. But that usually leads to questions about their life, my life, their past, my past. I have to lie. I've only had two, what you would call boyfriends in my entire life. One is Caleb Hunter whom I left behind a long time ago, before I became Megan Carpenter. The other is Dan Anderson whom I met during a couple of homicide investigations. He was one of the neighbors I interviewed and something just clicked. I tried to deny I had an interest in him, although he's big and muscular and handsome and not clingy and polite and a pleaser. None of that crossed my mind when he asked me out the first time.

Dan and I have been through some rough things together. Scary things. Things that either make you grow closer or tear you apart. He learned some of my secrets when we were being tortured by a crazy woman, but luckily she had drugged him so his memories are hazy. He forgave me for getting him into that mess. I don't know why. Yes, I do. He loves me. He's never said it but I can tell. At least I think I can tell. No one has ever been in love with me before. Not even Caleb. Dan has never grilled me about any of my past, or pursued learning about my family. He knows Hayden is my brother and to my knowledge has never asked Hayden about our past. Actually he's been extra kind and understanding and that scares the hell out of me. I'd rather face a maniac with a gun than feel the pain of real love. Love is foreign. Love is demanding. Love is weakness. Love is limiting. Love is beautiful and I feel guilty about holding it at arm's length. Holding Dan at arm's length. But I'm working on it.

I slow down and pull off onto the dirt shoulder. "Let's go get the ticket from your new boyfriend." I need to tease her now and then. It helps me keep my shit together.

"Stop it, Megan."

I drive off again, and she says, "But he was kind of cute. A little weird."

"A lot weird," I say. Gag me with a spoon weird. But then, she thinks Marley Yang is cute. I think Marley's disgusting and desperate. But useful. "You'd better not let Marley hear you say things like that." Marley was married when I introduced him to Ronnie. I knew he was married but I didn't count on those two hitting it off. And I didn't know he was separated from his wife. Or that he has children. But in my defense, I didn't really care. That's the kind of person I was.

But no longer. I care about people. Well, some people, anyway. And I hope Marley gets his shit together and doesn't hurt Ronnie. She's not as strong as I am. She's not as bitchy as I am. But one thing I can say for her. She never gives up.

I continue on Interstate 5, no traffic, no problem. "I'm sorry for teasing you, Ronnie. If I didn't like you, I wouldn't torture you," and that makes her smile. I'm beginning to think I could say "shoehorn" and she'd laugh. Nothing ventured...

"Shoehorn."

"What?"

"Never mind. Tittle said he recognized Duke."

Ronnie reminds me, "He said he recognized Thundercloud too. He might still have some intel for us. He said he'd call."

Yeah. He'll be the one breathing hard into the phone.

It's not hard to find the motel Rebecca rented but I drive past it. "Let's see if we can spot anyone around the Mom & Pop store." It's a longshot, but sometimes I get lucky.

I park in front of the store and there are no other cars around. That is, if you don't count the ones up on cinder blocks.

I'm about to get out when my phone buzzes in my pocket. The number is withheld. A chill travels down my spine. For some reason, I'm certain I know who's calling. It's him.

It's Wallace.

I answer, trying to keep the dread out of my voice. "Detective Megan Carpenter, who's calling?"

There's a pause and then a female voice answers. "This is Detective Anderson, Cincinnati PD. I believe you were looking to speak to Detective MacDonald."

"That's right," I say, relieved. I had forgotten all about the message I left earlier. "Thanks for calling back, is MacDonald available?"

"I'm afraid not, he retired last Christmas. I worked with him on the Greenwood murder, though. I believe that was what you wanted to speak to him about."

"Great, yes."

I give her the short version of the last few days. She gives me a "hmmm" that I find impossible to decipher when I mention Lucas's name. When I've finished bringing her up to speed, I ask her a couple of questions about her case.

"Lucas said there was suspicion the husband did it. Do you think so?"

"I don't know," Anderson said. "My partner certainly did."

"But you didn't have enough to nail him."

"That turned out to be the least of our problems. He killed himself not long after his wife was found."

"No kidding," I say, genuinely surprised. *Why the hell didn't Lucas tell me that?*

"After that, with no firm leads, I guess the momentum went out of the investigation. Most people took the suicide as an admission of guilt."

"Most. But not you?"

She hesitates. "I don't know. Lucas went back to Whatcom County. He seemed to think he was on the right track and then... nothing. I guess he hit a dead end too. Happens to the best of us, right?"

"Right," I say. And I'm thinking that Lucas isn't the best of us. I remember his boast about closing every case. What about this one?

Ronnie and I discuss the call briefly after I hang up. It's interesting, but there's still no solid link to her mom's disappearance. I remember why we're here and look up at the building.

Ronnie opens her door. "I'll go in."

"We'll both go in."

I go around to the side door first and look in the foyer and up the stairs. No one. No sound. I meet Ronnie at the front and we enter. The inside is the opposite of spic and span, with shelves stocked with mostly snack foods and Ramen noodles, all covered with a coating of dust. A cooler is near the counter filled with beer and sodas. A little woman comes from behind a shelf at the back of the store and says, "What you want?"

The lady is olive skinned, wrinkled, almost half my size, and three times my age. Maybe seventy years old, thin as a rail, dark hair worn close to the scalp. She's wearing an apron so large I can barely see her feet.

Ronnie and I take out our badge holders and hold them up. "Police, ma'am," Ronnie says, and the woman makes a shooing motion.

"No call police. You go."

Ronnie seems undecided what to do so I act as interpreter, pull my jacket back showing my gun. "Police business," I say.

She isn't intimidated by the gun but she motions us toward the front counter.

We meet her at the counter, and I show her my credentials again. "I'm Detective Carpenter and this is Detective Marsh."

She reaches for my credentials and I let her examine them. She takes a pair of cheap reading glasses from the counter and looks at the photo, the badge, and, unfortunately, the Jefferson County seal.

She pushes it back across to me and says, "You no police here. You go."

Ronnie leans against the counter. "I told you she wouldn't talk to us without the Health Department and Code Enforcement."

"You all alike. What you want?"

Ronnie pulls up the photos on her iPad and turns the screen where we can all view it. "Do you recognize any of these people?"

The lady glances at the pictures and then asks, "They in trouble. No come here."

"Look again," Ronnie insists.

She looks more carefully and then says, "No. Don't know."

I noticed her eyes when she looked at the photo of Duke. "One more time," I say. "Look closely. It's a crime to lie to a detective."

She points to the picture of Duke. "He come here. Rent apartment. I kick him out. Too loud and make a mess upstairs."

Ronnie zooms in on Vinnie's picture and points at it. "Does he come here? Did he rent with the other one?"

She shakes her head and puts the glasses back on the counter.

I say, "We need to look upstairs. We'll arrest them if they come here so you don't have trouble with them. Okay?"

She comes out from behind the counter and takes us to the door leading to the foyer for the upstairs entrance. She opens the door and walks away.

Ronnie and I check the upstairs rooms. It's a bust. Still dirty and no one home.

"It was worth a try," Ronnie says.

We're about to leave by the side door when I have a thought and go back into the store. The woman sees me and stops moving things on the shelf. I ask, "What did you mean police are all alike?"

"Man detective already here. He leave. Good riddance."

FIFTY-SEVEN

"Semiahmoo Resort, Roger Whiting speaking. How may I help you?"

"Turn the cameras off." The voice is unmistakable.

Roger goes into his office and looks at the monitors. A man wearing a red ball cap with a black hoodie pulled over it is at the employee entrance behind the resort. He picks up the call in the office and says, "I'm not supposed to be talking to you. You promised to keep me out of this."

"Turn the cameras off, Roger. I won't tell you again. I just want to talk. You have nothing to worry about. I'll stay on the line until you tell me they're off."

"Uh, okay." Roger logs in to the surveillance system and turns it off. "It's off. I can't keep doing this or they will get suspicious." No answer. "Are you there? Hello?"

"I'm right here."

Roger turns and his voice fails him.

"I know you've been talking to the cops, Roger."

Roger starts to protest but Thundercloud clamps a hand down on his shoulder and squeezes hard. "You gave Missy up, and they know I was living with her. They know I worked here. What else have you told them?"

Roger tries to pull away, but one hand covers his mouth and the other goes to his throat and shoves him backward into the desk.

FIFTY-EIGHT

I park on the gravel lot of the fabulous Ocean View Motel. The building is a squat, flat-roofed, boxcar type construction dating back to WWII, complete with peeling flamingo-pink paint, gingerbread trim, windows held together with duct tape, rusted A/C units, and the whole shebang covered in bird shit. It's a mile at least from an ocean view or any water unless the plumbing leaks. Ronnie makes a face, and I say, "It's perfect."

Rebecca calls. "Ronnie, are you at the motel?"

"You rented a nice place," Ronnie says sarcastically.

"You don't need to go to the office. There won't be anyone there today. Dad had them leave until tomorrow morning. The keys are on the bed in Room 4."

Ronnie says, "That's great. How'd he get the manager to leave?"

"He paid handsomely and gave the manager/owner a free night at the resort, meals included."

Rebecca says, "Oh, and one thing I forgot to do before you left here was to have you take my car. Megan's police car will scare them off. I'm sure you have a plan."

I'd thought of that but I didn't have a plan. "We'll wing it, Rebecca. I'll park my unit nearby."

Rebecca says, "Also, Dad had the manager put a NO VACANCY sign in the office window."

"Thanks, Rebecca. We'll stay in touch," I say.

The door to Room 4 is unlocked. There are two full size beds complete with six possible contagions. "So I guess Rebecca and Jack won't be joining us?"

Ronnie chuckles. "This isn't somewhere Dad would stay. He would burst into flames."

Good one. But that remark has me again thinking about Victoria. Where could they be holding her? I doubt her kidnappers have the money to buy out a motel for their purposes, but there are plenty of abandoned buildings and structures around here. I've had some experience with being held captive. It's not anything I want to think about.

Ronnie sits on the edge of one bed. "Is this really a good idea?"

It's either here or the Beverly Hilton. "Trust me." I open the curtain, signaling to the populace that this room is occupied.

Ronnie says, "Maybe this is unkind of me since I don't really know him, but this looks like a place Uncle Vinnie would stay."

My sentiments exactly. We're not looking for rich people. The kidnappers will be more at ease coming here. It's just the kind of place Vinnie would stay if he wasn't living in the back of a junked van.

Ronnie checks out the bathroom and opens a window in there for a breeze if we keep the front door open. She stands by the open front door and says, "I don't know about you but I could really go for a salad and a soft drink."

I could go for a pound of ribs and a box of wine. I don't see how she can eat salads. We can't order out and I have to move my SUV anyway. "If you can keep watch, I'll pick up something to eat."

"You know what I like. Don't hurry. We may be here all night," she says.

She jinxed us saying that out loud, but I agree. This is a Hail Mary Pass. I'm about to leave when a very large man steps inside and pulls the door to.

We both draw our guns, and he holds his hands up and says, "Hattie told me about Victoria Marsh, that somebody took her."

"Who the fuck are you?"

"I'm Vincent Lombardi," he says. "I'm told you've been looking for me."

We are speechless.

"Can I put my hands down now?" he says after a minute.

He's larger than the information we'd gotten on him. I knew the photos of Vinnie weren't recent but I wasn't expecting this. Vinnie is over six feet tall with bulging muscles. The face looks like the Vinnie we were told about, but Jack had told us Vinnie was Victoria's little brother. There's nothing little about this guy.

Before I can ask a question, he puts a large hand out to Ronnie. "I guess you're my niece. Ronnie, right?"

"You know me?"

"Of course. Vic showed me pictures of you growing up. And I've seen you in the news." He looks at me and says, "You're Detective Carpenter."

Ronnie takes his hand and says, "We've been looking everywhere for you."

"I try to stay under the radar. Where's Rebecca?"

FIFTY-NINE

Rebecca calls for an update. Ronnie tells her, "We found Uncle Vinnie. Or rather he found us. Maybe don't tell Dad quite yet."

"What did he tell you?"

"We haven't asked many questions yet. I'll call you."

"Here's an idea. How about we FaceTime and I can meet my uncle. I'll go out back."

Ronnie says, "I'll put it on my iPad so we can all see each other. I'll call you back in a minute."

Ronnie tells Vinnie and me what she's decided, and we all gather on the sofa with the iPad on the stained coffee table. Rebecca accepts the call and her face comes up in a box on the side of the screen.

"Hi Rebecca," Vinnie says, and Rebecca gapes, speechless. She's never met this man in her life.

She finally says, "Uncle Vincent."

"In the flesh. I've always wanted to meet you and your sister. I'm so sorry for not being around to watch you two grow up."

I look at this man and he has tears in his eyes and the sisters are dabbing at theirs. I say, "I'll let you talk. I'm going to watch the street." That's why we were here. We've found Vinnie but the kidnappers could show up at any time. Ronnie starts to stand but I say, "I've got this. You visit. When you're ready to ask some questions, let me know."

The curtain is still open and I lean against a wall where I can see most of the street without being seen. If someone comes up and looks in the window, they're in for a nasty surprise. I just hope Vinnie is what he appears to be. If he hurts my friends, I'll make him pay.

They've talked for ten minutes or more when Ronnie says, "Megan."

"I'll watch and you can ask the questions." If she misses something, I'll ask it.

Ronnie says, "First of all, Rebecca, where is Dad, and have you gotten any more messages?"

"Dad went for a walk in the woods. He said he needs some space. He's got his phone and if I get a call, I can put you on hold."

Ronnie says, "If you get a call, don't forget to record it."

"Gotcha."

Ronnie asks, "Uncle Vinnie, are you ready to answer some questions?"

Vinnie is still wiping at his eyes with the back of his shirt sleeve. "Anything I can do to help, I'll do. Ask your questions."

Ronnie doesn't miss a beat. She's thorough and asks for clarification when there is any ambiguity in the answer. She ends with, "Did you go to Semiahmoo Resort to see Mom?"

"No. Did someone say I was there?" he asks.

Answering a question with a question is usually a sign of a lie, or a delay tactic. But my gut tells me he's telling the truth.

"Did you and Mom have nicknames for each other when you were kids?"

Good question.

"Is that important?"

"Answer, please, and when we're done I'll tell you what we know. Okay?"

He nods. "Sorry. I'm a little awkward sometimes. Yes. We had nicknames for each other. She called me 'Luigi' like the character in the *Mario Brothers* video game. We played that every chance we got. Of course we didn't have anything like that at home but we had friends."

"And what was Mom's nickname?"

"Dinky. Because she was so little when we were kids."

"And you didn't go to the resort to see Mom?"

"Your dad owns the resort. I've never been there. I don't think I'd be welcome."

Ronnie pulls a picture up on her cell phone and shows it to Vinnie. It's the note left on Victoria's door when she went missing. She doesn't ask him if he wrote it. Good tactic. Let him talk.

"That's the nickname I called her, still do, but it looks like a child wrote that. What's that about?"

She ignores his question. "You were in Whatcom County Jail a few weeks ago. How did you get released?" she asks.

"I think you already know, but your mom bailed me out. We had lunch, talked about some things, and went our separate ways."

"What did you talk about?"

"Do I have to say?"

Rebecca, who has been quiet this entire time, says, "Uncle Vinnie, just answer the questions. Mom is missing and we don't have time to waste."

Vinnie's shoulders slump. When he looks up he says, "I don't know if Victoria would want me to talk about it."

For God's sake, spit it out.

"Well, I guess you'll find out eventually." Vinnie's eyes take on an angry look. "She said she was going to divorce Jack. She'd had enough. She asked me if I thought she should. She was worried about how it would affect you girls."

"We know about that," Rebecca says.

"Then you know that Jack and I don't get along. I don't like the way he treats her and she was kept from her own family. Sorry, but it's the truth."

No one speaks for several minutes, so I ask, "Do you think Jack could be behind her kidnapping?"

He doesn't answer right away. He thinks Jack could be involved. That doesn't mean he's right, but at least he's thinking.

"How long has my sister been missing?" he asks.

"Six days," Rebecca says.

"And she's missing from the resort and that's where you found the note you're asking about?" he asks.

"Did you leave it on her door?" Ronnie asks.

"No. I did not. I have never been to the resort. But something is starting to make sense."

Dragging things out unnecessarily must be a genetic trait in the Marsh family. They answer a question with a question, say "guess what" and "You'll never believe this," along with their innate intelligence. Maybe that's how geniuses think.

"I was on my way over here and saw Duke. Do you know Duke?"

Ronnie pulls up his photo.

"Yeah. That's him. He doesn't look like much but he's got an IQ that's off the charts. Dope and gambling are his Achilles' heel. Anyway, I saw him on the street getting into a black SUV a little while ago. I thought he was making a drug deal, but he didn't come out of the SUV."

I ask, "What about Duke makes sense to you?"

"Well, wherever Duke is, Thundercloud is nearby. They're thick as thieves. And that's what they do. Steal. Deal drugs. Rob people. And now that I think about it, it looked to me like that SUV was watching this place. I wouldn't put anything past Duke and Thundercloud. If they've hurt Vic, I'm going to kill them."

Ronnie asks, "Would either of them know your nickname for Victoria?"

Vinnie asks, "You think one of them put the note on Vic's door? To what? Frame me for her disappearance?" He doesn't need time to think about that. "Yeah. Duke knew I called her Dinky. She brought me money sometimes when Duke was around. The three of us were in jail at the same time. Duke, me, and Thundercloud. But I stayed away from Thundercloud. Completely crazy that one is. Everyone in the jail was afraid of him. We've butted heads a few times. He made some nasty remarks about Victoria and the guards had to break us up. What an asshole."

Vinnie makes fists. "Either one of them might have written that note to try and frame me. But I can't see Duke taking Vic. He's a coward. Thundercloud would be my bet." Vinnie gets a worried look on his face but he doesn't say anymore.

We hear a commotion in the background behind Rebecca, and Jack comes rushing out the back door, saying, "Rebecca. Come quick. Call Ronnie to come home."

SIXTY

Ronnie drives. She knows a shortcut only using part of Interstate 5 North then backroads. We make it to Cougar Point in twenty minutes instead of thirty-five. If I had driven, we would have made it faster even on the Interstate. When we pull up out front, Rebecca is waiting in the driveway for us. Vinnie stays in the vehicle.

"Oh, Ronnie!" Rebecca cries. "Dad's in the kitchen. Come quick."

Ronnie jumps out and chases after her sister. I get out and look at Vinnie. "You coming in?" I ask.

"I don't want to cause trouble."

"I'll protect you," I say, and pat my gun.

"I'm not afraid of Jack," he says, "I don't want to have to hurt him in front of my nieces. God knows what they've been told about me."

"Suit yourself," I say, and go after Ronnie.

Ronnie and Rebecca are standing around Jack, who is seated at the table. In front of him are Ronnie's laptop and a shoebox with bloodstained sides.

Another gift. The kidnappers are enjoying this. Jack has

gotten the money ready but they still push him with brutality. Jack looks like a broken man. Anger is the only thing propping his daughters up. I watch Ronnie's mouth set and see the murderous rage straining to be released.

Ronnie leans over Jack's shoulder and reaches for the box, but Jack's hand stops her.

Rebecca says, "A flash drive was with the box." She opens the laptop and starts a video.

The screen is dark and the sound of screaming blasts from the speaker.

A woman's voice yells, *"Hold still, damn it."* More screams and a different voice pleads. *"Don't do this. He'll pay. He'll get the money."* The first voice says, *"I'll cut your head off if you don't stop moving."* The other voice pleads and the panic in the voice is palpable. *"I can get the money. Just let me talk to him. I can take you to the bank. I have the money in the bank."*

Another scream and then the picture zooms in on the scene.

A woman wearing a ski mask and camouflage jacket has another woman spreadeagled on the floor while a big man holds the woman down. The man is also wearing a ski mask and camo hunting fatigues. The woman on the floor is naked and filthy.

I want Jack to stop the video so I can see them better but it's impossible to stop looking.

The man kneels in the woman's back with one knee on her neck crushing her face into the floor while the other woman kneels on the naked woman's forearm. She's holding a small hand ax, and I watch in horror as she raises it overhead and brings it down on the other woman's wrist. The screams that follow are animalistic and taper off to a whimper and then are stilled. The naked woman goes limp, and the man says, *"You were just supposed to get her fingers, you bitch."* The hatchet wielding one says, *"Shut up. You don't have the stomach for this. Besides this bitch had it coming. I hope she bleeds to death."* The man says, *"Give me that."* The camera jerks and then crashes to the floor and the screen goes blank.

Ronnie pulls the box over in front of us, and Rebecca says, "I can't. I just can't. I'm sorry."

She leaves the room but Jack just sits, dumbstruck.

Ronnie lifts the top from the box and lets it fall to the table. Her hand goes to her chest and she lets out a wail and starts pacing, alternately clutching her fists and grinding her teeth.

Rebecca comes back and stops Ronnie's pacing and hugs her tightly while Jack sits staring at the box that contains a pale hand with a wedding band still on the ring finger and the small finger is missing. Tears fill my eyes and my heart goes out to this family. If Victoria is still alive, she's being mutilated, slowly, painfully, one piece at a time.

The sisters are a wreck so I ask, "Jack. What happened? I'm sorry to ask but we may not have much time." I cringe at my own insensitivity but it's the truth. The kidnappers might be preparing another *gift* for Jack as we speak.

He looks at me and sucks in a deep breath and lets it out. "Can't you see what happened? What is wrong with you?"

"I guess I deserve that, Jack. I'm truly sorry." I am. "When you feel like it, please tell me and Ronnie how..." I stop there. I don't know how to ask how he got the hand so I just come out with it. They can hate me but I'm going to find Victoria. "How did the box get delivered? Did you have the cameras recording?" He's struggling to keep it together but the kidnappers are upping the game. That means I have to be insistent. "Talk to me, Jack."

Thankfully, Ronnie and Rebecca come out of it enough to talk.

Rebecca says, "Dad went for a walk in the woods behind the house. There are no cameras back there. He came in with the box and couldn't speak. Who could do such a thing?"

Feral animals can. The human kind. I say, "Where did you find the box, Jack?"

Rebecca says, "He hasn't told me. He said to call you and he hasn't spoken until you got here."

"Okay. We're here, Dad. Tell us," Ronnie says.

He takes Ronnie's hand and I don't think he's going to speak, but he does. "In the woods. A man. The box was on a stump and it struck me as odd that someone had left it there, but then I knew what it was. I didn't see the man until he spoke to me. He said I seemed to be having trouble obeying so he thought he would give me a hand. I suddenly knew what was in the box. I never thought they would do it. I asked him why and he laughed. He asked if I needed more proof of life. I started to go toward him. I wanted to kill him with my bare hands. He told me if I touched him, I'd get the rest of her in pieces. He asked if I had his money. I told him I had it. He said to give it to him and he'd let her go. I told him I wanted to see her. I'd give him the money if he'd take me to her. That was probably stupid, but I thought if I give him the money now, what's to keep him from killing her. I did the wrong thing, didn't I?" He looks like he's coming apart with grief and guilt and hopeless impotence. I've been there.

"You did right, Jack," I say. "Did you get a good look at him?" I ask but I'm hoping he didn't. If he let himself be seen all deals are off.

"It was the man. Not the woman. He was wearing gloves and a ski mask and a camo outfit."

"Could you see his eyes? What color?" I ask.

"What color? Hell. How could I know?"

"Anything distinctive about him?" I ask.

"Yeah. He's cut my wife's hand off and is threatening to kill her. I'd say that's distinctive enough. Wouldn't you?"

"Did you call Lucas?"

He shakes his head, and Rebecca immediately gets on the phone.

"We need him," I say. "Before he gets here can you tell me anything else. Anything at all."

"That"—he points at the flash drive—"was taped to the box."

He has been twisting a small piece of paper in his hands. He smooths it out and lays it on the table for us to read. Typed on it is one word.

TOMORROW

Rebecca finishes her call to Lucas and says, "He'll be here. He said not to touch anything."

Whoops.

A man's voice comes from the kitchen doorway. "Hi, Jack."

SIXTY-ONE
MARCH 2023

Whatcom County

The storage unit listed on the piece of paper Lucas had taken from Len Thundercloud's trash was the last one on a row of units. As he had expected, most of the businesses were closed, with the exception of the tire place. The unit on the bill was shuttered and looked like it hadn't been in use for some time.

He drove past it and pulled to a stop outside the tire place. A beefy guy with red hair wearing blue overalls sauntered out, giving his car a look up and down.

"Help you?" the guy said. He had a surprisingly high-pitched voice for a guy who had to weigh better than two-ten.

Lucas badged him. The guy didn't look too perturbed, which meant he probably wasn't the owner. He confirmed that when asked, and told him his name was Kayce Wallis.

Lucas asked Wallis if he had seen a black Nissan pickup truck recently.

He shook his head. "You mean a customer, or just in general?"

"Either."

"Sorry, can't help you."

Lucas pointed over at the shuttered unit. "You know who owns that one?"

Shrug. "Think it's vacant. Guy was there clearing it out a couple weeks ago."

"Can you describe him?"

Wallis looked over at the unit, calling up the memory, then looked back at Lucas. "Average height, maybe forty, dark hair. I think he had acne on his face."

Lucas nodded. Wallis wasn't telling him anything he didn't already know, but he seemed to be open and honest, which was good. He took his phone out and got Len Thundercloud's DMV headshot up, then held the screen out for him to have a look at. He tilted his head, thought about it, and said, "Yeah, that's him."

"Ever see him before last week?"

"Not that I remember."

"I don't suppose you have a key for that unit?"

"Sorry, guess you'd have to see the landlord for that."

"You know if he's rented it out yet?"

"Don't look like it."

Lucas smiled. Wallis wasn't falling over himself to be helpful, but he respected his straightforward manner.

"Thanks for your help." Lucas peered over his sunglasses. "You look a little familiar. You ever... help us out with anything?"

Wallis met his gaze and gave him the answer he was half expecting. "I did some stupid shit in my younger days."

"But not anymore, huh?" Lucas said, looking beyond him at the garage.

"No, sir."

"Good man. I'm just going to have a look around, you mind keeping an eye on my car?"

Wallis gave his car another look over and shook his head slowly. "I don't mind, sir."

Lucas walked over to the empty unit and examined the fresh padlock on the door. It was new, and it was definitely locked. He would try the landlord later but he didn't expect to find anything back there.

He walked around the back of the units. There was a partly asphalted road that petered out into a dirt track. He walked fifty yards along the track to see beyond the trees that encroached onto it and saw another structure with wood siding and a corrugated sheet metal roof. A faded sign advertised *Jessup & Co Salmon Cannery*.

Lucas turned and looked back toward the back of the line of units. He could hear the high whine of some kind of power tool from the tire place. No other signs of life. He took his phone out and googled Jessup & Co. Nothing came up other than a local history website which mentioned the place had closed in 1972.

He walked the rest of the way to the structure. The siding was rotted near the ground and the roof was rusty and holed in places, but it had weathered the last half-century well, considering. The front door was sealed with a sheet of steel that looked as though it had probably been there since '72. He walked around the back and found another door. This one wasn't sealed. And it had a padlock on it.

A new padlock, just like the one on the unit.

SIXTY-TWO

Vinnie remains in the kitchen doorway waiting for a response. Jack turns his chair sideways not looking at Vinnie. Rebecca takes Vinnie's arm and pulls him back into the hallway. I follow as she leads him down the hallway to the front of the house.

Rebecca says, "Uncle, something horrible has happened."

"To Vic?"

"Let's go out front and sit on the porch and I'll tell you. I need to sit down."

Vinnie stands looking toward the gate, hands in his pockets, jaw clamped shut.

"The kidnappers were here less than an hour ago," Rebecca says. "Dad said a man in the woods behind the house left a shoebox and told Dad he would kill Mom if he didn't start obeying."

"Obeying what?" Vinnie asks. He looks from Rebecca to me. I keep quiet for now.

I see tears appear in the corners of Rebecca's eyes, and she tells Vinnie everything that's happened from her and Victoria going to the resort, finding out Victoria was missing, the notes, the severed finger, and finally the video of the kidnappers chopping her mom's hand off. Vinnie sits and puts an arm around her shoulders.

"They cut her hand off, Uncle Vinnie! I just don't understand what's going on. I feel so helpless and useless and I haven't been a good daughter..." She sobs loudly, and Vinnie pulls her head against his chest.

"You did good. You got things going," Vinnie tells her. "I'm so sorry I didn't come here as soon as your mom talked to me about a divorce. I should have talked this out with your dad. I know it's not an excuse but I didn't want to make matters worse for her. And I didn't want you and your sister to hate me for..."

He doesn't have to finish. Rebecca gives him a tiny smile. "It's a good thing you didn't fight with Dad. Ronnie would beat you up."

Vinnie squeezes her tight. "I guess there's no point in my going back in there. Unless you want me to? I can go back to town and start searching."

"Stay, Uncle. You can help us come up with a plan here. Dad's got the ransom money together."

"You'll have to take me to town today. I'm not staying here."

"Dad will have to get over himself. And you will too. This isn't about you. It's about Mom so no more of this crap."

Vinnie shakes his head and says, "Yes, ma'am."

"Let's go in and sit at the table," I suggest. "Rebecca will get you some coffee. You don't have to say anything to Jack if you don't want."

We get up to go inside and then I hear the gate opening. A dark SUV comes down the driveway followed by two police cars and a K-9 Unit. Vinnie tenses but Rebecca takes his hand.

"I called them."

The SUV stops and Lucas gets out with a grim look on his face. He's ignoring me for once, eyes firmly on Vinnie. "Well, look what the cat dragged in."

"Hello, Sergeant Lucas," Vinnie says. "Long time no see."

"Not long enough, Vinnie. How long have you been here?"

"What are you doing to find my sister?"

"Well, Vinnie, that's what we need to talk about." Vinnie steps toward the driveway and Lucas says, "Don't even think about it." Lucas holds an arm out and says to Rebecca and Vinnie, "After you."

Rebecca leads the way. I bring up the rear.

Jack and Ronnie are still sitting at the table in the kitchen. "Dad, I've invited Uncle Vinnie to stay with us." Jack gives her a sharp look. She says, "It's not up to you. I've invited him and he can help us. You need to listen to what he has to say. Please, Dad. For Mom's sake."

Jack pushes another chair out for Vinnie, and the tension between the two men is electric. Vinnie puts his big hands on the tabletop and says, "I'm sorry for what you're going through, Jack. I know you love her very much. And she loves you." Jack's glare morphs into a pitiful look and tears stream down his frozen face. "I hope we can let our differences go and work together. It's up to you, Jack. I'm willing if you are."

Lucas sneers and says, "How heart-wrenching. You're going to make me cry." He looks from one man to the other. "I don't care if you work together, Vinnie. You're going to tell me everything I want to know or you'll be eating jail food again. Understand? Don't leave."

SIXTY-THREE

Ronnie and I sit on the back deck with Vinnie while Lucas talks to Jack. A small crime scene army is spread out on the grounds, working a grid search.

"I think Lucas suspects me," Vinnie says.

"That's crazy," Ronnie responds.

"Is it? You suspected me until we talked. How do you know I'm not lying?"

"You're family," Ronnie says.

She doesn't know how family can betray you. Jack is a dick and a liar and controlling, but I'd swap that for my parents any day.

Vinnie puts a hand on hers. "That doesn't answer my question but thank you for saying that, Ronnie. It means a lot."

"Tell me about you and Mom."

We listen to Vinnie's story about his and Victoria's childhood and hear a different side of Vincenzo Lombardi than I'd heard thus far. Vinnie was changed when he came home. He'd never gotten along with his parents, but he avoided them more often now. And not just his parents: he avoided his friends, his church, and worst of all he avoided Victoria.

Vinnie was injured in Fallujah when he accompanied a SEAL team on a mission as their medic. His injury was such that he was put on painkillers. The addiction gene hadn't missed him. The horrors he saw committed by both sides in Fallujah, coupled with the painkillers, created the depression, PTSD, and paranoia he still experiences to some degree. He'd tried to reach out to Victoria a few years ago when he was in jail.

He'd been sent into war as a naïve eighteen-year-old, witnessed and participated in atrocities, and when it was over he was sent home, dumped out on society, and didn't know how to live among civilized people. Every time a siren went off, he ducked or dropped to the ground looking for cover. He had night terrors and the Army had made him all better with more drugs, feeding his addiction even further. I'm amazed he didn't implode with everything that he went through, but he'd made some steps toward recovery. He was going to Narcotics Anonymous meetings but found a veterans group that were as messed up as he was. It seems to be helping.

"I thought I was going to spend the rest of my life in prison. Then Vicki saved me. I've never visited her at her house after she was married, but whenever I could get my shit together, we saw each other periodically and she kept me apprised of my nieces. When we got together it was at restaurants and coffee shops and city parks. I thought it was because of my... issues. But then I began to suspect she wasn't unhappy with me. She didn't want your father to see me because he disapproved."

He takes his wallet from his back pocket and pulls some pictures out and shows them to Ronnie. "That's you and Rebecca water skiing. You couldn't have been older than ten." He shows her another. "That's a picture of your mom and me when Victoria graduated from high school." He seems lost in reverie. "Your father must have put pressure on her not to see me. He never came with her and I got the hint."

"Why does my dad want to keep you out of our lives? Did you have a falling out?"

Vinnie doesn't answer. Instead, he shows her another photo. "That's me in Army basic training. Vic and I dreamed of getting out of that house so I picked the Army. It's the only other picture I've managed to keep. If Lucas thinks I had anything to do with Vic's disappearing, he's wrong. I would be more prone to believe she left Jack on her own. She was very unhappy the last few times I talked to her. She always steered the conversation to how I was doing, or her charity work and how proud she was of her girls. She showed me some newspaper clippings of Rebecca joining Jack's law firm and one of you in your uniform. Then there were several of you and Detective Carpenter in the newspapers and on television. Vic said she was happy you'd made a life of your own. She loves you and Rebecca very much."

I'd always thought I had a sucky life. The cause of my bad upbringing was housed in a women's prison, but Ronnie's family was still okay-ish and loved her and wanted good things for her and was proud of what she'd accomplished. My mother wasn't proud of my becoming a detective. Not really. She was only thinking of ways to use me for her benefit. I sincerely doubt she's proud of Hayden either.

I'd asked Hayden how he was doing now that he was living and working in Port Townsend. He'd said, "The grass isn't always greener on the other side. I've seen and done things I'm not proud of. Being here is no different. You carry your monsters with you."

He would never tell me what he'd done, what he'd seen. But I can imagine it must have been bad enough to change the happy boy I remembered into a bitter man. It must be the same for Vinnie. I guess we all have things in our past that have made us who or what we are. Sometimes those things are positive, sometimes scarring, sometimes dangerous to others.

My past has followed me with a vengeance. Twice now I've had serial killers come after me by harming people close to me. They wanted to kill me because I'd ended someone close to them. I'd hoped to spare Hayden from that but what I thought was the right thing to do concerning him had backfired. Ronnie's dad was doing the same thing. Trying to mold his girls into what he thought was good for them. He would one day regret trying to design a life for his girls in his own image; pushing his wife's family out of the picture. I can testify that bad decisions come back and bite you in the ass.

SIXTY-FOUR

Victoria is startled awake by something dropping beside her. She didn't hear anyone come in.

"Put those on."

Victoria uses her feet to push herself into a sitting position. She cradles her injured arm against her bare chest and looks up at the slight figure of a woman standing in the doorway.

The woman says, "You don't have all day. Get dressed. There's some food in the bag too. Don't eat the wrapper."

Victoria recognizes the woman but doesn't remember her name. If her captors think she can identify them, she won't get out of here alive. A black trash bag is by her feet. Inside are a blouse and jeans and sandals she had brought to the resort. Underneath the clothes is a sleeve of crackers that have been crushed into crumbs. The woman watches and laughs.

"I know they're not gourmet crackers, but at least you've got your own clothes. Now get dressed or stay naked. I don't really give a shit." The woman is holding a bottle of water. She tosses it across the room and leaves.

Victoria retrieves the water and crackers and resists the urge to devour the cracker crumbs. She isn't going to give this woman the pleasure of seeing how degraded she feels. Awkwardly, still trying to adjust to doing everything with one hand, she struggles into the jeans and top. It seems to take forever, but when she's finally clothed, she takes a measure of comfort in the feel of personal privacy, of not being subjected to nakedness like an animal. She slips her feet into the sandals. The small feeling of normalcy brings tears to her eyes. Maybe they weren't going to kill her. Why would they feed her and let her get dressed if they intended to harm her?

Her hunger overcomes her pride, and Victoria sits against a wall tearing the plastic sleeve open with her teeth. She shakes cracker crumbs into her mouth and struggles to get the cap off of the bottle of water. She'd done her best to ration the water that was in the pail, but it is gone. Between gulps of water and cracker she wipes her mouth with the sleeve of her shirt and looks at the stain on the arm of her Ravella silk blouse. Jack had bought the blouse for her on a trip to Rome many years ago to celebrate the opening of his first law firm. The blouse is soft to the touch, and Jack told her it was beautiful, like her, and it matched the color of her eyes.

That was back when he still knew she was alive. Back when he respected her as a partner, a mother, and a wife. Back when he still loved her. He told her Ravella is the Italian word for rebel. He said she was his beautiful Italian rebel and he loved her for being so headstrong. She laughs at the comparison of that woman with this one and tears stream down her cheeks.

She'd kept the blouse even though Jack had told her to get rid of it. He said it was old. She could afford a new one. She'd trans-lated that to mean "she" was old and he could afford a new wife. A prettier one. Maybe one with the spine to stand against him. She'd stopped wearing the blouse in front of him but would never dispose of it. It held remembrances of past happiness. A life full of love.

Victoria wishes the woman had turned the lights off. She

doesn't want to be visible. The only value she has to Jack is that she is his and he will never allow anything to be taken from him.

"Oh, Jack," she says, and her voice echoes in the emptiness. "What happened to us?"

She loves him and probably always will. If only he still loved her. She vows that if she gets free—when she gets free—things are going to be different. She will become the woman she was before meeting him. Her daughters need to see the strong side of her. They should never be anyone's property. Ronnie has already made that happen; made her own place, not relying on the family name, not relying on Jack. Rebecca is oldest but slowest to rebel and so, Jacks proudest achievement. He always said he loved both of his daughters the same but that was a lie. If you didn't do what he thought should be done, he resented you. He had warmed to Ronnie lately, but he still resented her for disobeying him and refusing to study law and join the family business. He didn't come right out and say it but Ronnie knew it was true. She was intuitive. She'd started coming home less and less over the last few years. But she called her mother and sister in between visits. They were Marsh women. They shared a bond.

As famished as she is, she puts the remainder of the crackers down. It's hard to eat when your heart is in your throat. She wonders if she'll ever see her daughters again. She didn't tell Rebecca she loved her their last night together. She'd intended to tell Rebecca about the divorce on the horizon but had lost her nerve and now it was too late. The family is already broken. If she had told Rebecca about her intentions, Rebecca would feel responsible; take it as a personal injury.

She leans her head back against the hard wall and closes her eyes.

SIXTY-FIVE

A uniformed officer comes to the door and says, "Lucas wants to see him," and he points at Vinnie. Ronnie gets up and leads the way inside. She says over her shoulder, "Just answer his questions the best that you can. Don't elaborate and don't let him get you angry. Anger won't help us. Save the anger for Thundercloud."

Jack wanted nothing to do with Vinnie and was glad when Lucas told him to show Crime Scene where he'd met the kidnapper. The tension was lowered with the removal of one antagonist, but now Jack had been replaced by Lucas's dour countenance.

"Your niece said you spotted a vehicle in Bellingham where someone looking like Duke was getting into an SUV," Lucas says.

Crap! I didn't want him to know about that. And now I'm not sure if Lucas knows we met Vinnie at the motel. Ronnie and Rebecca exchange a look, and Rebecca looks chastened.

"When was that?" Vinnie asks. Good deflection.

"Were you in Bellingham today?" Lucas asks.

"I was there this morning."

"Why were you there?" Lucas asks.

"I don't have to tell you my every move, Sergeant. I'm not on probation and unless you have a warrant for me I can get up and walk out that door."

Lucas is taken aback. "Why... your sister is kidnapped and you don't want to help. Is that right?"

"I never said I wouldn't help. Treat me with respect and I'll answer your questions. Otherwise, I'm out of here."

Vinnie looks at me and I see he's having Lucas for breakfast.

Lucas looks down at the table, collecting his thoughts, or maybe eating crow. He's bitten off more than he can chew with Vinnie.

"Okay. Sorry, Mr. Lombardi. Can we get back to you seeing Duke in Bellingham, please?"

"I never said I saw Duke. Just someone that looked like it might be him. But he was there one moment and gone the next."

"Did he get into an SUV? This Duke lookalike."

"Rebecca must have heard me wrong. Like I said, the guy was there and then gone. I didn't pay that much attention."

Lucas isn't giving up. "Did you know Duke has a warrant out for escape?"

"Escape from where?"

Lucas's scowl is back. "I'm through playing games, Vinnie. Did you see Duke in Bellingham or not? It's an easy question."

"I've answered your question. Just because you don't like the answer doesn't change anything. I saw someone that looked like Duke and then he disappeared."

Lucas leans forward and rests his palms flat against the table. "Do you have an idea who took your sister?"

"Thundercloud and Missy. I thought you'd figured that out by now," Vinnie said.

"And you have no part in what they're doing?"

"I'm here talking to the police. Do you think I would be

here if I was involved? You're not stupid, Sergeant. Just because I've had some issues in the past, it doesn't mean I would harm my family. I'm not going to listen to this any longer."

Vinnie stands to leave the room, but Ronnie takes his arm and leads him into the hallway where I can hear her whispering and Vinnie protesting loudly, saying that he's leaving.

"Way to go, Lucas," I say, and earn a dirty look and so I press on. "We've spent all this time looking for him and you piss him off. So what's your plan now?"

Lucas doesn't miss a beat. "Now we pay the ransom."

"It's about time," I say.

"You have no idea what's going on here," Lucas says. "I've got a murder to add to this kidnapping now and you're running around playing detective, spooking all the witnesses."

I'm struck silent.

"That's right. The resort reported a fire. Roger Whiting was just found burned to death in his office. The surveillance system was toast. What a coincidence. Every time I turn around, one of you is turning off the surveillance recordings. I'll need to know where all of you were today. A complete account. You're now possible suspects so don't get in my way or I'll arrest you until I can check your alibis. Got it?"

I open my mouth to respond to that, but decide I'll just say something I regret. Instead, I turn around and walk out to the front porch. Perhaps the fresh air will cool me down, make me less likely to wring Lucas's fucking neck.

Ronnie's sitting out on the porch with Vinnie. As I step outside, she's patting his knee, "I told you not to let him get to you, Uncle."

Vinnie puts a hand over hers. "He didn't. I just didn't want to tell him anything more."

"Uncle Vinnie, I think we're going to need his help."

"Maybe help from the sheriff but not him."

"Do you know something I don't?" Ronnie asks, and Vinnie squeezes her hand.

"The SUV I saw Duke get into belongs to Lucas." He nods toward the black SUV parked in the driveway. "I think Lucas is behind all of this."

"Who's behind what?" Rebecca asks, coming onto the porch.

Ronnie looks up at her sister. "Uncle Vinnie says the SUV he saw Duke get into is Lucas's," Ronnie says. "He thinks there's something off about Lucas."

"Something off?" I repeat, looking at Vinnie.

He's quiet for a moment. Then he simply says, "I know what desperation looks like. And I see it in Lucas."

I ask Vinnie, "You think Lucas could be behind this whole thing?"

Before Vinnie can answer, Lucas comes out, followed closely by his team. The search team heads to their cars and Lucas stops and faces us. "Mr. Lombardi, I apologize for being sharp with you. Mr. Marsh doesn't believe you've had any ill intentions toward his family and is convinced you are helping with the search." He hands Vinnie a business card. "If you think of anything that can help me, please call. My personal cell phone number is on there as well."

With that Lucas gets in his SUV and drives away.

Ronnie says, "I'm convinced."

Rebecca says, "Yeah. Lucas is not helping."

Jack comes outside and leans in the doorway. "Good. He's gone."

Vinnie stands and says, "I have an idea where Duke might go."

Ronnie says, "Uncle Vinnie will stay with Rebecca and Dad. The kidnapper has been here twice. I don't want my family getting hurt."

Good thinking. We'll know where Vinnie and Jack are.

SIXTY-SIX

Vinnie agreed to stay with Rebecca while Ronnie and I went back to the Mom & Pop store. He didn't want Jack to meet with the kidnappers alone, and Jack didn't trust Vinnie to go alone with the money.

We arrive in the area of the store, and I park a block away.

"I'll go in alone," I say.

"The hell you will," Ronnie says. "Someone killed Roger to keep him quiet. I'll bet it was Thundercloud. It seems he always knows what we're doing and where we're going."

We go in the side door, guns drawn, and quietly take the stairs. Ronnie checks the other rooms, and I check the room where Duke said Vinnie had card games. Nothing has changed since I was there with Lucas. Vinnie has misled us.

"I can't believe Vinnie would do something like this. He can't be trusted. Everyone is lying to us."

I say, "We need to know more about Vinnie and Lucas. Vinnie doesn't trust Lucas but I don't think Vinnie was telling us everything."

"I have an idea," Ronnie says, and makes a call. "Lieutenant Sitzman, please?" Ronnie says. "Yes. I'll hold."

"I hope Sitzman doesn't spread it around that he's checking on Lucas. Longbow and Captain Roberts are close friends with Lucas. The police station and jail are like a bucket full of holes. But if Lucas finds out, he can stuff it."

Sitzman comes on the line.

"Lieutenant Sitzman, this is Ronnie Marsh." She puts it on speaker.

"Miss Marsh. It is Miss, right?"

Best pick-up line ever. Right up there with "do you come here often" and "you must have fallen down from heaven because you look like an angel."

She says, "Lieutenant, I need some help and I thought of you. Can you keep something confidential?"

"Sure. I was hoping you'd call. Better yet, maybe you can come by and we'll discuss this over coffee. Or lunch."

Ronnie's tone turns serious. "Sounds nice but I have to ask a favor. Not even your bosses can know. I need to ask you something about Sergeant Lucas."

SIXTY-SEVEN

The call lasts only a few minutes. Ronnie asks Sitzman about what happened to Lucas's wife, and the answers are a whole lot more than we had bargained for.

It turns out Mrs. Lucas didn't just die. The official version of the story is that Joyce Lucas killed herself with a gunshot to the head; but not before killing their daughter, Maisy. Any instinctive sympathy I might have felt for Sergeant Lucas dissipates quickly as I read between the lines of the other things Sitzman has to tell us.

Like the fact Lucas's wife had a million-dollar life insurance policy, that he had returned to work only a few weeks after the deaths of his wife and kid, and that he had interfered a lot in the investigation while on leave. Sitzman doesn't come right out and say it, but he heavily implies that Lucas's ex-partner quit rather than be part of what he thought was a cover-up.

Ten minutes and a promise to go for coffee later, we drive away from the Mom & Pop store.

Ronnie says, "I can't believe no one said anything about this."

What I'm having trouble with is why Sheriff Longbow

assigned this case to him. I don't get a bad feeling about Long-bow. Or the jail commander, Roberts, for that matter. If we had known what we were just told I would have had a lot of questions.

I say, "I wonder if we can get copies of the murder/suicide investigation?"

Ronnie answers, "Sitzman might be able to access them but it sounds like Lucas was never much more than a suspect. He wasn't arrested or even suspended without pay. He was put on leave until the investigation was over and he was cleared."

He was cleared. How in the hell did that happen? Lucas's eight-year-old daughter was strangled, and his wife was shot with a gun from his lockbox at home. He lived in a cabin in the sticks. No neighbors to hear the gunshot or screaming or fighting. Lucas had taken out the insurance policy on himself and his wife five years earlier. One million dollars would have very high premiums. I have the insurance policy the sheriff office gave me. Twenty-five thousand won't go a long way but I'll be dead so it won't be my money. I've made Hayden my executor and everything will be left to him.

"Let's call Lucas's old partner, see if he'll talk to us."

Sitzman has texted the number for Lucas's old partner and Ronnie puts the call on speaker. Retired Detective Larry Stroud is sitting in a bar. I can hear darts being played and some occasional raised voices. His voice is a little slurred but he's willing to talk to us. The first thing I notice is there's no love lost between him and Lucas.

"So what can I tell you that I haven't told countless others? No one listens so what's the point," Stroud says. "Just let it go and save yourself some sleepless nights. What I did."

I ask, "Did you know the Marsh family on Cougar Point?"

"You're not from here, are you?"

I wait.

"Everyone knows them. Jack Marsh is a big shot around

here. Does your interest in Lucas have something to do with Jack Marsh?"

Ronnie speaks up. "Victoria Marsh is my mother. She was kidnapped six days ago. Lucas was assigned the case by Sheriff Longbow."

Stroud is quiet.

"Sergeant Stroud?" I say.

"Retired," he says. "I wish you hadn't come to me asking questions about Lucas. I took an early retirement so I wouldn't have to be involved."

Ronnie speaks up. "We're pretty sure Len Thundercloud, Melissa Milligan, and Duke Scanlon are her kidnappers. They sent Mom's finger to us along with some pictures of her being held captive. Today they sent us her hand."

Stroud is still silent.

I say, "We heard you were a damn good detective. You don't get that kind of praise unless you care enough to do a good job. How would you like it if you came to me for help and I said I wanted to keep out of it?"

"Okay, you don't have to keep busting my balls. I was just thinking. I assume you do that." The phone sets down on a hard surface and I hear laughter and chatter in the background, Stroud gets back on the line. "Let me go outside so we can talk. This is a cop bar and some of 'em are friends with Lucas."

Stroud goes outside and traffic can be heard in the background and some wolf whistles. The whistles sound like they're coming from Stroud. "Now. Where was I? Oh yeah. I gotta tell you first off that if Duke and Thundercloud are involved, you got problems. Sorry, Detective Marsh. But those two aren't wrapped too tight. For that matter, Lucas isn't well-adjusted either. Maybe I shouldn't be talking about an old partner like this but if another woman's life is in danger, I'll spill all his secrets."

I'm growing impatient. Does everyone around here beat

around the bush so much? "So tell us about Lucas's wife and daughter's deaths."

"Lucas's wife died from a gunshot wound to the head. Right temple. The daughter was only eight years old. She was smothered with a couch pillow. The little girl had fought very hard, so it would take some strength to hold her down on the hardwood floor."

The image he's planted will be in my head for days. Kids are my weak spot. Puppies are next in line.

"Were there other injuries on either victim?" Ronnie asks.

"There were. It didn't seem to matter to the sheriff. I still have copies of the coroner's report. I wanted an inquest but the sheriff nixed that. Longbow and Lucas are butt buddies. Fishing, hunting, gambling, drinking, and chasing tail. Excuse my language."

"What kind of injuries?" I ask.

"Old bruises. I got medical records on the sly after it looked like the investigation was going in the toilet. The wife was on antidepressants and had been in and out of therapy since the daughter was born. Of course the therapist wouldn't talk to me, but some of the neighbors were happy to spill. Lucas was one mean son of a... Sorry. Bad habit from when I was on the job."

"I understand," Ronnie said. "We do that all the time too."

Liar. Ronnie wouldn't say poop if she was knee deep in it. But she's doing good keeping this guy talking.

"Medical records showed past broken bones in her hands and feet. The little girl had the same things. The notes said the patients had tripped or ran into walls or doors. Clumsy is what the reports said. I asked Lucas about the injuries, and he got angry that the hospital gave me the records. No believable explanation of how those injuries had occurred."

I hear him take a deep breath before he continues. "This still pisses me off. If they'd have let me dig a little, Lucas would be behind bars."

"Tell us what you have. Maybe we can do the digging," I say.

"Who are you again?"

We give him our names and that we work for Jefferson County Sheriff.

"The kidnapping you're working is in Whatcom County. How'd you get permission to step on Lucas's toes like that?"

"Our sheriff and Longbow are acquaintances from a while back. Longbow deputized us."

He says, "Does Longbow know you're looking into Lucas?"

"Not yet," I answer, and he laughs out loud until he starts coughing.

He gets under control. "You'd better watch your back is all I can tell you. Okay, I'll fill you in on the case I was building against Lucas."

Larry tells us he responded to the police call to Lucas's place. When he arrived he got a bad feeling that the scene was staged. After thirty-five years in the job, he trusts his instincts. He didn't care much for Lucas even then but they made do. He said Lucas was always wanting more. More money. More women. More credit and glory. He was always talking about his investments and was on his phone constantly checking his stocks etc. It was annoying but when Lucas was working, he was one of the best detectives Larry had ever known. Sharp. Intuitive. And he had a cadre of snitches and people in high places that owed him favors.

Retired Detective Stroud tells us Longbow put Lucas on paid leave for several weeks while the deaths were investigated. Lucas was told to stay out of the investigation but he was interviewing the coroner and other officers that had worked the scene. Stroud saw the case was being shoved under the rug. The coroner ruled it murder/suicide, the wife killed the daughter and then killed herself, and that was that.

But Stroud wasn't satisfied. He called in some favors and

found out Lucas had taken out a large life insurance policy on his wife five years before. He informed us that the insurance policy had a suicide rider. But that rider expired after eighteen months.

The insurance company had their own investigator look into the claim and the insurance investigator thought the same thing Larry did. This all stank. They managed to wriggle out of paying out on a technicality.

"How much did that cost Lucas?" I ask.

"A cool million," Stroud replies.

I let out a whistle. A million reasons to kill his wife, and it was all for nothing.

"And Sheriff Longbow didn't think this was all suspicious?" I ask. "The whole thing, and then the insurance not paying out?"

"I'm sure he did but it didn't matter. Lucas had an airtight alibi for the day of the deaths. He was with a snitch. The snitch was also one of Narcotics' confidential informants and he vouched for him."

"One last question, Larry. Was Lucas's wife right- or left-handed?"

"Now you're getting it. Left-handed. Look, I got to go. Good luck. We didn't talk." With that he hung up.

Ronnie puts her phone away. "Do you think Larry or Lieutenant Sitzman will tell Lucas we were asking questions about him?"

"Larry? Hell no. Sitzman? I'm counting on it."

Whatcom County

As soon as Lucas walked through the doorway of Dr. Wright's office, he could sense things were different today. It was hard to articulate but it was like the sun had come out after a spell of bad weather. He noticed that the bookshelves behind her were empty. Cardboard boxes were stacked in the corner of the office.

Stephanie Wright was wearing a teal blouse today and, for the first time, a welcoming smile.

"Thank you for coming in," she said, standing up and beckoning him in. "I appreciate you moving our session."

Lucas closed the door behind him, "Not a problem, I was in the neighborhood." He glanced at the pile of boxes. "Moving to a bigger office?"

"Moving to a bigger state." She smiled.

Lucas paused for a second as he was pulling out his chair to take this in, then nodded and sat down.

"Guy could take that personally, you know."

Wright beamed, and Lucas suddenly realized this must be what she was like when she was talking to someone she actually liked spending time with. The severity in her demeanor was completely gone,

"A position came up in LA. My fiancé lives down there, so it's a no-brainer."

"Congratulations," Lucas said. "It's great news." No lie.

She smiled again and put her hands down on the desk. He noticed her notebook was nowhere to be seen. "Anyway, I wanted to see you before I left, because I wanted to know that you're still making progress."

"I'm getting there, Doc."

"And the case you're working?"

Lucas shrugged. "It's a challenge."

"You're not getting anywhere?"

"Not exactly."

"What does that mean?"

"Aren't we here to talk about me?"

"This *is* about you. You coming to see me was a condition of you returning to work so rapidly after your tragedy. The work is a part of that."

Lucas spread his hands in surrender. "I can't really talk about it."

"I understand. But if it would help, you *can* talk about it. I can't divulge any information you give me, whether it's about a live case or anything else."

Lucas watched her face. For the first time, he felt like he had a slight edge on her. He sensed something in her: a curiosity. Perhaps if he indulged that curiosity, she would give him something too.

He leaned forward. Glanced at her pad. "How do you think I'm doing. Really?"

She drew back a little, pursed her lips, the smile fading. Her voice regained the professional tone. "I already told you. I'm pleasantly surprised at the way you've adjusted."

"Surprised enough to sign off on me before you go? Or do I have to start over with someone else."

"I'm thinking about it."

He nodded and sat back. "All right. You're familiar with the basics of the Olivia Greenwood case?"

Wright smiled. "Sergeant, it's not that big of a place. Everybody within a fifty-mile radius knows about the murder you're investigating."

"I think I know what happened. But I can't prove it."

"You know who abducted her?"

"I think I know some of the players. Here's the thing: her husband had a girlfriend, and a shitload of debt. I think he hired somebody to kidnap her and ransom her. Only, he never intended to pay the ransom. They were to hold her long enough for it to look convincing and then kill her. Then he would get the life insurance payout."

"You think that's what happened?"

"No, I think that's what was *supposed* to happen. Something went wrong. She got away from them somehow, she was killed trying to escape. The plan got screwed up. Of course, the husband killed himself, so he can't help us identify his partner in crime."

"But you know who it is."

"I have an idea," Lucas said. "But..." He opened his hands again. "I can't prove it. So he's going to walk."

"And how does that make you feel?"

"How does it make me feel?" He took a long breath through his nostrils and looked out of the window, pretending to mull it over. "It makes me feel professionally frustrated, I suppose. But it is what it is. You can't close every case."

"You can't close every case," Dr. Wright repeated in a

hushed tone, as though he had just elucidated one of the secrets of the universe.

* * *

Lucas was in the car when Sheriff Longbow called him a half hour after leaving Dr. Wright's office. He had just finished reading an email from the life insurance company. Or at least, he had finished reading the first paragraph of the email, which had hit him like a dump truck.

> …due to the ongoing investigation, we regret that we are unable at this time to finalize settlement of your late wife's policy. If you would like to discuss…

The words seemed to scramble on the screen after that. In his mind's eye, they danced around and then reassembled into a picture of one million dollars going up in smoke.

"Fuck."

When he saw Longbow's number flash up, he thought about ignoring it. But he knew Longbow would just keep calling. He took a moment to compose himself and then answered.

"I guess congratulations are in order."

If only you knew, boss. If only you fucking knew.

Lucas cleared his throat and tried to sound jovial. "I'm getting a raise?"

"Not this decade. Dr. Wright called. She's signing off on your report. Says she's satisfied you're a well-adjusted human being. One day you'll have to tell me how you fooled her."

"I guess they give those psychology diplomas out to anyone these days."

"You coming down to the station?"

"In a while," Lucas said as he pulled to a stop at the curb. He looked out of the passenger window at the house across the street. As he watched, the door opened and Len Thundercloud stepped out, folding his arms and glaring back at him from across the street.

"Lucas?"

He remembered he was still on the line to his boss. Without breaking eye contact with Len Thundercloud, he replied. "Just got to take care of a couple things. I'll see you in an hour."

SIXTY-NINE

I'm still deciding what to do next when Ronnie's phone rings and makes the decision for us.

Ronnie answers, "What do you mean he's gone?" She puts the call on speaker.

"Uncle Vinnie. He said he was going for a walk to clear his head and he never came back. Dad is furious. I'm sorry but I can't keep an eye on them both."

"No one blames you, Rebecca. Do you have any idea where Vinnie might be going?" Ronnie asks.

I butt in. "How long has Vinnie been gone?"

"He went for the walk as soon as the two of you left to look for Duke."

Ronnie asks, "Do you have a phone number for him?"

Her silence is the answer.

Well, crap! "We just left the apartment over the Mom & Pop store but no one has been there." So he distracted us while he disappeared. Suddenly, I have a hunch I know what's happened. Vinnie thinks he can find Victoria all by himself, and for whatever reason, he doesn't want us getting in the way.

Ronnie asks, "Is Dad still there?"

"Let me check." The call is silent for several minutes then she comes back. "He's not in the house. I'm going to check around the property."

I ask, "Is his car there?"

The line is silent again, then Rebecca says, "Oh crap. His car is gone and I looked in his office. The bag of money is gone too. Can you come and get me? Or meet me somewhere?"

Vinnie's gone, Jack's gone, the money's gone. Great. This is all looking wonderful.

I understand Rebecca's need to do something. But it will cause us to lose time. "Hang on, Rebecca." I put her on mute and ask Ronnie, "By any chance did you put your dad's phone on your locator app? According to Rebecca, he's been gone at least thirty minutes."

Ronnie fires up her iPad and pulls up the program. "He's heading toward the resort. Why would he leave without telling us?"

I can think of several reasons. The most likely of which is he's gotten a call from the kidnappers and is on his way to drop the money off.

"Ronnie, you keep an eye on Jack and I'll drive." I drive faster.

"You're going the right way, Megan. He's stopped. We'll come across him in about fifteen minutes."

I step on it and trust that a policeman won't stop a marked police car.

Ten minutes later she says, "He's just up ahead."

"I'm going to call him." She starts to call him, stops, punches a few numbers and then cancels. It's her choice but if it was mine, I wouldn't call. At least not until we get closer. He's either okay or he's not. If he's not okay, he may not be able to call for help. If he is okay, he will be too embarrassed to call us. Strike that. I can't imagine that man being embarrassed. We can't get there any faster. I'm already pushing a hundred miles an hour. Any more and we'll lift off. Neither of us suggests calling Lucas.

Agonizing minutes later Ronnie points through the windshield. "There he is."

I slow down. I don't see anyone in the driver's seat. I drive across the road and off on the shoulder facing Jack's car. A head pops up and a pale, frightened face looks at us.

Ronnie and I get out but Jack remains seated, both hands gripping the steering wheel, head on a swivel.

We approach and I motion for Jack to roll his window down, but then I see glass on the ground beside the driver's window.

SEVENTY

I pry Jack's hands off the steering wheel, and Ronnie gets in the back of my vehicle with him. It takes a minute for him to stop babbling, talking to himself mostly. My phone rings. It's Lucas.

"What are you playing at, Detective Carpenter? I thought we had an agreement."

I prepare myself to get the riot act. "Mrs. Marsh will be in some real danger now but I guess you can't be bothered. You were supposed to call me when the kidnappers made contact. I should go to Sheriff Longbow with this and have you two escorted to the county line by an armed deputy. You're done here. Do you understand me?"

I can't help but think of some of the old Westerns where the sheriff would say, "Get out of town by sundown. And don't come back."

I say, "Why are you only worried about what we're doing instead of getting off your high horse and doing something yourself?"

The line goes dead. Ronnie says, "You hurt his feelings."

I'll hurt more than that if he messes with us. "I was out of line. I'll apologize after we get Victoria back safe."

Jack's head is down in his hands. He sounds ashamed. "What have I done? I should never have let you, any of you, get involved. I should have left the money and waited for their call. I demand you stop at once."

What the hell?

Ronnie turns on him. "And what would you have done when they got your money and killed Mom? What if they had killed you? You were sure glad when we came along to save you. Weren't you, Daddy? Tell the truth. You need us. All of us."

I don't think her dad was prepared to be basically told to shut the fuck up. He doesn't protest.

Ronnie calls a wrecker for his car and tells them to tow it to Cougar Point and leave it in the driveway. There will be no police. There will be no report. She gives them a credit card number.

Jack says, "They called. It was a woman, this time. She told me to leave the money twenty paces in the woods. Over there. She said I'd find a bag and I should put the money in it and go home and wait for their call. I got here and put the money in another trash bag and left it where they said, but I couldn't leave until I knew Vicki was safe. Next thing I knew a truck pulled off the road a little ways behind me. A man with a ski mask ran into the woods. The whole thing seemed unreal and I started to get out and confront him and he shot at me. The only reason I survived was Vinnie."

"Vinnie?" I repeat. This is moving way too fast for me. "Where did Vinnie come from?"

"He must have followed me. He knew I was going to make the drop and he must have been hoping they'd lead him to Vic. Anyway, he broke cover and knocked me out of the way. Another guy with a gun showed up, took him away."

I get out and check Jack's car. There are two holes in the passenger side quarter panel. Two small holes in the passenger window, and the driver's window was a jagged hole. There were at least four shots sent his way. *Idiot.* I get back in my vehicle in time to hear Ronnie say, "It's okay, Dad."

He responds, "It's not okay. I've killed her. They got their money and now she will pay for my stupidity. Why do I do this? What's wrong with me?"

"They could have shot you, Dad, but they didn't. There's still a chance Mom will be released."

I ask, "How long ago did this happen?"

He says, "I'm not sure. Maybe ten minutes."

"A wrecker is coming for your car. You can ride home with them. Go home, Dad," Ronnie insists.

"I want to be there when she's found. They've got my phone number if they want to call."

Ronnie reminds him, "They've got the money. They were supposed to release Mom. She might get home and you won't be there."

Jack says, "In other words you don't need an old man who screws things up."

"The smart thing to do is go home. You and Rebecca will be there waiting for her. Rebecca is going out of her mind with you taking off like you did. We'll keep looking but I can't do my job if I'm worrying about you and Mom and Rebecca."

Ronnie's making perfect sense. Jack may be a hotshot attorney but he's out of his league here. And just when I think he can't be any more mistaken, he says, "I think it's time to call the FBI."

Ronnie turns on him. "No. It's too late. You've done enough. Now you have to trust us. We're your best hope. Maybe your only hope. Just look how far we've come. You shouldn't have stayed behind to confront them. You never let anyone else tell you what is best. Now I'm telling you. You're going home. I'll call you a Lyft and you go straight home. Don't call anyone. Especially Lucas."

Jack looks defeated.

Ronnie calls a Lyft for her dad and he gets out. "I gave them your phone number, Dad. They'll be here shortly. I'm sorry but you're grounded."

SEVENTY-ONE

The woman enters the room again and finally, Victoria can put a name with the face. It's like the dreamlike haze of the last few days suddenly evaporates and she can see clearly for the first time.

Missy something.

It was on the nametag on her blazer at the resort. Victoria hopes Missy doesn't see the recognition in her eyes so she looks down.

"It's time, princess. Get on your feet and don't look at me. My boyfriend might decide to get rid of us both. Understand?"

Victoria gets up but keeps her eyes downcast. "It's time for what?"

"Time for you to get poor and me to get rich."

Victoria thinks of how much pleasure this woman, and the man, have taken in her humiliation and pain. She doesn't believe she's going to be released. She is being taken somewhere to be killed. She has to get out of here and she weighs her chances of taking this smirking bitch on. Missy won't expect her to fight back.

She's had more time than she needs to consider her life.

First her parents told her she'd never amount to anything. Then she'd met Jack. He was great, loving, supportive, considerate. For a while. And then he became just like every other man she'd ever known. He was the boss. She was his maid. His to do whatever he wanted with. Kept helpless, unable to go out on her own. She'd had the girls and her maternal instincts told her they were her life. She'd given up everything. But as they left the nest a deeply hidden part of herself started to push its way to the surface. She realized she didn't need Jack. She didn't need her house, the money, the life. She just needed to be herself and hope her girls would still love her. She'd worked up the nerve to tell Jack she was leaving him and that took more courage than what she needs to do to this little bitch. Missy isn't going to keep her from moving on. No way. Her remaining hand curls into a fist and she takes a step forward, just as two men enter. One of them, she hasn't seen before. The other man she recognizes only too well.

"Vinnie," she cries out. "Oh my god, what have they done to you?"

Vinnie is bleeding badly from a cut on his head. It looks like he's been pistol-whipped. As she speaks, the man holding him at gunpoint pushes him roughly forward.

"What the hell, Duke? Why is he here? This isn't the plan," Missy says.

The man apparently called Duke shoves Vinnie again, harder this time, and he falls at Victoria's feet. Vinnie looks up at his sister. "Hi, Dinky. Found you."

Duke cracks the gun barrel down on Vinnie's head. "Shut up, asshole."

"What's happening, Vinnie?" Victoria asks.

Vinnie struggles to his feet and spits blood on the floor. "Just a misunderstanding, sis. I'll sort it out."

Another man wearing a black ski mask comes into the room, holding a gun and a black bag. From his build and his voice, when he speaks, Victoria knows this is the man who cut her finger and her hand off.

"I thought I told you to come alone, Duke," he says.

Duke points his gun at Vinnie. "He knows too much, Len. He saw Marsh handing over the money and got in the way when I tried to shoot him."

"Is that right, Vinnie?" Len asks.

Victoria knows their names now. She knows enough to realize that this is very, very bad. It means they have no intention of letting either her or her brother walk out of here alive.

Vinnie struggles to his feet in front of Victoria and turns his bloody face toward her. "Are you hurt?" She shakes her head. Vinnie faces the others. "You've got your money, Len. Why don't you let her go. She doesn't know who you are."

Duke says, "That's bullshit. She knows enough. She knows our names. The police will show her the mugshots. I say we kill them and split the money. Equal shares."

Missy says, "Why should you get an equal share, Duke? You're as useless as a dead battery."

Duke gives her the finger and Len says, "In the hallway. Both of you. Now."

They shut the door behind them leaving Victoria and Vinnie alone. Vinnie wraps her in a bear hug. "I'm sorry about this."

She's shaking from the adrenaline rush. One second she's going to fight for her life, and the next she's facing three crazy people, two with guns. "Are these friends of yours?"

"Not friends. Just desperate psychos."

"They're going to kill us, aren't they?"

"The one with the ski mask is Len Thundercloud. He's insane. The other two are just greedy. If it was just Duke and Missy, I could talk to them."

Victoria says, "Maybe they'll leave us locked in here while they make their getaway?"

"They're coming back in a minute. If I know Thunder-cloud, he will have Duke do the dirty work. If Duke comes in by himself, I'll distract him and you make a run for it."

"No, Vinnie. Absolutely not. I won't leave you behind."

"Jack got the money together. He really loves you, sis. Maybe he'll be a better husband now. Maybe you won't have to leave him. But he's still a dick."

Vinnie hugs her, and she draws her hand back with a gasp.

"Sorry. I forgot the hand. I'll make them pay for that."

"I don't want to do anything but get home to Jack and my daughters. If that woman comes in again, I'm afraid of what I might do to her."

Vinnie says, "She's the one who set you up at the resort. I think the plan was to pin this on me. They left a note that was supposed to be from me."

Victoria says, "So they can't possibly let me go."

Vinnie doesn't reply. He knows they're both as good as dead.

"But if they know the police are on to them, maybe they'll just run. Nothing has to happen."

"Listen, Vicki. The police won't help us. The guy running the investigation... I think he could be in on it. Your daughter, Ronnie, is in town with another detective and they've been beating the bushes. I've met with Jack and he's changed. At least, he didn't throw me out of the house. But what I need to tell you is that no one can help us. It's just you and me. Like when we were kids."

"Vinnie," she starts, but he cuts her off.

"We don't have time for this. I have a plan, and you're going to have to trust me. When I start this you run like hell. Turn right down the hall and keep going. There's an exit and it's not far from a wooded area. Hide in the woods until they're gone. No matter what you hear just run. I've got nothing to lose but you have two beautiful daughters."

Victoria puts a hand on his arm. "You've met them?"

"I have. We've all been searching for you. It's a long story but they're still trying to find you. That's why you need to run when you can. I was supposed to be rescuing you and that's what I'm going to do. You've rescued me all of my life."

"I'm glad you're here, Vinnie. Thank you for coming for me, but I wish you hadn't. Are the girls okay? They must be so worried."

"They're fine. Wonderful girls. You did good raising them. Don't worry."

Vic says, "Ronnie might find us any time now. I pray she doesn't. These people are dangerous. I'm always afraid for her."

"She seems to be able to take care of herself, sis. Look at all the things she's been involved in and always comes through."

"That's what I mean. She's not afraid of anything. She gets it from her father."

"I seem to recall you giving Denny Sanders a bloody nose in grade school." Vinnie chuckles. "He was two years ahead of you in school but he was the one who ran off crying."

Just then, the bolt on the door slides back. Len steps back into the room. He's removed his mask now, so Victoria guesses the decision has been made: they're dead. He looks different than she had imagined him, with dark hair and an acne-scarred complexion.

"You made your decision," Vinnie says.

Len points the gun at him. "It isn't personal."

"Can I ask one question, first?"

Len thinks about it for a second, then nods warily. "Sure."

"You think you can trust those two?"

"I trust one thing, Vinnie. Money."

Vinnie stares back at him. "You know they've been fucking behind your back, right?"

Len's eyes narrow. Before he can say anything, Missy

appears in the doorway. She's carrying the black bag now, and suddenly Victoria realizes it looks familiar.

"That's a goddamn lie. He's lying, Len."

Len turns so that he can look at her and keep his eyes on Vinnie.

Victoria sees the ghost of a smile on Vinnie's face, and something much more overt on Missy's: guilt.

"This has been going on all along, hasn't it? You and him against me from the beginning."

She takes a hesitant step toward him. "Len, I swear—"

Len knocks Missy onto her butt. She drops the bag on the floor. Vinnie backs Victoria against the wall and shields her, and at that moment she realizes why the bag looks familiar. It's Jack's. It must contain the ransom.

Missy cringes with her hands up, pleading. "Please, Len. You can have it all. You don't have to do this. Please."

"How did the police get my name? Huh? Was it you or Duke?"

Duke appears in the doorway, a pistol in his hand. "She's not your problem anymore, Len."

Thundercloud turns but Duke is faster. The first shot hits Len in the neck and blood erupts like a fountain. Thundercloud drops the gun and both hands go to his neck. His legs fold and he goes down on his side with his hands still trying to stem the flow, his mind not knowing he's a dead man. Duke steps close and kicks the gun out of Len's reach. "You always thought you were better than me."

Len tries to speak and coughs up blood. His eyes fix on Duke and his voice seems to be coming from underwater. "You're a dead man..." Blood trickles down his chin and he smiles. "When I tell—"

Duke shoots him in the face. "Len Thundercloud. What a joke. You're just a cloud now. A ghost. How about that?"

Missy is trembling all over, her face a mask of fear.

"Thank you, Duke. He made me be with him again. I didn't want to but he forced me. He's evil. Oh God, he was going to kill me."

Duke shoots her twice in the chest and she slumps back against the wall.

"You never did know when to shut up." He turns the gun toward Vinnie and Victoria. "It's not too late, Vinnie. I don't have a problem with you. We can share the money. I'll take care of your sister. All you have to do is kill those two meddling detectives when they show up."

"She's my niece, Duke."

Duke looks incredulous. "So what? You don't owe this bitch." He waggles the gun at Victoria. "She kept you away from your family just as much as that asshole husband of hers. You don't even know your niece. You and me are friends, Vinnie. I'm the only real family you've got."

Vinnie doesn't speak. He just holds Victoria's body against the wall with his own.

"Okay. I understand you being mad at me for punching you around. But it was the only way I could get you in here. Thundercloud would have killed you if I brought you here all nice-like. You help me get patched up and when I get better you can punch me. How's that?"

"I don't want to punch you, Duke."

Duke says, "Okay. How about this? We don't kill your sweet sister. We can use her to get even more money. How much do you think she's worth?"

"Stop pointing the gun at her, Duke. I can reason with her and she won't tell. In fact, she's divorcing him. She can have some of the money to start a life of her own. No one ever needs to know. You and me will be rich. With that kind of money just imagine what we could do. Hell, we could start our own cartel, Duke."

"That sounds good, Vinnie. But I still need you to kill those two cops. They know too much. And I'm going to have the plea-sure of killing that shitbag Lucas."

Vinnie shakes his head. "If we kill a cop, we might as well put a gun to our own heads. They'll never stop looking for us. Right now you can come out of this with a lot of money. This was all Thundercloud's doing. Missy was in on it with him. Victoria will swear you killed them in self-defense. They were going to kill her. I'll say I came here with you and we stopped them. They both had guns. You'll be a hero. You can keep the money, and her husband will give you a reward. Vicki will make sure of it."

"That doesn't work for me, Vinnie. I'm an escapee. I can't explain that. Or how I came by a gun as a convicted felon. The cops have to go. No witnesses."

"Okay. You can keep *all* the money. Stow it somewhere and we'll say these two must have hidden it. You can still get well on this, Duke. You'll do what? Two years at most. You'll get out of prison a rich man."

He turns the gun back on Vinnie and Victoria, shaking his head. "You'd turn me in and get the reward for yourself. Len was going to keep everything. He never was going to split the money three ways."

"Duke—" Vinnie starts, but it's too late.

Duke pulls the trigger. Vinnie jerks, then staggers back against Victoria, his hands going to his stomach. Their eyes meet and she watches the light leave his as he collapses on top of her. A trickle of blood runs onto her upturned face and she screams.

"Oh God, Vinnie. Vinnie! Oh God. Oh God."

Vinnie's body pins her to the floor, protecting her even in death. She holds her brother's head against her shoulder and turns her hate on Duke.

"You bastard. He wouldn't have told anyone. What is wrong with you people? You aren't human."

"I'll be a hero like Vinnie said." He steps closer and shoves Vinnie's body over with the toe of his white Reeboks.

"Take the money. I won't tell. I swear to God I won't."

"Of course I'll keep the money."

Victoria's face turns into a mask of anger. "You're sick. My daughter will kill you. She'll find you and kill you."

"She maybe will. Maybe won't. Now, be a good rich bitch and shut up and die."

He leans over and puts the gun to Victoria's forehead. She squints her eyes closed.

A shot rings out.

SEVENTY-TWO

"Are you hurt, Mrs. Marsh?"

Victoria's eyes open slowly, fearful of what she'll see. She's surprised to find herself still in the land of the living.

A man in his sixties is standing over the body of Duke holding a gun. He wears a sport coat and has dark, almost black hair.

"I'm Sergeant Mike Lucas, I'm here to help."

She just stares at him unable to speak.

Lucas holsters his gun, then examines her quickly and moves on to Vinnie, checking for signs of life. Missy is lying in a pool of blood, two holes in the front of her blouse. She's still alive, barely. Mumbling something, delirious.

Lucas glances at the other two briefly and decides he doesn't need to spend any time checking for life signs. Duke isn't moving. Len Thundercloud's head has been destroyed.

Lucas helps Victoria to her feet. She is trembling and her legs don't support her. He has to grab her before she falls.

"It's okay now, ma'am. You're safe. You're safe."

He gets her to her feet but she can't stand on her own. He

picks her up and carries her like a bride down a corridor, through an open door and outside into the fresh air. The sunlight is dazzling. She hasn't seen anything but gloom and murk for days.

Lucas sits her down on the side of a wooden bench and lifts her face to his. "I'll get you out of here. You're safe now. Is anyone else here?"

She shudders but doesn't answer.

A twig snaps and Lucas spins around, the gun already drawn. A man in overalls is standing twenty feet from them, his mouth gaping as he looks at the blood-covered woman with a missing hand.

"Jesus fucking Christ, what happened?"

Lucas takes out his badge and holds it up. "I've got this, go back to where you came from."

The guy looks uncertain and then turns and beats a hasty retreat. Lucas turns back to Victoria.

"Deep breaths. Slowly. That's it. You're safe. I'm with the Whatcom County Sheriff' Department. We've been looking for you, ma'am."

She buries her head in his shoulder and exclaims, "Thank you. Oh, thank you. Oh my god. I'm alive."

He pulls her tighter and comforts her. "No one can hurt you now." He releases her and lifts her injured arm gently to look at where the hand was severed and the stump tied with a tourniquet. Then he examines her face.

"I'll get an ambulance." He jerks his head in the direction the man in overalls went. "That rubbernecker is probably calling it in right now. Are you hurt anywhere else?"

The tears come in a storm of relief. Lucas takes a few steps away and uses his portable radio.

"An ambulance is on its way. Do you think you can walk to my car?" She gives a shuddering breath and nods her head. He helps her stand and puts an arm around her waist. "Let's get you in the car, Mrs. Marsh. Your husband and daughters are anxious to see you."

A black SUV is parked facing away from the entrance. A blue Chevy Tahoe is parked nearby. Lucas opens the SUV's door and helps her into the passenger seat. "I have to check on something in there. I'll be right back. Just breathe. Slow breaths."

"Please don't leave me," she pleads, and grips his arm.

He peels her hand free and says, "Just for a moment. You're safe. Try to be calm."

He goes back into the building. Victoria gingerly unwraps the bandana wrapped around her wrist and closes her eyes as it drops to the floor of the vehicle. She can't look.

Then, from the building, three gunshots ring out.

Victoria freezes in the seat.

SEVENTY-THREE

The wrecker arrives and takes Jack's car away, but we're still waiting for the Lyft to come because Jack refused to ride with the wrecker. Ronnie's phone rings. It's Longbow, so she puts it on speaker so I can hear.

"Lucas found your mom. She's alive."

The words don't feel real. I can tell Ronnie feels the same way. She looks like she's in shock, and then the relief floods into her.

"Are you serious?"

"Yes. Lucas has been shot."

"What? Where?"

"He got them all. They're all dead. Ain't that something?"

"Where is my mother?"

"Your mom's okay but she'll need medical treatment, there's an ambulance on the way."

"Text me the location. Thanks, Sheriff." She disconnects and a few seconds later her phone dings with the location.

"What's going on?" Jack asks, getting out of his car to find out what the commotion is about.

Ronnie says, "Mom is alive. According to Sheriff Longbow,

Lucas was shot. The kidnappers are dead. Mom's getting an ambulance. And I've got the location."

"Where?" I ask.

She gives me directions.

"Dad can go with us. Hurry, Megan."

In the distance Semiahmoo Resort appears over fields of yellow flowers, and I bounce the SUV over an expanse of crushed shells to the building Ronnie pointed out when we first came to the resort. She told me it was an abandoned salmon packing plant. I start to slow and Ronnie says, "Go around to the back."

Behind the long wooden building I come to a concrete bunker, with rusted steel doors seeming to be jutting from the earth and standing open. The black SUV belonging to Sergeant Lucas sits near the bunker, and a disheveled-looking blonde woman, who can only be Victoria, is sitting in the back of an ambulance with her bare feet dangling over the side. One arm is bandaged and held tightly against her chest while the paramedic talks to her. Her eyes widen when she recognizes Ronnie.

"Ronnie!" Victoria cries out, and reaches out for her daughter.

Ronnie rushes to her. They embrace gingerly, then she steps back and examines her mom's wounds, the swollen eye, the bruises on her face and neck, the busted lip, and the bandaged nose.

"Mom, it's going to be okay. They'll take you to the hospital and everything will be... will be..." Her eyes go to her mom's bandaged wrist—the place where her left hand should be. She breaks down and sobs, and Victoria pulls Ronnie close with her good arm, cradling her daughter's head against her shoulder, in spite of the pain it causes her.

Standing a short distance away, I feel like my heart is going to explode and tears threaten my eyes, but it's all over and I don't want to make a scene. This is what a family is supposed to be. I can feel the love like it's a tangible thing and not just an emotion. I'm happy for Ronnie and at the same time a little jealous and angry with myself that I hadn't done more. Some great detective I am. If Lucas hadn't interceded, this scene would have been so much different. Victoria might be dead and Ronnie destroyed. I grit my teeth and feel a lump in my throat at the thought. I tell myself it's okay. Everything's okay. She's alive.

A paramedic goes to work motioning Ronnie back. Ronnie comes to me and wraps me in a tight hug, and I love it and hate it and want to cry but I won't.

"How are you holding up?" I want to ask, but I feel stupid. Of course she's in another world with her pain and her relief. I don't know what to say so I keep quiet.

Ronnie releases me so I can breathe and looks from me to her mom. "Thank you, Megan. She's going to be okay. I'll never forget what you've done. Ever. You're family now."

Now I do break down in tears, but I pry her loose and see Jack standing alone.

Ronnie wipes a tear from her eye and smiles. "Isn't it wonderful?"

It might be, but there's still a chasm that has taken a long time to be excavated between Jack and his wife and her brother. I don't envy the Herculean task it will take to fill that hole in. Been there, felt that with my own brother.

The paramedic is trying to steer Victoria back toward the ambulance but she says something to him and comes to us.

"Mom, you need to go to the hospital. I'll ride with you if you like."

"Not yet. I need a moment. This must be Megan."

Once again I'm tongue-tied. I merely nod, and she takes my hand with her good one.

"We need to meet properly. Thank God there will be time. Thank you for being with my baby."

I wonder what the hell is wrong with me. I'm not used to being overwhelmed and my therapist had told me this is how I cope with feelings.

"Give me a moment," Victoria says, and goes to Jack, who is still unsure what to do. Victoria steps close to Jack making him look into her eyes, and she surprises me by slapping his face. He looks completely shocked, and she slaps him again and then falls against him until he puts his arms around her. I can't watch any longer.

The paramedic comes over. "That's your mom, right?" Ronnie nods. "We really should get to the hospital. She possibly has some broken ribs and I suspect she's malnourished and dehydrated. I'll get fluids going but I'm worried about infection."

The coroner has arrived, and I see Sergeant Lucas is talking to him and a uniformed officer. A bandage is strapped around Lucas's waist. He looks my way and nods, then a crime scene tech in Tyvek coveralls and a hood speaks to Lucas and they go inside the bunker. I've never been shot but I can imagine what it feels like. I hope it hurt.

Victoria and Jack come to us. She says, "Sergeant Lucas saved my life. Your uncle was shot protecting me." Jack pulls her closer and plants a kiss on the side of her face.

"It's okay, Mom," Ronnie says. "We should get you to the hospital."

"I just want to go home." Her eyes widen. "Is Rebecca okay? Have you called her?"

Ronnie says, "I'll find out which hospital they're taking you to and I'll call her to meet us."

"But..."

"Don't argue with me, Mom."

Jack says, "She's right. Let's go. We can talk on the way if you like." Victoria looks back toward the bunker, and Jack has to turn her toward the ambulance.

Victoria's knees weaken and Jack holds her up. "Vinnie's dead, Jack."

"I'm so sorry, honey. I am truly sorry. He seemed like a good guy. It's my fault. This is all my fault. I won't blame you if you hate me. But please let me help you. Don't leave me. Please."

She just says, "Oh, Jack."

Maybe I do forgive him. Maybe he can't help seeing everything through "Jack" eyes. I hope this has opened them. I look on and think that it's too bad it takes something of this magnitude to wake people up to what's important and what's small beans.

Jack leads her to the ambulance and they get inside. The paramedic gets in and closes the door. The driver leaves; lights and siren.

Vinnie was a hero after all the lies. He was lying to protect his sister and he ended up dying for her. I hope Lucas wasn't the one that killed him.

As the ambulance pulls away, I step back to visually piece together what's happened but I can't help but hear what Victoria tells them of Vinnie's death. Vinnie was killed protecting her. I suspect Missy, Duke, and Thundercloud are inside. Dead like they deserve.

Ronnie got the hospital information and called Rebecca.

"She'll meet us at the hospital."

Lucas comes from the bunker with the coroner. A paramedic is trying to get him to let them change his bandage. He doesn't look any worse for the wear. I need to talk to him. I'm not ready to let this go.

SEVENTY-FOUR
MARCH 2023

Whatcom County

"I told you I don't know nothing a blue Nissan or whatever," Len Thundercloud said, standing his ground in his driveway as Lucas approached. He was wearing a purple robe and slippers. Lucas was pleased to see he hadn't dressed up on his account.

"It was black," Lucas said. "And I'm not interested in that now."

"Then what the hell do you want?"

Lucas gestured beyond him at the door of the house, which was ajar. "Can we talk inside?"

Thundercloud's upper lip curled into an approximation of a smirk. "Not unless you have a warrant."

Everyone always plays that like a trump card; like it's a set of magic words that make the problem go away. It didn't often work out that simple, and it wasn't going to this time. Lucas took a step back and looked up and down the quiet street. A few houses down, an old guy was carrying a cardboard box full of books to the trunk of his car, moving painfully slowly.

Lucas took a step closer, so that he and Thundercloud were

less than an arm's length apart. "I could get a warrant, Lenny. I would start with one for the salmon packing plant."

Thundercloud stiffened at the mention of the plant.

"After that, I'd bring you and Duke in for questioning. Melissa too. She could tell me all about her job in Ohio. But then the wheels are in motion and nothing you or I can do will stop it. You want me to do that?"

Without saying anything, Thundercloud turned and walked back toward the house. Not waiting for an invitation, Lucas followed him.

A short hallway gave way to the living room. There was a worn couch and a threadbare carpet and a coffee table that looked like it might have been pulled out of a dumpster and dusted down. Thundercloud sat down on the couch. His eyes narrowed as he looked up at Lucas.

"Look man, whatever you think you know..."

"Where's your gun?" Lucas asked, looking him up and down. He already knew there wasn't one; not concealed in a robe. Otherwise, he would have frisked him before letting him walk inside.

"I don't own a gun."

"Right. Well, you just stay on the couch. I wouldn't want one to suddenly appear from a drawer, you know what I mean? Not before we've had a little talk."

"I don't know what the hell this is about, but—"

"It's about you and your buddies Duke and Melissa kidnapping and murdering Olivia Greenwood."

Thundercloud didn't flinch, didn't even blink. Lucas wouldn't have wanted to play poker with him.

"I don't know what the fuck you're talking about."

"You keep saying that. And yet you're talking to me. Because you're not entirely confident you got rid of all the evidence, are you?"

Thundercloud stared back at him, and Lucas knew if looks could kill he would be six feet under already.

Lucas started to pace around the perimeter of the room, never taking his eyes from Thundercloud. If he made a sudden move, Lucas would have his gun in his hand before he could take his first step.

"I couldn't work out the connection at first. A wealthy woman kidnapped in Ohio winds up dead in a creek thousands of miles west. Then I realized that was the thread I needed to pull. It was the one thing that didn't make sense, so I knew it had to be the key to the whole thing."

He stopped and looked out of the window at the street outside.

"Where's Melissa? She goes by 'Missy', right?"

When Thundercloud didn't reply, he continued.

"Maybe she's out looking for a new job, huh? Something more local. I know she was working in Edward Greenwood's office in Cincinnati until last week. She kept her ear to the ground, knew about Greenwood's affair. She knew his wife would leave him if she found out about it, and she told you, and you came up with a way to make the situation pay. You knew how it would look if his wife was planning to divorce him and she disappeared. He knew too. So you came up with the plan to kidnap her, then make Greenwood look guilty as hell.

"The fact you were all the way out here was a plus. Two- or three-days' drive, but what was the hurry? You had a twelve-hour head start heading out of the city after you snatched her from the Park Plaza, and after that everybody was going to be looking closer to home. And it wasn't like you were going to have to make the return trip."

Lucas stopped pacing and leaned against the wall, staring at his audience. Thundercloud wasn't giving anything away, wasn't admitting anything despite everything he was saying. That was a good sign. It would be important later.

"So you brought her out here. You told Greenwood to call the search off, knowing he could explain that once the kidnap was revealed. You held her captive in that salmon plant. I don't know exactly when you got there yet, but I'm guessing the Monday. She was in captivity just over a week. What did you do with her in there? Torture her? Rape her?"

Thundercloud's eyes narrowed.

"Don't act offended, I know you cut her fucking finger off."

Lucas scratched his head. "So you held her there for days. She ate there. She slept there. She pissed and shit there. She bled there. How'd you clean up, Thundercloud? You hose it down?"

Thundercloud's face betrayed not a flicker of emotion.

Lucas shook his head. "Not good enough. You should have burned the place to the ground. And even then..."

Thundercloud said nothing. Still. Lucas couldn't help being a little impressed. A lot of other guys would be protesting, saying they had nothing to do with anything he was talking about. He knew how to keep his mouth shut.

That was a good sign.

"It would have worked. You were going to take the payout from Greenwood and then kill his wife, and you knew the police would assume he did it. But something went wrong. You killed her before you got paid. What happened?"

No response. Not that he had expected one.

"I'm speculating here, and it doesn't really matter, but I think someone—probably not you—left a door unlocked and she got out. She didn't get far, though. You or Duke ran her down and she hit her head in the struggle. After that, she was no good to anybody. You dumped the body and hoped you would still get the money. But when Greenwood found out she was dead and that the police were looking at him, he killed himself. Leaving nobody and nothing who could tie it to you."

Lucas paused for effect, then reached into his pocket.

"Almost nothing."

He showed Thundercloud Melissa Milligan's ID card from Greenwood's company.

"That was all it took to make the connection. As soon as I had that and the salmon plant, I put it all together. And here's the thing, Thundercloud. It was a great plan. Olivia would have disappeared, you would have got paid, and Greenwood would have taken the fall. If somebody hadn't fucked it up, it would have gone perfectly."

Thundercloud waited until he was sure Lucas had finished before he finally spoke. His voice was calm, like he was commenting on the weather.

"So if you think this is true, why are we having this conversation in my house?" Careful not to make any sudden moves, he got up off the couch. He went to the blinds and looked up and down the street. It was empty of people. No police cars screeching to a halt. "Why aren't you arresting me?"

"Arrest you?" Lucas shook his head. "Why would I want to do that? No. I'm not going to arrest you. I'm going to make you a proposal. This time, I'm going to help you do it right."

SEVENTY-FIVE

The paramedic checks Lucas's bandage and they try unsuccessfully to get him to go with them. Ronnie and I go to see Lucas and he fixes me with a gimlet eye. "What do you want?"

"Aren't you glad to see me?" I say.

"No."

That's pretty plain. It's also not true. His ego demands I acknowledge what a fine specimen of detective manhood he is. He's still a dick. A dick-tective. He mistakes my smile for bonding. The only thing I feel like bonding with him is my fist to his face. Except I can't do that since he saved Ronnie's mom from being killed. Not until I confirm my suspicions.

"Inquiring minds want to know, Lucas," I say.

"You mean, how did I find them?"

"Sure, start with that."

He speaks as though he's in court, running through a prepared statement.

"In a nutshell. I learned Thundercloud was deeply involved in this. I checked and he worked for the company that owns this bunker. It was one of their old storage places for hazardous materials. Long since abandoned. What better place for a hide-away? I followed Duke here. I heard shooting. I came in and saw Duke pointing a gun at Mrs. Marsh's head. Vinnie and Thundercloud and Milligan were dead. Or at least I thought so. Mrs. Marsh was on the floor pinned under the body of her brother. I didn't know if she'd been shot but Duke was ready to kill her. I shot him. I got Mrs. Marsh out to my car and went back in to see if there were others. Maybe more kidnappers. Maybe more victims."

He touched the bandage over his abdomen and winced theatrically.

"Milligan surprised me. She had somehow gotten to Duke's gun and shot me. I shot her. End of story. I'll send a copy of my report to your sheriff and you can read it. If you have any questions please feel free not to ask on your way out of town."

While he was reciting this, the medic was giving me annoyed looks. I was annoyed too.

"Can I go inside and take a look, Lucas?"

"No. It's a crime scene. Mrs. Marsh has been found. Your services are no longer needed."

The medic tells him, "Sergeant, we need to take you with us. I want a doctor to look at that wound. There's an entrance and exit but part of the bullet could still be embedded and can cause you some real damage if it gets infected."

"Listen to him, Lucas. There are two other officers here and you've done your bit. Let your crime scene people take it from here. We're going to the hospital."

Ronnie says, "Thank you."

Lucas looks at me and grins. "You'll be her junior partner someday."

I don't care but that's never going to happen. "Probably. She's pretty sharp. For instance she noticed there's no bag of money out here. What happened to it?"

His eyes turn to slits. "There was no money when I got

here. Thundercloud must have hidden it after he took it from Jack Marsh. I guess Thundercloud wasn't going to share the loot. He shoots Missy and Vinnie and then shoots Duke, but Duke didn't die. Duke kills Thundercloud and goes in to finish Mrs. Marsh off but I stopped him. I heard gunshots when I arrived. Good thing I got here in time."

"Wow. It sure was," I agree. "I guess it must have happened the way you said."

Lucas smiles in acknowledgement. The smile evaporates when he realizes I'm not done.

"But I'd still like to see the scene. We've come this far together. And you'll need me to write a report verifying what I saw and heard. Right?"

We look at each other a long time. He's lying. It was probably Thundercloud who shot Jack's car up and took the money. If he planned to kill them all why hide the money? And why isn't Lucas putting together a search party to find it? He could be suffering a little shock after getting in the fracas here. But I prefer to think of him as a lying corrupt cop. It's just as likely that Lucas is the ringleader. No matter what he says, the investigation isn't over. It's just beginning.

The paramedic reappears and starts examining Lucas, and I take the opportunity to walk away from the ambulance with Ronnie.

"You don't want to go in there," I say. "But I have to."

"Don't tell me what I want," she says sharply, and then puts a hand to her mouth. "Sorry Megan. I didn't mean that."

Lucas was right about one thing. Ronnie wouldn't need me much longer. I'm glad and sad.

"No, I'm sorry," I say. "This is your show, Ronnie. How do you want to do this?"

"Lucas didn't give you permission to go in," she says, casting an anxious glance back at the ambulance.

"He didn't say we couldn't. And we're still deputized."

Just then, we see an officer dressed in a white Tyvek suit with a hood approaching the building. I show him my badge. Ronnie says, "Sergeant Lucas wants us to go in with you." The officer looks skeptical then shrugs.

"Don't track through any of the blood. And don't touch anything." He walks ahead of us mumbling, "Why not make it a party?"

"We really appreciate it," Ronnie says brightly.

The officer slows and says, "Just stay to one side and walk where I walk. It's just that Lucas was all over this place and it looks like it was more than once. He knows better than to muck up a crime scene. I guess he's getting short-timer syndrome."

There are numerous bloodstains on the concrete floor in the shape of a shoe sole. They all look like the same shoe until we come to a steel door set into a concrete wall. The door is open and there are several sets of bloodstains on the concrete floor.

The bodies of three men and a woman are sprawled on the concrete floor. Missy is unrecognizable. Her face is destroyed, and she has two bullet wounds in her chest too. Vinnie is in a pool of blood. He's been shot in the stomach. The two men were shot several times, head and stomach. I recognize Duke by his white shoes. Overkill. Anger. Psychotic. It's all the same. I can relate. I shot a serial killer and rapist in the crotch once. Actually several times. I gave him a man-cave where his manhood used to be. Maybe I went a little overboard. Nah.

One of the male bodies was shot—I count them—seven times. His face is destroyed and he's wearing a leather jacket. *Thundercloud.* Jack said the person who took the money and shot at him was wearing a leather jacket.

I examine the bodies again. Missy is lying on her side, right arm laid out along the floor with a semi-automatic in her right hand. Her other arm is behind her. Her head is turned slightly as if she was looking at Thundercloud. The gun bothers me. I could swear Missy was left-handed when I interviewed her. I squat and look more closely at the gun hand. The forefinger is on the trigger. I would have thought she'd drop the gun when she was shot, but I'm not a forensic expert.

Lucas said he'd gone back inside after he brought Victoria out to his car. He told Victoria he was checking on the kidnappers. That would explain why there are so many sets of shoeprints in this room, but only one set entering or leaving. Missy was armed and shot him. He shot her. Plausible. But why was Missy holding the handgun in her weak hand?

"How many guns did you recover?" Ronnie asks the crime scene officer.

"Two. Why?"

"In here or outside?"

"Both guns were in here," he says. "I can give you pictures when I'm finished and file a report."

"How many shots were fired?" Ronnie asks.

"I haven't gotten that far. There are shell casings all over the place. And don't touch anything."

"Was she just like this when you got here?"

"Why?"

Ronnie stares him down.

"Everything was just as it is except for detectives walking through my crime scene. Now I have to eliminate those pieces of evidence from the rest, so I'll need you to come to the station and let me get casts of your shoes."

"What's your name, officer?" Ronnie asks.

"Corporal. Corporal Wiener."

I hold back a smirk. The name fits so perfectly.

Ronnie says, "I'll tell Lucas you were very helpful. You seem to very good at this so I don't blame you for being a little impolite to us. I know it's only because you want to do the best job you can. If you can bear with us a few minutes, we'll be out of your hair."

He looks embarrassed. "Sorry. I just don't want to make a

mistake. Lucas knew better than to track blood around. I'll have to take his shoes and he'll be pissed off and yell at me. Never mind. What do you need from me?"

While Ronnie's blowing smoke up his butt, I'm looking around at the blood. I take my cell phone out. "Do you mind if I take a couple of pictures?"

"Be my guest."

I take a dozen photos, and when I can't reach an area without walking over his scene, he takes my phone and shoots the pics for me. He takes pictures of each face, and a full body shot of the one wearing the leather jacket. There's also an area beside the door that's especially interesting, because it's completely free of blood spatter. He sees what I see and takes shots with his own camera.

"Good eye, detective," he says to me, and I get a smile.

We thank him and go back outside. Ronnie kept her composure when she saw the mayhem, and didn't slip even a little when she saw her uncle Vinnie's corpse.

We get outside and Ronnie says, "The money was in the room during the shooting. Dad said it was in a black bag."

"I agree with you."

There was an impression on the floor where no blood spatter had hit. The same bloody shoeprints as the rest led to the spot and then to the door.

"We need Lucas's shoes," Ronnie says.

My thoughts exactly.

SEVENTY-SIX

Lucas is standing by the door when we emerge from the bunker. He looks pissed, but like Hayden told me once, "Better pissed off than pissed on." Lucas knows he doesn't have a leg to stand on to prevent us from viewing the crime scene.

"I told you to stay out of my crime scene," he says.

My crime scene, I think. Interesting choice of words.

"You don't order us, Lucas," I say. "We are working on this together. Complain to Sheriff Longbow all you want."

He seethes for a moment and then seems to calm down. "So. Find anything? Did I miss a big clue, detectives?"

I say, "We need to step over to your car, Lucas."

"Now, what's this about?" he asks when we reach his SUV.

I'd watched Ronnie's hand go in her pocket as she walked in front of me. I hope I know what that means.

"First of all, I'm sorry if I've pissed you off." *Not.* "Ronnie says I could make an enemy of the Pope." A smile threatens his lips but he kills it.

"Stop blowing smoke up my ass. Get to it."

"What will happen to you after this? Your old partner told us you're very close to retirement."

"You've been talking to Larry Stroud?" The pissed-off look is back.

"It's only fair that we know each other better. Don't you think so?" I say.

"Whatever he told you is horseshit. Larry was caught stealing from a dope deal. I didn't turn him in because he was my partner. He'd run into some bad times. Divorce. You know. So he retired, and I let it go. Whatever he told you about me is just vengeful crap. I know he thought I had something to do with my wife's and daughter's deaths. And thank you very much for reminding me. He was wrong. I was cleared. But I went through hell. So what's your point?"

Ronnie says, "Where's the ransom money?"

The question catches Lucas off guard and he hesitates a little too long before saying, "There was no money here. Your dad gave it to Thundercloud if I'm not mistaken. He must have hidden it somewhere before coming back here."

I give him a skeptical look that says *STFU*.

"There's Thundercloud's truck back in the trees. Go search it if you want. The money wasn't in the bunker, and I looked in the truck and it wasn't there either."

I hadn't seen the Chevy truck. It was pulled back in the trees about fifty feet. The driver's door still stands open.

I say, "We believe you that the money is not in either of those places."

Ronnie steps closer to Lucas. "So where is the money, Sergeant Lucas?"

"Sheriff Longbow will put me on medical leave. There'll be a shooting board. Maybe I'll take early retirement."

"It must be nice to have that many years in. I'm far from retirement. Unless I get fired."

He laughs. It isn't that funny. My getting fired appeals to him.

"I've known dozens of detectives like you, Megan. You'll go kicking and screaming when it's time to go. We all think we're making a difference. That this job wants us. Needs us. But that's a lie. This job just eats us up and throws us away."

This is not the Sergeant Lucas I've met. He was gung-ho. This one has one foot out the door already. Maybe ten million dollars has something to do with the new attitude. Or maybe I'm on the wrong path here. Maybe he's a devoted civil servant who has been wounded in battle and ready to hang up his shooting irons. Nah.

Ronnie opens the passenger door of Lucas's car and says, "You said we could search for the money. Is it in here?"

"Get out of my car! You have no right."

He's too late. Ronnie holds up a grease-stained red bandana. "Well, well. This belongs to Duke. What was he doing in your car?"

Just for a second, he seems to lose his cool. He knows that we know Duke was in his car. And the only way that would have happened would have been if they were together before the shooting.

"You put that there!" he shouts, too quickly. "Your finger-prints are on my door handle." He'll have a lot of time to prac-tice sounding convincing saying that at the trial, but I give him a 2 out of 10 right now.

"Bullshit, Lucas, you know Duke left it there because you know he was in your car. Care to explain how that could be?"

He looks like a grounded goldfish for a moment, his mouth opening and closing, trying to think of an excuse. Then his eyes narrow and a look of smug satisfaction crosses his face.

"Wait a second, look at that thing."

"What?"

"It has blood on it. Victoria's blood. She had it wrapped around her stump earlier."

I peer closer, being careful not to turn my back on Lucas. Goddamn, he's right. It wasn't obvious because of the dirt and the fact the bandana was red anyway, but there the stains are, unmistakably.

"Any more desperate accusations, Detective?"

I want to put my fist through his face. He was panicking there, before he realized he had a legit excuse for the bandana being in his SUV. Too late: his instinctive reaction betrayed him. A guilty conscience will give you away every time.

"We've got more, Lucas," I say, glancing down at his blood-stained shoes. We already have a shitload of circumstantial evidence. If we find the money, we'll hang him.

"You're bluffing," he says. He doesn't sound at all sure, though.

"Blood. Shoeprints. Fingerprints. The gun was in Missy's weak hand. Ballistics on the distance she supposedly fired the bullet from. We saw where the bag with the money was on the floor in that killing room. You admitted to killing Duke. We find his bandana in your car. How many others did you kill? Not counting your wife and daughter."

His features are a mask of rage but Ronnie doesn't move.

He swallows and his fists unclench. "What do you want?"

Ronnie says, "You really were a good detective, Lucas. Before you panicked when your wife wanted a divorce. What did she say? Was she taking your daughter and threatening to clean you out? We know you had money trouble before your wife died. We know her life insurance didn't pay out, so you missed the big payday."

I don't know if the part about the money trouble is true but it sounds plausible. She's getting good at this stuff. Lucas remains quiet. That's not good since he's a homicidal maniac and he's armed. The only thing standing between him and a death sentence is us. I'm not afraid to admit that I'm afraid. We may have pushed him too far. But how will he explain shooting us right outside of a crime scene with officers everywhere? He can't. I just hope he's cognizant of that.

"What do you want?" he asks.

"Three-way split," Ronnie says, and Lucas laughs out loud.

"If I had the money, why would you get a third each?"

"A third of ten million dollars is a lot of money, Lucas," I say.

He shakes his head. "You're trying to con me. Trying to get me to incriminate myself. You don't want the money."

I laugh and glance at Ronnie. "Looks like this guy didn't do his homework on me." I step in closer and lower my voice. "You think I'm some kind of incorruptible straight arrow? You don't know shit about me, Lucas. We're more alike than you want to admit. Everybody in my family is in jail or dead. I've bent rules, I've cut corners, I've killed suspects. So far I've been lucky—all of them have been ruled good shootings—but my luck will run out one day. You think I won't take three million dollars to walk away from all this? Some days I feel like I'd walk away for a buck-fifty and a jelly donut. Hell yes, I want the money, Lucas."

I'm pretty convincing, if I say so myself. I think that's because some of that is true. Maybe more than I'd like to admit.

He thinks for a split second and says, "Let's not do this here."

Ronnie says, "I'm fine right here. You get the money and we'll split it."

"You think I'm stupid?"

He takes his phone out and taps a few times, and my phone dings.

"GPS coordinates for a safe place. I'll meet you there in fifteen minutes."

Ronnie starts to speak, but I interrupt her before she blows this. "Fifteen minutes, Lucas. Have the money or we go to Longbow."

"Now, you listen. Closely. If you try to double-cross me,

you'll..." He shuts his mouth and turns his face away. "Fifteen minutes."

He gets in his SUV and we watch him drive away.

SEVENTY-SEVEN

We need to catch up enough to keep Lucas in sight so he can't ambush us. I see him a couple of miles ahead and he's driving like a madman. I get to the top of a rise and his car has disappeared. Ronnie pulls up the GPS coordinates using my phone. I turn off the main road where there's a cut in the heavy guardrail, and we follow the GPS along a gravel and mud road leading up a bumpy rise to the top of a cliff about seventy-five feet above the road.

A one-room log cabin can be seen in a small clearing. The cabin has seen better days. The tin roof is rusted with pieces missing. The porch boards look rotted out from where we sit, but the cabin commands a view across Drayton Harbor where dozens of boats are berthed. From up here I can see the little oyster bar where I'll never return. Lucas's dark SUV is parked beside the cabin but there is no sign of him.

The clearing around the cabin is hemmed with giant western red cedars, Douglas firs, hemlock, and ponderosa pines, some as tall as three hundred feet. It's as if the trees deliberately surrounded the cabin. We look all around for Lucas but he could be anywhere. Behind a tree. A large boulder. Or the rotted cords of wood stacked near the cabin.

"I don't like this, Megan."

"We're here now. Either way this goes it doesn't end well for him."

We draw our weapons and approach the cabin. I'm liking this setup less and less. I had hoped Lucas would meet us out in the open. Forcing us to walk through a door just makes it more likely that someone is going to get shot.

I try the door. It's unlocked. I push it and step back quickly, letting it swing open. Glancing inside, I can see it opens on what looks like a living room. There's nobody visible, but I can see a doorway to a small kitchen beyond.

"Come on out, Lucas. We made a deal," I call.

No response. I exchange a glance with Ronnie, then point at the ground, motioning, *Stay here*. I want to see what's inside, but I don't want anybody coming in behind us suddenly.

I step inside and look around. There's a couch and a television and a coffee table and nothing else. A floorboard creaks as I move into the center of the room.

Just then, there's a sudden cry and the sound of a scuffle.

I rush back to the door, where I'm greeted by the last thing I wanted to see.

Lucas has one arm around Ronnie's neck; with his other hand he's pressing his gun to her temple. Stupid. I expected an ambush inside the cabin, not out here. He waited for us to separate, then got the jump on Ronnie.

"You two made a big mistake," he says, looking a little too pleased with himself.

"Tell me about it. I thought we could trust you to stab us in the back sooner or later. You know, Lucas, you're not as quick as I thought you'd be. I wouldn't go so far as saying you're a dumbass, but I've been wrong before. Put your gun away and let's talk. You give us our share and we can make most of the evidence go away. We'll even say we messed up the crime scene. None of us wants to go to prison. And no one here wants to get dead. So how about it?"

"You have nothing to offer me."

"Oh yeah? How are you going to explain everything without our help? How are you going to explain the gun in Missy's weak hand? The clean floor where the money bag was? Face it, Lucas, you're the only one who walked out of there alive, and therefore you're the only suspect."

Lucas's voice sounds like he's telling a story. One he's making up as he goes. "Duke was in my car. I'd found him right before all this happened and made him tell me where Victoria was and who was holding her. I didn't search him as thoroughly as I should have, and he had a gun. He showed me where they were keeping Victoria. I told him to go inside to verify she was still there and still alive."

I make a face that says, *Not bad*. "And you heard Jack's car was shot up and figured Thundercloud was on his way back here. You decided to wait and catch them all at once. Of course the sheriff will want to know why you didn't call in the troops."

Lucas picks up the story. "I was afraid if Thundercloud saw police or heard sirens, he would just run with the money. Missy and Duke would kill Victoria."

Ronnie says, "And how will you explain my uncle Vinnie being in there in the bunker? Are you going to say he was part of the kidnapping?"

"It was always going to be blamed on him. He wasn't supposed to be there at the end, but maybe it worked out better that way."

"And Missy's weak hand?"

He shrugs. "I don't know. Maybe she was ambidextrous."

I roll my eyes. "Seriously?"

"You in a hurry to die?" he asks me.

"Not necessarily, but I want to get to the meaty part where you tell us how we die and what we did to deserve it."

"I'm surprised you want the details. But you're not normal."

And you are?

Ronnie says, "Let me take a stab at the next part of your story. Megan and I were working with Vinnie. We kidnapped my mom and drew Thundercloud, Duke, and Missy into the scheme, promising them a big share, but never intending anything but killing them."

"That would never work. Too many people were at the scene and saw the bodies. You two showed up later. But I'll say you two had Vinnie go ahead to kill Missy, Thundercloud, and Duke. He would be a hero. Jack would have to give him a big reward. Meantime you two would have the ten million just waiting to split three ways. Not with me. You two and Vinnie. Victoria would go home thinking you'd saved her life. But you didn't. I did."

Ronnie says, "Good story. So now you have the money for yourself and my dad will probably give you a big reward. You retire to some nice island where there is no extradition with the United States and live the life."

"It's not a perfect cover but it's good enough to buy me some time. You'll be dead and no one will be the wiser. You two could have taken the money and disappeared, never to be heard from again. And you *will* never be heard from again."

"Okay, Lucas. You win. But I have one question that's bugging the crap out of me."

Now he rolls a finger in the air. "Time's a wastin'."

"How did your daughter die? For real."

He opens his mouth to tell me to shut up and then something changes his mind. He gives us a shrug and a *what the hell* expression.

"Joyce, my wife, was cheating on me with another cop. I thought it was Larry. Those two were thick as thieves. He dated her first but I married her. I caught her coming in before daylight and she smelled like she'd just taken a shower. Our eight-year-old daughter was in the house all night by herself while my slut wife was out screwing someone. I killed her. I was angry. More than angry. I watched the life go out of her eyes when I knelt on her throat. Then I took my backup gun from the lockbox, put the gun in her hand and shot her. Maisy saw me do it. She was hysterical and tried to run to a neighbor's but I stopped her."

His lip quivers but he straightens his shoulders and shakes it off. "It felt good to tell someone. Especially since you'll never have a chance to repeat it."

Ronnie says, "Move in, Sheriff."

Lucas grins at her. "Nice bluff. You sound almost convincing, for a woman with a gun to her head."

"She's not bluffing, Lucas," Sheriff Longbow says from beside the cabin. He's holding a rifle pointed at Lucas.

The color drains from Lucas's face as he realizes we set him up before he set us up. He lowers his gun from Ronnie's head and takes a step away from her. She bends and picks up her own gun from the ground.

It had been Ronnie's idea. She called Sitzman and Longbow and gave him the coordinates, telling them to show up quietly, there might be something they'd be interested in hearing. I was starting to worry they were never going to appear.

"You won't shoot an old friend, will you?" Lucas says, pleading with Longbow.

"I will." Lieutenant Sitzman has come around the other side of the cabin with a shotgun pointed at Lucas's chest. "Drop the gun and put your hands on your head. You're under arrest for... for all kinds of shit."

Sheriff Longbow looks at Sitzman and rubs a hand down his face. "You're under arrest, Lucas. We'll read you the charges when we get to lockup. Put the gun down, my friend."

"I can't, Sheriff. Remember the times we fished out here? Those were good days. Before your Lisa died and my family died. We saw a lot of each other. We still can. These two don't matter to anyone. Don't you see? I have ten million dollars. We can retired on that." He turns his face to Sitzman. "You too. I'll cut you in. This job will kill you, son. You should be shooting these meddling bitches."

Longbow and Sitzman don't answer, and Lucas's shoulders drop. The gun lowers a few inches.

Sheriff Longbow says, "It's over, Lucas. Put the gun down and I'll try to get you some help. You've been through a lot. Don't do something stupid."

"I can't go to jail. You know that," Lucas says to the sheriff in a way that means some bad shit is about to happen. I train my weapon on him and see Ronnie is doing likewise. He's not walking away from this.

Sitzman is leaning forward in a shooter's stance and looks like he means business. Longbow's features are set and hardened. He's facing what every lawman fears and that's taking the life of one of our own. If he can't do it, I will.

Lucas hangs his head and his arm lowers, but before Sitzman can move in to disarm him, Lucas opens his mouth wide, the gun comes up, and he fires.

EPILOGUE

Vincenzo Anastagio Lombardi's funeral was a quiet affair, with the only outsiders being Sheriff Longbow, Lieutenant Sitzman, and Annie and Hattie from the Word of the Lamb Shelter. And of course, me, but I'm like family now. Even Jack says so. Asshole. But maybe I'm being too hard on him. Ronnie told me Jack is buying a new van and making a generous donation to the mission in Vinnie's name.

Victoria spent eight days in the hospital and needed more time. Rebecca had packed her hand in ice, but when Crime Scene took it they hadn't kept it cold enough. There was no chance it could be reattached. There are all kinds of new medical gadgets that will help her recover the use of a new hand. She only let the hospital keep her so long because of her broken ribs and nose that would need a minor surgery to repair. I know that unless she's tougher than I am, she'll carry the scars the rest of her life. Even with all the trauma and drama, she's come home as hardheaded as her husband. I think his controlling days are over.

Ronnie had stayed but I had returned to Jefferson County until the funeral.

The hardest part was over. The burial and service was hard on the family, and especially on Hattie who had not quite secretly been in love with Vinnie. Jack had sprung for several new outfits so she would have something nice for the service. She had surprised us all when she grabbed Jack's face outside of the church and planted a wet kiss on his lips. He took it calmly but during the graveside service I saw him wiping his lips with a kerchief and wrinkling his nose.

The family all stood with heads bent while the minister did his bit at the head of the grave when Sheriff Longbow put a meaty hand on my shoulder and led me away under the cottonwoods.

"I owe Tony one for recommending you and Ronnie as deputies. And I owe you and Ronnie one too. You have friends here now if you need anything."

We stand quietly, easy with each other's company, until he says, "That damn fool couldn't do that one thing right. Goddamn Lucas."

I understand what he means. Victoria lost a hand, but Lucas lost part of his face. He was a terrible shot and only managed to blow part of his upper jaw and cheek off and a piece sheared off going through his brain and lodging against the top of his skull. The gunshot wound to his side was determined to be self-inflicted. His wounds wouldn't keep him from going to prison. But that will be a long time. He has to heal enough to be seen by a psychiatrist who will then certify he's sane enough to stand trial, or should be kept in a box. After that there will be a trial and Ronnie and I will have to testify. I hope I don't snicker when I describe Lucas's injury. It's bad form in front of a jury.

The ten million dollars ransom money was found under the floorboards of the cabin. Now I know why Lucas wanted us to give him fifteen minutes. The money must have been in the SUV while we were ruining his day confronting him.

Longbow told us the death of Lucas's wife and daughter

will be opened again. Ronnie, my little genius, had recorded our entire conversation with Lucas at the bunker, and had set her phone to call Longbow and left the line open so he could hear the confessions outside the cabin.

They've got all the evidence they'll need to put Lucas under the prison. Or if he's lucky, he'll get the death penalty.

I still have some questions I'd like answered. For instance, who kidnapped Victoria from the resort? Was Roger involved? Was he the one that turned off the surveillance cameras? One thing seems clear, though: Lucas masterminded the whole thing.

It looks like he had solved the mystery of the murdered Ohio woman found in the creek. But instead of bringing her killers to justice, he had decided to take their idea and make it work this time, repeating the kidnapping plot and throwing suspicion on a guilty husband. Victoria having a brother with a checkered past was a bonus: Vinnie would have been the perfect patsy.

But, ironically, instead of improving on the plot, he fucked it up, big time. Still, perhaps he would have gotten away with it, if only it wasn't for us meddling... Jefferson County detectives.

Rebecca had said once, "Nothing like this happens to the Marshes." Well, I can tell you from experience, shit happens to everyone.

Longbow shakes my hand and says his goodbyes, but not before he tells me he needs new detectives. I'm not sure if he was just looking to the future or offering me a job. I didn't answer. Not for me. I'm going back home to Dan and Hayden and all of my friends. I like being a detective in Jefferson County. I like being a girlfriend. I love being a sister to Ronnie and Rebecca. I finally have a life and I don't want to start over.

I'd arrived at Cougar Point this morning to have breakfast with the family before the funeral service. I wanted to get in my car and go home, but I had ridden to the service with Ronnie and Rebecca and would need to go to Cougar Point to retrieve it. I'd already made my excuses this morning by telling the family that Tony was expecting me back by the afternoon. I'm sure he did, but the truth was I felt awkward. This family had a lot of talking to do and I didn't fit in with that. Besides, Dan was supposed to be coming back from a business trip later tonight and we had a lot of catching up to do. There wouldn't be a lot of talking.

The service is over and we all pay respects to Vinnie and go to Cougar Point where Jack has a feast catered in. It's lunchtime and my stomach is writing letters to its lawyer. We eat, drink, talk, they compare stories of the past, Victoria tells humorous stories about Vinnie when they were children, they cry, they drink and I sip some wine. Being with them makes me wonder what my life would have been like if I'd had a real family. But the past has never been kind to me. It only hurts or bring evil people out of the void.

Jack is drunk and raises his glass. "Here's to Sergeant Lucas, who bravely 'rescued' my beautiful wife from those bastards." His voice is thick with irony. "So, here's to you, Lucas. I wish you a speedy recovery and an even speedier conviction."

The moral of the story here is if you're going to kill yourself, don't use a gun. Guns are not very reliable. I've seen half of someone's head blown away and they still lived. They're a vegetable, but they still lived. My case in point, I give you thick-skulled Lucas. The bullet fragment penetrated one lobe of his brain. If he wakes from his coma, he'll be blind for the remainder of his life. Doc says his odds are fifty-fifty he'll live. Sheriff Longbow was mad the county had to pay for his medical care and for an armed guard round the clock in the hospital. It's safe to say the friendship is ended.

"To Lucas," I say again, and raise my glass in toast. *May you rot in hell.*

The celebration is winding down, and the Marshes want me

to stay the night before driving back to Port Townsend. I decline, using Tony as my excuse. They all give me a hug and thank me for the hundredth time and I finally get outside. Jack stops me.

"Megan, you're part of the family now. I can never repay you. I'm sorry you had to see me at my worst. I'm glad you're partners with Ronnie. You can look out for each other and I won't worry about her so much."

"I'm glad everything worked out." I have an unexpected wave of pity for this man. "Are you going to be okay, Jack?" He'll have one hell of a hangover.

My question takes him by surprise. "Will I... I'll be fine. Thanks to you and my daughters. Megan, if there's ever anything you need. Anything at all. Or if you feel the need to straighten some crotchety old man out, I'm here. I know you have your own family but I hope you'll consider this your home as well."

If he only knew about my family. "Thank you, Jack. You're not crotchety." He tilts his head. He knows I'm just being nice. He was a total asshole and he knows it. But now I think I could like him.

"Thank you for everything," he says again.

"If you keep thanking me, I'll never get home," I say with a smile. I'm serious. I don't do well with kindness or gratitude or farewells. Thankfully, he staggers up the steps and goes inside but then Ronnie comes out.

"How are you getting back to Port Townsend?" I ask.

She says, "I called Sheriff Gray and he gave me another week off work."

"Say no more. Call when you need a ride."

"Dad said he and Mom will bring me. They want to see where I'm living." She rolls her eyes.

"Well, they'd better not try to talk you into coming back here to live," I say. "I'll see you in a week. Don't worry about the case load on your desk. I'll do all the work by myself. I don't mind. That's what partners are for." I smile when I say this but the truth is I'm expecting a pile on my own desk.

"Megan, I couldn't have done this without you." She gives me a hug and a kiss on the cheek. I'm not that kind of girl and I don't like to be touched but I hug her back. No kiss.

She gives me a serious look. "By the way, Sheriff Longbow called me yesterday."

"Yeah? Does he need us to give another statement?" The paperwork is never over until you've killed a tree.

"No. He offered me a job. Lucas's job."

A lump forms in my throat. I'm silent and search for something to say. "That's great, Ronnie. You'll be closer to your family. I'd miss you, of course, but you should do what's best for you. Do what makes you happy." *I'll be fine. Don't worry about me. This is why I never get too close to people.*

"Will you shut up for a minute?" Ronnie says. "He wants to offer you a job too. He said it was time the department had detectives he can count on." When she says this her eyes light up. I can imagine her twenty years down the road, always a scowl on her face, just like Lucas. But that's not Ronnie. One of my professors in college once said, "People who are happy all the time either have something to hide, or they're insane." Ronnie's neither of those.

"Ronnie, I'm happy where I am. But thank Sheriff Longbow for me. When do you start?"

"You... want me to take it?"

"Well, I'm not going to beg if that's what you mean. You won't find a better partner than me. And Tony loves you. And what about Marley? Hayden told me he likes you and wanted to ask you out."

She chuckles. "I'm not taking the job, Megan. I'll be back in a week. Sorry, but you'll just have to put up with me." She punches me on the arm and it's all I can do to keep from hitting her back. I'm not a punching bag. Been there. Done that.

"One week. Then I'm coming to get you. Bringing hand-cuffs, an Armed Response Team, and K-9s."

"Okay. Okay. Tell Tony thanks for extending my stay. And no donuts for him, Megan. Promise me."

"Promise," I say, and remember a place on the way home I can buy him some. I get on the road before she starts crying and sets off a chain reaction.

After a few miles I've forgotten all about her, the family, the case, the look on Ronnie's face while she stood in the drive and waved. I tried anyway.

My phone rings and I tell Siri to answer. I hope it's Dan saying he's come home early but it's not someone I want to talk to. It's Nan, Sheriff Gray's secretary. I want to program my car to block calls from her.

"Megan?"

"That's who you called, isn't it?" I'm sorry I said that out loud. *No I'm not.*

"I wouldn't have called but Sheriff Gray wanted to be sure you were coming back today."

"What's up, Nan?"

"I'll let him tell you."

Then why didn't he call? What the hell. "Put him on."

"He just left to go to a budget meeting."

Here we go. Round and round. "Okay. Tell him I'll stop by the office before I go home."

"There's something else."

I hate it when people do that. Spit it out. "Okay."

"You had a mysterious visitor this morning."

I wait. I'm not biting this time.

"Do you want to know who it was?"

I wait with my hands clenching the steering wheel imag-ining it's her neck.

"He said his name was Wallace."

My breath catches in my throat and fear runs through me. I barely hear her saying, "Megan. Megan. Are you still there?"

"Here," I croak.

"He wouldn't give a last name. Or maybe Wallace is his last name. He was very attractive. In a mountain man sort of way. He said to tell you he was sorry he missed you at the restaurant in Drayton Harbor."

I can't speak.

"Megan?"

I don't answer. I drift across the lane and the stupid computer voice tells me and corrects my steering all at the same time.

"Do you know who that is, Megan? He said you would know him?"

I know him. He's my stalker. He knows things about me that could put me in prison. He's kept track of my movements and never fails to let me know that. But I don't say any of that. "Did he say why he was here?"

"No. He just said he would catch you later. He was looking forward to it." She pauses and I can imagine the smug look on her face. "You have an admirer, Megan. Is he single? I didn't see a ring. Does your boyfriend know about—"

I disconnect the call.

A LETTER FROM GREGG

Dear reader,

I want to say a huge thank you for choosing to read *Cougar Point*. If you did enjoy it, and want to keep up to date with all my latest releases, just sign up at the following link. Your email address will never be shared and you can unsubscribe at any time.

www.bookouture.com/gregg-olsen

I hope you loved *Cougar Point* and if you did I would be very grateful if you could write a review. I'd love to hear what you think, and it makes such a difference helping new readers to discover one of my books for the first time.

I love hearing from my readers – you can get in touch through social media, or my website.

Thanks,

Gregg

 facebook.com/GreggOlsenAuthor
x.com/Gregg_Olsen

PUBLISHING TEAM

Turning a manuscript into a book requires the efforts of many people. The publishing team at Bookouture would like to acknowledge everyone who contributed to this publication.

Audio
Alba Proko
Sinead O'Connor
Melissa Tran

Commercial
Lauren Morrissette
Hannah Richmond
Imogen Allport

Data and analysis
Mark Alder
Mohamed Bussuri

Editorial
Laura Deacon
Imogen Allport

Copyeditor
Janette Currie

Made in the USA
Middletown, DE
18 October 2024

62850210R00236